THE GOLDEN PALACE

THE GOLDEN PALACE

TOM MORRIS

A Journey of Beginnings

Book One
Walid and the Mysteries of Phi

WISDOM/WORKS
Published by Wisdom/Works
TomVMorris.com

Published 2016

ISBN 978-0-692-56948-1

Printed in the United States of America

Set in Adobe Garamond Pro
Designed by Abigail Chiaramonte
Cover Concept by Sara Morris

*To all who suspect there's much more
going on in this world than meets the eye.*

CONTENTS

I

Through the Desert

Egypt. Many years ago.

A lone horse and rider dashed across the bleak landscape. By the calendar, it was 1934. But from a look at the sand and sky, it could have been almost any time.

The sun was well along its silent morning rise. Its heat would soon slow their progress. But for now, the man and his strong companion were straining to cover as much distance as they could. Their task was urgent, and speed was required.

The rhythmic thuds of pounding hooves tossed wild sprays of sand into the air as Bancom al-Salabar urged his horse on through the endless dunes and the few outcroppings of rock that marked their path to the still faraway city. Bancom's robes pressed against his back and flapped with loud pops and cracks. Even the desert wind seemed to push them toward their destination.

This horse and rider were racing an invisible clock that marked the hours and minutes rapidly vanishing between them and the meetings on which everything would depend. Even a moment too late, and all could be lost, with many good people removed from the world and the kingdom's best hope extinguished.

To Bancom's relief, the air in the desert that day was a bit cooler than normal for this time of year. It was still hot, but not oppressive. After a short break around noon to rest, eat a little fruit, and drink from a small jug of water, he quickly remounted and continued to ride with the wind howling at his back. He had to get into the city as soon as possible. What could take three days by camel, he had been asked to accomplish in half that time. There were vital messages to deliver and men to set into motion many months before they had expected certain dramatic events to unfold. The time available to him passed like a handful of sand through widespread fingers as he now rode on.

Suddenly, he glimpsed up ahead in the distance what appeared to be five other riders on horseback. In this part of the desert, they were almost sure to be bandits. Most journeys across this wasteland were made with a reliable camel. Merchants, adventurers, and local tribesmen all depended on these slower animals for their regular conveyance through the ever-shifting dunes. By contrast, thieves always rode on fast and strong horses they had typically stolen, or purchased with purloined gain, in order to hit unprepared travelers quickly, take their money and treasure by force, and then disappear.

Bancom had a single small weapon tucked into his belt for protection, something easily concealed that would not arouse suspicions or provoke concerns when he arrived in the city and visited certain individuals. It would be no match for five heavily armed riders intent on intimidation and forcible theft. But it was the only obvious defensive tool he possessed.

The riders were approaching at an angle that would allow them to intercept him within minutes. And he couldn't turn back. The time for his mission wouldn't allow it. In any case, he was now many hours away from the large oasis where his race with destiny had begun. He was even farther from his friends who had already left their campsite by a different route, to the south, in order to evade anyone who might come looking for them. He couldn't veer much off the path he was on. And it was unlikely he could outrun all the horses of so many thieves, which were always chosen precisely for speed and power. Even if he could evade the riders and stay ahead of them, he surely wouldn't be able to outpace their bullets. There was really no way to avoid the looming situation, no escape route available to this man whose task was so important to all his friends, their cause, and the future of the entire region.

He had a bit of money in some small bags, in case he had to buy the silence or assistance of anyone he encountered along the way who might otherwise be of hostile intent. But it was nothing compared to what these men would want. Most likely, they'd take his horse as their prize and leave him alone in the desert to die, or else they'd simply end his journey, his mission, and his life with a single shot, on the spot, before making off with their plunder.

Bancom was a well-trained fighter, and was prepared for almost anything, but he didn't like these odds. In that moment, he cleared his mind, and then focused on what he would need for any chance of survival. The words of a legendary warrior and good friend, Masoon Afah, echoed in his head. It was as if he could hear the man's voice say, in a calm and deliberate tone: "Prepare and Perceive; Anticipate and Avoid; Concentrate and Control." Masoon called this "The Triple Double for Dealing with Trouble." His formula or "toolkit of wisdom," as he often put it, consisted in three pairs of actions, both inner and outer, that could make all the difference between life and death.

Prepare and Perceive. Bancom's preparation for a task and time such as this had taken many years. Like most of his close companions, he was a master of mental and physical strength, a well-trained warrior prepared for almost anything. And in this moment, by calling to mind his friend's advice, he was already beginning to follow it in ways that the situation demanded. His specific preparation for the upcoming trouble was now underway.

And his perceptions were unusually keen. He was mindfully aware of everything around him. He had noticed these oncoming riders before most other men would have, at a great distance, their images still tiny and distorted by the heat rising from the sand on even a relatively moderate day like this. He knew how to observe, and what to look for in the nature and movements of a potential adversary.

Anticipate and Avoid. He was already anticipating various scenarios of what might happen, and none of the options he envisioned was promising. It occurred to him immediately that the best way to have any chance of avoiding sudden violence on the spot might be to present himself as a fellow bandit, the sole survivor of a recent, unfortunate skirmish with a nearby armed tribe. He could say he was now looking to join up with a new band of marauders and lend his military skills to their own opportunistic endeavors.

This was the only tactic he could think of, but somehow it didn't seem right. He needed to find another path for avoiding the consequences that now threatened. He should focus his mind on what might be required at each moment coming up. He would have to control himself and the overall situation in any way he could, with calm confidence and resolute courage, keeping in mind his mission on this day.

Of course, as Masoon had also taught him, every action that would ready him for a dangerous challenge had to represent an ongoing stream of repeated behavior. Bancom was even now preparing himself in various additional ways, and continuing to perceive every aspect of his developing situation as carefully as possible. He was monitoring his horse, the surrounding terrain, and the oncoming riders with care, while he galloped on as if nothing unusual had been noticed. The inner act of anticipation was never to be neglected, as any threat might subtly change, moment-to-moment. Possible avoidance tactics should be rethought, depending on the evolving contours of the situation, along with the promptings of intuition.

Concentrate and Control. Clear danger can actually focus the mind. Great jeopardy can bring great clarity. An imminent threat of major scope can even slow our experience of time, oddly broadening out the horizons of the present moment so that we have more mental room in which to register, reason, and respond.

Many of us have felt a natural ability, an unconscious reflex that kicks in without our intentional contrivance, to rise above the immediacy of what seems to be an unfolding personal disaster of the most extreme sort and to view it with a strangely calm, almost anesthetized emotional detachment that can't be fully imagined by someone who's never been in such a situation. This is a tremendous gift, and often can be used to great purpose.

A further gift not suspected by most people is that a well-trained mind can create a kindred experience of emotional calm and enhanced mental space at nearly any time. It can then use the unmeasured, elastic gaps between moments as allies for dealing with any difficulty, however small or severe it might appear to be. We can give ourselves this gift whenever nature alone doesn't provide it—a fullness of time and space sufficient for dealing with what we confront—but only if we've skilled ourselves well in its creation. It's within the inwardly expanded moment that great things can be initiated and done.

There was no doubt about it. Bancom was unusually skilled in this, and he thought of himself as such. His concentration was complete. He was, at the moment, still in control of his emotions, and was not allowing the worst-case scenarios running through his head to elicit the reaction of mind-numbing fear that could overcome him more quickly than any adversary. As Masoon had often said to him, "Most battles are won or lost in the mind before their results become visible in the world." And that was a man who spoke from a vast experience of winning, while others lost. As everyone knew, Masoon's mind was a stronghold of surprising power. Now, due to his effective mentoring, so was the mind of this messenger.

Three rifle shots suddenly called out and signaled Bancom in a sadly universal language to slow and stop his horse. The five riders now approached him head-on, side by side, guns out and pointed straight at him. When they drew near enough, one of them called out, "Who are you and what's your business here in the desert?"

Bancom took a deep breath. In this expanded moment, he knew. He instantly felt a strong instinct to tell the simple truth. "I'm Bancom al-Salabar, and I'm carrying something of great value into the city."

The boldness of his answer surprised the men. They knew that their appearance would give him sufficient reason to believe them bandits. And here he announces that he's in possession of something that has great value. It simply made no sense. A second rider responded. "What could you be carrying that's of such great value when you have only two small bags across your horse?"

"It's nothing in the bags."

"What is it, then?"

"It's a message." Bancom remained calm and firm.

First one, then another, then three of the five opposing horses showed slight movement, but were restrained. The armed stranger who had just questioned him spoke again. "Who is to receive your message?"

"It's for an important man in the palace of the king."

"Who's the man?"

"The treasurer and high counselor."

"What's the nature of the message?"

Bancom was silent for a few seconds. "I must ask you a question if I'm to respond to yours appropriately, and with all due respect."

The gunman looked suspicious. "What's your question?"

Bancom spoke firmly, but without emotion. "If I can reflect your own challenge to me: Who are you? And what's your business here in the desert?"

Two of the men turned to each other and smiled. Never had they come across anyone who would be so daring in the face of their number and their weapons in a situation like this. Such a man was either crazy, or greatly to be respected.

One of the riders replied, "We're on horseback and armed, and we're dressed as bandits, aren't we?"

"Yes, you are."

"But things are not always what they seem," the man then said.

"I know. Who are you, then?"

"We're soldiers of the king, sent in disguise into the desert to find and arrest, or to eliminate the bandits who've been causing trouble and interrupting the normal commerce of the kingdom in recent days. They've committed murders on two occasions."

For a moment, Bancom was relieved and then, just as quickly, he was alarmed. He instantly realized how disastrous it would have been to pursue the first defensive strategy that had come to mind, to have lied and identified himself as a bandit in search of others to join. He would have been arrested or killed by these soldiers, with their distinctive orders, and if he subsequently protested that he had lied simply to protect himself, he would have had nothing with him to confirm his true identity and purpose. And they would then have found him to be a liar, a man who was not to be trusted.

In that moment, Bancom was having reinforced in his heart a lesson that we all have a chance to learn at some point in our lives. Truth is the only sure foundation for getting our footing in the world. Even lies that seem perfectly designed for avoiding trouble can cause many more problems than they avert. Bancom was glad he'd trusted his deeper instincts and his normal commitment to speaking the truth.

But his second thought, following quickly on the first, was that, while he might have been able to bluff bandits and appear to join up with them for a short time, to save himself and perhaps still get to the city to accomplish his mission, soldiers of the current king would surely shoot him as a traitor. Or at best, they would capture him and prevent his mission, if they at all detected his true revolutionary aim.

And yet, clearly, the truth had served him well up to now. However dangerous speaking the truth might appear to be, he knew that it's in the end typically more dangerous to depart from it. So, he'd continue to tell the truth, and he'd find a way to do it that still might allow him to emerge unscathed, if that was at all possible.

Bancom nodded his head in response to the soldiers and gave a small courtly bow. "I'm glad to learn who you are. I greet you as worthy guardians of the peace, and warriors for the good of the kingdom. As you can see, if you examine my appearance carefully, I'm certainly no bandit."

"You're on a strong horse."

"I'm a courier. And speed is required. I was entrusted with a message that I'm to give to the highest-ranking official at the king's right hand."

The big man quizzing him responded instantly. "So, as I asked you before, and you now may answer, what's the message you carry?"

"I can tell you what it is, although I may also ask you to explain to me exactly what it means. I know it has to do with the safety and integrity of the kingdom, in matters of domestic justice and foreign affairs. It's a simple but cryptic message whose intended recipient, I've been assured, will understand and appreciate it for what it is."

"Speak the message, then. Get on with it."

"The message is this: 'The Owl of Egypt is ready to fly.' That's all."

Two of the men looked puzzled, and yet, said nothing. Two more quickly glanced at each other, as if surprised. Bancom could see on their faces an instant recognition of the unusual phrase that he had uttered. The fifth soldier showed no reaction, and now spoke.

"Who is this Owl? And what's meant by his flying?"

"I'm sorry. It's not my business, as a mere messenger, and it hasn't been given into my power, to explain these words, but only to convey them. Those who are to receive the message, I'm told, will need no explanation from an intermediary like me. Whatever this means, I can assure you, as I've been amply assured, it's something exceedingly good for the kingdom. I've been led to believe, by honorable men, that those who hear it will be glad."

"Who are these men? Who gave you this message?"

Bancom's horse stirred. He pulled the reigns in a bit and said, "It was given to me by men from a distant place, whose veiled identities and circumstances prevent my being able to provide their names. But I've been reliably assured that they are great friends of the kingdom."

The first of the men to have spoken, the one who initially demanded Bancom's name, as well as the purpose that brought him into the desert, was one of the two who had shown a moment of surprise and a hint of recognition when hearing him say, "The Owl of Egypt." He now immediately replied, as if to fend off any further questions.

"Very good. That's good. Your answer, I think, will suffice. We'll respect your role in what may be a great service to the kingdom, however mysterious it might remain to us." One of the other soldiers looked at this colleague of his with perplexity and hesitation. But the man continued. "I can assure you that you'll not be granted entry into the palace unless you're expected, and so you'll be able to do no harm if what you say is false. And, if your words are true, we need to provide you with safe passage. Because of that, we'll grant you freedom to pass. But there's something you must agree to allow, as well."

"What's that?"

"You must let us follow you for at least the next few hours, in case you attract any of the bandits we're hunting. They're especially keen to find lone travelers, such as you will appear to be. We can protect you and your mission and, by trailing you, we also may find the men we seek. We'll ride behind you at a distance, so that our presence won't be detected as soon as yours is, by anyone up ahead of us, between here and the city. But if you get in trouble, you can turn and ride toward us. We'll see you and intervene."

Relief flooded through Bancom's entire mind and body. What had seemed to augur the end of his task, and likely his life, would now serve to protect and facilitate it. Things are indeed not always what they at first seem.

"I thank you and your comrades for your kindness, and agree with gratefulness to your proposed plan. I have a small pistol in my belt, but that's no protection from a band of thieves who could attack me along the road. Your proximity will be appreciated. I may be able to help you in your search, and your availability for support will surely help me. I can assure you that your kindness will be remembered."

Bancom had good reason to believe that at least two of these five men before him were secret supporters of his mission and would indeed now ride in his protection. They certainly appeared to have had a prior acquaintance with the unusual phrase, "The Owl of Egypt." So they must know more than, at present, they could say, in front of their puzzled comrades.

This greatly relieved messenger was playing a crucial role in a complicated plan involving a thirteen-year-old boy, his seventy-year-old uncle, and a major event that had been hoped for by many in the kingdom for years. The boy had left his village several days earlier with his uncle and a caravan of men and animals. He'd been told that they were going out to cross the desert, as they periodically did, to take goods to Cairo for sale. It was the boy's first journey across the vast desolation of central Egypt, and it had already turned into the most amazing adventure of his life.

At an oasis early in the trip, the older man, Ali Shabeezar, had begun to speak to his nephew at length about
life, its wonders, and its challenges. He had decided that it
was time to prepare the boy for what he knew would eventually lie ahead. Something must have told him, deep down,
that this preparation would soon be important, and should
now commence. There was vital wisdom to share, and deep
insight to pass on to young Walid. What was about to develop would make these conversations crucial for the welfare
of all.

Hours earlier in the day, an act of treachery by one of their
traveling companions had radically altered the established
timetable for a secretly planned political revolution that was
otherwise plotted to occur within a year. Walid knew nothing
of this revolution, or of the role that the men around him
were to play in it. And now it had to happen, right away.
Because of this, it was necessary for Ali to tell Walid some
things about the two of them and their family history that
had never before even been hinted at in the young man's presence. These surprising truths were due to be revealed soon,
anyway, by his parents in the normal course of events and,
most likely, within a few months. But the moment had come
much sooner than expected, with its own timing, and so, at
the second and final oasis where they were taking some rest in
their desert trek toward Cairo, the old man and the boy had
held the most unexpected conversation of Walid's life.

What he had heard, he could hardly believe. His uncle
Ali was a displaced king, known to supporters as "The Owl
of Egypt." And Walid himself was the rightful prince of the
kingdom. The boy was utterly stunned by these disclosures,
and would not have been able to accept them as true if they
had come from anyone other than his parents, or this man,

his dear uncle, whom he loved and trusted. He could barely take in what he was hearing as these revelations were made.

A long awaited overthrow of the current illegitimate government would have to take place much sooner, and at vastly greater risk, than had been anticipated. A fellow traveler and member of their group had slipped out of their camp before daylight, and a full day before their intended departure from the oasis together, to reach the city ahead of everyone else and betray their secret cause to the authorities. It was now vital for Ali to tell Walid all about what was going on, and in some degree of detail. Certain things would have to happen quickly.

No plan can anticipate every problem. And yet, suitable preparation can often mitigate disaster. There was a good chance, in the present case, that it might. Still, as Ali's old friend and messenger Bancom had just experienced, nothing worth doing is easy, or without its difficulties. A few hours before Bancom first encountered the armed men who now followed him, he had left the peaceful oasis and the large caravan of friends that had been slowly traversing the desert to indeed take their goods to market, as they did twice a year. But, as Walid had now learned, their caravan wasn't simply the normal group of merchants it seemed to be. Like many other things in the world, its ordinary appearance masked a very different reality.

The assemblage of men and animals currently making their own way out of that oasis, but initially in a very different direction from the path Bancom rode, was in reality the entourage and core revolutionary force of a dispossessed king. Their veiled primary mission originally had been intended to further cultivate and prepare their newest confederates in the capital city to help with their long awaited return to power, when its proper time would yet come. But a single man, acting from simple greed, had changed their hidden purpose on this trip from that of preparation to one that would bring either a new regime to the kingdom within days, or else, possibly, death to at least most of those on the caravan, and soon, without delay.

2

A Royal Heritage

The day had begun after the deepest sleep of Walid's life, a slumber of utter unknowing that was shattered by a man named Jazeer, who came running up to the tent the boy shared with his uncle and jerked open the flap as he nearly shouted, "Ali! Ali!"

The old man pulled himself out of an equally deep repose. "Yes?"

"Faisul is gone! And three camels are missing!"

Ali leaned up on one arm. "What about the things the camels were carrying?"

"He left some of the bags behind, but took one that had been on Masoon's camel, the special bag!"

The old man rubbed his eyes and sighed deeply and said, "I see. Go get Masoon and Hamid immediately. We must take action. And tell Bancom to ride like the wind. He'll know what to do."

The boy had been shaken awake by the first urgent words from Jazeer. He listened to everything and said, "Uncle, what's going on?"

"Don't worry." Ali began putting on his sandals, as he realized what he now had to do. The situation had to be explained.

He began gently sharing with Walid some secrets of their family history, and more about this news with Faisul and how it would create both an opportunity and a great risk. Ali told Walid many things that he had never heard before, and although he made the account as brief as he could, it was still a lot for the boy to absorb. Walid had grown up knowing only that one of his grandfathers had lived and worked far away from their small village, in the legendary capital city of Cairo, doing some important job that had never been named, and that he had died tragically in mid-life. But now, the boy could hear the full story—or, at least, most of it.

Decades past, Walid's grandfather in Cairo was actually the king of their land, as had been his father, and his father before him, going back through history. Walid's uncle Ali was now the rightful king, and Walid himself was not just a normal boy meant for life in a small village, but the true Prince of Egypt. As Ali spoke, Walid could hardly understand the words he was saying. How could this be? Why had he never been told any of it? Ali revealed, as quickly as he could, the secrets that would be so important now for Walid to know. But as the old man spoke, he recalled within his own mind much more than he could put into words in the brief time available before they would all have to leave the oasis where they had been camping.

Walid's grandfather, Malik Shabeezar, was a good and legendary monarch, an enlightened leader of his people. But he was tragically assassinated by a group of wickedly ambitious men who had long schemed to take control of the land for their own purposes. His wife, Queen Noori, and their young son, Prince Ali, had escaped at the last minute through the assistance of a palace butler and had fled to safety outside the kingdom with a small group of their friends, relatives, and helpers. Several months later, the queen gave birth to another son of the late king and named him Rumi, in honor of a philosopher and poet long admired by her lamented husband. She raised the baby well and educated him thoroughly, in the company of her older son, with a firm hope that one day they would return to the palace and resume their rightful reign over the kingdom.

The years passed and the two boys grew strong. Their mother had a habit of dropping little nuggets of wisdom into the time she spent with them throughout the day. Even in their childhood years, she would say such things as: Education is possibility. Knowledge is power. Your dreams can give you direction. Enjoy much, need little, and love greatly. Pour your heart into everything you do. Character is destiny. Everything starts in the mind. Guard and cultivate your soul, above all else. Excellence is the key to influence. What you do with the gift of life is ultimately your decision. Every choice matters. Actions add up.

She knew that not all these ideas would make sense right away, but she believed that exposure to them would make a difference, over the long run. She was preparing the boys for their own proper forms of greatness, in every way she could.

To this end, she gave them advice about life with words they could remember. And she often counseled them about their attitudes and actions. As they grew older, she would tell them about what she called "the simple mathematics of life." Fairness adds, unfairness subtracts. Kindness multiplies, unkindness divides. The brothers would sometimes have fun with her little pronouncements, and make joking alterations for their mutual entertainment, but that was just fine with her. From sheer repetition, many of these simple lessons would stay with them throughout their lives, and come to mind when they were needed.

One day while they were all preparing the noon meal, during his eleventh year of age, Ali asked his mother about destiny. He had heard some men speaking of it, and wanted to know what it is.

"That's a big question, my son." Noori smiled and patted her growing boy on the head, smoothing his hair. "Destiny has to do with the whole of life. It's about the experiences we'll have, the things we'll do, and the paths we'll take throughout this great adventure we're on."

She looked off into the distance and was silent for a moment. Then she said, "Let me explain. Some things happen to us. Other things happen because of us. Destiny is a fruitful combination of the two. We're never just puppets in a play written by others. We're not grains of sand, or blades of grass, blown about by the wind. We're free to act and create something new. Your destiny—the past, present, and future realization of your promise, your talents, and your choices—awaits your wise action, and your masterful creation. Act well, create beautifully, love always, and your destiny will be truly yours."

No subject of interest to the boys was forbidden. No question was discouraged. But there were some matters that could be revealed only when the time was right. This wise mother held a few things close to her heart and waited on favorable circumstance to provide the key that alone would unlock those hidden truths and help her sons chart their ultimate destinies in the world. On all the things they did discuss, Noori gave lavishly of her considerable knowledge and insights. She could tell that the boys both shared her sparkling intellect, her intuition, and her good heart.

After a passage of years, the exiled queen and her two sons quietly returned to a remote part of the kingdom, and lived in many ways as normally as any small family would, but without their true identities being known to their new neighbors—at least, not at first. Friends and supporters also gradually relocated to be near them, over a period of time, so as not to raise any awkward questions or suspicions. But the village they had found was lively and friendly, and was on a popular caravan path. Because of this, strangers and new arrivals were often welcomed into the community. And, as their distinctive story began to be shared, quietly, to a few trusted new friends, they found plenty of allies who pledged to protect them from any discovery or harm, and to help them in the future.

When the boys were at the proper age and level of maturity, Queen Noori revealed to Ali, and later to Rumi, the secrets of their royal birth, their history, and some other things that set them apart as a family. Her explanations awakened in Ali many old, almost forgotten memories of his early childhood, and now he understood images in his mind that had perplexed him for years. In time, the family story was told to Rumi as well, and when that day came, he, like his brother before him, took the news with great seriousness and conviction and kept all these things in his heart, as his mother had, for so long.

The older son, Ali, became tall and powerful in body, mind, and purpose, and eventually built a general store in their village. He later added a bookshop, so that with these combined ventures he could more easily gather the information and supplies he would eventually need in order to fulfill his mother's dreams, and now his own plans, for a restoration of their enlightened rule over the kingdom. The store also provided a discreet meeting place for quiet political planning and other related activities of a confidential, and even clandestine, nature.

The younger boy Rumi helped around the house and with the stores in any way he could, and also grew strong and exceptionally bright. When he wasn't playing with friends, he was often to be found in the bookshop, reading on his own and learning all that he could about the world. As time passed, he began to feel his own strong sense of personal calling, distinct from what he now knew about his family history. Eventually, through his extensive studies, he became a physician to the poor in their area. His mother understood, and she encouraged him. A deep sense of mission should be respected. Life takes us down many unexpected paths. And that's important, for without its many surprises, this world would not be nearly as interesting and challenging, or as full of opportunity as it is.

In his early middle years, a bit late in life, but delayed only because of his studies and dedicated work, Rumi eventually married a kind, intelligent young woman who lived near their village and, when the time was right, they had a son they named Walid—a bright, smiling baby that Rumi was sure would one day, as a man, rule the kingdom. He and his wife Bhati educated and prepared this son well in all the basics of mathematics, science, economics, history, geography, and politics, as well as in the arts, and in some of the simplest and most fundamental ideas of philosophy. Within their home, life wisdom was often in the air, as they continued the tradition of Queen Noori.

There were always bits of advice floating about: Know yourself. Do nothing in excess. To have a friend, be a friend.

Treat others as you would want to be treated. Anger is seldom a good counselor. Wisdom finds the help it needs. In everything, do your best, and release the rest.

Young Walid even heard such statements as: The ideal must guide the real. Truth is the foundation for trust. Meaning and purpose should lead the way. Relationships rule the world. Love comes first, and all else second. He didn't, of course, grasp fully everything like this that he heard his parents say, but his mind grew from being exposed to these things, as his father's had before him, and with the passage of time, he understood more. The seeds of wisdom long planted in his mind grew and germinated, and began to bloom into an inner strength that he would soon need.

Most of all, Rumi and Bhati taught their son to ask questions, think well, and remember what he learned. But these loving parents had not yet revealed to Walid, at his current age, the royal identity and possible future role that was his. Like Queen Noori had done with her sons, they had been waiting for what would seem to be the right moment. For the boy's safety and a normal childhood, they had postponed this crucial information until they could be sure that he was old enough to absorb it, keep it within his heart, and use it well.

He was now thirteen years old, but not by much. And he was going along with his uncle Ali for the first time on one of the older man's regular trips across the desert, in the company of other merchants, traders, and friends. Ali was sensitive to the concerns of the boy's parents for Walid's safety, as well as for his ongoing education on their trek across the sands of the kingdom. And so he had started teaching the boy, in his own way, during the journey, discussing some of the most crucial insights for life that can protect us and prepare us for the uncertainties that inevitably lie ahead.

There were several respects in which Ali was no ordinary uncle. He was surely, by normal standards of the time, an older man, but he was still possessed of great vigor, the strength of a much younger age, and an incredibly sharp mind, along with extraordinary wisdom, which he had been sharing with Walid at a new depth in their time together across the desert. They had talked of inner peace, life balance, the dance of change, the vast power of the mind, the nature of danger, the basic elements that structure everything around us, and the liberating consequences of self-control, among many other topics. The boy was developing rapidly in his understanding of the deeper insights that can properly guide us, as these conversations continued, day-after-day. Although Walid didn't realize it at the time, he was being prepared for great things that were very soon to come.

Their desert caravan was on a journey that had been intended to serve both economic purposes and, of course, unknown to Walid until now, strategic political ends, as a source of both important income and vital information for all the men involved. Plus, they had planned on this trip to expand their influence with certain people connected to the palace in Cairo. But the exact nature of their initial secret purposes had now been transformed, literally, overnight. This trip to the capital city had been meant as the last visit to the surroundings of the palace that these men would make for surveillance, finance, strategy, recruitment, and final planning before they were to launch a needed revolution, many months out, by their preferred and now well-established timetable. But in their many preparations, they had always remembered the old saying that, "Men plan and God smiles." Things don't always go as we expect. And we then need to adapt.

The pace of their plans had been instantly accelerated and

the nature of the trip completely altered when one of the newer camel drivers and helpers, the man named Faisul, awoke in the early morning hours before any of the others. He stole what he thought to be some highly sensitive materials, along with three camels, and slipped away from the oasis where they had all stopped for a period of rest. He left long before dawn to travel toward the city—a good two or three day journey to the east. His intent was to profit from betraying the men and the cause he had pretended to follow. While acting like a loyal supporter for months, he had been scheming to turn on Ali, in service to his own personal desires, and trade information about the group's political aims for what he hoped would be a great deal of gold from the guardians of the current regime.

Ali and his closest comrades had anticipated the possibility of such an act of treachery at some point, and especially during the most recent months when they had been gathering many new followers and helpers in preparation for the upcoming events. They had created for their protection an elaborate and clever scheme so that any traitor in pursuit of his own goals might also, though unintentionally, act in their favor.

In a bag that he stole, Faisul had earlier seen some money and what he wrongly thought to be a valuable collection of precious jewels, along with a letter addressed by name to men who clearly seemed, by the contents of the message, to be secret confederates of the rightful regent and soon-to-be-revolutionary, Ali Shabeezar. The letter to these men, who were in moderately high leadership positions within the current regime, alerted them to imminent action on the rebellion and impending take-over that it acknowledged they had long wanted, and schemed to make happen. It explicitly thanked them for any help in this upcoming event, and it requested immediately what was referred to as their important assistance in all these matters.

Faisul could not believe his luck. This was the written proof of a planned revolution that he had needed. The money and fake gems that were in the bag had been put there to allow any traitor to think that his theft of its contents would probably be seen by the others as mere robbery, and nothing more. He would be unlikely to even conceive that the other men might know exactly what he was doing.

He was now riding across the desert alone, taking the letter to the current king's most loyal men, in hopes of securing a generous reward for revealing this plot against the palace. But unknown to him, the concocted letter was addressed to individuals who were actually not confederates of Ali and his comrades at all, but rather independent conspirators within the palace who had been planning on their own to turn against their king and use again the quick and brutal tool of assassination, as their fathers long before had done, to accomplish their equally corrupt ambitions.

By giving the current king's vice-regents the carefully contrived letter, Faisul inadvertently would be seeing to it that the main rivals of Ali, and primary impediments to his plan, would swiftly be arrested, along with their cohorts, and prevented from interfering with his intention to restore the rightful monarchy. In addition, any brigade of soldiers who would then certainly be sent out to intercept the camel train in the desert would also have false information from the letter about where the caravan would be, and in what direction they would be traveling.

The messenger that Ali had sent out right away from the oasis, Bancom al-Salabar, had been a close friend for many years, and the older man knew that he could be trusted with the most crucial task of the moment. Because of that, Ali had provided him with a powerful horse and a mission to leave the caravan and travel fast, by a route unknown to Faisul, into the city. He was to arrive prior to the traitor and set in motion the events that now needed to happen soon, before any unwanted interference could make them more difficult than they were already going to be.

Bancom's job was to tell their central contacts in the capital that the time was suddenly upon them all for the long-planned restoration of kingship to the Shabeezars. He had been given a cryptic message using a code phrase for Ali that he would pass on to the right people, and it would instantly set everything in motion. He would then rapidly get the word out to all their secret supporters in the government and the military, as well as in other groups in the city, and with their help, he would be able to open the right doors for the arrival of Ali and his men. If everything went well, the throne could then be retaken by a combined force of the caravan's well trained warriors and their internal palace sympathizers, augmented by friendly forces within the military. And it would most likely take place while a top unit of the kingdom's army would be away, out of town, chasing cold trails in the desert.

Ali was different from most revolutionaries. He sought a victory of stealth and strategy, not one of terrible violence. So the details of everything that needed to be put into place were important. And the entire plan was, at present, on Bancom's broad shoulders, as he rode on through the desert with focus and determination.

But no plan can anticipate every problem. And nothing worth doing is easy, or without difficult and complicating challenges that can come as complete surprises, as they were all soon to experience. Great danger lay in wait for them, in a place and manner they never could have anticipated.

3

INTO THE MARKETPLACE

THE NEXT TWO DAYS WERE A BLUR OF ACTIVITY. BANCOM was followed to the edge of the city by the five soldiers who at first had seemed so threatening. They met up with him in sight of town, wished him well, and sent him on his way. In a surprisingly short time, despite his exhaustion, he was able to make contact with their most elevated and secret of supporters, the treasurer and high counselor of the kingdom. He conveyed his brief message and by doing so launched the preliminary events that were his job to initiate.

The camel train had also by now made its way to the far outskirts of the city, unseen by hostile forces and untouched by thieves. An hour or more from their destination, they broke up into eight groups of mostly three to seven men each, one of them including the young prince and the rightful king. These small groups took several different routes into town, with diverse arrival times, so as not to advertise their overall number, or give any indication that they were all together. If their traitor, Faisul, had by any chance managed to arrive first and tell those in power his news, the authorities would be searching for a large caravan, not for small groups of men approaching the city in different ways and blending in with all the other clusters of people who were daily on the various roads into the capital.

The morning was bright and clear. The sand under their camels even seemed welcoming. A light breeze cooled their faces. The boy had never seen the city, and as it came into view down below them, still at a distance, he was amazed at its evident size. He looked over at his uncle, and at a well-disguised Masoon Afah, their companion and friend who was well known throughout the kingdom for his legendary fighting skills. As he gazed also at the four other good men who accompanied them, Walid wondered with a sharp twinge of perplexity how their little band of revolutionaries could possibly take control of such a large and magnificent place, along with the entire domain of its kingdom.

The men brought their camels to a stop, and Walid spoke up. "Uncle, I'm concerned."

"What is it, my boy?"

"The city's so big and we're so small."

"Yes. What you say is true. But remember one thing. Our calling is much greater than any number of buildings or men." Ali spoke with real warmth and conviction in his voice.

"But how can we, who are few, have the power to act over all these people, who are many?"

"Power is multiplied by purpose. There's tremendous power in doing what's right. An organized few with a noble purpose and a focused plan can prevail over a vast multitude."

"Your uncle says it well." Masoon moved his camel up closer, having overheard some of the brief conversation.

Ali smiled. "Thank you, my friend. I think our young companion feels a bit overwhelmed by the size of the city that will soon be our home."

Masoon nodded at the old man and turned back to look at the boy.

"Your Highness, this is true?"

Walid sighed and said, "Yes, it is. I've felt a little over-whelmed lately, I admit, in many ways, but just seeing such a place lifts my concern to a new level."

"That's natural. It takes us all a while to get our minds and hearts around anything that's big and new. But I promise you something. You'll soon learn that this city is as large as it has to be in order to serve its many functions, and yet that it's also as well sized as it can be to act as your new home. In both regards, it's going to provide for your needs quite properly, as a prince, and then one day, a king."

Masoon gestured toward the distant buildings and bustle of people, and said, "Right now, there's already something about this city that's completely up to you, fully within your royal power. You can use your mind to claim it as yours. You can take emotional ownership of this place in your mind and heart. You have the power to do this with any place you ever find yourself. There's nothing here that should intimidate you. But you'll indeed find many things at which to marvel. In your spirit, you can own these marvels and take great com-fort in them."

Walid replied, "That's a good point of view, Masoon. And I needed to hear it. Thank you for it. I take great comfort already in being with you and Uncle Ali, and all the other men." He spoke with evident honestly, and added, "I'm sure that what you say is true. I easily forget that most of what the world is to me is really up to me and how I choose to think and feel about it. But this is a recent lesson, as you know, from Uncle Ali that I've been trying to remember and put into practice. New wisdom sometimes can take a while to work its way into my feelings. Now, I'll be able to use this insight in a new setting. I'll be able to put into action what I have learned from all of you."

The old man spoke up. "You'll soon have a chance to use many things that you've learned over the course of your life, and lately."

Masoon quickly agreed. "Every day is a test of what we've learned. And each new day is a classroom for learning more. We'll keep being tested to make sure we've learned not just with our heads, but also with our hearts and habits. Gradually then, over time, and by all the testing, we're transformed into teachers as well, while still always remaining the students we're meant to be."

"That's correct." The old man nodded his agreement. "To be a great leader you must always be a great learner. Then you can become the teacher and guide that every leader should be. Curiosity and a real openness to new things are the keys. Cultivate a healthy curiosity in all ways, stay open to new insights, and you'll do well."

"I'm sure curious to find out what life in such a place is like." The boy spoke honestly. "I'm also keen to see what will greet us when we arrive, as well as to learn how we can prevail. And I'm going to be open to this new experience, in whatever ways it will come."

"Then let's go on. There's much for all of us to learn and do." Ali turned to face the panoramic view of their destination and gently directed his camel to begin the final short walk that would bring them up to the large and always crowded marketplace spread out on the edge of town. The boy then followed with Masoon and the others.

There was as yet no way to communicate with the other groups that had gone in earlier, or with those who were still arriving at variously different entry points into the hub of kingdom activity. There would be, in fact, much for all of them to learn and to do.

One of Ali's most trusted friends, a former soldier of the kingdom named Hakeem, had arrived on the opposite, north end of the market, with six other men about an hour earlier. They stabled their camels near the marketplace, and split up into smaller groups in order to seek out their friends in what seemed to be hundreds of shops and stalls, and quietly make known their presence and new purpose. There were many merchants in the vast bazaar who were secret confederates and would know what to do in order to put into action the plan they had created together.

With Hakeem were Mahmood, Bashir, Zahur, a man known as Simon the Shepherd, Naqid, and Dubin, one of the older men. Hakeem divided them into three groups. He sent Dubin with Bashir to the western part of the market, and he took with himself Simon and Naqid. Mahmood and Zahur settled the camels into their temporary stable and then carried bags of garments in another direction.

Seconds after they had split off and were going their own ways, Dubin spoke to his partner quite seriously and in a hushed voice. "Bashir, I don't recall the exact sequence of things we've been assigned. What's our first order of business?"

Bashir lowered his head and whispered back with great energy. "I was thinking falafels, with roasted goat, peppers, onions, and perhaps some hummus with garlic on the side. And beans for an accompaniment would be nice."

Dubin laughed. "No, no, I mean, where do we go first to make our contacts?"

Bashir smiled. "I understand what you mean, and I'm

completely serious, my friend. We have the great good fortune to follow our noses straight to the stall of Karim, the cook. He's famous for his food, you know. We are to eat there and talk as if we're just normal merchants hungry for a meal, and then give him our message. I have these orders from Masoon and Hamid themselves. They know how to keep me on task with a job I'll enjoy."

"Yes, I've seen you enjoy such a task very much." Dubin cracked a smile again. "Your frame bespeaks this enjoyment in ample ways."

Bashir wagged a chubby finger in the air. "Any job that involves a falafel or two is certainly one for me." The man's capacity to eat was legendary, and so were the unpleasant consequences in his digestive tract that those around him would have to tolerate unless they could manage to stay decidedly upwind of him. Dubin recalled the last large pot of beans they had shared in the desert and had to chuckle, while he glanced around for any large, open area that might be nearby.

As they made their way through the crowded market, looking like either ordinary shoppers or visiting suppliers, other groups were arriving at different points in the area. They, too, were breaking into smaller parties and going about their business of making contact and passing on messages. Each group had its assignments. And all were important.

The many previous trips Ali had made to the city under the cover of normal trade had been opportunities for the elaborate planning with their friends in the capital that alone could secure for them what they now sought. But every minute they were in the crowded public market at this point was, in principle, a moment of risk. Someone not in their network could recognize one of them and, depending on how fast Faisul's revelations of a plot might have traveled, potentially alert the authorities to their presence. For this reason, the widely recognized Masoon was very well disguised, and even Ali was taking unusual precautions to shroud his face.

Throughout the marketplace, a dozen or more vendors and proprietors of shops were already leaving their stalls and kiosks. They were either closing early for the day, or else turning over operations to a son or daughter or friend, as they began to make their way apart from the crowds and toward the palace, where they could put into play their piece of the plan on short notice. Fortunately for all, it was a plan that had been designed for adaptation and last minute change.

The old man and the boy had just ridden up on their camels to an area where the animals could be fed, watered, and put into some shade to rest from their journey. Bags of woven goods were removed from the camels—beautiful tapestries and carpets—and Ali, Masoon, and two other men carried them over toward a large stall of home furnishings, a short distance away, but still within sight of the camel stop. Ali had asked Walid, Hamid and another man, Baldoor, who was good at managing money, to make sure the camels were settled in, and that their bill for the animals was paid in advance. It was understood that the two men with Walid were also acting as his bodyguards at this point, and that they should all stay close together.

This was understood by everyone, except, apparently, Walid.

As Hamid and Baldoor haggled with the camel attendant over exactly what they needed and were willing to pay for those services, the conversation was getting a bit more heated than Walid had expected. Apparently, the man in charge of the stable thought he had enough camels to care for already, and didn't want to receive more at that point in the day. He was demanding a greater than standard fee for his services, and Hamid and Baldoor seemed to believe it was all a ploy to separate them from more of their money than necessary.

While the men argued, a beautiful young girl about Walid's age suddenly caught his eye. She was walking through the market very close by with a nice looking man and a stunning lady who seemed like they could be her parents. The girl gazed over at Walid just long enough for him to see her face and feel his heart leap in his chest as he detected what was clearly a slight smile forming on her lips. For a moment, he forgot where he was and what he was doing. He was captured by this vision in front of him. And just then, several younger boys ran by her. One bumped up against an elegant woven basket she was carrying and caused it to drop to the ground. Without even thinking, Walid ran across the broad path separating them, bent down to grab the handle of the basket, and stopping close to the girl, held it out to her.

Her mother was at the moment exclaiming, "My goodness! These boys are so wild and careless!"

Walid looked up at the mother more attentively and was astonished at her beauty, which was like none he had ever seen. He also noticed the finely made garments she was wearing, her artistic jewelry, and the noble demeanor that she and her husband both displayed, even in a moment like this. He quickly said, "I'm so sorry. I'm afraid you're right. And too many of them grow up to be men who are no different. But not all boys are this way." The lady smiled at him broadly.

Turning back to the girl, who had not yet reached out for the basket, he said, "I saw the rascals knock this from your hands, and wanted to get it for you before it could become soiled or damaged."

The mother replied. "Thank you, very much. You seem like a fine young man, and one with honor." She looked at the girl, smiled again, and nodded her approval.

The girl then reached out to take the basket and said, "Thank you for your kindness. May I ask your name?"

"I'm Walid."

"Thank you, Walid. You're a true gentleman."

At this, the boy could feel himself blushing intensely. A mixture of embarrassment, pride, longing, and instant infatuation coursed through his body and made him feel a bit light headed. As he was about to be bold and ask her name, in return, the lady put her hand on the girl's shoulder and said to him, "We'd better be getting along now. It was nice to meet you, Walid."

"It was my pleasure to meet you and your daughter. And you, sir." He looked up at the man who had been standing silently through all this. The gentleman nodded his head and gave Walid a small but genuine looking smile in response. As they walked off down the marketplace path, Walid watched them go and gradually disappear into the crowds. He stood motionless, with absolutely no thoughts whatsoever in his head. He then brushed back his hair, took a deep breath, and said in a very low, barely audible voice, "Wow."

Just then, three stalls down and on a side street out of sight from the place where Hamid and Baldoor were still arguing with the man about camels and money, Walid happened to see an older gentleman run into the path, look quickly about, and then gesture right at him, motioning frantically. He shouted, "Help me! Help me! My little pet, my animal is loose! Please! I need you to help me catch him!" Without any hesitation, Walid rushed forward again to be of assistance.

The man waved him into an area between the two stalls, a darker passageway, saying with urgency in his voice, "Quickly! Quickly! He's here in the back somewhere, out of his cage! I can't catch him myself!" The boy ran between the stalls, and just as he said, "What are we looking for?" a bag was pulled over his head from behind him. Strong hands grabbed him. Something was forced over his mouth, around his covered head, and as he struggled and tried to cry out, he felt his arms being pulled backwards and tied together.

"Take him!"

"Quickly!" He heard muffled voices as he jerked around and felt his feet and then his whole body lifted up by what must have been two powerful men, who then dropped him roughly onto a hard surface. There was a sudden movement of air, and he heard the sound of something slamming down over him. Everything went black, as the noise of voices grew much quieter beyond the bag on his head. There was shuffling and he was being jostled now, but not directly. It felt like he was in a large box of some sort, and it was lifted up and carried. With a loud thump and a jolt, he knew the box had been put down again. Then a lurch and a rhythmic bumping told him he was on something like a donkey cart, being taken away from the stall. But, taken where? And who was doing this? And, why?

As panic began to replace shock and confusion, he remembered his uncle's advice that, when facing anything unexpected and scary, like the desert storm they had been through together, he should remain as calm as possible. He took several deep breaths through the bag and tried to slow his racing heart. He said to himself, over and over, in the quiet of his mind, "I have to keep calm. I'll get out of this. I will get out of this."

Then he had the thoughts, "Uncle's close by. Masoon's near. Hamid and Baldoor are here. Somebody will notice I'm gone, any second now. They'll find me. I'll be fine. I shouldn't be afraid."

But the fear he felt was altogether appropriate for the danger that now awaited him.

4

In Sight of the Palace

Nothing happens in this world without many contributing causes. But once the stage is set and everything is poised and ready, one action can seem to create, on its own, a major cascade of events.

The very moment Walid was taken, Hamid first noticed his absence. His heart leaped into his throat, and his feet were already moving toward the nearest stalls as he shouted, "Walid! Walid! Where are you!" Looking back, he yelled a bit louder, "Baldoor! Where's Walid?"

"I don't know! I thought he was right behind us! I don't see him!" Baldoor felt a tightening in his chest and began to follow Hamid at a quick pace, craning his neck in all directions to peer down the nearest pathways and through the crowds walking by.

"Stay here and look. Search quickly. I'll get Ali." Hamid broke into a fast stride toward their leader's position, bobbing and dodging the people strolling by, while visually scanning the mob of shoppers and vendors for any sight of the boy.

Masoon first noticed the approach of Hamid, and put his

hand on the old man's arm. He leaned into Ali's ear and said, in a low voice, "There must be some news or trouble. I see Hamid coming our way, and quickly. I'll handle it."

Ali simply nodded and continued to talk to the vendor of rugs and tapestries who was holding up one of their woven articles for a moment of inspection. Masoon took several steps in the direction of Hamid's progress, and, putting an index finger to his lips, met his intensely focused gaze. When they were face to face, now less than two feet apart, Hamid drew close and said, "Walid's disappeared. Baldoor's looking for him."

"How could this happen?"

"We were haggling over the price demanded for the care of our camels, and he was standing right behind us. Then, I turned around to speak to him and he was gone!"

Masoon looked back at Ali and the two men who were with him. They were already watching, aware that something had happened. Motioning to both of the men who were there primarily to guard the rightful king, Masoon said to Hamid, "Take these two with you to find him. I'll stay with Ali here for a moment, and then both of us will also join in the search. Some soldiers have been spotted nearby. Let's hope that Faisul's mischief didn't alert the authorities yet to be on the lookout for us. He could have identified Walid, or our young friend might have just wandered off. There's much here to see. But if he's been spotted and taken by the palace guard to be held hostage in order to stop us, then we'll have big trouble ahead."

The two other men reached them at that moment and Masoon said simply, "Go with Hamid. He'll explain." Then he turned to walk back to Ali and fill him in on the problem. The old man and the tapestry vendor both looked up as

Masoon approached. He spoke to the two of them equally, in a hushed voice. "Walid has suddenly disappeared. Baldoor is searching for him. I sent the men with Hamid to help. But we must learn quickly if the palace guard is behind this."

The vendor lowered his head and replied, "I think not, but it's possible. There were some soldiers nearby earlier, but they were regular troops who often police the market, not men from the palace guard. I recognized them. But there have been some kidnappings in town recently—some boys taken away, and rumors say they're sold into forced labor by someone in the government."

Ali replied, "This is not good. We have to find Walid as quickly as we can. His safety is of the utmost importance. With any delay in locating him, we'll need to change our plans, and there's very little time at this point. Things are already in motion."

The vendor nodded. "I'll send a few men to help. We should move with haste and yet not so quickly as to cause a scene and draw unwanted attention our way."

"I agree. And I thank you for the help." Ali gestured respectfully toward the man and then turned to walk with Masoon at a brisk pace back toward the camel stalls.

The heat in the box was now stifling, the darkness was oppressive, and the noise of travel was loud, as the donkey cart bumped over deep ruts in the dirt path. Walid suddenly became aware that his body was completely tense all over, as his head banged against the hard surface of wood beneath him with each big bump. His fear was making him nearly as rigid as the box that contained him at the moment. But he then came to the realization that this tension could just make things worse, and would have no positive impact on his prospects. So he made a conscious effort to empty his mind and breathe deep. He then relaxed his muscles sequentially, starting with his feet, and moving progressively up his legs to his torso, and out his arms, then through his neck and head. He focused on each spot of tension, and initially tightened it more, holding it in a squeeze, and then releasing it. His uncle had taught him how to do this, while once speaking to him about the importance of creating a place of peace within himself, and especially at difficult times.

Every few seconds, his body weight pitched onto his wrists and hands that were tied tightly together under him, and each time it hurt. But his deliberate breathing and ongoing relaxation efforts were having an effect. The loosening of his muscles seemed to dissipate some of the stress he felt. And he tried not to think about the pain. He directed his senses away from his body, and toward the outside of the box. As a result, he began to hear more of what was happening around him. He could detect bits and pieces of conversation a few feet away, but the noise of the cartwheels bouncing on the road obscured most of what was being said.

Right then, there was a bang and a jolt. The wheels under him seemed to have been lifted onto a path or road with a different surface. The cart stopped loudly lurching so much and the noises from the wheels were more rapidly rhythmic—clickety, clickety, clickety, clickety. He felt a turn, then another turn, and later on a third one, and then he sensed the cart slowing down and coming to a stop.

There was a muffled sound of banging, as if on a nearby door. Then voices. He could feel the box being lifted again and carried. He kept perfectly still and alert, noticing every sensation. He could hear the feet of two or three men shuffling across a hard floor, and their grunts and complaints. The box was tilted upward and he felt himself sliding down with his feet pressing the bottom of it. He was in this strange position for longer than he had expected. It felt and sounded like he was being carried up many stairs. Men cursed. There were more noises. Then, the box was set down roughly, not quite dropped, but he felt in his bones its impact with the floor. And there was a noise again of feet on the floor all walking away, and voices receding. A door shut heavily. He heard the distinct sound of a lock being turned. Finally, everything was silent around him for a few moments. Then he heard some shouting at a distance, and after that, it was quiet again.

Walid started thinking quickly about how to get out of the box. He pressed his feet against the lid, which he could feel was only a few inches above his toes. There was hardly room for a kick. But he tried first with his right foot, then his left, then the right again, and the left. He couldn't use his hands, since they were tied behind him, and he was lying a bit to the side. Just as he was about to try a kick again, he heard the sound of a latch being opened right beside him. There was a loud squeak, and light came bursting into the box as the lid was lifted upward. He twisted abruptly, as if to try to see what was happening, but the bag over his head blocked from his view the fact that another boy about his age or a little younger was at that moment leaning over him, holding the lid of the box straight up.

A low voice said, "It's Ok. Stay quiet. I'm Mafulla, your fellow captive. Let me take the bag off your head. They did the same thing to me."

Mafulla first untied a scarf that was over where Walid's mouth would be, and then pulled the bag off his head. The boy was a bit smaller than Walid and very skinny. He looked friendly, but also extremely concerned. He said, "Turn over a bit and I'll free your hands."

"Thank you!" Walid spoke the words in a loud whisper, then spit out some fibers that were in his mouth, and twisted to the side while Mafulla went to work on the rope that bound the arms of the prince. But, of course, he had no idea who this boy in the box might be. He was just treating the new arrival the way he would want to be treated by a fellow prisoner, or anyone. Within less than ten seconds, he had the ropes untied and Walid was raising himself up out of the box.

Mafulla offered him a hand and said, "Welcome to The Kidnapper's Hotel—the finest of its kind in luxury accommodations in all of Egypt, at least, up here in the penthouse."

Walid said, "What?"

The smaller boy looked a bit sheepish, but had a smile on his face. As he now stepped back to allow the new arrival enough room to get out and stand up next to the box, he added, "I'm sorry. I joke when I'm nervous. I'm just trying to make the best of a bad situation. But look around, it's much more spacious than the box. And I'm very glad to have some company."

Walid glanced around and replied, "I'm sorry. I'm just totally confused. What was your name again?"

"Mafulla. What's yours?"

"Walid."

"Hi, Walid. Nice to meet you. Do you come here often?"

Walid said, "I admire your ability to joke in a situation like this, whatever it is."

"Thanks."

"But, let's be serious for a minute. Where are we? What's happened to me? And who are the people doing this?" He continued to wipe loose threads from his mouth and face, and then rubbed his wrists, which were red and sore from the ropes.

Mafulla answered, "We've been kidnapped by some really bad guys. I've heard them talking outside the door. It sounds like they grab boys our age and sell us to some men in the palace who then turn around and sell us again, into forced labor, for a much higher price. The men here have been complaining that they should get more payment for each boy. I've heard them argue about it. Maybe it's because they recognized my own especially high quality, in mind, if not body."

"But where are we?" Walid was just getting his bearings, looking more carefully around the large, bare room.

"I don't know. We're somewhere in town. And it's always noisy down on the street, but muffled. I think we're on a second or third floor, and maybe an attic. I'm not sure. The street sounds come from pretty far below."

"That makes sense. It seemed like a long time they were carrying me up here."

"Yeah. I thought the same thing. I've tried shouting for help but no one down on the street heard me. And once when I did it, a big man came in and yelled loudly and threatened me and said something about cutting out my tongue, which is a body part I'm very fond of, so I've been quiet since then. There's only one small window up there, as you can see, and it's too high for me to reach. But now that they've left your box in the room, maybe we can use it to climb up and look through the window and figure out where we are."

"That's a good idea. And it is nice to meet you, by the way, despite the less than favorable situation. Let's get to the window. Maybe we'll see something to help us know where we are or what we should do."

Walid then immediately went into action, grabbing one end of the box. The boys slowly dragged it over to the window, as quietly as they could, and pulled it up on one of its ends, again, trying to make as little noise as possible. Walid cupped and intertwined his hands for Mafulla to step into, but instead, the smaller boy just looked confused. He said, "What are you doing with your hands?"

"Giving you a boost."

"Oh. Ok. I step into them?"

"Yes. Or I could just stand here in this strange position, whichever you'd prefer."

"Ha! You can be funny, too. Good. Let's hope you're also strong."

Mafulla carefully put one foot into Walid's interlaced hands and scrambled up onto the box, from where he could reach a low beam that he used to pull himself up to the barred window.

Within a second, he was whispering loudly. "Oh, my goodness! The palace! I can see The Golden Palace! It's at a distance, but there it is. And this is a nice angle on it. We're in a central location, in sight of the palace, just what I'd hoped."

"What do you mean?"

"We have a room with a view."

"Very funny, but please, let me look!" Walid whispered loudly as well. Mafulla instantly jumped down and then cupped his hands like he had just seen his new companion do. Walid looked at his skinny arms for a second, then, trusting that appearances aren't always a good guide to realities, put a foot gently into the boy's hands and climbed up onto the upright box. It took him a moment to get his balance there. Then, pulling himself up just enough by use of the same rafter beam, he too could see out the window and across a low building and beyond it. There was a great open square past it, and it was surrounded by busy streets and other low structures. And, beyond that, there was the most beautiful of all the buildings he had ever seen, glowing in the sun. It seemed to be made of golden sand, marble, and glass, with a roof of pure gold. It was shimmering like a beacon under the bright, clear sky. There were also flags of many colors flying in the breeze in front of it. It looked so amazingly impressive—like it was a monument to something very important, dignified, and even spiritual. Walid felt a flood of emotions wash over him, and started to speak.

But just then there was a loud noise outside the door, and the prince jumped down from his perch as quickly and quietly as he could. The boys slid the box to the floor and quickly moved it back to its original position in the room. Voices could be heard, angry words, and curses again beyond the locked door, and the sounds were coming closer. "They're in jail!" someone said, in apparent anger.

Another voice answered. "What do you mean, they're in jail? They're important officials!"

"It doesn't matter! They've been arrested!"

"Who would arrest them? What are they in jail for doing?"

"A man with three camels arrived at the palace an hour ago with the frantic tale of a revolt that's about to happen, and he had a message addressed by name to Caleeb and Neemar—a secret note about a coming revolution, and this letter proved they were involved."

"A revolution?"

"Yes! The king had them arrested right then, and they're in jail. The palace guard is out searching for accomplices. That means us!"

"I don't understand. What are you saying?"

"They're looking for us, to take us to jail for treason, now!"

"But we had no idea what Caleeb or Neemar were doing with the money from these boys, or why they were doing it."

"I know! But the guards don't!"

"We … we must have been providing the funds for their revolution without having any idea. We're business men, not traitors."

"They don't know that! And we can't prove it! They'll shoot us or hang us if they find us!"

"This is crazy! And now, we can't even get paid for these two boys that we have."

"I didn't think of that."

"What should we do?"

There was a sound of heavy approaching steps and a third loud voice. "You two, stop talking! We have to leave! Now!"

"What about the boys?"

"We can't worry about them."

"What do you mean?"

"We have to get out of here and save ourselves! Make sure the door is double locked. Then come, quickly!"

"But one of them has seen us. They should be killed."

"No, you idiot. We've always covered our faces in the room. There's no time to deal with them. No time! Do you hear me? Lock up and leave, now!"

Someone put a key in the lock. And there was the sound of a bolt being set. Then the boys heard footsteps going away, and finally silence.

Walid and Mafulla were almost afraid to breathe until that moment, when both together suddenly took a deep gulp of air. Mafulla spoke first. "Well, the good news is: There go our evil kidnappers."

Walid quickly replied, "And the bad news is: There go the keys to our door, with the kidnappers."

Mafulla said, "And, actually, the news gets even worse."

"What do you mean?"

"Those guys were room service. I mean, the food was pretty bad, but better than nothing, though, not by much. I was thinking about writing a complaint, but there was no stationery here in the room, which is another cause for a bad review, to be sure. But your point about the keys—now that I think about it, it concerns me just as much. What can we do?"

Walid stared at the door, and then looked at his friend. "First, we need to stay calm. Panic will keep us from thinking straight and it can lead to further thoughts like those you've just had of room service and hotel stationery. Everything will be fine. We need to be at peace and think. We'll somehow use what we have to deal with the situation."

"I'll follow your lead. I haven't been able to figure out any way of escape, and I've been here for two days before this." Mafulla spoke now with a tone of sincerity and obvious respect for his new acquaintance. "They've been bringing in a little food each morning, and a water jar and a bucket, which they always took away a couple of hours later. There's, of course, no food or water now, and no bucket. So we'd better come up with a plan pretty soon or the guy who wanted to kill us will eventually get his way without anybody lifting a finger."

Walid walked to the middle of the room and began to look around, as he spoke from the wisdom of recent conversations with his uncle. "Often, two can do what one alone can't. It's clear that we need to conceive of a way to get out of this room, and soon. I'm confident we can do it. Now we need to concentrate on what it will take and get busy consistently doing whatever needs to be done."

"Wow. You just said a lot." Mafulla began thinking aloud. "What do we have that we can use? We have the box. That's something new that I haven't had in the past days. They took mine away. Well, maybe this one is mine, but they needed it for you. And here it is."

"Yes, we have a box," Walid replied, waiting for what Mafulla might say next.

And the small boy continued. "We could, maybe, pull off one of the pieces of wood from the lid of the box without weakening it too much to be able to stand on it again. Then, one of us could climb up again to the window and use the piece of wood as a tool to break the glass."

"But there are still bars on the window."

"Yeah, but with the glass broken, I bet people on the street below could hear us call for help."

"Good idea. Good. Ok. Let's try that. And we can hang my belt out the window."

"That blue sash you have?"

"Yeah."

"I noticed it right away. It's nice. Why do you have it? I've never seen one that color."

"It's a traditional family color. I wear it in the hot weather like a belt, and in the cold at night out in the desert like a scarf, sometimes."

"But why hang it out the window? Do you mean to use it like a flag to say we've finally taken over this place?"

Walid laughed. "No."

"Or is it to be, like, laundry day? You need to dry it or air it out a bit?"

"Funny."

"Or, could you be, though I do hesitate to suggest this, and I don't at all mean to be critical, but could you be just the least little bit ... sartorially ostentatious, in an overly flamboyant way?"

"Sartorially ostentatious?"

"Showy, with regard to your clothing, or accessories."

"You, my friend, are both silly and extremely well spoken."

"I thank you."

"My reason for hanging the scarf out the window is simple. If anyone who knows me sees it, they'll realize I'm in here and come to get us."

"Oh."

"But, wait. I forgot to mention something important."

"What?"

"Before I take this off, I need to remove an object that's hidden by it, so don't be alarmed." Walid reached inside his broad, folded belt and pulled out a small gun, a revolver that had been given to him by Masoon.

"Whoa. You have a gun?"

"Yes."

"How is it that you have a gun?"

"An older friend gave it to me recently."

"Why in the world didn't you say so before now?"

"I didn't say anything, I guess, because I just wasn't thinking about it."

"But, we can use it."

"Yeah, I guess we can. Although, we need to choose our use of it carefully. It has only six bullets."

"We could shoot through the locks on the door."

"Maybe."

"What do you mean, maybe?"

"The door looks pretty thick and it's bolted from the outside, plus whatever other locks are used. I heard the bolt. I don't think we could shoot through all that wood and the locks, especially since we don't know exactly where they are."

"Ok. We could shoot the gun out the window to get attention."

"True, but it might be the wrong kind of attention."

"What do you mean? In the present situation, wouldn't absolutely any attention be the right kind of attention?" Mafulla looked completely puzzled.

Walid put the gun onto the floor and pointing away from them as he answered. "I came here from out of town with my uncle and some other men, and he could be in a bit of trouble with the law in the next few hours, until he's able to establish who he really is."

"He's in some sort of trouble?"

"He's not a criminal. He's a really good man, but some people in town may think differently, based on a misunderstanding too complicated to explain right now. If we shoot the gun, we might attract the attention of enemies who would not actually help us, but throw you and me both into another bad situation, and a real prison. Besides being unpleasant for us, that could also be hard for him and for something he's trying to accomplish."

"Oh."

"I think the gun's best saved for our protection, in case we need it and nothing else will do."

"Ok. You're likely right, Walid, given what you say. I didn't know all the details. Well, I still don't. But we won't try to shoot our way out, or fire the gun to get attention. We'll just break the glass of the window and call for help. We can use the gun barrel for that."

"Hitting anything with the gun might make it go off. It's too risky."

"All right. Back to the original plan, then. We'll use a piece of wood, shout for help, and tie your belt to a bar on the window, and let it hang out the building as a signal. Maybe somebody you know will see it and realize you're up here."

Walid thought for a moment. "We might not get a response right away."

"What do you mean?"

"There really aren't many men in town who would know it's mine. But those who do know will likely be out looking for me."

"How many people can recognize your belt?"

"Only my uncle and about forty or fifty other men, some who came with us by camel train across the desert, and others who are my uncle's friends here in town."

"That's actually a lot. Four people, maybe, at the most, would recognize one of my belts. Forty or fifty could do the job."

"Yeah, and they'll be pretty much everywhere looking for me. I was taken near where they were in the market, and they'll all be out trying to find me now, I'm sure—or at least, most of them; those who know about my disappearance."

"Ok, so let's get to work." Mafulla bent down and grabbed one side of the box. The boys dragged it back across the room again, put it up on one end under the window, at an angle against the wall, and, after much more effort than they had expected, they finally managed to pry loose from its lid a long thin piece of wood. Mafulla then took it and, with Walid's help, climbed up on top of the box again. Using the rafter once more to pull himself a bit higher with his right hand, he wielded the strip of wood in his left hand. From that position, he could hit the window glass with it. After three tries, with no apparent progress, he put his whole strength into striking the glass dead center one more time, and it finally shattered and fell in pieces onto the street far below. "All right, then!"

Walid said, "Good job!"

"Thanks. Toss me your belt." He dropped the makeshift tool.

Walid balled up his belt and threw it upward. The smaller boy caught it, readjusted his position, and within seconds had tied an end of it around one of the window bars and dangled the rest out through the opening and down the side of the building. It wasn't so long, but its brightness stood out against the dirty white color of the wall outside.

Walid said, "Now, you need to lift yourself up a little closer to the window like when we first looked out, and get as near to the opening as you can, and try yelling for help." He watched Mafulla then raise himself toward the opening.

"What should I say?"

"What do you mean, what should you say? Something like 'Help! Help!' would be a good start."

"Yes, of course. Forgive me. I wasn't thinking. It's my first time calling out to strangers for help from a small window high above a city street while imprisoned—too many new things at once. My mind was blank. It's just something like stage fright, I suppose." Mafulla directly faced the window, and with one hand cupped beside his mouth, shouted as loudly as he could. "Help! Help! Two boys are locked into a room in this building! Help us! Help us! Help! Help!"

The boys were both silent for a moment. Walid said, "Did you hear any reply?"

"No, not yet."

"Well, try again."

"Ok. Maybe a bit more urgency will do the job, more of a dramatic tone. More imploring." This time, he was even louder. "Help! Help! Help! Help! Two boys are locked into a room in this building and we need help to get out! Help us! Please! Please, help us!"

Both listened intently. Walid said, "Is there anything? Anything at all?"

"No. Still nothing. Look, you're bigger than me. Maybe you can yell louder. And you're obviously smart. Perhaps you can be more persuasive, more motivational. Should we trade places?"

"Ok, let's try that." Walid held the box while Mafulla shimmied down. He then gave Walid the two-handed boost so he could get up and approach the window.

Walid positioned himself, took a deep breath, and bellowed. "Help! Help! Two boys are locked in a room and need help! Walid and Mafulla need help! Help! Help! I'm Walid. My friend Mafulla and I need help! Please rescue us! Please, we need your help!" Hearing again nothing in response, he tried a second time, with more or less the same words, shouting still at the top of his lungs.

The silence was almost loud.

Just then, there was a faint noise at a distance below them, and shortly, in less than half a minute, outside the door, they both heard a faint sound as of footsteps approaching. But, rather than immediate relief, this created a sudden new worry. Could it be the kidnappers returning to do them harm? Walid jumped down from the box and picked up his gun, putting it behind his back.

They could both hear bolts unlatching. Then a voice shouted, "Stand back from the door, as far as you can and to the side! I'm going to shoot the remaining lock!" Three seconds later, the crack of a gunshot could be heard, and then another, and the door was kicked and flung open.

In the next moment, two guns were raised and pointed at each other.

"Walid! What are you doing here?"

"Bancom! What are you doing here? I'm so relieved! I was kidnapped and brought here."

"What?"

"I've been kidnapped! How did you find me?"

"I was across the street, out front, walking toward the palace when I heard someone yelling, but I couldn't make out the words, and I glanced over and saw a sash hanging out a window that looked like yours. I stopped for a moment and then heard shouting again and, this time, it sounded like you. I ran into the building with a feeling that, for some reason, you might be here and might be in trouble, and that I was supposed to help. And here you are."

"Yeah."

"But where are the kidnappers? And how did you get here?"

"I was in the market with Hamid and Baldoor and, while they were haggling with a merchant to stable and feed our camels, I saw a man who cried out that he needed help and, without thinking, I ran down the path to be of assistance."

"That sounds like you."

"Well, I ducked into a space between two stalls where he was directing me to go and then I was grabbed, with a bag put on my head, and I was thrown into a box and brought to this place to be sold into forced labor by some men who were kidnapping boys!"

"Oh, my."

"They got my friend Mafulla here before me, and a few minutes ago they all left in fear because someone said that the people they were going to sell us to are the men in the palace who were identified as secret revolutionaries by Faisul with his fake letter, and now they're in jail! And the kidnappers got out of here fast when they found out, but one of them wanted to kill us, and we didn't know how we were going to escape from this place, so we broke the window and took turns yelling for help."

"That's quite a story. I'm so glad I heard you and found you! I didn't know you were even here yet, or separated from the others. I've been elsewhere in town doing my own preparations for the big events to come. Now, we must get you quickly to where our friends should be. I'm sure they're very concerned." Bancom patted Walid on the arm and turned toward the door.

Mafulla looked confused. "Wait. Walid, who is this Faisul you just spoke about, and what do you mean about a fake letter, and how do you know this man, and what are the big events he just mentioned?"

"I'll explain everything later. We've got to get out of here now. This old friend, Bancom, is a good man." Walid turned to him.

"Bancom, what about Mafulla? He's good, too, and smart, and can be trusted."

Bancom looked at the smaller boy. "Where's your family?"

"We live not far from the edge of the city, on the northern side. I was taken from the market a couple of days ago. I was there with some friends at the time. I was going to sleep over at their house. But I got snatched. They may all be looking for me where I vanished, or they could have gone back home, hoping I'd reappear there. My family doesn't know I was kidnapped, but they're surely worried about me by now. They may be quite frantic—especially my mother, who worries a lot. Such things have happened recently."

Bancom replied, "Ok. You can come with us. That's likely best for the moment. And then, as soon as possible, we'll get you to your family."

"I could make it across town myself and go to their shop, or home."

"The streets might not be safe right now, or for several more hours."

Bancom turned to Walid. "We should first go to the safe gathering place, and then send some of the men to find your uncle and tell him you've been recovered and are unharmed. Perhaps someone could then get a message to your friend's parents that he's safe with us."

"Ok. That sounds good," Walid replied.

Mafulla was still trying to understand what was going on. He said, "What do you mean, safe gathering place?"

Bancom responded. "Things will be happening today and tonight that could make it dangerous for us to be seen in public. Tomorrow, everything should be fine, if all goes according to the plan. But if you can trust me and Walid for now, we can keep you safe."

"I trust Walid. And if he trusts you, then I will, too. Since I happen to be the only one here without a gun, I think that's a good plan."

Bancom smiled, "You're among friends. And we're good friends to have, as you've seen already. Tomorrow, we'll be even better friends to have, I promise you. But now we should go."

Walid looked up. "Bancom, wait. I need to get my belt down from the window."

"Yes. Ok. Just do so quickly, and then we leave."

Mafulla and Walid did their now well-practiced movement, with the hands of the skinny boy interlaced, giving a boost to his larger friend, who quickly mounted the box, untied the belt, and leapt back down to the floor with it in his hand. As they walked toward the door, Walid tied it around his waist again and tucked the pistol into its folds.

They had no idea what was just about to happen.

5

A Scepter and a Robe

Life is full of surprises. and sometimes they come in bunches.

Walid felt very grateful for the surprise of seeing Bancom's familiar face, and being rescued by him. The older man now led him and Mafulla across the room, through the door, and down a first flight of steep stairs. But at that very moment, they heard a commotion of muffled voices outside and ducked into a hallway off the landing that led to the last set of steps they would have to descend in order to leave the building. Bancom took Walid by the arm and grabbed the shoulder of Mafulla, pulling them both aside with a silent signal to remain quiet. The two guns were again slowly drawn, at about the same time.

There was a quiet shuffling of many feet downstairs, and within no more than four seconds, a number of large men with short swords, knives, and guns drawn rushed almost silently up the stairs and onto the first landing. Without hesitating, they ran up the second stretch of stairs as well, heading for the room where the boys had been held. They must know about the place and the room. Could this be the kidnappers returning with more men?

A voice rang out above them. "They're not here! They're gone! Search the entire building!"

Before the first word had been spoken, Bancom had already led the boys quietly from their hiding place and onto the lower flight of stairs, now blocked from the view of the intruders, and the three of them descended as quickly as they could without much more sound than a mere rustle of clothes and the faint creak of a stair. Walid had tucked his gun back into his belt, but Bancom's was still out. Near the bottom of the steps, Walid's revolver accidentally slipped out of its hiding place and hit the wooden stairs with a ferociously loud thud and a clatter. They all three froze at the noise, just as they heard a booming angry voice shout, "Stop instantly, or die!"

Walid and Mafulla stared at the gun on the step in front of them, as a wave of panic seemed to stop their ability to think. For Bancom, at the same moment, it was very different. He experienced once again a slowing of time, and in the expanding space of the present, he came to an intuitive realization of what he should do. He took a deep breath and calmly held his weapon in a ready position, hidden from sight against his chest. He would not turn around until he was prepared to begin firing toward the upper landing. He had four bullets left, and he would need to make each one count. Then, maybe one of the boys could pick up the other gun, and they would have six more chances to save themselves.

At that instant, they heard their adversaries rushing down toward them, and Bancom began to make his turn to take the one available action that might either free them from the situation or else lead directly to their deaths in the very next moment. But at the same fraction of a second, the voice they had heard yelled out once more.

"Bancom! Walid! What's happened?" It took a major effort to understand these words they were hearing. Then the same voice said, "Bancom! What are you doing here?"

It was Masoon. His voice was now clearly recognizable to both the prince and the messenger who was his agent of liberation. They had never heard his fierce and frightening confrontational tone before, and so had not realized, at the first shout, who it was.

"Oh Masoon! Masoon! You scared us half to death!" Walid put his hand over his heart.

Bancom suddenly laughed aloud like a crazy man and said, "It's so good to see you, my friend, and in that convincing disguise I would barely have recognized you. I was about to shoot you, or, more likely, give you the chance to shoot me, but I'd prefer to hug you, instead!"

Masoon was with several other men, weapons at the ready, and after a momentary pause they all continued down the stairs to where the escapees were standing still and experiencing the greatest relief of their lives. Mafulla, of course, had no idea who Masoon was, but he could tell he was likely a friend as soon as the big man called out Bancom's name. It was almost as if a jolt of electricity had shot through all their bodies as their emotions flipped from stark terror to instant relief on hearing the changed tone of voice in the shouting of that name and then Walid's.

Bancom did hug Masoon and he kissed him on the cheek and patted him on the back as soon as the great warrior approached him. And he began explaining to them all. "My friends, thank you for coming to us. I was walking down the street toward the safe house when I heard muffled yelling and stopped and saw a bright blue belt hanging from the upper window outside and it directed me to where the sounds had originated. Something told me it was, of all things, Walid's voice—it was just the strangest sensation—and so I went in and ran upstairs and got the door opened and found him and his young friend here. This is Mafulla, another kidnapping victim and a new trustworthy companion for Walid."

"Greetings, Mafulla." Masoon spoke for them all.

"Hi."

Bancom then said, "How did you find us?"

"Ali and Hamid and some men searched the marketplace when they realized that Walid had disappeared. The rug vendor who's our main contact sent some of his men to look for our friend here, and they interrogated a couple of petty thieves in the market about recent disappearances and kidnappings that have happened in the area. The criminals were only too happy to trade information for their lives, and we learned that the ring-leaders of the kidnapping business were the two men in the palace who had been plotting assassination and revolution. They were involved in various illegal enterprises to fund their ambitious plans, including this nefarious scheme."

"But how did you know Walid was here?"

"We sent a local contact, a man with connections, to the palace gate and he got in touch with the right people quickly. Some supporters in the palace guard questioned the newly arrested men right there in the jail, and, while still disavowing responsibility for any of the recent kidnappings, they reluctantly identified this building as the place where they had heard, they said, that abducted victims might be held before being sent elsewhere. Of course, they vigorously denied knowing anything about Walid. And yet, with their directions, it took us only a few minutes to find this place. We came in prepared to eliminate any kidnappers quietly in order to rescue Walid with as little commotion as possible. But it seems that you did our job for us."

"No, no, I'm no hero. The vermin were already gone when I got here. Apparently, they heard of their bosses being imprisoned and left quickly in fear that the palace guard would come for them next."

Masoon nodded and smiled. "A hero seeks to serve, and puts himself at risk for the good of others. You are a hero, my friend. But as to the kidnappers, we'll find them later and deal with them properly. For now, we need to get everyone to the place where many of our friends are gathered. Tonight is the time for the big changes, as you know. We need to have Walid in the secure location."

Mafulla had been standing quietly, listening to all of this. He turned to Walid and touched his arm and whispered, "Is it really Ok now?" He studied his new friend's face for reassurance.

"We're safe. We can go with these men, and everything will be fine. I promise."

The smaller boy nodded his head, with a very serious expression on his face. He was still a bit bewildered about all that was swirling around him, but he sensed that these were people he could trust.

The men put away their weapons and left the building in small groups and pairs, so as not to attract too much attention to themselves. Bancom and Masoon were with Walid and Mafulla and went first through the outer door and down the street. The others left a bit later and stayed far enough behind to seem unconnected with them, but still close enough to keep them in sight.

Within a few minutes of brisk walking, they turned down

a side street and continued along it until they came up to a big old building that looked abandoned, which they then entered by a side door. They made their way down a long hall and approached an internal door. Masoon knocked on it five times. Someone unlatched it and they all went inside.

It was a large room full of men sitting, standing, and lying about. Some were playing cards, others were cleaning weapons, and many were talking in low voices. As Masoon, Bancom, Walid, and then Mafulla entered the room, all the men looked up at them, first with surprise on their faces, and then big smiles. In the next moment, as Walid walked a little farther into the room and came to a stop, smiling with great relief to see so many people he knew in one place, all the men, as if on command, stood up together, facing the prince, and bowed. Many voices murmured what could possibly sound like the words, "Your Highness."

"What's going on?" Mafulla spoke to his friend in a stunned and hushed voice.

Before Walid could reply, Hamid walked up quickly and with a big grin on his face said, "Prince, it is so good to see you. We've heard some of what happened in the marketplace. I'll learn the rest from Bancom. You and your friend here, I would presume, are safe now." He then turned to a man behind him and said, "Hakeem, please go and tell the king that the prince is here with a new friend and is safe."

The new friend was standing there with his mouth hanging wide open. Walid saw him and laughed. "You look like a thirsty camel, Mafulla. Can one of the men get you a drink?"

"Your Highness? Prince? Why? What? Who are you, Walid?"

"Yeah, well, it's all sort of news to me, too."

"What do you mean?"

"I just found out days ago that I was born a prince, the

rightful heir to the throne of this kingdom, as such things are determined."

"But, how?"

"It's a long story. But my job, as I understand it now, thanks to my uncle, the rightful king, is really to be your supporter and servant, I mean, when we get set up, I guess, in that beautiful palace we saw outside our window, once the current residents are shown the door. And that should happen some time, I think, this evening."

Mafulla just looked stunned. He said, "I had ... no idea. You're a prince? I thought I was just untying and helping somebody like me."

"You were. I am somebody like you, Maffie. And I think that's what I'll call you, from now on, whenever the mood strikes me."

"Ok, but."

"I'm just like you. We're both royalty in the realm of the mind and the spirit."

"What?"

"I'll explain all that to you later, if you don't already know all about it."

"This is all totally new to me."

"For me, too, actually. But, right now, it's enough for you to know that I just have some special extra responsibilities that I'm still learning about, myself. I'll tell you the whole story when there's time."

"Ok, but man, oh, man. And, just to get clear on my own situation here: What will the current king, the one actually in power right now, think about all this, with you and your uncle and all these men?"

"I don't imagine he'll be too keen on it, but that shouldn't matter for much longer. He should be retired pretty soon."

"If you say so, Your Highness-to-Be."

The boys were given some food and drink and a couple of pallets that they could lie down on and rest while they continued to talk. Masoon came over and sat and spoke with them some, as did Hamid, after he had spent a few minutes with Bancom. A bit later, the king's trusted messenger and hero of the day was put in charge of watching over the boys and getting them anything they might need for the late afternoon and evening.

In less than half an hour, a messenger brought Walid word of the great relief and happy regards of his uncle, along with a request that Walid stay with Bancom for a while longer. The man apparently also had some instructions for Masoon. Then, about an hour later, most of the men left the warehouse with the great warrior to take care of the business of the kingdom.

Six heavily armed individuals remained in the building with the prince and Mafulla, under the authority of Bancom. They knew that, by this time, because of Faisul's report and letter, a large contingent of soldiers would have been sent out of town and into the desert to find a caravan of rebels approaching the city, and smaller units would be searching throughout the capital for any confederates of the rightful king. The men with the prince were prepared to resist and dispatch any hostile force that might enter their safe house. But they were also fairly confident that no such event would take place. They had enough supporters in the army and the palace guard to misdirect the search effort that was now underway, and to keep prying eyes far from their place of temporary refuge. But all those under Bancom's command were alert and carefully watchful, nonetheless.

Walid and Mafulla sat together over against one wall, talking more. The prince told his new friend all about Faisul and the theft that had set things into motion, and what his uncle had revealed to him as a result of the unfolding events. Mafulla took it all in and was amazed.

After a while, Bancom came over and gave the boys some pillows and told them they should try to sleep. The next day would be a busy one, and they would need to be refreshed. But the surprise and sheer energy of the past few hours, with all their events, would not allow sleep to come easily. So the prince and his friend lay awake and talked more. They told their life stories to each other. They each asked a lot of questions, back and forth, and both gave full and candid answers. Walid even shared a few bits of the wisdom his uncle had passed on to him during their journey across the desert together. The hours passed, and the boys finally grew weary and, against their own wishes, each of them fell deeply asleep for what seemed an eternity devoid of the passage of time.

As they slept, the evening around them was quickly becoming more active than any night the kingdom had ever seen. And about an hour or less before dawn, a runner came into the safe house with news for Bancom and his comrades. Their plans had succeeded brilliantly, quickly, and so far, without any loss of life on either side. The man relayed the whole story in at least a general outline, but in low tones, so as not to awaken the boys.

Stealth, speed, and the sheer number of their supporters, along with their confederates high in the government, had allowed easy access to the palace and a lightning fast occupation of the king's inner quarters. Masoon, Hamid, and a few others had been forced to render several guards unconscious, and these potential adversaries were then relocated immediately to the jail cells of the palace, along with several corrupt administrators who had been rousted out of their beds in nearby homes.

The usurper king, long a pretender to the rightful throne, had been whisked out of the city with two of his top assistants and their families, put on a boat, and sent on a long journey down the river. In the process, the deposed regent had apparently been convinced, quite thoroughly, that it would be strongly in his self interest not to return.

Supporters of King Ali had gone throughout the city with printed pamphlets they had secretly prepared, announcing a peaceful change of power. They told the story of the plots long ago and the historic assassination that had originally put into power the unjust, oppressive government that had now been long hated by the people. The pamphlet introduced the new and rightful king, as well as his nephew, the prince, explained the new king's wish to help the people gradually transition to a form of enlightened self-rule, and declared a one year tax holiday for all, in celebration of these wonderful events. It also went on to explain that much of the tax money collected in excess by the wrongful government would be returned to the people quite soon in the form of public works, jobs, and improved working and living conditions throughout the kingdom.

When the citizens of the city awoke to see these pamphlets on their doorsteps and under their doors, they read them with curiosity and then rejoiced with great excitement. Many took to the streets in jubilant celebration. There was music and dancing outside, all around the city, and food seemed to appear from all directions. A huge crowd gathered in the park in front of the palace and it seemed that all who were there were chanting, "Long Live The True King!" over and over again, punctuated at times by loud cheers.

Now it was Bancom's job to escort Walid to the palace, along with the other men who had been on guard in the safe house overnight. No one on the streets knew what Walid looked like, so it should be an easy task to get him to the palace. Even if there were supporters of the old regime at large and out in public, they would not likely make any trouble at this point, at least, not for these few individuals.

Bancom woke the boys and gave them a quick rundown of the incredibly positive news. Hearing all of it was a great relief to Walid, and Mafulla was able to shed some of the worry and stress that he had harbored, as well. They both ate a breakfast of figs and biscuits, and watched the men work as they readied themselves to leave. Despite all the good news, and a complete absence of any bad signs, the men with Bancom were still preparing as if for battle. One more cleaning and checking of weapons was followed by elaborate acts of concealment, as guns and knives were hidden under belts, robes, and in bags that could be carried inconspicuously. They didn't want to attract any attention on the streets. But they were prepared, within seconds of any alert, to fight a full-scale skirmish if needed.

Bancom then came up to Walid and Mafulla and asked the smaller boy, "How old are you, my son?"

"Almost thirteen."

"Almost?"

"Well, twelve. And, actually, I just turned twelve, to be completely honest. But I'll very soon be thirteen—at my next birthday, which is coming up quickly, less than a year from now. You know how time flies. And I am mature and wise far beyond my years."

"You look a bit younger." Bancom said. He was skeptical.

"Diet and exercise—and I limit my exposure to the sun. It can age you terribly." Even in these circumstances Mafulla could make a joke.

Bancom smiled. Then he said, "Do you know how to use a gun?"

"Yes. I have an uncle who's let me do target practice a few times. I'm a good shot. He was in the army long ago and kept a revolver for his own use. He didn't steal it, I promise. But he has it. And I've shot it."

"You have?"

"Yes. And I'm pretty good at it, but maybe I said that already. Bottles and cans that are nearby tremble when they see me with a gun. Even large rocks seem quite threatened." Mafulla was a little nervous around Bancom still.

"Good. Then you may take this if you promise to be very careful with it." Bancom handed him a small pistol, and a wide tan sash to be used as a belt. "Put this on like a belt, and fold it and hide the gun in it just as Walid does."

"Really?"

"You'll not likely need to use it, but it's better to have it and not need it than to need it and not have it. And, by the way, for your own safety and that of any innocent bottles and cans around, not to mention the poor rocks, the first two cylinders are empty. So, if you truly need to shoot, you'll have to pull the trigger three times to fire the first round."

"Ok. No problem. Thanks. I was almost getting used to being the one completely helpless, unarmed person around here, but this will make me feel more secure, I'm sure."

"Now, take this thin green piece of material, this ribbon, both of you, and tie it around your belts."

"What's this?" Walid held the strip of fabric and examined it.

"A secret sign that you're on the side of the new king, and are armed in his support. All our armed men will have a strip of green fabric somewhere on them, not a lot, but visible from the front of their garments for anyone who knows to look. It's a signal unknown to our enemies, if any still exist. Should a situation develop where you have to decide whether to trust someone brandishing a weapon, look for the green ribbon, and if you don't see it, then beware."

"When are we leaving?" Walid asked as he tied the fabric around his belt, at the front.

"In just a moment. I think all the men are ready."

Bancom then walked over to the others to confer one last time before they left their safe haven and ventured onto the streets. Two men would walk ahead of Bancom, Walid, and Mafulla, with a couple beside them, and two more a bit behind. The plan was that they would move down the street as casually as possible, and seek to appear, in conversation, spacing, and demeanor, as if no more than a few of them knew each other, and were actually walking together. As they all knew, prevention is the best way of dealing with almost any form of trouble.

Bancom came back over to the boys and said, "Ok, Walid, I mean, Prince, it's time. We should go. There was a robe, a crown, and a scepter awaiting your uncle when he arrived at the palace a few hours ago. And a place there now awaits you."

"Really?"

"Yes. There won't be a crown or scepter yet for you, I'm afraid, but that's Ok, because, really, who wants a metal hat and a heavy pole to carry around, anyway?"

Walid laughed and said, "Yeah. True."

Bancom smiled and added, "However, I do hear that there's a very nice robe about your size that's ready for your arrival, and I think it's in a color that will meet your approval."

"Bancom, you can be a funny man. I'm comfortable in

what I'm wearing right now. But, from the looks of it, Maffie could use a nice change of apparel."

Mafulla made a face and said, "Hey, the clothes I have on represent the latest styles. What's wrong with them?"

"Nothing that a little soap and water won't cure—or maybe a lot of soap and water. Meanwhile, I see something new and even more stylish in your future."

Looking down at the front of his very stained garments, Mafulla said, "I'll have you know that these clothes all bear marks of distinction, signs of a man of action ... except for one streak over here that may just be fig juice, a stain recently acquired in the time of rare leisurely indulgence that we've enjoyed since our arrival here."

"Well. It's time now for a change." Walid laughed. He grabbed Mafulla's arm, and they followed Bancom out the door.

6

ONE ANCIENT ADAGE

THE WALK TO THE PALACE WAS SURPRISINGLY EASY. Crowds were in the streets celebrating their liberation from an oppressive ruler, and no one took any special notice of the small group now making its way toward the center of power. But still, Walid's stomach was churning with excitement and more than a little anxiety. This was all new territory. And it was almost too much for a boy who had lived until now in a very small village far across the desert from anything like this. Every step was taking him farther into the unknown.

Even though Mafulla had lived in Cairo all his life, he was feeling something very much like what was going on in his new friend right now. He was almost in a daze, just trying to take it all in, as he walked quickly down these normally familiar streets that had suddenly taken on a strange tone and atmosphere. Shock, joy, and giddy exuberance were everywhere around them and had crowded out any sense of the ordinary.

Two newly installed guards at the palace gate recognized Bancom from a recent encounter in the desert. They smiled and swung open the ornate iron bars, as the men and boys sporting small green ribbons approached. One said to Bancom, as they drew near, "The Owl is here, and all is well." Then, two beautifully dressed soldiers escorted them across the gardens and up to the wide stairs outside the palace. Another two guards took over from there and showed them the way up to and through the massive front doors, where several more members of the current palace guard were standing.

Bancom preceded them into the huge entry hall, floored by light tan and white marble flecked with gold, and lit by many large chandeliers. They all stopped for a moment just to take in the impressive sight.

Walid said, "You could fly a kite in here."

Bancom replied, "Yes. You'd only need some wind."

"So, where's Bashir?" Walid asked, and immediately laughed along with Bancom at his own joke. The big man he had referred to was an old acquaintance known far and wide for his love of beans and for the spectacular consequences that often followed when he overly indulged in his favorite dish.

"Who's Bashir?" Mafulla asked.

"A friend of ours who eats huge amounts of food and especially beans, even though they create big trouble in him."

"Oh, I see. Enough trouble to get a kite up in here?" Mafulla caught on and played along.

Bancom said, "Enough for a dozen kites. A dinner with him by the river could launch an armada of sailing ships."

The boys laughed and Mafulla said, "Ah! So then, a well placed hot air balloon might fill up and take flight?"

Walid replied, "Definitely! But you wouldn't want to be anywhere near!" The boys both laughed again, and so did Bancom. That moment, Hamid appeared at the far end of the hall and waved them all in his direction.

"Where's the king?" Bancom asked immediately.

"Upstairs. Let me take you to him."

They followed Hamid through another door, down a hall-way, and up another enormous flight of wide, marble stairs. At the top, they crossed an entry hall, nodded a silent greet-ing at several soldiers, and entered another room through an open doorway whose massive door had been pushed back and was being held in place by boxes of ammunition put to a bet-ter use than had been anticipated.

Mafulla mumbled, "This is just amazing."

Walid said, "Yeah."

And then as he looked all around, Mafulla added, "I love what you've done with this place, already," and that made his friend laugh again.

At the far end of the long room, which was decorated beautifully with dark wood furniture and banners lining the walls, there was a large table and, around it, Walid could see Masoon, Baldoor, and several of the other men he knew from their trip across the desert. Then someone stepped to the side and he spotted his uncle Ali seated at one end, where he was signing a paper of some sort. At that exact moment, Ali looked up and saw the boy. He jumped to his feet and, followed by several others at the table, strode quickly across the room to his nephew, shouting his name and throwing his arms wide in greeting. Walid ran the last few feet and they embraced in a fierce hug, as Ali planted kisses on both the boy's cheeks.

"I'm so glad to see you, my boy!"

"Not as glad as I am to see you, Uncle!"

"I've heard that you had occasion to be very brave and resourceful since I last laid eyes on you."

"Yes! I was able to try out many things you've taught me,

and they worked well! But the outcome might not have been so good and quick without my new friend, Mafulla." Walid turned to gesture to him, and he motioned for him to come join them. As the boy walked up, smiling, Walid said, "Uncle, this is Mafulla. I also now call him Maffie." He turned to him and said, "Is that Ok?"

Mafulla said, "You're the prince."

"Mafulla, this is my uncle Ali, the new king."

"It's an honor to meet you, King Ali." Mafulla did a small bow as he said this.

Looking at the smaller boy, Ali smiled broadly and said, "Welcome to our new home, Mafulla, who is also called Maffie! You're hereby invited to stay as long as you'd like, and, of course, we'll find your family today and bring them here to the palace to reunite with you, where we can be certain that everyone is safe. You can give Bancom the full information he'll need to send for them. We've already sent word to them through the local police, where you'd been reported missing, that you're safe."

"Oh! Good!" Mafulla spontaneously said in great relief.

The king continued, "I just want to thank you for all that you've done to help see to it that you and my nephew here were rescued from your unfortunate captivity."

Mafulla looked overawed and very pleased, and a bit confused at the same time. "Thank you, sir, I mean, Your Majesty. Walid was brave, and we were a real team." He said these words and then suddenly realized that maybe he should bow again, which he did very quickly but awkwardly and with a little flourish that made Walid smile.

Ali also took note of this with a measure of inner mirth. He sensed something very good about the young man, and then turned and said, "Bancom, will you escort the boys and get one of the guards to show them where they can bathe and change into clean clothes?"

"Sure thing!"

"Then, I'd like to see them both an hour from now for lunch in the large royal banquet room, downstairs."

"You bet!" Bancom turned toward the door, then quickly turned back again. "Oh! Sorry, Ali! I meant to say: Yes, Your Majesty, right away!" Everyone laughed, including the king, as an evidently embarrassed but also self-amused Bancom led the boys toward the door. Royal protocol was going to take some getting used to.

Walid and Mafulla were led to adjoining suites where tubs had already been filled for them. A hot bath never felt so good. The boys each soaked and relaxed, and then cleaned off many days' worth of dirt, sweat, and grime. The soap stripped away everything down to the skin, and their bodies could now feel the fresh air once more. Meanwhile, new clothes had been brought in and laid out in wait for them—crisp, white, properly sized, and even smelling good.

Within minutes, Mafulla stood in front of a full-length mirror with golden gilded edges and modeled for himself the new garments, feeling the material and brushing away a few wrinkles. He was striking a few silly poses as Walid walked in. He said, "Stunning, don't you think? Really beautiful! I mean, of course, in a very manly way."

Walid just laughed.

And Mafulla continued, "I have to say, I look quite sophisticated, and almost regal, appropriately enough."

"Yes, you're very close to regal," Walid laughed.

The younger boy went on, "I think this place is starting to rub off on me. Is there any cologne around here that I could use? Something suitably strong, even robust?"

That made the prince laugh out loud again. Asking for cologne! Well, it was clear that his friend was now feeling comfortable in this very new and unexpected setting.

The boys were soon escorted back downstairs for the big lunch, but not before a butler had found Mr. Mafulla a rare and expensive bottle of heavily scented fragrance. It was a good thing there was a light breeze through the hallway, because the eager visitor splashed on enough to alert and attract young ladies from at least a mile away.

A hot bath, some clean clothes, and the prospect of a great meal can perk up the spirits of even the most exhausted boys, especially when they're in a palace and there's so much excitement swirling around. In the large banquet room this day, there were five long tables, each seating twenty men, and a head table with ten. At the king's table, Ali was in the center, with Masoon to his right, and Hamid to his left. Many other friendly faces were smiling around them. Bancom, Bashir, Baldoor, Hakeem, and Mahmood were already in their places. Walid, and Mafulla joined them in the two remaining chairs. All the other tables were filled as well, with men from the camel train, and friends from town who had assisted mightily in the events of the past few hours, as well as in the extensive and intricate preparations for this day that had been going on for years.

There was a series of toasts and cheers and Masoon stood up to say a few words of appreciation before they all got down to the serious business of their first big meal together since the quiet revolution of the previous evening and early morning hours. Everyone was tired but exhilarated at the same time. Specially prepared food, hot from the kitchen, was passed around and enjoyed greatly. Good cheer filled the room as stories were told around all the tables, tales of intrigue and uncertainty culminated by accounts of miraculous outcomes, over and over. At the king's table, Bancom spoke of his dangerous encounter in the desert with heavily armed men. Hakeem had experienced an unexpected meeting with some unfriendly soldiers at the market. Walid told them more about his own ordeal with the kidnappers and how Mafulla helped and Bancom saved the day.

"He almost shot Masoon!" Walid exclaimed, to everyone's sudden amusement.

"That's Ok. As his doctor, I've come to think the man's bullet proof!" Hamid shouted over the commotion and evoked even more laughter.

Masoon then raised his glass to Bancom, and the faithful messenger lifted his in response, both with big smiles on their faces. At that moment, Ali leaned over and whispered something to Masoon. The one man who would be greatly feared if he were not so loved by everyone in the room rose to his feet again and announced in a loud booming voice, "The King of Egypt will now stand to speak briefly, but has asked that all of you please remain comfortably seated." Three or four seconds of spirited and happy commentary from the men swelled throughout the room and then quickly faded to complete silence, as Ali rose from his chair and stepped a bit to the side of it.

That instant, several men started hitting their fists on their tables in rhythmic salute to the king. Someone shouted, "Long Live The King!" And with a thunderous roar, over a hundred other voices immediately responded, "Long Live The King!" Then there was a huge ovation of applause, cheers, and whistles throughout the room, along with a thunderous stamping of feet. The king stood tall and still, with a broad smile on his face, and slowly nodded his grateful acknowledgment of this spontaneous display of affection and admiration on the part of all the men who had worked so hard to change the course of history.

Lifting his hands, the king said, "My friends, my friends. Thank you. My family thanks you. I thank you. A grateful kingdom thanks you." He paused for a moment as they all settled down, and then continued.

"Right eventually brings might. We've seen this powerfully displayed in the past few hours. We few men have unseated an unlawful regime with no loss of life, and we now have the opportunity to rectify decades of corruption within the government. Without all the good people outside these walls who've resented that corruption and sought to resist it, we could not have achieved what we've accomplished in this short burst of well targeted activity. Together, we represent the interests of all the good men and women and children who live within the borders of our kingdom. It's now our job to help shape a society for them where goodness and fairness, justice and hope can prevail. Our victory today is not for us, and certainly not for me, but for all the citizens of the kingdom."

"Here, here!" Many men shouted their approval of Ali's words. Others turned to their fellows with various remarks of affirmation. Then, as the voices around the room quieted again, he went on.

"All of you know how I feel about our duties and responsibilities now. And you know how I feel about you, each and every one of you. Finally, I'm sure you know how I feel about my nephew here, Prince Walid, who will one day likely follow me as your king. It's our job to show him how good men rule. I have no doubt that, when his time comes, he'll improve on what he sees us do. He has a loving heart and a good mind, and I ask you all to help him learn to serve well."

Positive words could be heard all around the room. Men were nodding in agreement. The king paused for a moment and then spoke again.

"Every new sunrise will find us laying the foundations of responsible government and a good society. Each day we'll plant seeds for future harvests, and tend the plants as they grow. Let me remind you all of an ancient adage that's as applicable today as it ever was: Deep roots produce good fruits. What goes on under the ground, behind the scenes, invisible to the casual glance, is what will bring forth the visible results of all our efforts. Most people won't see most of what we do, day-to-day, but these roots will produce good fruits for all to enjoy. And the work of cultivating those roots begins today."

A big smile appeared once more on the king's face. And he said, "I thank you from the deepest places in my heart for your vital role in all this, and I'll be depending on you every day that I'm given to represent and shepherd the people of this land. May the kingdom long flourish and its citizens forever remember this day as the start of something new, something different, and something great!"

With that, Ali moved back to his chair and stood behind it. His words were met with an eruption of thunderous applause and cheers, as all the men leapt to their feet, clapping and shouting and stomping in happy celebration of their king and their victory. Walid was amazed and Mafulla was almost speechless for the first time in his life, as he looked around the room and just said, "Wow."

The king then leaned over and spoke to Walid. "Let's go up to my private chambers for a while. Just follow me. Bancom will escort Mafulla to a nearby room, and the two of you can spend more time together shortly."

Walid nodded his agreement. "Sure, Uncle—Your Majesty!"

Then Ali smiled and told all who were around his table. "We should leave the room together now and get to work. Time waits for no one." They all then turned toward the door as the applause continued and, following their king, filed out of the banquet hall. A few of them waved to the other men as they walked toward the door. The rest of the men could then be seen shaking hands, patting each other on the back, giving old friends big hugs, and talking and laughing as they too began to leave their tables, and eventually the room, to go forth and do the work of the day.

Up the stairs and down a long hallway, Mafulla was escorted to a large private bedroom with its own small sitting area and a big window overlooking the gardens outside the palace. As soon as he saw the window, his first thought was, "No bars. Nice." He smiled to himself and mused, "No one would need bars to keep me in here. This place is great." But then he thought of his family and hoped to see them in the palace soon, too.

Three doors up the long corridor, in a suite of rooms that Mafulla had just walked past, there was a large and elegant royal parlor where King Ali and Prince Walid had just sat down together. The king politely dismissed his new private butler and two guards, who quietly closed the doors as they left. The old man and the boy were finally alone again, at last.

Ali spoke first. "It's been a very eventful time, Prince Walid."

"Yes, it has," the boy replied.

Ali said, "Again, I'm so sorry you were taken from the marketplace and that I didn't know about it until it was too late to intervene and stop it."

"It was scary, Uncle, but in a way, I'm glad it happened."

"How so, my boy?"

"It gave me a chance to use some of the things you've taught me—some ideas about living in the present moment, bringing yourself inner peace with your own mind, using what you have to deal with a problem, and even putting to work your seven secrets for success!"

"Good! I'm pleased to hear this. Did the ideas work well for you?"

"Yes! I reminded myself that I needed a clear conception of what I had to do, along with a strong confidence, despite how things looked, a focused concentration on what it would take, and all the rest. And the many thoughts you've shared with me worked almost like magic!"

"Very nice."

"I'm so glad that you and I had such time to talk on our trip across the desert. I've learned a lot of great stuff from you, already."

"I'm happy for that. It's always been my intention to share with you some of the most important things I've learned, and so much starts with the power of the mind and how we control our thoughts, emotions, and energies."

Walid said, "It was my mind that kept my body calm when things were crazy and scary all around me. Even reminding myself to breathe deeply and relax my muscles and visualize something good and peaceful was very important when the kidnappers had me in a closed box and were taking me to their hideout. I kept reminding myself how you've taught me that it doesn't matter so much what happens to us as how we think about and respond to what happens. I could hear your voice saying that we can't control the day, but only what we make of the day. That got me through a lot."

The king said, "Good. Very good. It's also wonderful that,

in addition to making it safely through those unexpected adventures, you found a new friend along the way."

Walid smiled. "Mafulla's a fine person, I can tell, and he's smart. He can think on his feet. He makes silly jokes when he's nervous, but he can also use his mind creatively and well."

Ali looked pensive and said, "Would you like it if I offered his family the chance of a palace education for him at your side?"

"Is that possible?"

"Now that I'm king, many things are possible."

"That would be great! I'd love it. I need a good friend here who's about my age."

"Yes."

"I mean, I like being around the older men, but there's something special about having somebody my age to talk to. And he's a lot of fun."

Ali nodded in recognition. "You know, they say that having a friend in your life doubles the good and cuts the bad in half."

"That makes a lot of sense."

"Friendship is one of our greatest gifts. I know that you've seen how Masoon and Hamid do so many things together. They're great friends, and have been for years."

"I've always wanted a friend like that. Well, you're my friend, for sure, but I mean, someone more my age."

"Yes, yes, a friend who's about your age is important to have. One of the greatest philosophers, the man Aristotle, said that it was crucial for friendship that people share important things in common, and be roughly equals in most ways. Of course, as a prince, you'll have no complete equals of your age in the kingdom, officially, in terms of your role or status, but there are many ways in which a good, creative, and intelligent boy like Mafulla can be, in most relevant respects, an equal. And it's good to treat him as such. You must always remember your extra duties as a prince, but you and he can share many things in common. I think it will be quite beneficial for you to have classes and tutorials together here in the palace."

"It's funny, Uncle, that friendship is so important, but we meet our friends almost by accident, or coincidence, and sometimes even in bad situations, like being kidnapped."

"Much in life is like that, my boy. On the surface, things can seem random, and accidental, and even at times terrible, but beneath appearances, there can be deep patterns in how things happen. We often get just what we need when we most need it. The most difficult situations can sometimes bring us the most wonderful results. This certainly seems true of the kidnapping, which did lead you to Mafulla. Things and people come into our lives when the time is right."

He continued. "Where many people see luck, I see destiny. But that's something we've talked about, and as you may remember, something that has two sides: What happens to us and what happens because of us. I'm confident that it was part of your destiny and Mafulla's that you meet each other at this point in time. And, perhaps, you had to meet in very difficult circumstances in order to see the depth and character, and the resourcefulness, in each other."

"Yes. That makes sense."

"You've done something remarkable together already. And I'm confident you'll do many more such deeds."

Walid said, "Crazy unexpected things do seem to happen a lot these days. And, as you've taught me, they're rarely what they at first seem. I'm glad I've learned the lessons of wisdom to stay calm and attentive and seek the truth beneath the illusion of surface appearances."

The king replied, "Wisdom is a great tool for any situation. We can't overstate its importance. It helps to center us." He then stood, while indicating that Walid should remain seated. He took a few steps over toward a big window near them and looked out through it for a moment, taking in the view of the city spread out beyond them. On the main street nearby, he noticed a donkey cart slowly making its way, and that sparked a thought. He looked back at Walid. "Have you ever seen the wheel of a wagon, and pondered the way it's constructed, and how it works as it moves along?"

Walid said, "I guess so. But I'm not sure. Do you mean how it has a central hub and spokes that go from there to the outer rim, and it all turns together to roll forward?"

"Exactly. And this provides us with a useful image for our lives."

"How do you mean?"

"Life is like a big wagon wheel that's always turning around. People who go through their days without wisdom dwell on the outer edge of the rim, and they're flung about, up and down, with great highs and lows, as the wheel turns. They can often barely hang on. Wisdom moves you closer to the middle of the hub, centering you spiritually and emotionally. The wheel will still spin, but you won't be whipped around through those huge ups and downs like most people are. Wisdom can then give you strength as it brings peace to your heart and guides you in all things."

"Wow, Uncle, I like that image a lot. The wheel will always spin, but we're better off being at the center of the hub. That way, we don't get flung around with such big highs and lows."

"That's it, my friend. And this is why wisdom means so much to me. Those without it experience unnecessary extremes in their thoughts and feelings. It's better to have a measure of inner peace—the oasis within that we've discussed. With it available as a centering and calming force, you can make wiser decisions, and not always live at the mercy of powerful emotions that are fleeting, and often false."

Walid thought for a moment. "I'm guessing that good friends will share healthy, positive feelings and help each other deal with the negative ones."

"Yes, they do exactly that, if they're wise. And this is another important point. Genuine friendship requires a measure of wisdom in the hearts of both the friends. Foolish people can't be true friends. The unwise can have fun with each other when things are going well, and can even help each other in various ways when things are tough, but no one can be a real friend, of the deepest and most genuine sort, without having a measure of wisdom, and also virtue, or simple goodness. The good and wise you can count on. The corrupt and unwise, you can't."

He went on to add, "I think you and Mafulla are off to a good start. I feel that he's a special person, from everything I've heard and seen, and I encourage you to get to know him as well as you can. You may have with him that rare example of a real friend."

"Speaking of Mafulla, Uncle, can we invite him in here for a minute? I know he's eager to see his family soon, and I wanted him first to be able to talk a bit more with you—my family here—for a moment."

"Certainly. Bring him in if you'd like. You can go get him now. But first, speaking of family, I want you to know that I've sent a message to your parents with all the details about what's happened, making sure they know you're safe and well. I'll find out by reply when they'll be able to join us here."

"Good! I was just going to ask you about them! What are they going to do, now that we're here?"

"They'll be coming to be with us."

"Really?"

"Yes, and I'll know more about when it will all happen once I hear back from them."

"That's really great."

"You're right. But you'd better go get your friend if you'd like him to join us for a bit. I'll have some meetings to attend soon."

"Right away, Your Majesty!" Walid grinned as he jumped up, and ran out of the room and down the hall to where Mafulla was waiting, in a comfortable small suite. He was at the moment sitting in a big stuffed chair, looking over a book of photos featuring world capitals.

Walid stuck his head in. "Hey, Maffie, Uncle Ali, I mean, the king, has asked that you come into his private chamber with me."

"Am I in trouble?"

"No."

"Is my family here?"

"Not yet."

"Does the king need my advice on kingly things?" He slowly stood up.

"You're too funny. He just wants to see both of us for a minute."

Mafulla looked skeptical. "You're sure there's no problem. I'm not in any trouble at all."

"Why? What have you done?" Walid pretended to look concerned.

"Nothing! I promise!" The boy showed mock panic as he glanced quickly around the room and added, "Whatever it is, I didn't do it, touch it, take it, or say it. I'm sure I didn't even think about it."

Walid just laughed and said, "Nothing's wrong! Come on!"

Mafulla bent down and adjusted the book where it lay on a table. He let out a big breath. "Ok. Whatever you say. You are the prince, after all. So if there is a problem, I have a friend in high places. Right?"

"Right."

"And you have the job of making sure I'm off the hook."

"Yes."

"And I mean every hook, should there, by any chance, actually be a hook."

"Ok, already. There's no hook and no trouble. Let's go!"

Walid held the door for his friend and motioned him forward. Mafulla moved through the open doorway with his eyebrows strangely high on his face, in a funny sort of expression or gesture of what must be ongoing uncertainty, however real or pretended. The prince couldn't help but smile. The boys walked back down the hall and through a sort of entry room and then into the much larger and more ornate space where the king had just finished speaking with an attendant.

"Please, take a chair, boys."

It was all that Mafulla could do not to say to Walid, "Which one would you like? I think we can lift the red one." He certainly thought it. But, he behaved himself and sat down quietly, and in precisely that one.

The king smiled and clapped his hands together. "Thank you again, Mafulla, for all that you did to help get the two of you rescued. You boys both thought on your feet, took action, and were very brave."

"I'm grateful to be free, Your Majesty. And I'm thankful for my new friend here, fellow high-class kidnap victim, Prince Walid."

The king chuckled at the boy's boldness in making jokes at

such a time, and in this setting. He was, like Walid, a spirited young man.

Ali said, "Freedom is indeed something for which to be grateful. I think most everyone throughout the entire kingdom will be thankful to be free of the oppressive rule they've struggled under for years. In a sense, the whole kingdom was kidnapped decades ago by greedy thieves, and only now has been released."

"That makes sense, Uncle." Walid's political education was going on now in almost every conversation he had with the older man.

Ali looked from one of them to the other, and said, "I want to be sure that you boys both understand the concept of freedom, especially after what you've been through. It will help you to know why we've done what we've done, and also to grasp more fully what we're going to be doing now in the palace."

Mafulla spontaneously asked, "What would you tell us, Your Majesty?"

The king smiled and said, "Thank you for asking. Here's today's life lesson for the both of you. There are two kinds of freedom: freedom from, and freedom to—the freedom of release, and the freedom of aspiration. I often refer to them as the lower freedom and the higher freedom. The purpose of the lower freedom, which is, most often, good in itself, is to provide for the higher freedom. Many people don't understand that. They fight for the lower freedom and ignore the higher form."

"Could you say more about that?" Walid looked very interested, as he often did when he heard something new.

Ali answered, "Certainly. In the past day, you've just experienced the first kind of freedom—the freedom of release—

on two different levels, one immediate, and the other, only a bit less so. First, you've been freed from a locked room, and, second, you've been freed from a corrupt government, whose administrators conspired in such a way as to imprison you in that room, with only their selfish gain in mind. Both these examples of the first kind of freedom provide for the second kind. You're now free to aspire to and accomplish many good things. And it's entirely up to you how you'll use this new-found freedom. You are boys, still, and should have fun, and run about and play games, and explore the world around you. But you're also old enough to start trying to improve the things around you. Never forget that you have your freedom in order to make your world better."

Walid turned to Mafulla and said, "Uncle Ali taught me not long ago the importance of goal-setting. We need a clear conception of what we want to make happen, for the good of others as well as ourselves. A strong sense of purpose, he said, can guide us to great things."

Mafulla responded. "I like that." He turned to the king and continued. "It seems to me that so much of the time, we have no idea what we're going to do next, except that we're basically doing today what we did yesterday, and we'll do tomorrow the sorts of things we did today. This idea about goal-setting means that there's much more available in life than just going along and repeating the past, out of habit."

The king replied, "That's correct. And when you set goals, you're an active participant in life, a true partner in the enter-prise."

Walid nodded his agreement. "Maybe that's what freedom is for."

"Yes." The king nodded his approval.

The prince then asked him: "Can you give us some advice

about what should guide us in setting our own goals for the future?"

Ali nodded and said, "Yes. Everything we do or think is in a context. The better you know your context, the better you can set goals for the future. Think for a moment about the biggest context of all. If we can understand why we're here on earth, why we're alive, it's much easier to set goals well and properly, in relation to the big picture." The boys looked very attentive. So the king continued. "The deepest of thinkers, across cultures, and through history, hint that the ultimate meaning of life is creative love, or what we can think of as a form of loving creativity. We've been lovingly created to be loving creators. We're here to do new and original things, things that are expressive of the best in us, and things that demonstrate proper love for others, as well as ourselves."

He then repeated the point to emphasize it. "We're here to create lovingly, and love creatively. That, in the view of many wise people, is our main purpose on earth. So, always ask yourself, when making any big decision, or setting any new goal: 'In doing this, will I be acting in a loving way? In doing this, can I be acting in a creative way?' Creative love—loving creativity—that should be the core of your existence and action in the world, a guide to everything you do."

Both the boys were clearly taking all this in. The idea was so big that they could barely get their minds around it. The king paused for a moment and continued, "Without setting goals for yourself, it's impossible to be usefully creative at the highest level. And you'll never set the right goals for your life unless you follow the path of love. Ultimately, this is the purpose of freedom." He paused and asked, "Do these ideas make sense to you?"

Walid responded. "I think so, Uncle. This is deep. And it's

clearly important." He looked at his friend and said, "How about you, Maffie?"

"This makes a lot of sense to me, too, but no one's ever spoken to me in such words before. I like thinking in this way. It makes me feel that I can do great things with my life."

The king smiled. "Well, good! I'm certain that you can indeed do great things, each of you and, most likely, the two of you together. I feel that many great things are in your future. But, perhaps, this is enough time spent being philosophers together, at least for the present! You boys need some freedom right now to explore the palace!" The king stood up, and so did the boys. He added, "Mafulla, when your family arrives, I'll send word to you both. But, as for now, you should probably go wander the palace, and just look around."

"That sounds good," Mafulla said.

Walid added, "Thanks, Uncle Ali. That's very … loving of you—creatively loving."

"Yeah, thanks, Uncle—I mean, King Ali!"

The king said, "Oh, and Mafulla?"

"Yes, Your Majesty?"

"Your cologne is delightful."

"Thank you, sir." The boy bowed quickly, then looked at Walid and quickly lifted his eyebrows twice at his friend, and then followed him out the door with a spring in his step.

Ali chuckled to himself as both boys left the room in high spirits.

7

A Magical Spell

THE BOYS WERE STANDING TOGETHER IN A LARGE AND mostly empty hallway. "Why is there no queen with your uncle the king?"

Mafulla asked Walid this question as they looked at an old tapestry with a geometrical design that appeared to be from ancient times. It was one of many works of art to be found all around the place, on the walls, and on tables, adorning rooms and lining hallways.

Walid said, "I'm not sure. He was married long ago, but his wife died from a serious fever before I was born."

"That's too bad."

"Yeah. And he never remarried. I think he's been too busy planning and preparing for the revolution all these years. That's been his full time job. And it's really been his life."

"Ok."

"He's traveled a lot. And he's always reading and learning. He's also spent a lot of time with my parents and me. I guess he never had time to meet another lady who could become his wife. And, maybe he didn't want to marry anyone else. I don't know. I've never really talked to him about it."

"I see. But it's a shame."

"Yeah."

"People like queens."

"I suppose so."

"Maybe you'll be the next king to have a queen."

The girl in the marketplace flashed through Walid's mind. But he didn't know her name, or where she lived, or anything about her. He just saw her face vividly in his memory and felt a strange mix of gladness and sadness moving around in his heart.

He said, "Yeah, maybe. We should check outside the palace later to see if all the girls who want to be queen one day are lining up already to meet me. "

That made Mafulla laugh.

Walid added, "I may have some difficult choices ahead."

His friend replied, "I'm sorry to say this, but I doubt the young ladies of the kingdom even know about you at this point."

"Really?" Walid played along, looking serious.

Mafulla quickly responded, "But we can change that."

"How?"

"You should advertise. 'Future King Needs Beautiful Queen.' Or, pull out all the stops: 'King-To-Be, and Friend of Mafulla-the-Great, Needs Gorgeous and Loving Queen.' Then they'd show up by the hundreds and you could have your pick. It would be like a national contest. And I could take The First Runner-Up to be Mrs. Mafulla Adi. That could be The Amazing Consolation Prize."

"Is that your last name? Adi? I didn't know."

"Yes, and the future name of the second most beautiful girl in the land—or the most beautiful, in case you decide to go for brains instead of beauty."

"I think I'll go for both."

"Ok, then, the second most beautiful, and second most brainy girl in all the land—but a very close second, nearly a toss-up, almost indiscernibly different from the queen, in the minds of most onlookers, and my own, I'm sure."

"Where do you get words like 'indiscernibly'?"

"I am a man of the world, my friend. Pay attention and you can learn much from me."

Walid laughed.

"The words 'Indiscernibly different' mean that you can't really tell, or discern, the difference."

"Thank you, Professor Adi."

"You're welcome. But, seriously, speaking of all these beautiful girls I might end up evaluating in the future for the great honor of becoming the next Mrs. Adi, if I could some-how wrangle a Duke title or something, which would allow me to offer to make the lucky girl a Duchess, or some other such honorific, that might help my case a lot. I mean, there have to be some serious benefits from knowing the prince."

"We'll see about that, Possible Duke Adi. I don't know if we even have titles like that in our kingdom."

"Well, Earl, or Baron, or Count might work. Possibly, Satrap Adi."

"That's Persian."

"Oh. Ok. Maybe, Governor Adi?"

"That implies actual work—you know: governing."

"Oh. Yeah. True. Well, scratch that one, I guess. This is not as easy as I thought. But maybe a title isn't necessary. I suppose I could just rely on a magical spell. I have talents, you know. So, if you need a little something extra for attract-ing the ladies when Queen Time rolls around, I'll be glad to help."

"You are sometimes unbelievable."

"What can I say? I try. Believe me."

A palace guard came around the corner at just that moment. "Prince Walid, your friend's family is here, in the reception parlor in the main part of the palace."

"I'm not sure yet where that is."

"The two of you can follow me."

They walked down the long hallway, turned a corner, and descended some wide marble stairs. A short distance from there, they entered a wide doorway into a spacious but comfortable room where they could see several people standing in front of a long blue sofa, all looking more than a little bit awkward and nervous.

"Mom! Dad! Uncle Reela! Sammi! Sasha!" Mafulla threw open his arms and rushed to the group, where there was much exclaiming and embracing. Walid hung back to allow the family reunion to proceed without any interference from his presence. He could hear excited statements being made, left and right.

"My son!"

"My boy!"

"Thank goodness you're safe!"

"We didn't know where you were or what had happened to you!"

"We were worried sick!"

"We were frantic! And all our friends were helping look for you!"

Mafulla said, "I'm so sorry you were worried!"

His mother replied, "It's not your fault! We heard what happened!"

He hugged her tight and said, "It's so good to see you!"

Someone said, "I can't believe you're in the palace!"

"Man, we thought you had disappeared completely!"

"We didn't know what was going on!"

Voices were tumbling over each other as they all exchanged greetings and expressed relief and happiness to see each other. Emerging from the pack of hugs, arm-squeezings, and back pattings, Mafulla called out to his new friend: "Walid, come over here and meet my entire family!"

The prince approached them with a big smile on his face. Mafulla gestured to him and said, "This is my new best friend, Prince Walid."

Walid said, "It's so nice to see all of you!"

"Thank you so very much for helping our boy to escape to safety!" Mafulla's father put his hand over his heart as he said this.

"He helped me more than I helped him!" Walid replied.

"He's such a good boy and we were all just terrified that we would never see him again!" Maffie's mother was now smiling and crying at the same time. Seeing her face, Mafulla moved back to her to put his arms around her again.

Walid nodded his understanding. And at that moment, little Sasha spoke up: "Are you really a prince?"

"That's what everybody's been telling me. And, whether it's true or not, I'm at least in a palace and everyone calls me 'Prince,' and that's good enough for me!" Walid grinned and picked up Sasha and whirled her around in a big circle as she laughed and squealed.

Sammi was a little shy, but he said, "I like your palace a lot."

Walid told him, "I bet you'd like some of the food we have here, too, Mr. Sammi. But I don't know … some people don't like fancy baked foods and sweet desserts. They prefer plain, ordinary food."

"I like the fancy sweet things! Do you have any here?"

"I think we can find you something you'll enjoy." Walid turned to look at the royal butler who was standing close by, near the door.

"I'm sorry, sir, but do you think the kitchen staff would mind putting out some dessert items for a hungry boy?"

"Not at all, Your Highness. I'll have them do so right away." The man turned to leave, and Walid had a thought.

"Just a second. You know, these good people might all enjoy a little bite to eat, so, if it's not too much trouble, could something be brought around for all of them?"

"Yes, Prince Walid, I'll see to it immediately." He did a small bow and walked briskly away.

"Wow, that's nice." Sammi was clearly impressed.

Mafulla's mother said, "You don't have to go to any trouble for us. Getting our son back alive and well is more than enough."

"This is no trouble at all. I'm sure the kitchen is stocked with lots of food, and many of the former residents of the place are not here to enjoy it. I'm sure the cooks will like being busy and knowing the food won't go to waste."

Just that moment, Hamid walked through the door, smiled, and said, "Hello, everyone. Please excuse me for a second. The king will be in shortly. He wanted me to tell you that he's glad you're here. And, in case it might help to know, the proper way to greet the king is with a short bow. It's not appropriate to reach out to touch the king, or to offer to shake hands, but he may reach out to you, and if he does, then it's permissible to respond. When he stands, you stand. If he sits, you keep standing, unless he asks you to sit, and then you do so. Is everyone comfortable with all this?"

"Yes, yes, we are. Thank you." Maffie's father spoke quietly. "We're just very honored to be here." Mrs. Adi reached down and picked up little Sasha and held her in her arms. You never know what a four year old might do.

Two palace guards suddenly entered the room and stood on each side of the door. Within a second, the king walked in, with a big smile on his face and outstretched arms. "Welcome! Welcome to all of you! We're so happy you could come to be here with us. You have a fine boy in Mafulla, and we're glad to know him."

"Thank you, Your Majesty." The father bowed and spoke at once. And Maffie's mother mouthed the words silently, with a small bow herself, "Thank you."

Mafulla's dad then spoke again. "I'm Shapur Adi, and this is my wife, and Mafulla's mother, Shamilar."

"It's so nice to meet you. And who are the others?"

Shapur gestured. "This is my brother, Reela Adi, and these little ones are my other children, Sammi and Sasha." Reela smiled and bowed.

"It's a great pleasure to meet you all!"

The king moved to the side and sat down in a large golden yellow arm chair. He was wearing a bright red and gold robe, just to mark this special day, but there was no crown on his head. He had decided to use the crown only for ceremonial purposes and a few extremely formal occasions. Even the robe would not be everyday attire in the palace, but at the outset of the new monarchy, he thought it might be a nice touch of reassurance to people.

As he sat, he said to the family, "Please, all of you, sit down and be comfortable." And they did, variously positioning themselves on the long blue sofa that stretched out behind them, and on two flanking chairs. Walid and Mafulla sat on the floor in front of the sofa. One of the guards looked like he was thinking about bringing Walid a chair but then decided to stand still and allow the prince to be the boy he still was.

The king began to speak to the family about the adventures the two young men had gone through together, and the bravery of their son. He turned to Walid and Mafulla now and then for a specific detail, and wanted to make sure they all knew how thoughtful and capable Mafulla had proved himself under very difficult circumstances.

Mafulla's mother put her hands over her mouth three or four times, barely able to imagine the danger her son had encountered. Sasha and Sammi each said, "Wow!" two or three times.

Then the king delivered his surprise. "We're so impressed with your son, and we think he and Walid are getting along so well, that we would like to propose taking up his education at this point here in the palace. He can join Walid in classes and with tutors. He'll have the palace library available to him, as well as science labs and other resources not yet readily available elsewhere. We can include him on informational meetings and he'll get a chance to speak to some of the top experts in each field who live in our kingdom or visit here. He can even sleep down the hall from the prince as much as he likes, and be around for everything that happens at the center of kingdom affairs. We think he's capable of great things, and want to offer you the chance of an education for him that could make this possible."

At first, the family sat in silence, stunned.

"May I have your thoughts?" The king rested his hands on his lap and looked expectantly at Mafulla's father, mother, and uncle, who all had nearly blank expressions on their faces.

Shapur said, "Your Majesty! I think I speak for the whole family when I say that we're totally overwhelmed by your generosity. This is an opportunity beyond anything we could have imagined for our son."

Mafulla looked like it hadn't sunk in yet. His mouth

was open, but he was simply speechless. Walid saw him and thought, "Thirsty camel."

His mother said, very softly, "If I may speak, Your Majesty?"

"Yes. Please do."

"This is so overwhelmingly kind of you that I don't know where to start, but I do have one question. Would Mafulla have to live at the palace for this wonderful education, or could he possibly still sleep in his bed at home?"

"He can do anything you'd like. There are times when he would benefit from being here overnight, or even for a few days, but we can develop a schedule that meets your needs in every way."

"We live not so far away, and I suppose we could bring him in for lessons each morning, and then pick him up in the afternoons."

Shapur suggested, "Or, perhaps we could start out allowing him to be here for a more total immersion, and see how that works for all of us."

Shamilar then asked, "But if he was sleeping here in the palace, could we still see him as often as we'd like?"

The king said, "Oh yes, I assure you. You can visit him any time, and he can go home whenever you would like. Our aim is to provide for him and your family a wonderful opportunity, and nothing at all difficult, unpleasant, or burdensome."

Mafulla seemed to wake up from his trance. "You mean, Your Majesty, I'd get to stay here in the palace, almost like I was a minor honorary junior prince or ... a duke or something?"

The king chuckled. "Well, yes. You could have your own room, the one you spent some time in today while I was with Walid, near the royal bedchambers, just down from what will be Walid's room, and you'll have full access to all the facilities and benefits of palace life."

"Oh, wow. Mom, Dad, how about we give it a try? Between school and work, I'm away from the house most of the time already. This way, I'll get the very best possible education, and I'll learn a lot from life around the palace, more than I could learn any other way, and I could maybe spend every weekend at home, or every other weekend, or something like that—whatever we'd like."

The king then suggested that, to provide for some regular spending money, Mafulla could also have a part time job in the palace, as a component of this new arrangement, if he would enjoy that. The Prince would also have chores to do, and would be provided with comparable spending money as a result. This suggestion evoked another round of gushing thanks and words of astonished appreciation from nearly all.

The conversation went on for a few more minutes and everyone enthusiastically agreed to let Mafulla stay and enjoy a full run of the palace and begin a new phase of his education, with many weekends at home, and more frequent visits with family whenever anyone wanted to see him, or he wanted to visit with any of them.

When the king was satisfied that all was in order and everyone was in agreement, he stood up, and the rest of them did so, in response. He thanked the family again for coming and bid them farewell for the moment, assuring them that Mafulla would be well cared for whenever he was in the palace. The boy's mother and father in turn thanked the king profusely, bowed deeply, and had big smiles on their faces as Ali left the room.

Before they could say anything else, the food prepared for them appeared, as if by magic. It was carried in by six waiters and placed on tables around the room, along with jugs of water and juice, and some other beverages for the adults, in case they wanted them. The headwaiter bowed to the family and said, "Courtesy of His Majesty, please enjoy a royal snack!" Then he and the other waiters left the room.

"Thank you, my good man!" Mafulla smiled broadly and, turning to his family, said, "Just let me know if you need anything else and I'll see to it immediately." They all looked surprised and then laughed aloud at his mock presumptuousness and instant familiarity with the royal way.

He said, "What? I seek to serve and aim to please!"

Mafulla's uncle laughed again and said, "For a boy who doesn't like any of his chores around the house, this is a nice change already. It's good to have a faithful servant in high places who aims to please!"

Everyone had a feast from the "royal snack" that had been laid out for them. They talked and laughed for nearly an hour more before Mafulla's dad suggested that they should be getting back home. His mother commented that the visit had been truly magical. And Mafulla remarked that it was funny she should say that, because earlier, he and Walid had been talking about magic in their lives. Walid smiled at the private joke and knew that he now had a friend who would be of enduring entertainment value.

They briefly made plans to bring Mafulla a few of his favorite things from home for his upcoming stay at the palace. And he promised Sasha and Sammi more playtime on the grounds for their next visit. Everyone hugged Mafulla again and, after making sure it was allowed, they also embraced Walid. Then the butler on duty escorted the family down the hall and all the way to the outermost doors, where friendly guards took over and walked them out to the external gates and bid them farewell for now.

Public celebrations were still going on outside the gates, as throngs of people sang, chanted, and talked about their joy over the changed monarchy. Most families had older members who remembered the former Shabeezar reign, or had heard family stories that had been handed down about those good times in the past. The mood all over the city was festive.

There were a few people, however, who had benefited in selfish ways from the corrupt regime and were not at all happy with this sudden change in the government. One of them was across the street from the main gates of the palace as the Adi family was escorted out with a show of great respect. He thought he recognized them from somewhere, and made a mental note of them as he memorized each of their faces. If they were friends of this new monarchy, or perhaps of the king himself, they might become useful.

In fact, at that very moment, he decided to summon a colleague from down the block to follow these people home and report back the location of their residence. Knowledge, after all, is power, as it has often been said. And those who least deserve any degree of power are often the most focused in its pursuit.

8

Time and the Golden Mean

We measure time, and it has a way of returning the favor. It silently takes our measure by laying the grid of its progression over the flow of our lives to allow us to see whether we've made our own distinctive forms of progress in growth, wisdom, and positive action—or not. As an old Hindu proverb tells us, true nobility consists not in being superior to some other person, but in being superior to our own previous self. Do our months and years tell a tale of accomplishment, growth, and flourishing, or merely of passive, inert existence, tethered by habit and bound to the past?

The early days in the palace saw all kinds of positive movement and accomplishment on the part of its new residents. Previous staff members were interviewed and many were retained, though a few were helped into other occupations, and two, sadly, had to be jailed. It seems that they had sought to exploit the commotion of change for their own purposes, and had been found hiding valuable items in their work areas, in preparation for smuggling them out of the palace.

Discoveries were being made all over the place. One day, the king summoned Walid and Mafulla into his private rooms and surprised them each with a gift. A short time before he was appointed to the lofty position of treasurer for the kingdom, one of Ali's old friends, Baldoor, had been looking around various palace storage areas at the king's request and had found a locked closet in the basement that was stocked with all sorts of luxuries. They had apparently been purchased by the previous regime from various European makers, with a concentration of valuable items that had originated from Switzerland, France, and Germany. Among these treasures was a large cabinet filled with small boxes of beautiful and well-made wristwatches. Ali knew the usefulness of these timing devices for coordinating activities within the government, and immediately gave many of them to his top administrators and their assistants for daily use, including, of course, Baldoor.

The life Ali had lived back in the village with Walid's parents and their friends had a much slower pace of activity, and most things could be done by the position of the sun. The phrase "I'll meet you in just a bit" was commonly used, as if everyone knew at least the approximate length of "a bit." The rhythms of their previous routines had allowed the continuation of this rough sense of time and its passage that has governed most of the human adventure. In the palace, however, greater precision was needed, to allow many more coordinated activities to be fit into the average day. Now, a normal workday for most of the men was an extraordinary rush of meetings, decisions, and events of great importance. People's comings and goings had to be organized to the greatest possible extent and they had to be able to meet with each other easily and at the right times.

After the king had distributed various timepieces to the top palace staff and other important individuals, there were a few quite special watches he had kept aside. With some research, he had determined a proper use for two of the remaining items. So, when Walid and Mafulla stuck their heads into his door, he was ready for them.

"Come in, boys, come in!" The king beamed at them from across the room. He was sitting at a desk and had been reading. He gestured toward some chairs and said, "Please, have a seat."

The prince and his friend plopped down energetically on the nearest indicated chairs. "Why did you want to see us, Your Majesty?" Walid was a little breathless, and so was Mafulla, since they had just run across the entire palace, and bounded up some major stairs after being summoned by a guard to go see the king.

"I have a break now between meetings and wanted to take a little time to talk with you about a topic of great interest and importance. And, in addition, I have something for you that's relevant to the topic, if you'll allow me to present you with a small gift."

Walid grinned and said, "That's very nice! What do you have for us?" He was always eager to hear about new things, to experience nice surprises, and especially, to receive unexpected gifts. His excitement came through in his voice.

The king held up his right index finger and said, "I'll get to that shortly. Let me first ask you both a few simple questions. I want to talk with you briefly on the topic of time, regarding its nature and passage. We need to think deeply about it together for a few minutes."

Mafulla turned to Walid and said, "Well. It's about ... time."

Both Walid and the king chuckled at his almost inevitable cleverness, or at least, at his reliably best efforts in that direction. The king then furrowed his brow and said, "This is my first question: How is time to be understood? Does it move? Is it like a river that flows past us? There's one picture of it that suggests it does. Imagine that we're standing together on a bridge over a fast moving river, all facing in the direction from which the water comes. The current brings us what has been the future into what is now the present, right under us on the bridge—representing the time in which we exist now—and then takes that moment behind us, into the past. On this picture of time, we human beings are in a deep sense still, positioned as we are, relative to its passage, and time is moving at first toward us and then away from us, but always in the same direction."

Walid said, "That sort of makes sense. Time flows on like a river."

Mafulla said, "And we do normally speak of the passage of time. It moves, and it passes us by. Some say it flows. Others say it flies."

"Yes, we do talk like that, but consider another image." Ali continued. "What if time is more like a long twisty road, and it is we who are moving along it? On this view, it is motion-less—it's a dimension through which we pass—and we're the ones moving, as we make progress along it. The future is that part of the road up ahead, the part we haven't gotten to, and can't yet see. The present is under our feet now, easily visible to us. And the past is the part of the road we've already walked—either we ourselves, or we human beings, through our ancestors, whose memory we now may, in part, retain, and whose history we can recall. Is this what time is like?"

Mafulla made a face and said, "Hmm. That makes sense, too."

Ali continued. "And, yet surely, it must be one or the other of these images that's true. They can't both be. Time moves, or it doesn't. Which is it? We have a puzzle. And if it's time that moves like a river, could something speed it up or slow it down? If instead it's we who move along a motionless road of time, going from past into future, could we then, at certain points, go more quickly, or slow down?"

"These may be puzzles without easy answers!" Walid was instantly fascinated.

Ali smiled. "Now, consider another question: Do you know what it means when someone says to you, 'I'll be with you in a moment'?"

Walid said, "Yes, of course, Uncle." Mafulla nodded his head as well.

"So, how long exactly is a moment?"

Both boys looked surprised and perplexed.

The king was warming to the topic. "We all live in the present moment. The past moments that were once present have all gone away, somewhere or somewhen." The king smiled with almost a look of mischief when he pronounced the last word. And then he said, "These past moments are no longer with us. And the future moments that we'll at some point experience as present are themselves not yet here, any of them." He put his hands out in front of him and began to bring them slowly together until his fingers were all touching, and his palms were flat together, as he said, "We have only the present moment, one point in the overall sweep of time, as our current dwelling. That is our grip on reality, where our existence as souls in the world objectively resides. You can subjectively live in the past or in the future with your thought. But as to where or when you're doing the thinking: You are here, and it is now."

The boys sat silent, listening and thinking, taking it all in.

Ali continued. "The present moment, the point in time

designated by the word 'now,' seems to be the special location of real objective being, the point at which we are most fully and intensely attached to this world, and connected in a unique way. But what's the true story about this present moment in which we uniquely live? How big is it? How long is it? It certainly doesn't go on forever. There will be many future moments beyond it, like tomorrow, and later today, and a few minutes or even seconds from now, just as there were past moments before now. The present moment is therefore certainly limited in its size, or span, or duration."

"That sounds right," Mafulla said, hesitantly.

"But does it have a span at all?" The king asked. "Can it? And, if so, how long is that span, between the past and future, that span of solid temporal ground on which we now stand? Surely, it has some measure. We can't exist, here and now, if we are poised on nothing. It's surely something, this present moment, and it must have some sort of substance, or area, or room, on which to stand. And yet, here we have another puzzle. Does the present moment actually have any real duration, or thickness, any real extension, or length? If it truly separates the past from the future, it must. Something without any length or width or thickness can't truly separate any two other things. If the present moment is in some sense a wall between what has been and what's yet to come, then surely it must have that one crucial characteristic of a wall—some sort of thickness. Correct?"

"I guess so." Walid spoke softly and with hesitation.

Mafulla spoke softly as well, at this point, saying, "But walls have thickness and height and a length by which they stretch on for a certain distance." His voice trailed off.

"Yes! And now, let's think of the thickness of this wall in terms of the distance, or measure, between the side that faces the past and the side that touches the future's next moment. If you think that this wall of the present, this one moment of time, in the strictest sense has some form of length, or duration, then it would surely have to be the shortest possible length. Anything longer than a shortest possible length could, in principle, be measured and, at least in thought, divided into two still shorter lengths. But then, what was one moment would really be two. And that makes no sense. So, the present moment must be without any divisible length at all. And yet, how can that be? It would be like a geometrical point, which is theoretical and not an existing thing in the real world! We do say 'at this point in time,' but can we possibly mean that in a literal way? Is all the fullness and solidity and scope and depth of our existence in the world balanced on a mere single mathematical point? But a point without any length or any extension whatsoever is just a theoretical abstraction, an idealization—and such abstract idealizations are not to be found in physical reality. They're mental constructs, playthings of thought, and our lives are surely not that!"

"Oh, my." Walid responded. It's safe to say that the boys were in a state of complete puzzlement. They had never heard anything like this before. But the king went on.

"This moment in which I now speak: Is it thick? Or is it thinner than the edge of a razor? Is it deep? Or is it shallow? How much can happen in it? And, consider this additional question: Do we all live in the same present moment, or could we in this room actually live in different present moments that merely touch and, perhaps to some extent, overlap?"

They were all silent for ... a moment, and then Walid spoke up again. "These are very, very hard and confusing questions."

Ali pressed forward as the eager teacher that he long had been. "Yes. You're right. But are they difficult questions because they're about things you've never experienced, like questions about exotic birds or animals who live only in far-away, remote parts of the world, or perhaps, are they like questions about distant and strange things in the universe studied by science that you've never yet heard about?"

Mafulla promptly answered, "No, not at all. These are questions about something very familiar that we live with every day. We're supposed to know what time is. And in one sense, we do. We're around it all the ... time." That last word brought a slight smile to his face but he was otherwise very thoughtful and perplexed in contemplating these things.

Ali went on. "I don't want to make you dizzy, but consider this. Some moments seem amazingly full. Others appear relatively empty. Some strike us as abbreviated. Others feel like they've been stretched. When something happens that's life threatening, many people speak later about having experienced an expansion of the present moment, as if time slowed down almost to a stop, and a ripe fullness of the immediate instant swelled outward to encompass more territory than they ever would have thought possible."

Walid said, "I sort of felt that recently, when I was confronted with sudden danger."

"Me, too." Mafulla chimed in.

The king paused and then spoke again. "Now, let me ask you this: Have you ever noticed that, when you're really enjoying yourself, time seems to fly by rapidly, but when you're bored, or doing something you don't like, anything that feels unpleasant, time seems to creep and crawl slowly, as if on its hands and knees?"

"Yes!" Both boys answered at once.

Walid added, "That's the way it felt now and then on some really hot days, crossing the desert."

The king replied, "Exactly. This shows clearly that our

experience of time can be quite different from time itself. No matter how much fun you have, or how terribly bored or uncomfortable you are, every second, minute, and hour is presumably the same objective length as any other second, minute, and hour. Whether you're excited, or bored, or miserable, or scared, a person nearby would find his clock or watch ticking at the exact same pace. And yet, in our experience of time, certain hours or days can be very different from others, in how we sense the passage of time, and that all depends on what's going on inside us, in our thoughts and feelings, and not on what characterizes the pathway, or the river, of time itself."

Walid remembered their many previous conversations and said, "You mean that, with time, as with so many other things, appearances can be very different from realities?"

"Yes, that's correct. And, as a consequence of this, most people have trouble keeping accurate track of time, and managing their time well. In fact, our use of time is one of the toughest challenges we face in life. We all have the same number of minutes in every hour, but some people can get a great deal accomplished in that length of time, and others fall far short of what they could have done. Some people use their lifetime well and achieve great things. Others allow time to slip away from them and squander one of their most precious resources.

"In addition, there's one thing that you'll notice as you grow older. The people who seem to waste their own time the most flagrantly will try also to take it from you, and waste yours, as well. You need to be aware of this and to be very careful around anyone who would abscond with your time. It's one of the few things in the world that, if stolen, is absolutely impossible to get back. It can never be recovered from a thief."

"Wow, that's true," Mafulla said. "But I'd never thought about it."

Walid jumped right in, adding, "And I suppose that, for the same reason, if I give my time to a friend, to help with a project, or just to listen to his problems, then that's one of the most valuable things I can ever give."

"That's right and very wise. Investing time in an activity, or with a person, is imparting a very precious, limited resource. Always remember that. We must use our time well, or we'll look back on our lives with regret. Some things are worth our time, and others aren't. Be careful with your time, and protect it well, but don't hoard it like a miser. It's to be used and given to worthy pursuits and to the people you care about. That's what it's for."

Mafulla commented at this point. "My parents have always invested a lot of time in me. I've seen other kids whose parents gave them very little time, and those kids usually grow up with problems."

Ali replied, "You're right. Good relationships require a substantial time investment. And all children need it, if they're to develop well. As we grow up, from our earliest days, we benefit greatly from the time that parents and other older adults might give us."

Walid said, "I bet that's one reason you've always given me so much time, Uncle. You want me to have those benefits."

"That's correct. And I enjoy your company. I see great value in you as a person. The time we spend together signifies all of that. These days recently have been very busy and there's been less time to share. But you and Mafulla have had extra time to explore with each other and learn about this new place, and that's good. Things will settle down soon and we should have more time to talk again as we have in the past, and as we're doing right now. It's sad when people who care about each other are kept apart by the pressure of hectic and urgent circumstances. Sometimes, it happens. We get out of balance. Then we act to restore the balance."

The king looked thoughtful. He said, "Perhaps the most important advice I can give you today about time is this: One of the greatest challenges is to manage your time well. And you can't do that unless you manage your emotions well. That, in turn, requires managing your thoughts. Most people seem to assume that our thoughts and emotions just come to us, and we have no control over them. But the truth is that we can have great control over them. And yet, like many things, mental and emotional self control is an art, a skilled activity. You get better at it by practicing it." The boys quietly took this in.

The king then looked off into the distance for a moment and said, "When we govern our thoughts properly, that allows us to do the same with our emotions. And since it's mostly our emotions that cause us to make decisions and choose one activity over another one, the action of governing our emotions well allows us to govern our time well. The busier you get in life, the more you realize the importance of this."

Ali looked at Walid, then at his friend, and now addressed the smaller boy. He said, "You know, Mafulla, palace life is different from life out in the remote country village where Walid and I have lived for so long. I'm sure it's even different from your family's daily life."

"Yes, it is." Mafulla responded right away. "Things are always going on here. It's impossible to get bored. We never know what's going to happen next."

"Indeed, it's very busy in this place. That's why it was important to me that we have this little talk about time. I want you to understand that, when your formal school sessions start very soon, and when you begin to have more responsibilities around the palace, it will be important for both of you to be able to show up when you're needed. It will be more crucial than ever for you to be able to plan your day and use your time well. And, with that in mind, we have a problem to solve."

"What's that, Uncle Ali?"

"Right now, whenever I want to see you, I send a butler or guard to find you. But there will be circumstances when I want to alert you that I need to see you, not right away, but after a certain passage of time. And there's no easy way to do that now. If I sent a guard or one of the other men to find you, and he said that I wanted to see you in an hour and a half, what would you do to make sure you arrived on time?"

Mafulla said, "Counting one thousand one, one thousand two, with sixty of those in a minute and sixty minutes in an hour, is probably not the solution. It would get tiring, for sure. And I might lose count."

Walid smiled and followed up with the comment, "I don't know what we'd do except maybe stay near one of the large clocks in the palace and wait for the time to pass, checking the clock now and then."

"Yes, and that would be both inconvenient, and a very inefficient use of your time." The king got up and walked over to a couple of boxes on a table nearby. "That's why I've decided to give each of you a present today."

Mafulla grinned. "I like this place better and better."

Ali said, "One of the men found a locked closet in the basement, and in it were many nice things that had been purchased recently from various countries in Europe, along with other items that had been received as gifts from around the world. From Switzerland, there were many wristwatches, those small clocks, or timepieces, you can wear on your arm. Have either of you seen one of these?"

"I've seen a couple." Walid responded.

"I've caught sight of a few in town and at the market, usually on the arms of important men, and two different ladies." Mafulla had a very serious expression on his face as he remembered.

"Well, I would like to give each of you a watch to wear every day."

The boys both looked surprised. Neither of them had ever seen anyone of their ages wearing a watch. The king handed a dark blue box to Walid, and then one to Mafulla. They opened the boxes as quickly as they could, and within each there was a striking, highly polished rectangular steel watch with a black strap. Each of the watches practically glowed as it sat on a small cushion of stuffed fabric, with its strap encircling the cushion as it would a wrist.

"Oh, man, this is beautiful!" Walid couldn't help exclaiming, on first sight of his watch.

"It's unbelievable! Look at this thing!" Mafulla was just as excited.

Ali explained, "The time has already been set, and each of these has been wound. You need to rewind your watch every morning, using the winding crown on the side, being careful not to tighten the spring within it too much. When you feel resistance, often at around twenty or thirty quick turns, give or take, you should stop. If you forget and the watch stops running, you can pull out the crown and reset it, using a palace clock, or your friend's watch, to determine the correct time, and then rewind it. Properly cared for, these fine instruments will serve you well for many years to come, and then perhaps one day your child, and even, farther into the future, a grandchild."

"Wow, Uncle, this is so amazing. It's really, really beautiful."

"Yeah," Mafulla said. "Really."

"I'm glad you both like them. Now I must show you a little trick."

"What is it?"

"Most people don't give boys your age such nice watches, fearing that the rough and tumble life you lead might cause the crystal, or the glass over the face of the watch, to break. These small mechanisms are expensive to purchase, and can be quite costly to fix, even if only the glass is damaged. But a few years ago, a British polo player in the country of India asked for a special watch to be made that could withstand rough sporting activities, and the result is this amazing rectangular creation that you have in your hands."

"Interesting," Walid commented.

"Now, Walid, allow me to hold yours, in order to show you a trick." He gently handed his watch to his uncle and the king took it with his right hand. Using his left thumb, he pushed sideways on the case, and the main part of it slid in the direction he was moving it, while the black strap and a steel plate now visible underneath the case stayed immobile. The king then became a real magician and flipped the watchcase over and slid it back into place with a click. Suddenly, they were all looking at the highly polished, solid steel back of the watch where the face had been. Engraved on it was a beautiful royal crown and, below the crown, the Greek letter Phi, which is shaped like a large zero with a vertical bar through the middle of it, and extending a bit out of the circle, both top and bottom. Ali showed it to each of the boys and then gently handed it back to Walid.

He said, "Wow! How did you do that? And what's this on the back, a picture of a crown? And something else, an interesting shape." The prince spoke up as he examined the quickly transformed timepiece.

After Ali had returned the watch to Walid, he took Mafulla's, and did the very same trick, handing it back as well. "This unusual watch is called a Reverso. You can reverse the front and the back when you know you'll be engaged in some form of rough activity, so as to protect the glass, and then reverse it back again when you want to be able to see the time. The little winding crown that sticks out on the right of the case when the crystal faces you is what you use to wind up the spring in your watch daily, as I mentioned, turning it upward from the front. But if you push the opposite side of the case in the direction of the winding crown, the case moves outward, sideways, and then you can flip it over. You just reverse those movements to get it back to the way it was."

"Gee," Mafulla said. "That's pretty wild."

"But now, if you'll notice, on the backside of the watch, we have these two engravings—an intricate one that was done in Switzerland by the makers of the watch, and the other, a simpler one, that was done for me yesterday evening by a local jeweler I know and trust. The image of a royal crown came from the maker, and the man who is now the palace engraver added the Greek letter Phi at my request."

Walid said, "The engraving of the royal crown is beautiful, and the Phi is … mysterious."

Ali nodded. "The crown of course symbolizes the fact that these particular watches were ordered from their Swiss maker for the use of royalty. I've been told that the Prince of Denmark recently had one made with such an engraving. And the King of England may be planning to order one soon, also with a crown engraved on the back. The Phi symbol represents something very interesting that I love about the watch itself, and also stands for something else that's independently quite important in its own right."

"What is it?" Walid's curiosity, as always, was keen.

Ali lifted another small box from the table nearby, and pulled from it a watch in most ways identical to the ones that he had just given the boys, but with a rose gold case surrounding a shimmering black face. He held it up to display to the boys, bringing it close to them.

Mafulla said, "Wow. Double wow."

Walid chimed in, "Yeah, triple that for me. It's just like ours but black and gold. It's really, really beautiful."

The king ran a finger around the external case design and said, "The beauty of the case is in part due to the special gold from which it's made, but it's also a result of the shape and proportionality of the design, in addition to its meticulous finish."

"What do you mean?" Walid asked.

"The width of this particular object stands in relation to its length in a ratio of 1 to 1.618. Or, at least, that second number is conveniently rounded down to what's called three decimal places, since the actual digits to the right of the decimal point marking the exact ratio will go on literally forever, like time itself, perhaps. It represents what's called an irrational number, something that's of interest in its own right. We can discuss it on another occasion, if you'd like."

Walid said, "For now, could you say a bit more about ratios?"

"Certainly. If this watch were perfectly square, having the same length as width, the ratio of the width to the length would be 1 to 1. If the length were twice that of the width, the ratio of width to length would be 1 to 2. This is somewhere in between and has a ratio of 1 to 1.618, and so on."

"Ok. I get it," Walid said. "So, this is a very strange ratio."

"And it's an important one."

"Really?" Mafulla said.

"Yes. This particular ratio, again, the proportion of the width to the length, is of such great importance that it's widely referred to as 'the golden ratio.' Sometimes it's called 'the golden mean,' or even 'the divine proportion.' It's believed to be that significant."

"Why is that?" Walid asked, as the boys gazed at the watch.

Ali replied: "The ancient Greek artist Phidias used this ratio in his sculptures and in the famous and greatly admired building in Athens called the Parthenon, a temple built in honor of the goddess Athena, whose construction we think he designed and supervised. So, it's customary to use the Greek letter Phi, his initial, to represent this ratio, or proportionality. The most fascinating thing about it is that so much of what we find interesting, attractive, or beautiful in both art and nature conforms to the proportion of the golden ratio."

"Who exactly was Athena?" Walid asked.

The king smiled. "She was believed to be the goddess and thus divine patroness of wisdom, courage, inspiration, justice, mathematics, strength, skill, the arts, and strategy in war, among other things."

"Wow. That's a lot," Mafulla said.

"Yes, it is," the king replied. "And so, Athena was of great importance to the Greeks. You can well imagine that her temple was a revered and holy place."

"Uncle, I've never heard any of this before." Walid's interest had clearly been piqued. As he looked down at the watch, he asked, "Can you tell us more about this proportion thing, the golden ratio?"

"Surely. To our knowledge, it was first defined explicitly

in writing by Euclid around 300 BC right here in Egypt, in the city of Alexandria, although it's been said that the Greek mystic and philosopher Pythagoras also understood it, before him. A great mathematician in Baghdad, Iraq, a man called Al Samawal, also famously wrote of it in the twelfth century, expressing it as a fraction: 1 + the square root of 5, over 2: a fraction whose decimal expression is 1.618."

"Whoa," Walid said.

"Do you boys know squaring and square roots?"

Mafulla replied, "It seems like a good time for a joke of some sort, but I can't think of one, so I'll just say no." Walid smiled and shrugged.

Ali also smiled and nodded and said, "Well, then: In mathematics, squaring and square roots are related. The square root of 4 is 2, because 2 times 2, or 2 squared, as we say, is 4. The square root of 9 is 3, because 3 times 3, or 3 squared, is 9. The square root of 5, by contrast, can never fully be expressed except with a symbolic abbreviation. Because of that, the fraction Al Samawal discovered to express Phi, the fraction involving this number, is called an irrational number."

"Interesting." Walid looked deeply impressed, but felt that he was on the edge of his ability to understand what he was hearing.

The king continued. "As I mentioned, the Parthenon was designed and built in several ways according to this ratio, 1 to 1.618. The Great Pyramid in our own land embodies it as well, from a time long before the creation of the Parthenon. Famous paintings also can be shown to obey its boundaries. An ideal human body, one that would be seen as especially beautiful, offers example after example of it—the distance from the top of the head to the shoulders is approximately 1.618 times the distance from the top of the head to the bottom of the jaw line. The width of the nose of a beautiful woman, from one extreme to the other, stands in this ratio to the broader width of her lips. The bones in our fingers and hands, and various proportionalities concerning our height and torso, can also be cited. The examples go on and on. And then, all this gets even more interesting and mysterious."

"What do you mean?" Mafulla was now clearly caught up in this description as well.

"An Italian mathematician, Leonardo of Pisa, also known widely as Fibonacci, discovered something that, it turns out, several Indian mathematicians before him had also recognized, a curious sequence of numbers that starts with 0, 1, 1 and then continues in such a way that any further number in the sequence, after the beginning, is the sum of the previous two numbers. For example, the series goes:

0, 1, 1, 2, 3, 5, 8, 13, 21, 34, 55, 89, 144, 233, 377, 610, 987 ...

"And you'll forgive me, I'm sure, if I can't continue by memory."

"Jeepers, Your Majesty. You did a lot more than I could have," Mafulla said.

The king replied, "The series itself also goes on forever. 5 is the sum of the two previous numbers, 3 and 2. 8 is the sum of 5 and 3. And so on. What's really interesting is that these numbers in sequence seem to play all sorts of hidden roles in nature, even helping us to understand the shapes of various plants and the idealized breeding patterns of some insects and animals. And here's something very strange, indeed. If you begin taking the proportional ratios of subsequent pairs of numbers in the Fibonacci sequence, you get a convergence toward 1 to 1.618—Phi, or the golden ratio."

"This is just too much," Walid said, and his mouth hung open.

"You now look like a thirsty camel, my friend." Mafulla was grinning.

Ali smiled at the two of them and said, "Walid, I've heard you comment many times on how beautiful this palace is."

"Yes, it's the most beautiful building I've ever seen."

"It was built in all its major exterior dimensions and in many interior aspects just like your watch case, in accordance with Phi, the golden ratio. Many of its furnishings were also designed around the ratio. The table here embodies Phi. All of this around us was conceived of and made by my great grandfather, a brilliant man, and his father before him, a known philosopher and mathematician. They've surrounded us with the golden ratio."

"So ... there's more than one reason that this building is called The Golden Palace." Walid spoke with a tone of respectful astonishment.

"My boy, you're completely right! I'm not surprised that you picked up on that so quickly. Nearly everyone in the kingdom thinks it has its name just because of its exterior color at certain times of day. But this is the deeper reason."

He paused for a moment and then looked at Walid. "I'll say just one more thing about this number, and that will be all for now. Do you know the family name of our old friend, Masoon?"

The prince answered, "No, now that you mention it, I don't think I've ever heard it."

"It's Afah. He's Masoon Afah, and has been so named since he was born."

"Oh."

"Now, if you take the name Afah rendered in the English

alphabet, the most widely used on earth and most commonly employed for political and economic dealings, and you map numbers to the letters, starting with A = 1, B = 2, and so on, the name "Afah" corresponds to the sequence: 1, 6, 1, 8, the first four numbers of the golden ratio."

"What?"

The king continued. "In Arabic, of course, the name Afah means 'protector' or 'strength'—and I think you would agree that this is an unusually appropriate name for our friend. When he's with us, we have a special strength and a golden protection."

"This is almost spooky." Walid looked very serious.

"Almost?" Mafulla said.

"There are many things we don't fully understand. And some of those things are among the most important realities of all. In fact, as you've heard me say before, it just may be that some of the easiest things to understand in the world are among the least important, and some of the most difficult to understand are among the most crucial. So it's wise of us to ask questions and think hard, and occasionally to be reminded of special things around us that we don't normally pay much attention to, like the nature of time, and the golden ratio."

He looked at both boys. "Since one particular mystery, the proportionality of the golden ratio, has played such a role in our family's history and in the design and construction of this palace, it's quite appropriate that its classic symbol, the Greek letter Phi, is engraved on each of your watches. In part, it will remind you of the hidden patterns around us that can mean so much, especially when we acknowledge and respect them. And, of course, if you're seeing it on the back of your watch, that just means there's something else hidden that must at some point be revealed."

"What?" Walid asked without thinking.

"Well, of course, the face with the time on it." Ali smiled again as the boys both laughed.

He then said, "Keep track of your time, and use it well. You have a new tool with which to do that. You can leave the boxes here, which I'll keep for the moment, so you won't be bothered with carrying them, and I'll send them to your rooms later. Fasten the strap of the watch around your wrist, allowing just enough wiggle room for it to be comfortable on you, and you can begin wearing your new timepiece right now, in the fullness of the most mysterious present moment."

Walid and Mafulla each took a few seconds to put on their new watches, these precise little machines that could measure that most familiar but perplexing of things, the ongoing passage of time—or, of life through time, whichever it might be.

Ali rose from his chair, and then so did the boys. He said, "I think it's now time that you two go on about your day. And I have some important meetings to attend. But I want to see you in my private dining room for dinner at exactly six o'clock."

The boys both said, at the same time, "Yes, sir!"

Walid added, "And not a moment later."

Mafulla, of course, had to add, "Whatever exactly that means!"

9

A Visitation

Practically everyone who lived outside the law, even partly, or else at the edge of it, knew of Ari Falma. If there was ever a king of the illegal underground economy in the kingdom, it was Ari. His father was a thief, and his father before him. He boasted the criminal version of a royal lineage. In connection with anything unlawful, the Falma name was heard. He had uncles and cousins and even a brother working for him in the most extensive crime family Egypt had ever known.

The capital city was famous for its huge market. Ari was known for his alternative black market, a network of connections and warehouses where items of worth could secretly be bought and sold without government knowledge, or the oversight and taxes that would diminish his profits. It was Ari who had arranged a big kidnapping scheme for a couple of corrupt palace officials, the criminal operation that had snagged Mafulla and Walid in its net.

Ari himself was a small, slender man, of less than average height, but he was typically accompanied by armed associates, strong muscular men who always carried with them various weapons for the sole purpose of using them as often and as brutally as they could. Their boss was a blackmailer, a racketeer, an extortionist, a greedy mastermind of robbery and counterfeiting, and a supplier of any illegal substance or weapon needed by the seedier elements both within the kingdom and well beyond its borders. He was in reality an international criminal whose entire enterprise was now threatened by the political revolution that overnight had removed the previous, deeply corrupt monarchy from power. He had even been involved in devious schemes hatched by the prior king himself, as well as by some of his trusted administrators who had sought to topple him.

In political matters, Ari didn't choose sides. He always instead chose whatever money and power might be available to him, regardless of who it was that he would have to work with and what he might have to do to get these things. And now he was deeply worried. Many sources of revenue had been completely eliminated by the sudden palace takeover. The corrupt administrators he knew were out of power. Most had left the kingdom. His important contacts in the palace were gone. And many lucrative activities that had been ignored or protected by friendly soldiers and policeman were now in jeopardy. Something had to be done. He needed leverage. He required a plan.

That was why he had a man follow Mafulla's family from the palace gate after their visit, and across town to their house. And it was the purpose for his personal visit to see them a week later. Claiming to be a top representative of the government and sent by an associate of the king himself, he easily gained entrance to their home, and then, conjuring up all the charm of which he was capable, he spun a tale of intrigue that captured their attention, as well as their imaginations. Sitting comfortably with them, after enjoying some characteristic hospitality on their part, he spoke of the reason for his visit.

"Mr. and Mrs. Adi, I've come to see you with the news that the king needs your help in a highly secretive and confidential way. I've been asked to visit and speak to you today by the king's treasurer, who has sent me, I can assure you, on his majesty's own orders. It's been discovered that, due to the surprisingly quick takeover of the government recently, some forces who are actually opposed to the king have been able to masquerade as his supporters, and retain or secure powerful positions in the monarchy's offices."

"Oh, my," Shamilar said. "That's terrible."

"And it's dangerous," Ari said.

"Is our son safe?"

"Yes, he's completely safe, for now." Ari, of course, had no idea what she was talking about, but would spin this mention of a son to his advantage. He continued. "We know that there are some traitors among us, but not yet who they are. We need to find out—the sooner, the better for everyone, including of course, your son. And the clandestine operations required in order to accomplish this will be costly. The king wants to keep these expenses off the official books so that there will be no possibility that those suspected can themselves glean the information that an operation is underway to expose them. There are objects and services that have to be bought and sold in order to fund the investigation. And this needs to be done in secret, far from the palace and any watchful eyes that might be there."

"I can understand that," Shapur said. "It makes sense."

"Mr. Adi, we know you to be a very successful merchant. I myself have seen you at your rather spacious shop in the market."

"Thank you, sir. I'm blessed to own a good business."

"I've also heard that you may have a large open area in the back of your shop where you keep many surplus and recently arrived goods."

"Yes, that's correct. We have a lot of room in our building, and much space that we don't even use."

Falma nodded and said, "This is good. We were wondering whether you could allow some of our men into the shop, if at all possible, under the guise of friends of a friend who are starting their own small business. And, of course, in a sense, this will be true. Their story will be that you're allowing them some space in the back of the place for their start-up venture. If asked, they'll say that their business has to do with security and transportation. If you're ever questioned about them, you can say the same, and be assured that your representation is accurate enough. So, we're not asking you to lie about anything. We'd never ask that. And, for your gracious cooperation, the men, in turn, will be available to give you extra help whenever you need it."

Shapur said, "I would be honored to be of assistance in this way."

Falma continued. "Excellent! Now, remember, these men will be engaged in the work of which I've spoken. Their activities will be secret, and it will be better if you don't even know their names or what they're doing. This will allow us, in complete safety, to fund a full investigation of potential treason and then pursue it vigorously."

Shapur answered again with eagerness. "Whatever the king needs, I'm most happy to provide, in whatever way I can. As I'm sure you know, he's doing us such a great favor by educating our son with the prince, and allowing him to live in the palace alongside the future king, as his friend and companion. We'll do whatever you ask, and with gladness in our hearts."

Falma, of course, knew nothing at all regarding their son and the prince, but was glad to learn of it. The connection now spoken of could be important. He smiled and said merely, "I thank you and the kingdom thanks you. But I need to ask one more thing of you both."

"Anything at all, sir."

"You must not mention this meeting or these secret activities to anyone outside this room, including your son, who should be kept at a safe distance from these events, for his own protection. Nothing should be said even to the king. His Majesty has instructed the treasurer of the kingdom that this secret project is never to be mentioned in his royal presence. There may be listening ears anywhere, and this operation must be kept from them, so that it can succeed, however long it takes."

Shapur responded, "Absolutely. My wife and I will say nothing to anyone about this endeavor. We're pleased to allow it to develop under the humble roof of our shop."

Rising to leave, Ari smiled and said, "Thank you very much. You're most gracious. Our meeting today will be as if it never happened, aside from the kind service you'll be providing by allowing our men to come into your shop. They'll arrive tomorrow and ask for you, saying that a mutual friend has sent them."

"That's fine. I'll expect them. And, again, it's my honor. I look forward to seeing my new associates."

Shapur walked Ari out of the house and bid him farewell, not knowing that he had just been conscripted into one of the biggest criminal enterprises in the history of the kingdom. Falma's network of crooks would be able to take care of some of their most sensitive and lucrative operations far from any locations where illegal activity had ever been suspected, and even under the cover of palace favor that would certainly extend over the Adi family and their business. Plus, no one would know. They would be able to do new things in such a context and make up for the income that the palace revolution had taken away from them. The kingpin of crime smiled, and actually chuckled as he walked away, congratulating himself on such a brilliant plan.

It had been a bright sunny morning, with a nice breeze blowing through the palace windows. The boys had been told that their new school lessons would begin mid-morning, at 10, but that they should be in their palace classroom by 9:30 for introductions and orientation. As usual, they woke up not long after dawn, ate together in the royal family's small private breakfast room, and then went out to practice their soccer skills. At about 8:30, it occurred to Walid that he should reverse his watchcase and check the time. Seeing they had only an hour before the start of their new school experience, both of them ran upstairs from the gardens, cleaned up quickly, and were the first arrivals in their new palace classroom at 9:20.

Two minutes later, the next person to enter the room brought the equivalent of an electric shock to Walid's entire body. The man initially had a very serious expression on his face. But then he stopped just inside the door and smiled broadly. "Hello, boys. I'll be your teacher and main tutor here in the palace this year." He stepped to a nearby blackboard, picked up chalk, and wrote his name, while saying, "I'm Khalid El-Bay." He pronounced his last name as if it were spelled 'B-u-y' instead of 'B-a-y' and explained, "The prime vowel in my name sounds much like the first one in the word 'father.' But my preference is to be very informal here, so please just call me Khalid."

"Hi, Khalid. It's nice to meet you," Walid said, as he felt a bit dizzy.

"Yeah. Hi." Mafulla chimed in, completely unaware of his friend's inner reaction.

Looking first at Walid very carefully and then at Mafulla, he said, "You both seem familiar to me. Have we met before?"

Walid could hardly think. He said, "Yes, sir. In the big marketplace recently. A young lady who may be your daughter was holding a beautiful basket, and some boys ran by her, knocking it to the ground. I came over and picked it up for her. I'm Walid Shabeezar."

"Oh. You're Prince Walid. Yes, yes. I do remember that day vividly. What a remarkable first meeting! You were so kind with your assistance to our daughter, Kissa."

"Kissa?"

"Yes. Her name means 'sister of twins,' but her two older brothers were not with us that day. I had no idea, of course, that you were the prince, or at least, soon to be such. My wife Hoda spoke highly of you several times later that day. She was especially impressed by your gracious and courtly manners."

"That was nice of her, and it's very good of you to tell me." Walid blushed with a surge of heat across his face.

"Not many young men would show that sort of helpfulness to a stranger in a public place."

Mafulla spoke up. "You may have seen me in the marketplace before, as well. My father runs a big pottery and furnishings store there and I'm often in the market, either helping out, or sometimes just hanging around. I'm Mafulla Adi, official best friend of the prince."

"It's nice to meet you as well, Mafulla. I've heard of you."

"Really?"

"Yes. And a few others whose parents now work in the palace, serving in top administrative positions, should be joining us shortly." Khalid looked out the door and said, "Oh, and here they come, now."

Three boys about Walid's age came walking down the hall and then up to the door, followed at a short distance by two more. Walid smiled broadly as he saw Hamid's son Malik, and Masoon's boy Haji, along with Bashir's son, Bafur. "Hey, guys! This is a nice surprise!"

They all responded with big smiles as well. "Hey, Walid." "Hey, man."

He had known them from their old village, and didn't realize that they had already relocated to town this soon after the revolution. They must have just arrived in the city. He had never been in a class with them before, though, because he had been completely home schooled until now. And, even though they had lived on the other side of the village, or a bit outside it, on that far side, he knew them fairly well. But the other students who came in after those three were completely new faces he hadn't seen before. There were two of them, one named Jabari and the other, Set. Jabari was the smallest of them all, and Set was a strong looking boy.

Khalid asked them to take seats and then he introduced himself to the rest of them. He also explained that there is another small palace class that meets occasionally for younger children, who are being mostly homeschooled, and that it's taught by a different instructor. Then he went on to add that, in the past, there had been a class later in the afternoon for a few older scholars, but that there happened to be no young people of that age involved in palace life right now. So this class would be the only one of boys held throughout the week.

"So, where are all the girls?" Mafulla could not help but ask, and the other boys grinned at his boldness.

"They're meeting elsewhere in the palace, to be taught by my wife."

Walid felt a tingle again throughout his body. He wondered whether, at that very moment, Khalid's daughter was already in the palace, in some other room, awaiting her first hour of class. His heart rate increased a bit at the thought.

"How many girls are there?" Jabari asked, right away.

"I'm not exactly sure, but I think they'll have about the same number that we do."

He smiled and then went on to say to the boys, "We'll be working together first from 10 AM each day until 12. Then we'll take a short lunch break, and get back together from 12:30 until 2:30. Some days, we'll have an additional hour, always announced in advance. But, regardless, it's a relatively short period of time each day, so we have to concentrate and work hard in the few hours we have. There's a lot we'll need to accomplish in our time together."

Khalid moved some books around on his desk and said, "We'll be studying language, science, mathematics, literature, art, and some philosophy together in our sessions. But, before we get started, let me ask you to take a sheet of paper from the stack I'll pass around now, and a pen, from a bundle also coming around, and write for me on one side of the page a short account of who you are, what your favorite subject in school is, and any hobbies you might have. Then I'll ask you to take turns reading aloud your brief compositions, and that will help serve to introduce each of you to your fellow students."

Walid put his favorite subjects as literature and philosophy. Mafulla named science and history. Malik liked art and science, and Haji's favorite subjects were history and politics. The other boys' essays were all interesting. Bafur said he liked to study food, and was learning to cook. His dad Bashir famously loved to eat, and had become the Secretary of Agriculture and Food Supplies, with extra oversight duties for all the kingdom's restaurants and food shops. Maybe Bafur would become a chef and open his own place.

The boy, Set, like Walid, said he loved philosophy, and quoted Socrates, saying, "The unexamined life is not worth living." Walid thought to himself that he would have to get to know this guy. Jabari wrote that he liked science chiefly because of astronomy. But he also liked music and poetry. Most of the boys said they loved soccer, or as they most often called it, football. They would be able to have some good games together.

Some of the boys played musical instruments. In addition to the three who were from near Walid's village, the other two had grown up in the capital city, like Mafulla. Walid liked what he saw and heard as the others read their short essays. But he liked most of all knowing that the girl from the marketplace was likely somewhere nearby, under the same roof, doing the same thing now that he was doing. Maybe he could soon see her again. It felt like destiny. It was very exciting to think about, but also a little scary at the same time.

In what seemed like a flash, it was noon, and lunch was ready for the boys, as wonderful aromas beckoned from a nearby room. They all dashed into the small class dining room, ate with relish and speed, and had almost twenty minutes remaining to go outside to kick a ball around and get to know each other better. At 12:28, Khalid, who had been watching the informal play that was quite lively and engaged for a first day of school, stood up, clapped his hands, and told the boys it was time to reconvene for their lessons inside. As they quieted down a bit and began to walk toward the door, they could just manage to hear the laughter of girls nearby, beyond a high wall. Walid's heart jumped a little, and he smiled.

The afternoon went by as fast as the morning had. Khalid was an engaging teacher, a great storyteller, and more fun than he had looked to be at first. He gave a brief introduction to each area they would study together, posed some of the central problems they would examine in each of these areas, and finally sent the boys off with some new books and a keen curiosity about what would happen on the next morning. He even assigned some preliminary reading for the coming day. Both Walid and Mafulla were now really looking forward to their lessons.

On their way back to the royal family residence area, Mafulla asked Walid whether he thought it might be possible for him, or the two of them together, to visit his father's shop in the marketplace that afternoon. "I miss the place," Mafulla said. "I'd often hang out there after school. And, even though I know I can't get there as much now, it would still be nice to visit for just an hour today and tell dad about the class and our new teacher."

Walid eagerly agreed to ask about it. He found a butler who conveyed the question to the king, and in no time at all they had their answer. They were both given permission and an escort of three trusted soldiers, serving as palace guards, to take them the short distance to the market. The butler handed Walid a note from the king that, unfolded, said, "Don't help chase any lost animals." He had to smile at that. And he showed his friend the note.

Reading it, Mafulla looked surprised and said, "Did you get caught that way, too? You didn't tell me that part of the story!"

"Yeah, but what do you mean by 'too'? Is that how they got you?"

"Yep." They both laughed, as Mafulla said, "We're such idiots."

Walid replied, "But we're idiots with good hearts."

"True."

The prince looked around and lowered his voice. He said, "Look, I know the marketplace is normally safe, and we have armed escorts today, but no one can predict what might happen in these early days of the new government, so I sort of think we should also take our guns under our belts and put on the green ribbon."

"Really?"

"Yeah."

"Ok. That's smart, I guess. It pays to be safe. But are you sure it's all right?" Mafulla said.

Walid replied, "Definitely. The king wants us to be as safe as possible."

They both went to their rooms, found their small guns, tucked them into their belts, quickly tied the thin green ribbon on, in case it was still a sign being used by friends of the king, and met at the top of the stairs. From there, they walked down together to find their guards, who were dressed in fairly rumpled civilian clothing, so as not to attract any unwanted attention. The guards all noticed the green ribbons, but thought it was likely something the boys had just continued to wear as a memento since the day of the revolution, or else that they had them on simply to signal to any friends of the king that they were with guards, who were armed in service to him. It actually didn't occur to any of these three men that the boys themselves might now be carrying weapons. In the context, it just didn't cross their minds.

A long wooden donkey cart had been brought up so that they could sit in it and make the journey more quickly than the thirty or forty minutes it could take to walk to the market. It would also be a form of transportation that would help them blend in with the crowds on the street and not stand out as having come from the palace. The king had a few automobiles available to him, but any of them would create too much attention at this point. They were kept in a large garage behind the palace and had not yet been used since the revolution.

Ali was well aware that any obvious friends or close associates of the new monarchy would be viewed by some in town as enemies, at least until he had a chance to demonstrate the benevolent nature of his reign. And, even then, there was a criminal element in the capital that had flourished under the former, corrupt regime and they would always resent members of the new government and their associates. Operating under the philosophy that the best way to deal with trouble is to avoid it, all precautions would be taken whenever the boys left the palace grounds in these early days.

Less than twenty minutes of easy travel, bumping along the crowded streets, brought them to the edge of the market that was closest to the Adi family shop—"Adi Pottery and Home Furnishings." That's what the sign would say if they had a sign. But the shop was so well known that no sign was needed. Mr. Adi could be seen just inside with a customer. Mafulla jumped from the cart and walked quickly toward the store as their three escorts visually scanned the street, one with his hand on Walid's shoulder until he could be sure that the area was clear of any threat or danger.

"Dad!" Mafulla caught sight of his father stepping out the door of the shop and waved.

Shapur turned with a look of great surprise. "Mafulla! My son! What are you doing here?" Mafulla walked toward him and then quickened his pace to grab and hug his father, while Walid at first stayed where he was, near the cart, to give them a private moment of greeting. He also spoke a few words to the head guard.

Mafulla responded to his father with a big smile. "I missed seeing you and got special permission to make a short visit this afternoon with Walid. We're going to just hang out for a while."

"Good! This is very good!" As soon as he said these words, smiling broadly, Mr. Adi remembered that he had those new men in the back doing their secret work, undercover. He grew inwardly nervous that his older son would ask too many questions, so he took the initiative to block any inquiries. He quickly said, "There are some new men in the back, taking care of extra work for me, so that I have more time with customers and staff, while they're also starting their own small business."

"Really?"

"Yes. It's a favor I'm doing for a man in town who may become a good customer. I'm letting them use that space back at the rear door. In turn, they provide extra eyes and ears, and hands when I need them."

"That's new."

"Yes. And quite useful. Having them here will allow me more time to visit with you today! It couldn't have worked out better! It's so good to see you!"

"Thanks, Dad! I didn't know at all about this new development." Mafulla glanced over into the store and asked, "Are they good men? Do they fit in well around the shop?"

Shapur quickly said, "They seem to do their jobs well. And this is just a temporary favor. But meanwhile, I have more time for the family."

"This is very nice, Father. You work so hard."

"Wait, what is this beautiful watch that you have on your wrist?"

"It's a gift from Walid's uncle. He gave one to each of us to help us manage our time in the palace and wherever we go. It's called a Reverso. The case flips around to protect the crystal whenever we're playing a sport." Mafulla did a quick little demonstration, back and forth. "You like it?"

"Yes! Indeed! But it's such an extravagant gift! Let me see it more closely." As Mafulla held his wrist close, his father said in a low voice, "Oh. Oh, my. It's so elegant."

"Yeah, it's great. And comfortable on my wrist. I hardly even feel it, and it's so convenient to have."

"I'm very glad for you, my son. Your benefactor is quite generous."

Just then, Walid joined them and exchanged friendly greetings with Mafulla's dad. He also quietly told him about their military escort, pointing out that two of the guards were standing at a short distance, talking and appearing to browse at the next store over while keeping a wary eye on the boys. One casually wandered into the Adi shop to look around, nodding to the boys and Shapur as he passed them.

After Mafulla had a chance to say a quick hello to an old friend working in the shop, and Walid looked around the store for a minute, Mr. Adi suggested they go down the street for a few minutes to have tea and biscuits together.

Mafulla said, "You can leave the shop in the middle of the day like that?"

"Yes, it's wonderful! I have a piece of new-found freedom!" Mr. Adi put on a good front with a happy face, but inwardly his stomach was churning with worry that if they stayed around the shop, the boys might pry too much into the activities of the new men. It was the first time he had ever felt anything like this. Otherwise, it had always been just wonderful to have Mafulla around.

Secrets have a way of tying knots in the fabric of ordinary life, interrupting any flow of calm enjoyment, and creating unpleasant emotions that inevitably distract us from our normal engagement with the people closest to us. Mafulla's dad was trying to do the right thing, in allowing this undercover activity to take place in his shop, but he was already feeling uneasy about it. Some of the new men didn't actually seem to be the type to work in government, or to represent the king's values. They were rough looking and were a bit crude and brusque in demeanor. And even though they customarily spoke in low voices, Shapur had heard enough to know that their language wasn't always suitable for a family owned retail establishment. He had thought of gently asking them to please be more careful with their words, but instead had mostly kept his distance, not wanting to interfere in any way or be a problem for the greater cause.

Mr. Adi did not know that, across the street, and two small shops down, some new merchants who just moved in were really the king's men and were watching over his shop to make sure he was safe. They had bought their store and set up their sandals and leather goods business a few days after the revolution, and they seemed like two very nice brothers. They had gone around and introduced themselves right away to all the neighboring shopkeepers as Mumar and Badar Sakat. Mr. Adi was not aware that they were also trained military men and keen observers, well armed, and prepared to defend him, his family, and his shop from any threat that might materialize.

All Shapur knew was that these new neighbors were friendly and made some extremely nice sandals. They had come in and set up their business just days before the new men arrived in the Adi shop, and so they didn't know how unusual it was for Mr. Adi to take on several new associates at once, and especially people who did not seem to be old friends or family members. Among the few old employees in the store, there was occasional hugging, kissing of cheeks, playful banter, and good fun. These new men kept to themselves, were fairly quiet, and seemed not to interact with the normal customers who came through the front door. They were a bit odd, but not so much as to alert Mumar or Badar to potential trouble in these early days. And yet, it was a situation they had both noticed. For the first time in the history of the shop, there were nearly as many people coming and going through the back door as through the front. And the brothers had noted that this level of back alley activity was not to be seen at any other store on their busy road.

As Mafulla, his dad, and Walid walked down to the little place where they could have tea and biscuits and talk uninterruptedly, they first approached the Sakat Sandal Shop where Badar was outside sweeping the area in front of the door. Mr. Adi said a cheerful hello, and introduced his son and Walid to the man, who was very happy to meet them. He called Mumar out of the shop and introductions were completed. As they walked off, Mafulla caught Walid's eye, tugged at the green ribbon on his belt, cocked his head back toward the men they had just met, and held up two fingers, wiggling them so they would be noticed. Walid responded with a knowing nod. "Interesting," he thought. "I wonder what's going on."

Turning to his father, Mafulla said in a low voice, "Dad, I think you have some new protection, courtesy of the king."

"What? Oh, yes, protection. Certainly. The men who came with you today will also surely watch over me as well while we're together. I noticed them slowly following us while we were at the sandal shop."

"No. I mean, yes, that's true, but it seems like there's also some more permanent protection for you now, as well."

"What do you mean, my son?"

"Do you see the small green ribbon I have on my belt and that Walid has on his?" Mafulla put his finger on the thin piece of bright fabric.

"Yes. I see it."

"The men escorting us today have that on their belts as well."

"They do?"

"Yes, but so do the Sakat brothers at the sandal shop."

"What does this green ribbon mean?"

"It's a very secret sign, known only to the most trusted men around the king, so it must stay a secret, but I can tell you as my father that it means 'Armed in service of the King.' The men at the sandal shop are providing armed protection, probably looking out for you and mother and keeping our store safe."

"This is such a surprise! They moved in two days after the revolution."

"That was after the king had decided he would invite me to stay at the palace and be educated with Walid. He must have believed that this might make you and the family to some extent vulnerable to enemies of his rule, and so he sent these men to watch over you all."

"That's extraordinary. I had no idea. Are we in real danger?"

"No, I don't think so, especially with the two of them being here. I believe the king just likes to be cautious."

Shapur thought to himself, "They could be there to oversee and guard the operation underway in my back room. But, then, the nice man from the palace didn't approach me about allowing this activity until a week after these men moved into their shop. Hmm. Well, the protection must indeed be for me, as Mafulla suggests."

Then a realization suddenly hit him and he said, "But, my son, you are wearing a green ribbon."

"Yes."

"Are you also … armed?"

"Yes, sir." Mafulla spoke in a low voice.

Mr. Adi stopped in his tracks and raised his voice, but only a bit, saying in a tone of great concern, "But you're twelve years old! This is dangerous. What sort of weapon do you have? Who gave it to you?"

"Don't worry, Mr. Adi." Walid stepped up and joined the conversation. "I was given a small revolver some time ago for personal protection, by the man providing the closest security for my uncle. Then, after Mafulla and I had been kidnapped, and when we were being rescued, another trusted aid to the king, the man who got us out of the locked room where we were held captive, he gave one to Mafulla as well, but with the first two chambers empty for the sake of extra safety."

"But is this safe?"

"Yes, sir. We're to use these items only in dire circumstances and grave danger, if that should ever happen to us again. And we've both been given a refresher course in gun safety, to be doubly cautious."

Shapur looked at Mafulla and said, "You're absolutely sure that you can be careful with this dangerous thing?"

"Yes, Dad, I am. I'm very cautious with it."

Shapur let out a deep breath and said, "Good. Good, I suppose. I have to admit that I'm surprised, and even shocked by this, but in light of recent extreme events, I think I understand. There's so much new to take in. We must sit down and have our tea and biscuits and talk more. There's so much going on."

They were at that point only a few feet from the door of

the teashop and, following Mr. Adi, they entered, placed their order, and sat at a table near the window. He turned to his son again, with a look of great concern.

"So, you truly promise on your honor that you're being extremely careful with this thing you have in your possession?"

"I handle it with the utmost care, Father, and I almost never carry it these days. Only this afternoon, leaving the palace to come to the marketplace, where we were both grabbed by the kidnappers not so long ago, we decided it might be prudent to be as prepared and safe as possible."

"I suppose that's sensible. I see what you're saying. But your mother will worry so much."

"Do we have to tell her?"

"Secrets are difficult, my son, and especially with people you love. It's best to be honest. That treats your loved ones with respect."

As he said these words, Shapur felt a strong inner conviction that it was wrong to keep the real activity in his shop secret from his son. He needed to live up to the lofty and true words he was speaking about the importance of honesty. So, he looked around the shop where they sat, and then in a low voice he said, "There's something I must share with you, and with Walid, since he's your best friend now. I was asked to keep it secret, but in light of what I just now rightly said to you about secrets, I think I should tell you."

"What is it, father?" It was Mafulla's turn to look worried.

"I will feel absolutely terrible if telling you this endangers you in any possible way, but I can't imagine how. So, let me begin."

"Please do."

"A man came to the house and told your mother and me

that he had been sent by the treasurer of the kingdom, on orders from the king himself, to visit us and ask me for a favor."

"What sort of favor? I haven't heard anything about this." Walid spoke up immediately with a twinge of concern.

"The man said it was top secret and told us the king had asked that it never be mentioned in public or even in his royal presence. He said that top officials suspect some disloyalty in the palace, and worry about treasonous activity, and need to investigate their suspicions to identify anyone who may be serving the king under false pretenses. But, they have to raise the money to do this investigation quietly and off the official books, to keep the information from prying eyes on the part of anyone under suspicion."

"Really?"

"Yes. And so the man asked me if I would be willing to receive a few men to work in the back of my shop on this operation, with the cover story that they are starting their own business and, for the free use of my space, they will in turn help me with odd jobs. In a sense, the cover story is true. These men are starting up a business to fund an investigation of these problems in the palace, and they're indeed now and then being helpful to me, but I'm deeply uneasy about them."

"Why? What are they doing?" Mafulla was already troubled about what he was hearing.

Just then, the tea and biscuits were served, with jam on the side. When the man who brought their treats had left, Mr. Adi looked a bit worried himself and answered his son. "They just seem more than a little shady. They don't appear to be the sort of men to work for King Ali. They're quite profane and crude in their behavior. And they're very secretive in everything they do. I just have a bad feeling about it all. But I want to do my duty for the king, in case this is all legitimate and necessary business for the kingdom, as the man who visited assured us. I've simply come to have my doubts."

"Who is the man that visited you and requested this favor?" Walid asked. He needed to know because he was already planning to speak with his uncle about it all.

"He gave only his first name—Ari. He said he works for the treasurer, but that it's all very sensitive and secret and he was not free to reveal anything else concerning his identity, for my protection and his."

"I'll look into this for you, very carefully." Walid assured him. "This doesn't sound right to me. I don't think my uncle would turn your place of business into a lair of intrigue and secret investigations."

"But he said the king doesn't want this spoken of in his presence."

"I'm sure that doesn't apply to me. We speak freely on everything, and in absolute privacy. It's different between the two of us."

"Ok. Good. I understand. I deeply appreciate your help."

Walid said, "I think that the first thing we should do is to make some indirect inquiries at the sandal shop. In case what's going on at your store is not what it was said to be, those men need to know that something suspicious may be happening. We don't have to tell them what you've told me—not yet, at least. They just need to be alert to any problem that might be developing. If the men in your back room are not who they were represented as being, and if they're not doing what they were said to be doing, then we need to find out who they really are and what they're in fact up to, and we need to find out soon."

At that moment, one of the three palace guards who were

along on this little excursion, and who until now had been keeping their distance, suddenly stepped into the shop. He came close and looked at Walid and bent down close and said, "I'm sorry. There's been an incident. We need to get you and your friends to safety right away."

Shapur spoke first, asking, "What did you say?"

"The three of you, come with me."

10

PREPARATION PAYS OFF

AT EVERY MOMENT, WE SHOULD BE PREPARED FOR almost anything. The world is in many ways a kaleidoscope of change, and at any time, something completely unexpected can happen. Our challenge is to be strong, keep our bearings, and act with reason. But acting with reason doesn't always mean proceeding slowly or even acting in a way that seems reasonable to others.

When the guard suddenly came into the teashop, addressing the prince, and telling him that he, Mafulla, and Mr. Adi must leave for a safe place right away, they immediately stood up from their table. "What's happened?" Walid wanted to understand what was going on.

"I'll explain. You must first come with me to the wagon, quickly, all three of you. We have little time."

They moved toward the door, stepped outside, and were joined by the other two guards along with, surprisingly, the Sakat brothers, who motioned them down the street, away from the direction of the Adi store and the sandal shop, and around a corner onto a side road.

Badar Sakat said, "In less than a minute, the cart should meet us. When it arrives, all of you get in and go to the palace right away."

As they walked briskly down the road, Walid said, "Please, tell us what's going on. You have a green ribbon."

Badar held up his hand and spoke, as they continued to walk. "I'll explain. My brother and I are on an assignment from King Ali to watch over and guard the Adi shop, just as a precaution." He looked over at Shapur and said, "I'm sorry I didn't tell you this, but we were trying to stay as far under-cover as we could. You're in no specific danger, but the king is cautious and wanted to provide you with protection. We're both military." Mr. Adi nodded his head in response.

Badar then looked back at Walid and said, "Just now, a man came from the Adi shop with a broken sandal strap, and he crossed the street to our store, saying he wanted to get a repair immediately. The second he entered the door, I recognized him as a wanted criminal of the worst sort and excused myself, tell-ing him I had to get my brother Mumar, who does the repairs. I went into the back and told Mumar who he is and, when he was taking off his sandal, we sought to restrain him in order to handcuff him. There was a violent scuffle. He wounded me with a knife that he suddenly produced, but I'm going to be fine. He also cut Mumar lightly. The man himself, however, unfortunately died in the struggle."

Walid interrupted. "He died?"

"Yes. It was unintentional, but there was no alternative way to stop him than with great force. Thankfully, there were no other customers in the shop or close by outside."

"Oh, my." Mr. Adi spoke up. "Who was the man? What did he look like?"

Badar replied, "He's a big man, very muscular, tall, with a

bushy mustache, no beard, and a very large long scar on his left arm."

"Goodness! I know him. He's one of the new fellows who've been working in the back of my store."

"Did you hire him?" Badar was eager to put together some of the puzzle.

"No, no. As a favor to another man, I recently allowed some of his associates to use the back of my store for a short time while they were starting up an enterprise of their own, whose many details were mostly unknown to me. In return I was told that they would provide extra help for me. I didn't interview or hire any of the men myself. I don't even know the name of the man you mention, but he's one of them. And I always felt uneasy when he was in the shop."

"Was the man who asked for this favor a criminal of any sort?"

"Oh, heaven's no! I mean: I hope not! He represented himself to me as a good and honest man, and as being involved in a legitimate enterprise, but again, all the details he didn't tell me."

"May I ask: Why would you agree to such a big favor, especially for a man you didn't know well?"

Shapur glanced at Mafulla and, looking back at Badar, took a deep breath and spoke softly. "He said it was for a secret investigation the king is doing. I wanted to help the king."

"What was the name of this man?"

"I don't know his family name, but he said that I could call him Ari."

"Interesting. There's a major crime figure with that name."

"Oh, no."

"He's a small man, intense features. He can be quite charming, people say."

"Oh, no. No, no, no. That sounds like the man."

"Ok. You felt uneasy around the scar man for good reason." Badar said to Mr. Adi, and continued. "We don't know for certain whether the Ari you granted the favor to is the same man as the criminal I have in mind, but it sounds like it, and we don't know whether there are more felons among the new men in your store, from which the scar man came. If there are, we also don't know what they will do when they discover that their associate has simply disappeared on his short errand. We had to hide the body temporarily. We can't compromise our cover. And we can't allow you to go back to your store in these uncertain circumstances. It's safer for you all to go to the palace until we get this sorted out."

"Yes, I understand. But—Oh! It just occurred to me: My wife has been out shopping, and she was planning to come to the store this afternoon, very shortly, with our children, Sammi and Sasha! My brother Reela was going to drop them all off and then go on to some business he had nearby." Mr. Adi was clearly alarmed. "They should be there soon at the shop, if they haven't already arrived!"

As soon as he heard those words, Mafulla just broke from the group without a word and went running down the street, back toward the store, as fast as he could go. And he was very fast. Everyone just stopped, stunned at his reaction.

"Wait!" Badar shouted at him.

"My son! Where are you going?" Mafulla's father cried out, as he stood frozen in place with his hands outstretched.

In the next instant, Walid shouted, "Maffie! What are you doing?" And with no answer in response, he hesitated for a second then also started running in pursuit of his friend.

"No, no, no!" The tall guard who had come into the tea-shop yelled out toward them and then hastily said to one of the two other guards, "Stay here and wait for the cart. Bring it and the driver to the sandal shop. Wait there for my signal. The rest of you come with me." He turned and jogged quickly and with vigilance in the direction of the boys, accompanied by a fellow palace guard, along with Mumar, Badar, and a very worried Shapur Adi.

Mafulla ran through the front entrance of the Adi store and nearly crashed into the elderly man who had helped customers there as long as he could remember. "Oh! Mr. Kaza! Is my mother here?"

"Why, yes, Mafulla, she arrived a couple of minutes ago, saying she was early. Her brother just left. I told her that you were here and that you and your father and your friend Walid had gone down the street for tea and should be returning soon."

"Where is she?"

"She took the children into the back to speak with the new men."

Mafulla felt his heart leap into his throat and a jolt of dizziness shot through his brain right before a nearly supernatural clarity took over his consciousness. He knew he had to protect this old family friend and associate, and so he said, "Mr. Kaza, would you mind going down the street to the office supply store and getting us a new record book for inventory, right now? Dad needs it. I'll be here for you."

Kaza looked a bit surprised but said, "Certainly. I'll go this second."

"Thank you." Mafulla nodded at the man, and watched him walk toward the door. Then he experienced the sensation of time slowing down all around him as he took a deep breath and walked directly through the store toward the door that opened into the back area. If he could just walk back there like nothing was wrong, put a big smile on his face, and greet his family with enthusiasm, he could likely get his mother and brother and sister out of there before anything might happen. These men could be seriously dangerous, and who knows what they might do when they realized their friend had disappeared, or, worse yet, if they found his body?

That second, he felt a hand close around his right arm. A whispering voice said, "What are you doing?" Walid gasped for air.

Mafulla whispered back with authority. "Stay out front. I'll pretend everything is fine and get my family out of here. Wait for us." Walid let him go and watched him approach the back of the store, and then, with a feeling of great uncertainty, returned outside to wait.

The moment Mafulla walked through the inner door to the back of the shop, he took in the entire scene. His mother was talking to a small man on the left side of the room. Two larger men were working in the back of the area. One was sitting at a desk near the rear outside door, over close to a corner of the rather large space, and the other was moving several boxes from the door to the other side of the desk, and then stacking them up.

"Mother! Sammi! Sasha! Hello! Hello! Hello! I'm so surprised to see you here!" Mafulla looked gleefully happy and his tone was exaggeratedly joyful.

"Brother, brother, brother!" Sammie and Sasha whirled around and hugged Mafulla's legs and stomach, jumping up and down.

His mother turned around with a big smile. "Mafulla, my dear, dear boy! Kaza told me that you're visiting today! What a great and completely unexpected treat it is to see you! When did you get here?" Shamilar then also grabbed her son and squeezed him tight.

"About an hour ago! Walid and I decided to take a break from our new schoolwork and come to the store just to hang out for a couple of hours."

"Where's your father?"

"He's down the street with Walid. I'd like to show you something down there, just for a minute. You'll love it. But you have to come right now. Please, follow me and bring Sammi and Sasha."

"Really?"

"Yes! We need to go quickly. You just have to see this one thing. You won't believe it." Mafulla had adopted the jolliest tone he could manage under the circumstances, and still displayed a big smile, despite his frantic inner panic.

"I was just talking to this nice man who is starting his own business, and your father's letting him use some space back here."

Mafulla nodded and turned to the man and said, "Good, good! Dad told me! It's wonderful to have you here in the shop!"

Out of the corner of his eye, he could see another man come in through the back door, and this new arrival started whispering into the ear of the fellow who had been moving boxes, and who was now standing still with a gravely serious look on his face.

The small man said, "It's so kind of your father to allow us to start up our new enterprise here in this spacious area."

"Yes, thank you. He loves to be of help to others. Look, I'm so sorry to interrupt your conversation," Mafulla said to both his mother and the man, "But I've not seen mother and the kids for a while, and would love to take them out for just a few minutes, to visit and show them something I have for them."

The man smiled and nodded his approval. But the two

other men approached suddenly, walking up close to all of them, and the one who had just come in said, "I'm afraid no one's leaving right now."

"What?" The small man looked and sounded shocked. "What are you saying? This is the gracious family who owns the shop, and they come and go as they please."

"Not right now." He glared at Mafulla as he spoke. One hand was behind his back as he continued. "Abdul left a while ago to have his sandal repaired down the street. He's not returned."

"That's of no concern to these fine people!"

"Yes, it is. And I'll tell you why."

The smaller man turned to Shamilar and said, "I'm so sorry for this unacceptable interruption."

"Someone may soon be very sorry for its reason," the larger man said, and then he continued in a menacing voice. "I went out to get more of the boxes that had been delivered and I saw the sandal makers both leave their shop. And I wondered how they could do that if Abdul wasn't back. I was curious. I watched them go down the street and I followed them."

"What in the world does this have to do with the Adis?"

"I'm telling you. The sandal makers went to a teashop and spoke to some other men, and one went in and got Mr. Adi and this boy here, along with another one. The sandal men then met up with them, and they walked off together. I turned around and went quickly back to their shop and discovered it was locked. So I broke the lock to look for Abdul. And there was no one. But I noticed the floor had just been washed. It was still wet. I found the trash out back, and many wet cloths were in it. Some of them seemed to have large stains on them that could very well be blood. There was no sign of Abdul anywhere or, at least, no … other sign."

Mafulla's right hand had slowly moved toward his belt. His mother and the two small children were listening to all this with increasing looks of worry on their faces. Shamilar said, "Oh, my. "

The man stared right into Mafulla's eyes as he said, "Something's going on. And not one of you leaves here until I learn what's happened to Abdul."

The small man looked frantic. "These good people have nothing to do with Abdul, nothing at all. They're helping us. We have a legitimate business here. There's no cause for alarm or any unpleasantness. Abdul could have gone off to do anything. You don't know."

He quickly looked over toward Mrs. Adi. "Please excuse this coarse and unnecessary talk. There's no reason to be concerned."

"Abdul's not your brother, is he?" The larger man raised his voice and gave his smaller associate a fierce look. "I want to know what's happened to him, and I want to know now!" He then revealed a long, menacing knife that he had been holding behind his back.

Mrs. Adi gasped. Sammi and Sasha held on to their mother for protection. The little one said, "Mama!"

Mafulla quickly pulled out his gun and lifted it toward the larger man, at this point not even noticing another individual, who had been working at the desk and was now standing a bit to his left, closer to his mother and the small children. A whooshing sound was the only thing that heralded the lashing of a leather whip that knocked the gun out of Mafulla's hand. And in a flash, the small man had bent down to grab it up off the floor.

"What's this? You have a gun? What are you doing with

a gun?" The small man hissed out the questions and now looked even angrier than his large colleague. His face had instantly transformed into a hideous expression. "Stand still, and don't move."

He first pointed the gun at Mafulla and then, backing up, lifted it to Shamilar's head. The children both screamed and ran to Mafulla, grabbing him and making it difficult for him to move or do anything in reaction. This all happened so quickly, he hadn't even had a chance to think. He didn't notice that both the man with the knife and the one with the whip were at that moment slowly approaching him. He was focused on the gun that was now pointed at his mother's head.

Then there was a booming voice. "Stop right where you are!" It was Walid shouting, and he sounded much older than his age. Mafulla twisted his head toward the inner door and saw his friend entering, with his own gun drawn and pointed at, first the small man, then the other two. He was moving it back and forth to keep all of them covered. "Put down the gun and the other weapons!" He yelled out this command like he wasn't outnumbered three to one at the moment.

"I'll put down the likes of you!" The small man practically spat out the words, turned Mafulla's gun toward Walid, and pulled the trigger.

Click.

"What?"

Click.

"Useless!" The man threw the gun to the floor where it hit a rolled up rug, and then he jerked a knife from his own belt, which he began raising toward Shamilar's neck. Walid had his revolver now aimed at the small man's head and instantly pulled his own trigger twice, as quickly as he could.

Click.

Click.

The small man lowered the knife and yelled out, "Their guns are not loaded! They have no bullets!"

The other two men moved at that instant to grab Mafulla and Walid, but right after the second click and the man's shout, just a split second before the prince could squeeze his trigger a third time, there was a loud crashing sound. Glass shattered in a nearby window as two doors elsewhere in the room were being opened. All eyes turned toward the window, where they could now see a rifle barrel appear, and at that moment, with everyone distracted, six armed men burst into the room at once. Three came through the inner door behind Walid, and three through the back door with guns out, as several of them shouted at about the same time, "Freeze or Die!"

It all happened with lightning speed. The words "Drop your weapons!" from several voices now boomed through the suddenly crowded space. The criminals were instantly surrounded by guns held at their faces, and could not even try to react.

In a flash, two of the men who rushed in had revolvers to the head of the small, knife-wielding man.

"Now! On your knees! All of you!" The three palace guards, the Sakat brothers, and the donkey cart driver—another member of the palace guard, as it turned out—were all over the men, skillfully and roughly subduing them, shoving them to the floor, tying them up, and rendering them immobile. As this was going on, Mr. Adi ran over to his wife, putting away the pistol he had been given, pushing it down into his belt, and then hugging her, as he reached out for the children.

Sasha was crying loudly, saying, "Daddy, Daddy, Daddy!"

Sammi was putting on a brave face, but tears were also rolling down his cheeks.

Shapur exclaimed, "My dears! My dears! I'm so glad you're all safe! I was so frightened for you!"

"My husband! You've saved us!" Shamilar exclaimed, as the two little children ran to their father and grabbed his legs.

"I'm sorry you had to go through this, but you're Ok now!" He covered them with kisses, including Mafulla, who embraced his father tightly.

"Mafulla! I can't believe you ran back here by yourself!" Shapur said.

"I couldn't let mother and the kids be in danger! I had to act quickly!"

"But weren't you afraid?"

"Yes, of course, but I did what I thought I had to do. I didn't really even think about it. I just acted."

Mafulla then turned to his friend. "Walid! What happened to your gun?"

The prince looked a little sheepish. He said, "I decided that your two empty chambers were a good idea for extra safety, so I took out two of my bullets a few days ago, as well. I knew I'd have to pull the trigger three times to shoot, and I was just about to do it when the men all burst in."

"Wow," Mafulla responded, and he let out a deep breath.

"Yeah. I'm so glad I didn't have to shoot that evil little guy. He was standing too close to your mom, and I'm not sure that I'm that good a marksman."

"Boy, oh, boy!" Mafulla still could hardly believe what had just happened.

The head guard turned his attention to the Adi family and Walid and said, "I'm just happy that you boys had some form of protection with you. I'm sure that, as a result, you were able to delay these men a few crucial seconds. And that's all it took."

Walid replied, "I'm even more glad we had all of you backing us up, as the real protection here."

The guard smiled. "Your uncle always says, 'It pays to be prepared,' and that's been proved true again today. We had no idea that you'd be facing some of the worst criminals in the kingdom on a simple trip to the market. But we're able to handle the situation." The guard then turned to Mafulla's father.

"Mr. Adi, how did these men get into your store?"

Shapur repeated the story that he had already told Mafulla, Walid, and Badar, but this time with more detail, adding, "It was obviously all just a lie. I was deceived."

The guard thought for a moment. "We'll discover what these men were really up to here. But my guess is that they were using your store as a safe place to conduct illegal enterprises. This Ari of whom you speak is most likely Ari Falma, the top crime boss in the kingdom, a corrupt and dangerous man. This was likely his scheme." He paused and looked at the men bound on the floor and said again to Shapur, "With your permission, we'll replace these men we're arresting with a couple of our own, who can sit for a few days in the back of your store, in case any more of their fellow criminals show up. And they'll also help you out when needed. The Sakat brothers, of course, will continue their work as well, with increased vigilance now, and they'll always be available as your protective backup."

Badar Sakat chimed in. "Ari Falma may never show his face here. But he might send someone to check on things. And, if so, we'll now be ready for him. We would advise you to keep the family away from the store for a few days, until we're sure that you're all safe from any unpleasant repercussions that might result from today's actions."

Mr. Adi nodded his head. "That sounds wise, and I thank you for your ongoing concern and protection."

Walid spoke up. "Mr. and Mrs. Adi, I'm so sorry if my friendship with Mafulla has led to any of this. I'll also make sure that you're safe."

The criminals had all been bound and gagged and were lying quietly on the floor, fuming at what they considered their terribly bad luck, when Mumar walked up to them. He looked down and announced: "In case you simpletons haven't figured it out yet, you stand accused of attempted murder against the prince of the kingdom, a crime of the worst possible sort. It's not a good time to be you, but then again, that's likely a general truth in your miserably wasted adult lives."

The palace guards got them all up off the floor and hauled the bound men outside to the waiting donkey cart, where they were officially placed under arrest for the attempted murder of the prince, as well as of civilians, and for other crimes against the kingdom. The guards didn't know any of the men's names, but at this point they didn't need to. It would, however, have been good if they had learned at least the family name of the small man, whose stature, character, and general disposition were all shared by a brother with the given name of Ari.

II

THE UNEXPECTED

SOMETIMES, THE UNEXPECTED HAS LAYERS LIKE AN onion. When enough of these are peeled back, you may eventually arrive at the utterly unlikely, the completely unbelievable, or perhaps even something truly mysterious. There are many times when the exceedingly odd can hide deep beneath the ordinary, leaving only small hints until we decide to dig down and discover what's really there.

People often tell us that we should expect the unexpected, which is great advice in the most general sense but, of course, in any more specific sense is in principle impossible. And this fact itself would make it even more unexpected if you could actually pull it off. There will never cease to be surprises. And that should be no surprise.

Mafulla was supposed to be reading. Walid was indeed doing so.

"When were you born?" Mafulla asked, while staring straight at his friend.

Walid looked up from his book and blinked. "1921."

"I mean, what month and day?"

"August 13."

"Wait. Do you realize something odd about that?"

"Sure, it's an odd number."

"What?"

"The number 13 is an odd number—always has been, and always will be."

"No, no, no. I mean that there's something a lot odder."

"Like what?"

"August is the eighth month of the year, right?"

"Yeah. So?"

"So you were born in the eighth month, on the thirteenth day, in the twenty-first year of the century."

"Ok."

"That makes your birthday, 8-13-21."

"Yes?"

"Those are consecutive, sequential numbers in the Fibonacci Series."

"What?" Walid made a slight face.

Mafulla sighed. "The Fibonacci Series, or The Fibonacci Sequence. It's that number sequence your uncle told us about when he gave us our watches. Remember? 0,1,1, and then, boom, every subsequent number is the sum of the previous two, like 2, 3, 5, 8, 13, 21, 34, and so on."

"You remember all that?"

"Yeah. I'm a numbers guy. Come to me with all your math questions. It's that big, infinite series of numbers found in crazy places in nature whose ratios, in pairs, approach the golden ratio. And that's the famous mathematical thing that lies behind so much of the beautiful and impressive stuff in the world, like our watches and the palace."

"Oh."

"And now, it comes to light that it somehow involves your birthday, or that your birthday involves it."

"So, my birthday is in this way among the beautiful and impressive stuff in the world."

"No. I'm not suggesting here that your birthday, or you, could by any stretch of the imagination be considered beautiful or impressive."

"Still, that is super odd. I sure didn't know my birthday was a series of Fibonacci numbers."

"You mean they never sang, 'Happy Fibonacci Day to You' back in the village on your special annual celebrations?"

"No, I'm afraid not."

"What a shame, and a lost opportunity."

"How do you think up these things?"

"Wait, wait. Hmm. In addition, my friend, it's now 1934. The number 34 is the next number in the same series, in case you're interested—and even if you're not. It's still the very next number. And then, of course, if you subtract your birth year, 1921, from the current year, the difference is your age right now: 13. And, again, it's a Fibonacci number, the same as the middle one from your birth date."

"Ok, That's pretty strange." Walid looked mystified, or maybe just confused.

"Yeah, it's strange. Or, like I said, it's odd, really odd."

"It probably doesn't mean anything."

"Yeah. Or maybe it does."

"What could it mean?"

"I have no idea. Look. There's something you need to know. I don't have all the answers, even though by now you might think I do. I'm a genius only up to a point. Then I'm pretty much just like you."

"Ha! You mean, like, beautiful and impressive?"

"Well, now, you got me. I can't quite say no, to be true to at least half the equation here, but that's not what I meant."

"You do think about some really odd things."

"Sometimes."

Mafulla sat silently for a moment, then continued, as Walid was about to get back to his reading. "Here's an odd thought, in the sense of strange and almost random. I wonder what was in all those boxes."

"What boxes?"

"The ones the big guy was bringing into the back of my dad's store when everybody almost shot everybody else."

"Oh, those boxes."

"Yeah. I wonder what was in them."

"I guess the palace guards know. I'm sure they went through everything right away."

"Yeah, but I think I'd like to know, too."

"Why?"

"Curiosity."

"Curiosity?"

"Yeah, the engine of civilization, art, science, and all discovery—the goad to know, the itch to find out."

"Ok, Ok. We can probably find out—after we do the reading we've been assigned, if you can redirect your itch."

"You sure are disciplined about schoolwork."

"This may come as a surprise, but all of us ordinary non-geniuses actually have to work to learn. Our brains don't just produce ideas from thin air like yours."

"Don't be jealous. I have a simple process."

"Which is?"

"I figure that if you read everything carefully and I ask you the right questions, then, as a result, I'll know what I need to know."

"That may be true, if I answer."

"Of course you'll answer. We're friends. So answer this: Were you really going to shoot that guy—the evil little guy holding the knife to my mom's throat?"

"Yeah, I think I was. I was less than half a second away from it."

"Very cool. And more than a little scary."

"What do you mean?"

"You were going to try to save my mom. You were willing to do something extreme for my loved one. But it would have been extremely risky."

"Yeah."

"So, I guess that's the deal—that can be our deal."

"What?"

"You tell me the important stuff in our reading assignments and you take care of the bad guys when necessary, but only when absolutely necessary, and I'll be your math guru, your idea guy, and I'll hook you up with the girl of your dreams when the time is right. I should throw that in. Plus, I'll point out any possibly important oddities you may need to know, not for school, but for life."

"Like random facts about strange numbers and birthdays."

"That could mean something."

"Yeah. I just need to figure out how I got so lucky."

"It might not be about luck, my friend, but perhaps destiny."

"Yeah. Ok. I can buy that. Now, let's read."

"You're just attracted back to that page because the book you're holding is more or less proportioned by the 1.618 thingy. You know, width to length: 1 to 1.618."

"How do you know that?"

"How else? I measured and calculated. That's our book."

Walid laughed. "If you say so. But then, here's the problem. You should be attracted to it as well, since the golden ratio thing is supposed to be appealing to everybody."

"I am attracted to it! I can sit and look at this book all day. I like the shape. I'm just having trouble actually reading it. I need someone to read it to me."

"I'm not doing that."

"No, no, I had in mind more like a beautiful girl about my age."

"Really?"

"Yeah. Or maybe two of them: One to read and one to feed me fruit and maybe massage my feet while I listen."

"Gee."

"But between the feet and the fruit there would have to be some hand washing, of course. Or maybe I need three helpful young ladies who could be specialists in reading, fruit, and feet. But then, I could imagine needing a fourth for beverage service. It would get a little crowded in here. You might have to excuse yourself."

"I still don't know how you come up with all this."

"It's a gift."

There was a knock at the door.

"Enter."

"So sorry to interrupt, Prince Walid, and Mafulla, but the king would like to see you in five minutes, in his office."

"We'll be there." Walid answered.

"This is new."

"What?"

"I didn't know the king had an office. We're always summoned to his private living quarters, you know, his sitting room, or the dining room. I didn't know there was a kingly office."

"There has to be a place where he can concentrate on office-ial things." Walid pronounced the word weird like he was making a joke, a very embarrassingly lame joke.

"Wait. Are you doing an exceptionally weak form of wordplay? Office? Offic-ial? That's clearly my speci-al-ity, not yours."

Walid closed his eyes and spoke like he was reciting a poem.

> "We can play with words like the toys
> that we had as much younger boys.
> No lexical constabulary
> can police our vocabulary
> and prevent us from having those joys."

Eyes still closed, he smiled.

"Walid! You're making that up as you say it?"

"Yeah, pretty impressive, don't you think?"

"Ok, while the rhythm doesn't completely work for me, still, it's very creative and more than enough. You're officially in the club."

"I'm afraid to ask."

"No, no, the very exalted 'Genius-Up-To-A-Point Club.' And I have to admit, it's nice to finally have another member. I was getting a bit lonely. It was a drag, year after year, to be in it all by myself. But, I have long enjoyed being president of the organization, which I hope will continue, if I can count on your vote."

"I wouldn't think of voting for anyone else. But, look, my Reverso says we should leave."

"Funny, my Reverso just uses its hands to signal me. It never actually says anything. In fact, it's completely silent, except when I put my ear right up on it. And then I just get Tick, Tick, Tick. I can't image how yours actually says things in some way to you. Do you mind if I ... watch?" Of course Mafulla emphasized this last word, drawing it out.

"Ok, that was as bad as mine, and you have to admit it."

"But, certainly, it's timely humor, nonetheless, you must admit."

"Jeepers."

"I like winding you up with a few jokes."

"You can stop now, this second, in fact. Or, to put it another way: Please, oh please, oh, won't you reverse-oh your tendency to joke so, oh, Jolly Good Fellow?"

"Oh! Oh! Indeed. Consider me stopped like a broken watch. Now. Please. Lead the way." Mafulla dropped his head and gestured for the prince to go ahead of him out the door.

It wasn't much of a walk down the hallway, but they had to pass the king's private living quarters and go around a corner and a bit farther down a second hall. Walid knew the way. The boys always enjoyed looking at palace artwork when they went anywhere. This hall in particular had some great tapestries along its walls. The door to the office was open and they could see into it as they approached. The king was making notes on a large pad of paper. Masoon and Hamid were there with him, sitting in chairs facing him and talking, when the boys arrived right outside the door. A guard standing beside the door smiled at them, bowed slightly, held up one hand, and mouthed the words, "Just a moment."

Mafulla whispered to Walid, "We have no idea, of course, exactly how long that is. But we can wait." Walid just smiled and shook his head.

It looked like the men might be reporting on something to the king. The conversation went on for a minute or two more, and with words of agreement, along with a nodding of heads all around, Ali stood up, and so did Hamid and Masoon. The two of them then turned toward the door.

"Walid! Mafulla!" Masoon greeted them right away. "I've been hearing all over the palace how you both helped apprehend those dangerous criminals in the market, and with amazing bravery."

"Yes! I have, too!" Hamid added immediately, "Congratulations on your effective and courageous actions! Good for you."

"Thanks," Mafulla said. "But I just managed to pull out a gun and hold onto it for about one second before some guy lashed it out of my hand with a whip. And then Walid charged in like he was a whole army."

"Yeah, and all I did was click through two empty chambers in my gun. Then the real army showed up."

Masoon smiled and said, "Well, you acted like true warriors to confront those men the way you did, and you definitely made a difference, keeping them together in that room and slowing them down until the palace guards could arrive. Your part was much appreciated and has been talked about a lot by the men."

"Really?" Mafulla said.

"Yes. It's unusual for boys your age to get into the middle of such action. And you did very well. In some situations, mere survival is success, but you did much more."

Walid replied, "Thank you, both. We're glad to have been of any help at all in stopping what was going on at the store. And we were happy to get out of there alive." He sounded genuinely proud and grateful at the same time.

"I really appreciate the men who came in and saved us." Mafulla spoke with humility and a clear tone of gratitude. Then he smiled and added, "But you know, they may have also saved those evil crime guys from a major smack down. I was pretty worked up and, given another minute or two, I'm sure I could have cleared the room, you know." As he said this, he crouched a bit into what he must have imagined as a fighting stance and bobbed back and forth.

Everyone laughed, knowing the way Mafulla was, and

Walid said, while laughing, "You could have cleared the room?"

Mafulla said, "Yes, but perhaps like your friend Bashir." Everyone laughed again as he explained, "I was experiencing severe stomach bloat at the time, bad pressure in the lower regions, and within a minute or so, I suspect the whole room would have cleared out, or else a different sort of rescue would have been needed."

They continued to laugh, and Hamid actually snorted, provoking further laughter, then he shook his head as he dropped his gaze to the floor, his stomach still bouncing from the mental vision that Mafulla had evoked. Masoon, still chuckling, put his hand on Walid's shoulder and said, "Well, I know your uncle has some business for you both, so we'll leave you now and hope to see you later on today or tomorrow."

Walid replied, "That would be good! I miss our times of talking around the campfire out in the desert."

"So do we!" Hamid patted Walid on the back and gave Mafulla's arm a quick touch of friendship, and then he and Masoon walked away down the hall, and the king motioned for the boys to come in.

He said, "You young men continue to be spoken of as heroes around the palace."

"Well," Walid reflected. "That's good, but I wouldn't mind at all some nice, quiet, non-heroic days around here now."

"Excellent! This is exactly what I have in mind for you."

"Really?"

"Yes. I have a task for you both that will require your diligence and care, but will not likely call for gunplay or even strenuous exertion."

"What is it, Uncle? What can we do?"

"Sit, boys, and I'll tell you." They both sat down and the king stroked his beard for a moment. Then, he explained the task at hand. "There are many things stored in the palace, in different places, but most of the storage areas are in the basement. The previous administration kept basic records of the contents in these various storerooms, but we're not sure of their accuracy. We need to check them against what we now find in the rooms. I have the record books and will have them delivered to your rooms later on today. I would like you, tomorrow after school, to begin to go through the major storage rooms on the basement level and check the records against what you find there. You'll have a key to each room in the front of the record book, and they're all labeled. Make notes in the book if things are different from what they're represented as being. And then bring me the corrected record books by the end of this month. Can you do this for me?"

"Yes, of course, Uncle."

"Sure thing, Your Majesty," Mafulla said. "It'll be interesting."

"Good. And keep track of your hours. You'll be compensated. You'll be officially working as my assistants in doing this."

"That sounds important," Mafulla said.

"It is."

"King Ali, may I please ask a question?" Mafulla made bold to speak up, but was at the same time properly deferential to this man he liked a lot and admired, and who was also the monarch of the kingdom.

"You may ask anything, and at any time."

"Thanks. Here's my concern. The palace guards took boxes out of my father's store, boxes that had been delivered and were being stacked up by the bad guys when we burst in and took them down—the guys, I mean, not the boxes."

"Yes." The king smiled again at the always entertaining young man.

"Is there any way I can find out what was in those boxes? I have no idea why I want to know, but I really, really do."

The king said, "I think that can be arranged."

"Great."

"Those boxes, I've been told, are actually stored in a room near where you'll be doing your inventory. You have my permission to open any of them and examine their contents. But do be careful. I understand that the men opened one or two and found weapons. But many other boxes remain unopened."

"Thank you, Your Majesty. We'll be very careful. And if there's anything there that's of particular interest or value, we promise not to sell it on the open market, for personal gain, despite the evident good it could do for our bank accounts." Mafulla spoke with mock gravity.

"Good. I appreciate your kindness. And, please, if you would, make that a general policy. I don't want anyone out and about, selling things from the palace. I would hate to have to buy back some of my own stuff, or anything that belongs to the kingdom."

The boys both smiled at the king playing along. And Mafulla said, "That's reasonable, Your Majesty. Agreed."

"There's one more thing."

The boys sat and looked expectant.

"I want to talk with you both about your recent display of courage, if you have just a few minutes."

"Yes, of course," Walid answered for them both as Mafulla nodded.

"Good! I've listened with keen interest to the reports of your deeds. You were certainly very brave."

"Thanks," Mafulla said.

The king continued, "And, you may not know this, but the great philosopher Aristotle thought of this quality, courage, as one of the chief virtues, or strengths, that we need to bring to our daily lives, in order to live well. He also believed that, associated with each virtue, there are two corresponding vices, or weaknesses—a weakness of too little, and a weakness of too much—a deficiency and an excess."

"That's very interesting." Walid couldn't help but speak up, as his mind focused in on these thoughts. "Could you provide an example?"

"Easily. Consider the virtue of generosity in the face of need. The weakness of too little that's associated with it would be something like a miserly stinginess, an inability or disinclination to part with anything to help provide for others what they might need. Then, the weakness of too much that's associated with this virtue would be something like a grandiose, careless, or extreme profligacy in giving, lavishly providing much more than is needed, and in the process emptying your own supply of money, or time, or resources, or energy."

"I see," Walid said.

The king concluded, "The virtue of generosity is a mid point between too little and too much. It's a happy medium of just enough, and as such, a strength for living well with others. The other two habits, the extremes, are weaknesses that create vulnerabilities in our individual lives, and in our lives together."

Walid said, "I've never thought about it before, but that makes sense."

"Aristotle suggested that this is the contour of virtue, universally. For any given virtue that's to be cultivated in our hearts, there will be two associated vices, or weaknesses, to be avoided."

Mafulla was nodding his head. "That really does sound right."

"Now, think about courage for just a moment." The king smiled. "And, yes, Mafulla, you know what I mean, even though you can't precisely specify the length of time I denote."

Mafulla raised his eyebrows twice in a distinctively funny way, but sat quietly at this point to listen and learn.

"Courage is a virtuous response to danger, like generosity is a virtuous response to need. And again, there are two extremes to be avoided—the extreme of too little, and the extreme of too much. Too little courage is timidity. None at all is sheer cowardice. And then on the other side, going farther than the proper borders of courage is the territory of temerity. Going on even a bit more is an unhinged, crazy, foolish rashness that's completely careless, or even blind to danger as well as to the legitimate, important concerns of prudence—or a proper care about ourselves that we often and rightly think of as a healthy self-interest. The virtue of courage avoids both a deficiency of spirit and a mindless excess."

The king paused. "Does this still make sense?"

"Yes, sir," Mafulla said.

"Yes, Uncle, it does to me, as well. In our responses to the world, it's a weakness to either fall short or overshoot the mark. Extremes should be avoided. There's a middle way that's virtuous, or strong."

"Exactly. Some people say there's a 'golden mean' or perfect point of balance between the two extremes."

Mafulla asked, "But what's the difference between this golden mean and the golden mean of Phi, the ratio of 1 to 1.618?"

"Oh, yes. It's another but related meaning of 'mean.' The word 'mean' can mean different, but sometimes similar, things."

Mafulla laughed and said, "Oh?" He looked pleased at the king's convoluted statement, and yet at the same time, his expression seemed to be one of mild puzzlement, whether real or feigned.

"I should explain. It would be mean of me to do otherwise."

Mafulla grinned and said, "I like your turns of phrase, Your Majesty. You have a way with words."

"Thank you, Mafulla. I just realized that I sound like you." The king smiled conspiratorially. And then he continued. "In the context of virtue, the concept of a mean refers to the middle ground between opposite extremes. It's called golden because it's in this place that great value is to be found. The proportionality of 1 to 1.618 is sometimes called 'the golden mean' a bit misleadingly, since 'mean' usually connotes something different in mathematics. It's more normally called 'the golden ratio' because of its own distinct association, as a ratio, with beauty and value of a different sort."

"I see. I think." Mafulla smiled back at the king.

"Good. Now, I should come to the point of my lesson. Your actions in the marketplace, both of you, were in many ways very courageous deeds. There was nothing mean, in a different sense of the word that connotes deficient, or lacking, about them. But they were also a bit rushed, and could even be considered in some respects to have been relatively rash."

"Oh. Yeah." Mafulla looked chastened.

The king continued. "You did run headlong into danger without taking time to organize your efforts or energies, or to form a plan that could be agreed on by all present, so that you would have the safety of support and backup."

Mafulla replied again. "It was all my fault, Your Majesty. I was scared for my mom and Sammi and Sasha and so I ran to the store without really thinking what I'd do when I got there. I was afraid there was no time for anything else. But when I did arrive, I began to hatch a plan."

The king said, "Yes, I understand completely. Your intentions were quite noble. And as I told you when you first came back to the palace, I'm overjoyed at the outcome of the events. And I'm proud of you. I just want you both to understand that, in some ways, you may have been toeing the line between courage and rashness in your actions."

"I see," Walid said.

Ali continued. "I do find your efforts that day to be, in the vast majority of respects, completely commendable, even highly praiseworthy. And things certainly turned out well. But never let positive results block for you the importance of analyzing a situation like that after it ends, and learning from it whatever you can."

Walid nodded his understanding. So did Mafulla.

The king concluded, "The next time you're faced with an urgent need in the midst of danger, perhaps you can find a way of responding that's just as courageous, and has just as positive an outcome, but without subjecting yourselves to quite the same level of extreme risk. Prudence, or prudential wisdom—which just amounts to rational self care—requires a consideration of all the basic values involved in a situation. You know your families and many other people would have been terribly grieved if your actions had led to either of you being severely injured, or even losing your life. Then, you would not be around in the future to do other good things, and come to the rescue of other good people. We need you to be with us for the long term."

"Boy, I never thought about it that way," Mafulla said, immediately.

"I hadn't either," Walid replied.

Mafulla reflected, "When you do really think about it, things easily could have gone badly wrong. And then all the young ladies of the kingdom would have been in mourning for a very, very long time."

The king and Walid looked at each other. Mafulla quickly added, "I'm sorry. You know me. I joke when I'm nervous. And even thinking about how close we were to disaster churns me up a little inside, like Bashir after one bean too many, I suppose." He looked at Walid, who laughed and shook his head.

"I understand completely," the king said as he smiled. "And it would indeed have been very difficult for all the young ladies, I'm sure."

Walid let out a deep breath and said, "Thanks, Uncle, I mean, Your Majesty, for talking with us about this. We were lucky that things turned out so well. Next time, if there is a next time, we'll try to be much more careful. I understand now how courage and care should go together. I have to admit I've never really seen that before."

The king nodded in approval and added, "Sometimes, extreme circumstances call for equally extreme measures. And at other times, we can mitigate risk by using all the resources available to us. It's important to remember that when something dramatic happens and we make it through a bad situation with mostly good consequences, we most often recall everything through the perspective of those positive consequences. And we can tend to view all our actions, as a result, in a celebratory manner. But it's good to remember everything that happened, look closely at our actions and reactions, and ask ourselves if we could do it differently, and perhaps better, the next time. All good warriors do this after a battle. Great athletes do it after a competition. Review and reconsider. It's important for any of us to do it as well. Self-examination can lead to self-improvement, and that's always a good thing. How we perform under pressure helps to define us. But how we improve our performance through time defines us even more."

Mafulla said, "Wow. That makes a lot of sense. I suppose I ran to the store without really thinking, when I realized that my mother and the kids might be in danger, because it was just such a big surprise. It was so unexpected. I should have planned a response with the others, even if it had to be fast."

The king said, "I understand. When we're sufficiently surprised by a situation, we can surprise ourselves with how we react. But there's something else here that's also important to realize. Life is full of surprises. The better prepared we are for the unexpected, the better we can respond, rather than just reacting without thought."

He went on, "A very wise man once taught me that I should often do worst-case scenario thinking. How could things go wrong, and what would be the best response in each situation? He didn't mean that we should obsess about the negative. And we shouldn't do this sort of worst-case scenario planning with our emotions all worked up, actually anticipating that terrible things will indeed happen, since most often they don't. But if we can think through possible responses to bad things we might face, ahead of time when we're not under the real pressure of dealing with them, we benefit. Then, if a situation develops where we don't have time to think, we'll already have done the thinking necessary for the proper response."

"That sounds like a very important thing to do," Mafulla commented.

"Yes. Worst-case scenario thinking is helpful, and healthy. On the other hand, worst-case scenario believing is not."

"That's really wise, it seems to me." Walid spoke with a measure of enthusiasm about the idea. "It's like what Masoon means when he talks about preparing for trouble."

"You're exactly right, my boy, and it's of great value." The king paused for a moment and smiled. He then glanced down at his watch and said to both of them, "We may have philosophized enough about all this for the time being. But please continue to reflect on these things. And always feel free to bring me any questions you might have. I mean it."

"We will," Walid replied.

"Definitely," Mafulla said, as he inwardly appreciated the king's words.

"Good. Then, to sum up: Be courageous in everything. But also be prudent. And be prepared. Now, I suppose you're both eager to get back to your school work so that you'll be sufficiently prepared for your next class."

Mafulla looked very serious. "Yes, Your Majesty. That would be prudent. We should be getting back in case Walid needs my help, to tutor him in the fine points of the assignment, if necessary."

At that, Walid laughed so loudly he hiccuped. The king chuckled as well and rose from his chair, as did the boys, and they quickly took their leave of the king, with good wishes expressed all around, and a reminder of dinnertime for both of them.

Then, when they were only a few feet down the hall, King Ali called out, "Oh! Boys! I forgot to mention that we have some important and unexpected guests arriving right before dinner, and they'll be joining us for our evening meal, so please be on time or even a bit early."

"Yes, sir!" Walid responded.

Mafulla whispered to him, "I wonder who the guests are."

"I have no idea."

"So, we're now expecting a situation where we don't know what to expect. Mental magicians of the mind that we are, we're officially expecting the unexpected." Mafulla grinned.

In response, Walid smiled and took a deep breath and exhaled loudly.

They had no idea of the truly unexpected things that soon awaited them.

12

A DINNER OF DELIGHT

A CONVERSATION THAT TRULY ENGAGES YOUR MIND CAN energize you for hours or even days. It can bring a new level of concentration and enjoyment to everything else you do. The mind is a lot like the body and requires a regular experience of peak use, or it grows flabby and out of shape. Raised to a new level, it seems to have more power, and can function more effectively in every way.

Deep conversations in particular seem to stretch the mind and expand it. An active discussion in-depth about any topic fundamental for life in the world can awaken your perceptions and thoughts more generally, and benefit you in everything you do. Whenever the king had one of these talks with the boys, they seemed to have, as a result, new energy and insight for anything they were doing. And this was especially paying off at school.

Each day, Walid and Mafulla had been enjoying their classroom work together, and they both really liked their teacher, Khalid. All the boys in their small class seemed interested in the work and, so far, they all got along remarkably well, which is, as some of them knew from unfortunate experience, all too rare in most school settings, or almost anywhere else in life. The classroom, like the palace around it, was an oasis of good feeling. They had a lively, active group, and everyone contributed to the class discussions. Their assignments for the time between classes were well designed, but they often took longer than the boys thought they would. And yet, in the end, even the students themselves realized the importance of the work.

It was good that Walid and Mafulla had such a great relationship with the king, and such a nearly idyllic school experience to this point, because there were forces surrounding them that were very soon going to impinge on their lives in frightening ways and test them severely. In order to have any chance of meeting these challenges, they would have to rely on what they were learning from both the king and the classroom.

After their talk with the king about courage and surprise, the prince and his new best friend got right back to business and spent more than an hour finishing up their homework. Mafulla seemed to have a new mental focus, and hardly spoke during the entire time. Fortunately, Walid did not, after all, need any tutoring help from his younger colleague, and both the boys got their assignments completed by bearing down and concentrating.

Walid retained enough presence of mind that, despite a total immersion in the reading assignment and, after it, some challenging math work, he remembered to glance at his watch now and then to keep track of the time until dinner. With about half an hour left, he gave a reminder to Mafulla, and they both were able to finish and clean up before joining the king and some other guests for the evening meal.

They often got to sit and listen to various kingdom officials give their reports informally to the king over dinner. Or sometimes, visiting dignitaries would entertain them all with wild stories from faraway places. Ali considered this a vital part of their education, and it was almost always interesting to be present at these dinners. Tonight should be no different. Or at least, that's what the boys thought. In fact, it would be very different, and, because of that, dramatic in its own distinctive way.

The boys were the first to arrive at the private dining room. They were told by the king's assistant and head butler, a man named Kular, that they could take their customary seats, which they did. He asked about their day, and they gave him some highlights, as they would often do. And then, in turn, Walid inquired about his day. "Oh, you know. The same old, same old—hovering around the pinnacle of power, taking care of royalty, meeting top people from all over the world, as usual. It's been just one of those ordinary days." He would almost always say this, or something like it, with a slightly comical expression.

Suddenly the king came striding around the corner of the doorway with a puzzled look on his face. He said, "Walid, there are some people here who say they know you. Would you be willing to take a look and see if they're at all familiar? We have escorts to take them out of the palace, if they're not."

Walid and Mafulla had risen to their feet as soon as the king appeared, as was their custom, and Walid replied, right away, "Um, sure. Ok, no problem, Your Majesty. Who do they say they are?"

"Well, you might not believe me if I told you. But you can see for yourself." Looking back outside the door, the king said, "You may come in and let the prince confirm your identity."

"Walid!"

"What??? How??? Mom! Dad! You're here!"

"My son! My son!" Both parents were exclaiming with joy and relief and pride in their voices as they moved quickly, arms open, in the direction of the prince. Bhati was wearing a beautiful pale yellow and golden gown, accented in royal blue, whose diaphanous sleeves were fluttering lightly as she glided across the room. Rumi was dressed formally as well, and not in his normal small village attire. He looked as regal as Bhati as he walked toward his son with a huge smile on his face, though hanging back just a touch to allow his wife first access to their boy. Walid shoved his chair out of the way, and practically ran around the table to meet them. The room was full of hugs and kisses as the king and Mafulla smiled broadly and nodded their heads at each other in approval of this happy event.

"Oh, let me look at you! You've grown in the time you've been gone!" Bhati was gushing her approval at Walid's appearance. "You're so handsome, just like your father!"

"Mom, you don't have to say that. It's just great to see you."

"No, I mean it! It's been too long since I set my eyes on my favorite young man in the world!"

"And we've heard of your incredible exploits!" Walid's father, Rumi chimed in.

Bhati put her hand over her heart. "A desert storm! Eluding hostile forces! Kidnapped and escaped! Breaking up a famous crime ring! My goodness, I hope things can calm down for you, my son!"

"I do, too!" Walid laughed. "I'm all for a stretch of uneventful, ordinary days at this point!"

Rumi said, "You've been a good student to many wise

counselors, and it's all paying off. We're very proud of you."
He patted the boy on the back and beamed with all the pride
of which he spoke.

The king then said, "Allow me to introduce you both to
Walid's partner in crime … fighting, and all other things, Mr.
Mafulla Adi, Esquire."

Bhati exclaimed, "Mafulla! We've heard so much about
you! It's wonderful to meet you in person!"

"Thank you!" Mafulla replied with the same enthusiasm.
"It's very nice to meet you as well. But, how do you know
anything about me?"

Bhati explained, "The king sent two dozen soldiers to come
get us and escort us to the palace. They were dispatched from a
base closer to us shortly after he took power, and your bravery
in captivity with our son was well known by many of the men.
Word travels on the wind, as they say, and in many other ways.
Ali also sent messengers and several communications since
then. We're current on many of your heroic exploits but certainly want to know more!" Walid's mother spoke in a musical
rush of words that were like a magic waterfall.

The king encouraged them all to be seated, and a lively
conversation bounced around the table all through dinner
and afterwards. Walid's parents brought everyone up on the
news from home, and the king did the same, concerning palace and kingdom events. The prince then told his mother
and father about all the things that had happened during the
caravan across the desert. He was almost breathless in reciting
some of the lessons he had learned from his uncle, and much
of this, Mafulla was hearing for the first time, as well. Bhati
was eager to learn all about the new classroom experience the
boys were having, but first she drew out from them the details
of their recently eventful day in the market.

She then asked about their beautiful watches, and both boys gave her the whole story of the history of the Reverso, showed her how they could flip the cases, explained the engravings, and of course Mafulla gave a short discourse on the golden ratio. He started to relate it to Walid's birthday, but something held him back. He didn't know why he was hesitating, but decided not to go there in his explanations—not yet, at least. For one thing, it was maybe just an entertaining oddity, as far as he knew, but for another thing, maybe not, and he couldn't simply blurt out something that he didn't really understand, and that might soon be of importance to all of them.

They talked for hours, and no one wanted to leave, but the time finally arrived when the king suggested that the boys had better go look over their work one more time for school, and prepare for a good evening's rest. Walid's parents would be staying in rooms down the hallway from Walid and Mafulla, and they could all continue their conversation in the morning before class. There were hugs all around once more, exclamations of happiness, relief, and joy, and wishes of a good night's sleep for everyone.

The boys walked back toward their rooms, and after only a few seconds alone, Mafulla said, "You didn't tell me about all that amazing stuff your uncle said in the desert."

"I told you some of it."

"Well, yeah, but a lot of it, I'd never heard before—the emotional telescope idea, the balance image of the tightrope walker, the nobility and humility stuff, all the details about the royalty of the mind, the four elements and four kinds of people, and the image of the tiger. It's all pretty incredible."

"Yeah, it is."

"What else are you keeping secret?"

The beautiful girl in the market, Khalid's daughter, flashed through his head, but Walid quickly said, "Nothing! I wasn't even keeping that stuff secret. It's just that we've been so busy, I haven't had a chance earlier to tell you about all of it. I've told you some of it, but the rest was coming. It was going to be an important part of my contribution to The Education of Mafulla Adi."

"Well, all right. Just because I'm a genius up to a point doesn't mean that I already know everything. When you learn something important, you've got to clue me in, and then I'll take over and figure out how we can use the information for our mutual profit, the good of the kingdom, and the undying admiration of young ladies everywhere."

"Ok, I promise I'll be quick, henceforth, to share anything important that I learn, and anything that Uncle Ali's taught me that I may not have mentioned yet. I'll say something as soon as I'm aware that I've got something worth saying."

"Ok, good deal—even though, generally, that shouldn't reflect an absolute policy."

"What?"

"Remaining silent until you have something to say that's truly worth saying. I can't take an environment of almost complete, nonstop quiet on your part."

"Ha."

"You see? Even utterances like that have their place, and fill the void." He said the last three words with a very dramatic voice.

"The void," Walid repeated, and shook his head, with a laugh.

At that point, the boys had arrived back at their rooms. Mafulla came into Walid's room where they had been studying earlier, as usual. He wanted to take one more glance over his preparation for tomorrow and collect his books and note-books.

"Have you seen any of the girls who are in the palace school?" Mafulla suddenly asked this, out of the blue.

Walid said, "Not yet. Well, maybe I caught a glimpse of two of them, at a distance, one day, down a long hallway, but just for a second. They keep the girls pretty separate, away from us, I guess. Why do you ask?"

"I was just thinking at dinner what a great mother you have, and what a great wife for your dad she must be, like my mom, too, and then I was thinking we're really lucky to have moms like that. And, you know, maybe one day if we keep being lucky, we can also find wives who'll be that great. That's all. I was just thinking. I mean, you gotta plan ahead."

"Yeah, I guess. But my dad was pretty old when he met my mom."

Mafulla said, "My dad was really young. His father started our store, and he met my mom when he was not much older than me, when he was working there, in the store. So maybe, it's getting near the time when some lucky girl will have the chance to, you know, improve her life tremendously by meeting me."

Walid laughed and said, "You crack me up."

"It could happen. You never know. But it's not like I'm out and about that much. I mean, I'm here in the palace or on the palace grounds most of the time. And that's great and all, but when you and I leave this immediate environment and go out into the larger world, we tend to get involved in things that are not exactly conducive to romantic encounters, like when everybody's pointing guns at everybody else. So, I was just wondering about the talent here in the palace."

Walid had to laugh again at Mafulla's use of the word 'talent.' He said, "Well, the king's sending us off to examine the storage rooms starting tomorrow. Maybe we'll have a chance to look around the palace more generally, and, who knows, we might be able to have a close encounter or something. I wouldn't mind that at all."

"Good. That sounds like a plan."

Walid was silent for a few seconds and then said, "But I guess I've got something to sort of confess."

"What?"

The prince felt a fleeting moment of embarrassment, with a hot flush in his cheeks. He fought through it and said, "Ok. Well, now that you've given me some grief about keeping secrets, even though I wasn't, I guess I should tell you about Khalid's daughter."

"What about her?"

"So, you might remember that on the first day of class, I recognized Khalid as a man I had seen in the market the first day I got to town."

"Yeah. I remember that."

"And that day in the market, he was with a really beautiful lady, which I guessed correctly was his wife."

"Ok."

"And they were walking with a really, really knock-out great looking girl about my age, which he said is his daughter, Kissa."

"You didn't mention at all the knock-out great looking part."

"No. I guess I didn't."

"So, that's the secret?"

Walid hesitated and then said, "Actually, no. There's something else."

"What?"

"I think I should definitely call dibs on Kissa, since I saw her first and everything, and we sort of already have a relationship."

"What do you mean? What kind of a relationship?"

"Well, you know, I met her because I was being a little bit gallant and everything and ran over to pick up a basket she dropped when some boys bumped into her and knocked it out of her hands. And she obviously thought it was at least semi-heroic of me, and I could tell that maybe she liked me right away."

"Did she say she likes you?"

"Well, no, of course not. I just met her for a couple of minutes. And her parents were standing right there. But I could tell from her eyes, and her smile. And, you know, I had a feeling."

"Wait. How many girls are there in the palace class for our age?"

"I've heard there are seven, same as our class."

"Ok, then. One for you and six for me. That seems fair. So, I grant your wish. You may have dibs on this one. Of course, she hasn't seen me yet, but I promise I won't turn on the magic with her. I'll respect your choice. You have nothing to worry about."

A knock at the door interrupted this elevated train of thought.

"Enter."

The door opened a bit. There was a familiar voice. "I'm sorry, Prince Walid, but someone left a letter at the front gate for Mafulla, and when I took it down to his room just now, he wasn't there, so I thought to check here." The head butler then stepped into the room and smiled and said, "Ah. There you are, just as I suspected," and handed the sealed envelope to its intended recipient.

"Thanks, Kular," Mafulla said.

The butler nodded deeply and looking back at the prince asked, "Is there anything else I can do for the two of you?"

"No, but thanks for asking. Just have a good night," Walid replied.

"Yeah. Have a good one," Mafulla said.

The butler did a small bow, and saying, "Your Highness," slipped back out through the door. As he was leaving, Mafulla looked carefully at the envelope that had his name written across the front and said, "Who would drop off a letter for me, at the gate, at night?"

"Your harem of six in the girls' class? Or, an especially eager member of that group? One of your lovely fans?"

"Very funny. They haven't seen me yet. Wait. It's no girl. This is my mom's hand writing." He began to open the envelope and pulled out a piece of paper inside it.

"What does it say?"

"Hold on. Let me get it unfolded. Ok. She has nice handwriting. Look at the even script, and the artistic loops." Mafulla turned the page toward his friend.

"Yeah, it's nice. Read it already."

"Ok. It says, 'Dear Son: I don't want to alarm your father, so I haven't mentioned this to him, but strange things may be going on in the neighborhood. I just wondered if you could find out from the king whether our home, as well as the store, is being watched by soldiers or the police. It's, of course, a wonderful thing that they're monitoring the store for our protection. I just think that things are happening near our home that they should know about. Again, I didn't want to worry your dad, since he's had so much on his mind lately, but if you could check into this, it would be wonderful. I've asked Reela to drop off this note to you on his way to see some friends nearby. We hope you're doing well, and look forward to seeing you again soon. Love, Mom.' And that's it. Huh."

"I wonder what she meant by 'strange things' in the neighborhood?" Walid said.

"I can't imagine. Do you know whether the house is being watched?"

"No. I don't know, but I would guess so. At least, since the recent events at the store. Let's ask Uncle Ali tomorrow."

"Boy, I didn't expect anything like this. I hope they're all Ok."

"I'm sure if they sensed any clear danger, they'd come to us quickly, knowing that we'd respond."

"Yeah. I guess you're right. We should just go to sleep now, I suppose, and we'll ask the king in the morning."

Walid thought for a few seconds and said, "You know, crime fighters need secret identities, so people can't mess with their families."

"What do you mean? Like, disguises or something?"

"Yeah."

Mafulla looked impressed. "Wow. I hadn't thought of that. And I think you're right. We need masks or something if we're going to keep up this adventure stuff, and maybe special code names."

Walid laughed and said, "Code names. That sounds good. I could be The Desert Viper and you could be …"

"The Windstorm." Mafulla uttered the words with great drama.

"Good one. Spooky, fast, unexpected, dangerous, powerful."

"I would offer a small suggestion, though, Prince Viper."

"What?"

"I think that, in light of your birthday strangeness, and

the fact that we live in and operate out of The Golden Palace and all, you should call yourself The Golden Viper."

"The Golden Viper?"

"Yeah. The Fibonacci Viper doesn't have quite the ring you want. And The Phi Snake just sounds weird. The Desert Viper is great, but now you, as a matter of fact, are based in the city, not the desert. I like The Golden Viper. It rolls off the tongue and can inspire fear in all who hear it."

"Ok. Good. I like it, too. The Golden Viper it is."

Mafulla looked like he suddenly had a great thought. "The girls of the kingdom are going to go nuts over these new identities."

Walid looked skeptical. He said, "Yeah, maybe, but remember, they're secret identities. So they couldn't know it's you or me."

"Oh. Yeah. Good point, unfortunately. Well, that's really too bad. It sort of takes the wind out of my sails, as they say on the river—or the Windstorm out of my desert." Mafulla picked up his books, let out a deep breath and, walking over toward the door, said, "I'm pretty much too tired right now to think any more tonight about fighting crime, anyway. Maybe I should just say: Goodnight, Prince of Crime Fighters, otherwise known as The Golden Viper."

"Night, Stormie."

As Mafulla walked out the door and down the hall the short distance to his room, the head royal butler appeared once more outside Walid's threshold. The door was still open. "Please excuse me again, Your Highness."

"Oh, hi, Kular. Sure. What's up?"

"The king has sent you some record books. I promise this will be my last visit of the evening, short of something quite dramatic and utterly necessary."

"No, no, that's fine. I was expecting these at some time tonight. Thanks. And again, have a good evening."

The butler said, "And a good one to you, Prince," as he handed him a surprisingly heavy little box of palace storage record books, and then turned and left, closing the door behind him.

Walid put the box down on the side of his bed, opened it, and saw a smaller box inside, on top of the record books. In it were two flashlights with a short note: "In case these are helpful." He pulled out one of the flashlights, tried it successfully, and put both of them on a table next to the bed. Then he removed the small box and pulled out the first book underneath it. It was labeled, 'Basement: Palace Guard Short Term Storage Room.' There was another note attached to it: "Walid, you don't have to inventory this one. But it's where the Adi boxes are and it's just a few feet away from the other rooms. A key is in the book, like the others. Protect all the keys. Your Uncle."

The next book below it was labeled 'Basement: Storage Room One.' The prince lifted it up as well. Under it was 'Basement: Storage Room Two.' By the size of the record books and the depth of the box, there could be a dozen or more rooms represented here.

A sense of adventure slowly overtook the prince. And he thought to himself, "I wonder what in the world is in all these rooms."

They would likely have to check the Palace Guard Short Term Room first to satisfy Mafulla's curiosity about the boxes from his parents' shop. He might make a lot of crazy jokes about being a genius up to a point, and having magic available when needed, but he did often have a strangely powerful sense for things. And so, his concern about the boxes might be a sign of something important, just like the weird birthday stuff that probably isn't a sign, but maybe is. You never know with Mafulla. Jokes and silliness can easily mask something very interesting and serious going on beneath the surface, something that could be powerful and shouldn't be dismissed. The king clearly saw something in Mafulla, too, from the very beginning, since the day of his introduction to the palace. And the king knows people pretty well.

Walid then realized that he felt extra tired and put the box and the books on the floor and lay down on his bed. He picked up his diary, a small notebook he often wrote in, and made a quick entry for the day, jotting down only a few sentences. Then he put it back on the table beside his bed and rolled onto his back, closed his eyes, and went limp all over.

In the midst of his exhaustion, his brain started swimming with little mysteries and facts that didn't seem to really go anywhere: The golden ratio, Reverso watches, the letter Phi, that guy Fibonacci, Aristotle's reasoning about virtue and courage, and the other Ari, the guy who would probably be really mad about his secret crime operation being broken up at the Adi store. He thought about his parents here in the palace and how glad he was to see them. Then there were those boxes and their secrets, and Mafulla's mysterious letter tonight from his mom, and all these storage rooms, and the girl Kissa, the beautiful girl Kissa, daughter of Khalid, here in the palace for school, but at the same time seeming so far away. And there was the secret identity idea, and something about Masoon, something that can't quite be named yet, but maybe something like unfinished business with him, and maybe Hamid. And, surely, one empty chamber, not two, is enough for proper gun safety.

And, finally, with a few other ragged realizations, the

thoughts slowed, and time itself bogged down a bit, and the gaps between the thoughts grew longer. Then Walid's consciousness was reduced like someone turning down a volume control on a radio, and it was all shushed and silenced into the needed quiet of deep, sound sleep where the thought beyond thought could happen and maybe start to make sense of it all.

13

Pieces of a Puzzle

Relationships rule the world. We can do things together that we could never accomplish alone. People who forget this reduce the circle of their potential impact. Those who remember this truth and act on it expand their influence. Mafulla was sitting in class thinking about all his new relationships, with Walid, and the king, and some of the other men and boys he had recently met, when he suddenly realized that Khalid was talking, and he instinctively looked up at him.

"So, all of that having been said, this is the question: If A is greater than B, and B is greater than C, then what's the relationship between A and C?" Khalid turned and looked at one particular face in the room.

"Mafulla."

"What? Oh. Ok. Let me think for a second."

"That's fine. Just tell me what you know, or take the time to think it out. If A is greater than B, and B is greater than C, then what's the relationship between A and C? It should be simple."

All the boys smiled and snuck glances at each other, except Walid, who alone seemed to have an expectant, curious look on his face as he gazed over at Mafulla who, now it seemed, was ready to answer. "Um, Ok. I remember what the book said. But it seems to me that A can be greater than B, and B can be greater than C, and yet there could be no relationship at all between A and C, since maybe they've never met, or if they have, it could be that A is just not interested in C at all. Or maybe they did meet and C was rude and A got mad, and so they have nothing to do with each other."

Most of the boys snickered. Hamid's son Malik caught Mafulla's eye and gave him a thumbs up. It was a good thing that Khalid was a relaxed, easygoing teacher, understanding, and positive. He said, simply, "Very funny." Khalid then glanced at all the other boys and looked back at the comedian. "Now, think logically. A is greater than B. B is greater than C. What can we conclude about A and C?"

"Other than being among the letters most picked on by math and logic books?" Muffled laughter around the room was followed by a serious look from Khalid. Mafulla changed his expression and replied, "Ok. Sorry. I know what I'm supposed to say: A is greater than C. But I really think it all depends."

"What do you mean?"

"A could be greater than B in one way, like in size, and B could be greater than C is some other way, like, value or cost, and we wouldn't know from that information by itself how A and C relate to each other in either size or cost, or any other way."

"This is unexpected, well said, original, and completely correct." Their teacher was clearly impressed.

The boys in the class now looked blank, except Walid, who was smiling and nodding his head. Khalid continued on.

"In order to derive the math book's expected conclusion that A is greater than C from the information I just gave, we have to hold steady the way, or respect, in which the items are being compared. There has to be a uniform scale or standard of comparison. Mafulla, your answer shows me you're really thinking today, even with your little misadventures in what could have been an attempt at humor. When we're doing simple mathematics, a uniform scale of comparison is typically assumed, and that's true in the book we're using. But in life, it can be dangerous to make too many assumptions."

"Why is it dangerous?" Walid asked right away.

Khalid smiled broadly and sat down on the edge of his desk. "Ah. Good question. First of all, look: we have to make assumptions in life, all the time." He turned to the largest boy in the class and said, "Bafur, did you know for sure that I would be here today if you got up out of bed, got dressed, and came to class?"

Bafur was caught off guard by the question and looked a little confused. But he said, "Well, you're always here on class days. I guess I just assumed you'd be here today."

"Yes. Absolutely. We assume things all the time. And that's fine. We must. We just don't have time to establish everything by evidence and explicit reasoning. And we couldn't anyway, even if we had the time and energy. We assume that the basic laws of nature will operate tomorrow, and even later today, like they have in the past. We can't prove it. But we have to assume it."

At this point, several of the boys seemed puzzled.

Khalid continued. "Most of life would be impossible without assumptions. Walid, when you get up in the morning and look at your watch to check the time, you assume that the watch is running normally and so you trust the time it indicates. But you can't know that someone didn't sneak into your room in the middle of the night while you were sleeping and reset the hands of the watch by an hour or two. And yet, when you glance at your watch to check the time in the morning, you just assume that no such thing has happened, without even thinking about it. You get up and get moving, sure that you know the time. You're certainly justified in most circumstances in making such assumptions. It would be crazy to go around really doubting and questioning everything. There are not many things we have to do in life, in order to live. But there are a few. We have to breathe, eat, and drink water. And, in addition, we have to make assumptions." He paused for a second.

"But sometimes, the making of assumptions is both illegitimate and dangerous. It's simply the result of laziness, haste, carelessness, or unjustified blind trust, and a failure of the will—a failure to summon and use the energy it takes to question and investigate." Khalid was clearly warming to the topic at this point.

"Pay attention to when you hear people use the word 'assume'—especially in its past tense: 'assumed.' You'll most often hear it come out of the mouths of people who have just made a big mistake based on false beliefs that they easily could have corrected with a little time, energy, and attention. They'll say, in protest, or in a vain effort to explain an error and excuse themselves from its consequences, 'I just assumed …'—and they often say this in a plaintive voice, as if they're merely innocent victims of a capricious reality that betrayed their simple trust. But to almost everyone listening to them, the question will occur instantly, 'Why did you just assume and not check?' We know that appearances don't reliably give us realities. People don't always do what they say they'll do, or what we think they'll do. Things aren't often the way we imagine they should be." Khalid looked from face to face. Then he concluded, with one parting shot.

"Those who don't go to the trouble to check something they're taking for granted, and basing important actions on, often end up saying, 'But I just assumed ...' and by then, they're usually not the only ones who wish they had been more careful."

Masoon's son Haji said, "But, Khalid, how can we know when it's fine to make an assumption, and when it's just lazy, or even dangerous? I think that's what Walid's really asking."

"Ah. This is why we need wisdom, or the skills of life discernment. There's no universal rule that's easy to apply here, except this: Consider how much is at stake. When you're basing an action on an assumption, ask the question, 'Is it safe to assume this?' Think about the potential cost of your assumption. Ask yourself: 'What will be lost in case I'm wrong?' If the stakes are high, if the risks are too great, then double check rather than assuming. Triple check. Spend the time and energy to make sure you aren't taking for granted something that's really false. That's the path of prudence. A foolish assumption is the doorway to disaster."

Khalid paused and said, "This is our philosophical lesson for the day. Allow me to repeat it for your edification and personal growth. A foolish assumption is the doorway to disaster."

The boys sat looking at Khalid. And he said, "Haji, what's a foolish assumption?"

"The doorway to disaster?"

"Yes."

"Mafulla, what's a foolish assumption?"

"The wide open, devilishly deceptive doorway to disaster."

"Good. Remember this. Don't make foolish assumptions.

Prudence takes the time to check vital beliefs before moving forward."

Walid recalled hearing the word 'prudence' recently. It was when the king was talking about courage and how we need to be guided by a sense of all the values that are at stake in a situation. What Khalid was telling them about now seemed to be related in interesting ways.

Walid spoke up again. "Khalid, I recently had a conversation with my uncle where he was describing what courage is, and he said that to be genuinely brave, you have to be guided by prudence. I guess that when you're trying to do the right thing, you can go wrong by making too many assumptions about the situation you're in, assumptions that can turn out not to be true, and then you end up with a mess or even a disaster. As a result, you can wind up not being brave but foolish."

"That's a very good point, Walid. Prudence is an important feature of the path of wisdom in life. I wish we were all born into the world wearing an expandable wristband that had printed on it the words: 'Proceed Boldly But With Caution.' That simple rule of conduct is a key to life. It often means questioning, investigating, and double checking beliefs."

He then looked around the class and said, "In the basic math or logic problem I was posing to Mafulla, the problem concerning the 'greater than' relation, he pointed out to us that without making certain assumptions, the question could not be answered. In life, especially in situations of uncertainty and risk, we have to be careful about what assumptions we make. But in class, I think it's … safe to assume right now—that it's time to get back to our math lesson!"

Khalid did this sort of thing now and then. Someone would ask a question and he would launch into a philosophical response that was pretty interesting. And it was often something that Walid and Mafulla needed to ponder. But eventually, he always pulled the discussion back to the lesson plan and whatever book they were studying.

The rest of class went on normally after that. Mafulla, in characteristic form, made a few more of his creative jokes along the way, but nothing that derailed the lessons or got Khalid off on any more of his big tangents. The boys were concentrating well and their work, as a result, was flowing. The time really flew by.

Before they knew it, class was dismissed for the day and Walid and Mafulla were on their way back to their private quarters. Their plan was to collect a couple of the storage room record books and go start their new job of taking inventory in the mysterious basement area where stuff had been stashed away, likely for years. They were both experiencing a glimmer of curiosity about what they might find there.

They first stopped in to the royal residence area's smallest dining room to get a snack, then kicked a ball up and down the long hallway outside it a few times. After that, they went to Walid's room, picked up three of the storage room record books, and put them into a bag along with the two flashlights the king had given them. On their way out, Walid asked the nearest staff member for directions, a younger man they hadn't seen before, and told him what they were off to do. He provided them with a clear description of how to get to the basement door, and they headed off on their first official assignment from the king.

First, they had to go down the nearest flight of stairs to get to the main floor, then along three consecutive hallways that seemed to go on forever. Finally, they arrived at a large, dark wooden door with an old brass plaque on it that said,

"Basement Stairs." Mafulla looked at Walid, made a face, and said in a mock-dramatic, spooky voice, "The Doorway to Disaster."

The prince laughed. "Khalid used that phrase in class today."

"Yeah, when talking about foolish assumptions," Mafulla replied.

Walid said, "I think we're completely reasonable in assuming that the basement of the palace is a perfectly safe place to go. We're on orders to work there, after all."

Mafulla looked comically dubious, and made a universally symbolic bow and sweeping hand gesture that communicated exactly what his accompanying words said. "After you, then, my good friend. I assume you'll be fine leading the way."

Walid opened the door and they both saw that it led to a very short stretch of hall at whose far end was a long staircase that descended into a dimmer light. The prince took a step forward and then held the door for Mafulla, who said in a hushed but overly dramatic voice, "Well, here goes nothing! The Golden Viper and his faithful sidekick Windstorm prepare to descend the mysterious stairs to new discovery and great adventure."

"Ha!" Walid had not thought about those new names all day, and had to laugh as soon as he heard them. He said, "Let the great adventure begin!" He then saw a light switch on the wall, flipped it, and a string of electric lanterns flickered on to provide extra illumination for the stairway. He took hold of a dark, old hand railing and began to walk down the wide staircase. They could already see that the basement was a big place with a high ceiling that had multiple corridors off a main open area, and many doorways stretching down along the halls.

But then Walid suddenly stopped. He froze in position and whispered, "Wait. Do you hear anything?"

"Yes. I do." Mafulla whispered back with a very serious expression on his face. "The sound of you whispering."

"No, crazy man, downstairs."

"I didn't hear anything."

"Oh. Ok. I thought I did." Walid turned and began walking down the stairs again, but more slowly and carefully, with his full attention available for any slight sounds that might be heard.

They got to the end of the stairs and something felt strange. Walid announced in a firm voice, "If there's anyone down here, I'm Walid Shabeezar, and Mafulla Adi is with me to do some work."

"Oh, good!" A voice came from around a corner. And so did Haji and Malik, each of them holding what looked like a dark colored ball in one hand. "Nice arrival announcement. Very professional. Complete, and courteous, even." Haji smiled.

"What are you guys doing down here?" Walid asked in a surprised tone of voice.

"Shh. Not so loud." Malik answered. "This is where we sneak away to play bocce ball when it's a little too hot outside. Come, see."

Walid and Mafulla followed the boys around a corner and there, in a hallway stretched out in front of them, were two lighted lanterns and several thick and beautiful Persian rugs lining the hard tile floor, pulled up against each other. There was a small ball, and also several larger balls, clustered on the rug farthest away from where they now stood.

"What's bocce ball?" Walid asked.

"It's a game from ancient times. You roll that little ball, the pallina, and then try to roll the other balls as close as you can get to it." Malik explained this much, briefly, and then basically ran through all the main rules.

Haji said, "Come on, let's do a game together as teams of two. You and Mafulla against me and Malik."

Walid said, "That would be great, but we have a lot of work to do down here that my uncle gave us, so can we just do a few practice rolls today? You can show us how. We'll challenge you guys next time. But we're really in a rush to get started with the work, so we don't get in trouble."

"What work are you doing in the basement?" Malik was curious.

"Just boring stuff with record books and some old storage rooms."

"Oh, Ok. We'll do a few rolls and let you guys get to work. We were going to leave in a few minutes anyway. Walid, you roll for me, and Mafulla, you roll for Haji."

They had fun doing this for about ten minutes, and then Walid excused the two of them, to get to work. They found Storage Room One, got out the record book for it, unlocked the door, entered, and saw boxes and boxes of large, industrial looking kitchen pots, pans, baking dishes, serving platters, tableware and other things that might be used for cooking and serving meals at palace banquets.

Suddenly, Mafulla remembered something, and spoke to Walid in a low voice. "I thought we were going to start in the Palace Guard Storage Room. You know, to look at the boxes from my dad's store."

"Yeah, we were. But maybe it's a good idea to wait for Malik and Haji to leave before we open that one up," Walid replied.

"Oh, good idea. We can go in there once we have no back-up."

"That's not what I mean," Walid said.

Mafulla pointed out, "You know, they're both pretty strong."

Walid raised his hands, palms up, and said, "The guards didn't put the bad guys into the storage room, just the boxes of their stuff."

"Ok. Whatever you say, GV."

"GV? Oh, Golden Viper. Thanks, Gutsy Gusty."

"Jeepers! Nice one. Gutsy Gusty. Two words, same letters, different order, with perfect meanings for your little bit of sardonic humor."

"Thanks. And I'm just as impressed with 'sardonic,' old friend."

The boys then got to work in the first storage room, checking the record books which, fortunately, recorded just the overall number of boxes in the room and the general nature of their contents, but not individual items. They glanced over the list: Boxes 1-5, Serving Platters. Boxes 6-14, Plates. Boxes 15-25, Pots and Pans. Both boys were totally relieved. Most of the boxes were either open or unsealed, so doing their job would be easy. If they had been given an item-by-item inventory to check, and there were lots of boxes to unseal and open, that could have taken weeks or months, with all the rooms they would have to go through. So this whole job might go much more quickly than they had initially thought. That meant less money, of course, but lots more free time. And that was a pretty decent trade-off for these two, a truly welcome result.

Walid looked up from the first book. "The record book says there should be 34 large boxes in here. It looks like the boxes are all numbered on their sides. So I guess we can do our job by counting the boxes, checking the numbers, and eyeballing the contents of each one, to see if they contain the stuff the record says they contain." It sounded like a good plan. Mafulla agreed and they got to work. Before long, everything in the room checked out.

There was an internal door on the right wall of the storage room. Mafulla jiggled the handle and it opened into an adjoining room that looked pretty much the same as the one they were in, but with more boxes all over the place. "This must be Storage Room Two," he surmised. "How many boxes does the record book say it should have?" He asked the question as he stepped into the darker space, illuminated only by the light from Storage Room One.

Walid took the second record book out of his bag, putting back the first one. He followed his friend up to the doorway, and opened the book to its first page. He squinted and answered. "It says here that there should be 55 boxes of office supplies in this room."

"Uh, oh."

"What do you mean, Uh, oh?" Walid tensed up and snapped on a light switch for the second room, which he had just noticed was located right outside the door frame. Brighter, but still dim, light illuminated the new space. "What is it? What do you see?" Walid whispered.

"No, I just see more boxes, but the number you gave me sort of surprised me."

"What number?"

"55."

"Why?"

"We just inspected Room One with 34 boxes. Now we're apparently in Room Two, with 55 boxes—and those are sequential Fibonacci numbers: 34, 55."

"Oh. Ok. I'm still amazed that you remember this stuff, but it's surely just a coincidence."

"Wait, there's another door."

"We didn't bring the record book or the key for Room Three."

"We didn't need a key to get in here just now. The inside doors may not be locked—just the outside ones. Let me try the handle."

"I'm not sure about this."

"Why? We have all the keys back at your room. We're supposed to inventory all the storage rooms. We'll just look into this one right now and do the inventory work on it tomorrow."

"Ok. I guess."

"Don't be a worry wart. The fate of the world as we know it may hang in the balance here." Walid shook his head while Mafulla walked across to the next side door and turned the knob. It seemed locked, or at least stuck. He tried it again, and shoved his shoulder against it. Then, with a pop, it creaked open loudly. He quickly said, "I didn't break it."

Slowly pushing the door ajar, he peeked into the room beyond it, and then opened the door more widely. This room was clearly bigger and there were lots and lots of boxes. Driven by curiosity and a kind of strange sense that there was something going on, he said, "Flip the light." Walid did, and Mafulla quickly started looking over the boxes. "40, 41, 43—wait, there's 42—44, 45." He continued counting out loud and moved on to a separate stack of boxes that were closer to the back. Walid stepped farther into the room and just listened. Mafulla's counting became even quicker and more mumbled.

"What are you doing?"

"Just a second."

"83, 84, 85, 86, 87, 88. Wait."

"What?"

"There's no 89."

"What do you mean?"

"The first two storage rooms contained the exact numbers of boxes that are sequential numbers in the Fibonacci series, 34 and 55. The next Fibonacci number is 89. Add 34 and 55 and you get 89. This room should have 89 boxes, but there are only 88."

"Well, that could just mean the numbers in the first two rooms are a simple coincidence, like I said. If this room had 89 boxes, then, Ok, that would be maybe too much for just a coincidence. But it doesn't. 88 isn't a Fibonacci number if 89 is—right?"

"Right."

"So there's no bizarre stuff going on here after all."

"Yes, there is, and it's even more strange. The Box Number 89 is mysteriously missing." Mafulla nodded his head, wagged his index finger in the air, and spoke with complete confidence.

"Come on. You're really getting carried away with this. How do you know there even is a Box 89?"

"There's one way to find out for sure." Mafulla strode across the room to the next interior door and grabbed it so hard he practically pushed the knob out of the wood. He swung this door open with another loud creak, flicked on the light switch, and entered the room quickly.

"Are you going to count boxes again? It looks like there's really a lot in this room. It's way bigger."

"Give me a minute, would you? Genius, even genius up to a point, has its needs. You should know. You're in the club. Just don't blow your membership now. I can simplify this." He disappeared behind a stack of boxes in the new room and started looking over even more, this time stacked high in rows through the room. He didn't even try to count aloud. He looked at the written numbers on each box and followed the rows to get to the highest numbers. Walid just stood in the doorway, waiting.

"Oh, man. I was right." Mafulla called out from the back corner of the room. He walked quickly back toward Walid. "I was right!"

"What do you mean?"

He pointed toward the back. "There are 144 numbered boxes in this room—exactly 144. I saw the highest numbered box, and it had on the side the number 144. There's no 145. And it didn't stop at 143 or lower. But 144, my friend, is the next Fibonacci number after 89. 55 plus 89 is 144. This series of rooms contains boxes stored on purpose in a Fibonacci sequence arrangement. And there's exactly one box missing from Room Three. We now know that."

"Well, maybe we don't actually, for sure, know it. But I'm starting to think that, yeah, you might be right. You could be onto something."

"Thank you."

"But, come on, even if you are right, then, so what?"

"What do you mean, so what?"

"What's the big deal? We expected some boxes to be missing, or at least mislabeled, right? That's the whole point of an inventory, to find out what's here and what's not, and then write it all down."

"But you're missing my main point, and my secondary, almost main point."

"Which is what?"

"Something very strange is going on. So far, it looks like there's just one box missing—one, single, missing box that interrupts a well known mathematical sequence, the sequence related to Phi, to the proportions of this palace, the Great Pyramid, our watches, and, remember, it also contains your specific birthday."

Mafulla stopped mid-thought. Then he continued, "You can know that something's going on without knowing what it is."

"I guess."

"It's just very strange that the storage rooms are arranged in this odd series. And it's every bit as strange that one box is missing."

"Well, maybe you're right. But where's the missing box and why is it missing?"

"When we discover that, this puzzle will start coming together." Mafulla was sounding more and more sure of himself.

Walid was thunderstruck. He said, "The Palace Guard Storage Room! We have to go there, now!" Mafulla instantly knew he was right.

The boys quickly retraced their steps through all the inner doorways, closing the doors, and going back to Room One, then leaving through its outside door and locking it back up carefully. They looked around. They were at the beginning of a long hallway. All the doors they could see seemed to be sequentially numbered storage rooms.

Mafulla said, "Let's go back closer to the stairs. I'm guessing the palace guards don't want a long walk when they bring something down here for temporary or short-term storage. And they'd likely be the ones to have first dibs on convenience."

"Smart."

Walid led the way. Back near the staircase, they went into

a closer hall and there it was. The plaque on the door said, Palace Guard Storage Room. Walid took out the matching book, removed the key from its front pocket, and opened the lock on the door. Right inside was a light switch. This room was the biggest yet. There were long walls of crates and boxes under some sort of rope mesh. And there were many others that weren't covered. Over to the left, up against the wall, were all the boxes from Mr. Adi's shop. There was a simple sign taped onto one: 'Adi.' Walid and Mafulla spotted it right away.

The first two boxes were open. One was full of knives, military looking knives of the sort that might be used for general purposes and even in battle. Each was in a holder. "That's a lot of knives." Mafulla marveled at the contents of the box. The second box contained revolvers, again looking like they were military issue. Most of these were in holsters, some not. And there were a lot of them, too.

The boys looked at nearly twenty more large boxes of stuff that had not yet been opened. The king said it was fine, so they got to work, pulling back sealed flaps. Most of the thick sided cardboard boxes were just an outer wrapping for wooden crates inside them, crates that were strong enough to hold heavier contents.

Mafulla said, "No wonder they had a big guy moving these boxes. Some of them are really heavy. He must have had a few on rolling pallets, or something—I don't remember noticing—and, even then, they'd be hard for one guy to handle."

Walid answered, "Well, he was kind of an ox."

"Yeah, true."

Mafulla had been trying to move one of the larger boxes and was obviously having a little trouble.

Walid noticed and smiled. "Wait. Is there something that can't be moved by a powerful desert Windstorm?" In response, Mafulla made a ridiculous muscle with his skinny left arm. He was doing a sort of bodybuilder pose, and Walid had to laugh out loud.

"Ok, stop commenting and giggling and help out here." Mafulla pointed a finger at Walid, and right away he got to work. They pulled back the box flaps, and peered through the sides of crates. They went through six boxes of rifles, several more crates of ammunition held in metal boxes stacked inside, and then a few containers of ammunition belts. There were even more knives and revolvers. After going through the first few boxes, the boys had realized that there were identifying abbreviations on the outsides of most of them, so you could know what contents to expect.

Walid paused and said, "Were these guys going to start their own war?"

"Maybe. But it could easily be that they were just buying and selling this stuff, or stealing and selling it— for a bit more profit. Maybe they were gun runners, among, I'm sure, many other unsavory things. I bet all this stuff's worth a lot of money."

Walid thought for a second and said, "I'm guessing that the Ari guy is really mad about losing it."

Mafulla said, "I would be. I mean, if I were a criminal."

"And so it's safe to assume he wants to get it back like crazy."

"Yeah. Good bet. I just hope he doesn't think my mom can help."

"What?"

"You know, her note about the neighborhood?"

"Oh, yeah."

They had asked the king that morning at breakfast about whether anyone was watching Mafulla's house. The king had said that, yes, there was a house across the street from his home and down the road a very short distance, but still well within sight, where small teams of palace guards were taking turns on duty to watch over the Adi family home and the neighborhood more generally. Mafulla showed the king the note his mother had sent to him, and Ali promised he'd have his men look into the situation right away.

Walid said, "I hope your family can stay out of that Ari guy's mess from now on. They've been through too much already."

"Yeah, I hope so, too." Mafulla then changed the subject back to the business at hand. "Well, we've got just a few boxes to go."

"You're right. Let's get to it." The next box they examined had 'Rev' on the outside, for revolvers, and another had 'DGR:HND-GRN' on the outside. Opening it, they saw the word 'DANGER' in red paint all over the wooden crate inside the box, and in black the words 'Explosive Grenades' were stamped every six inches or so along the boards.

"Ok, let's not touch this one any more," Walid advised.

"Good idea," Mafulla said. "I'm not in the mood to blow up today." He gazed around their immediate area and added, "There's just one more box left. And look at this." He pointed.

"What?"

He then bent down and looked more closely. "The end where most of these have been labeled has had its own marking scratched off or something."

"Yeah, I can see what you mean."

"But the other side is up against the wall where there still might be some indication of what's inside."

"You're right."

"So, if we can push it very gently away from the wall, maybe we can still find out the safe way what's in it. At this point, I'd rather have some idea of what's there before just opening it up."

Walid replied, "Or we could just quit now and leave it alone. This isn't one of the rooms we have to inventory."

Mafulla scrunched up his face and said, "No. We've gotten this far. I think we should at least try to find out what's in this last one."

"Ok. If you're still curious."

"Let's move it out just a little bit so we can see if there's anything written on the other side. But let's do it carefully." Walid was concerned, but he moved into a better position to help.

They grabbed the box by its sides and started to slide it around. And that led to a first surprise. It didn't feel nearly as heavy as most of the others. It was almost light by comparison.

"Ok, this is strange." Walid was bending over and looking at the end of the box that had just been pulled away from the storage room wall.

"What?"

"Where we've been seeing abbreviations that sort of make sense, there are just two English letters and a space."

"Let me see." Mafulla moved into position, as Walid stood up and stepped back. He bent over, then squatted, and twisted a bit to look.

"Oh my. My, oh my." Mafulla stood up and turned to Walid, and looked like he had just seen a ghost.

"What is it? I just saw the letter Y, and on its right a space with an underline mark, and then the letter X."

Mafulla said, "Do you know what that is?"

Walid looked puzzled. "Well, in the English alphabet, X usually comes before Y, in the normal alphabetical sequence, and there's nothing in between. Here, X and Y are reversed and there's a blank space in between, with a low underline mark, like something's supposed to be there. What does that mean? Y space X—what could this possibly stand for?"

Mafulla said, "It's from the Greek alphabet. They're not English letters."

"What do you mean?"

"I looked it up and studied it after your uncle told us about Phi and gave us our watches."

"You looked what up?"

"The Greek alphabet."

"Really?"

"Yeah. The next day I was staring at the Phi symbol on the back of my watch and got inspired to do a little research. These are Greek letters, the letter Upsilon, the one that when capitalized looks like a Y, and the letter Chi, which in its English representation is spelled with a 'Ch' but it's pronounced like it's a 'K,' followed by 'eye' and it's the letter that looks like an X."

"How do you know all this?"

"I love languages, among many other delights. And here's the thing. In the standard sequence of the Greek alphabet, there's a letter in between Upsilon and Chi, and it's the letter that goes in the empty space where the underlining is."

"What is it? What's the letter?"

"Well, that's where things are suddenly sort of scary-strange."

"Why? What do you mean?"

"The letter is Phi. You know, the one that Rhymes with My-Oh-My."

"No way. You're kidding me."

"Nope."

"So you're saying that this box is indirectly marked with a Greek Phi, but in such a way that no one will understand it who doesn't know the Greek alphabet?"

"That's exactly it, my friend. So after we take a moment to get over being weirded out to a major degree, we need to open it, now."

"Ok. But it is kind of spooky at this point, I have to admit."

The boys gently tore back the cardboard flaps and, rather than seeing either military stuff or a wooden crate inside, they just saw another, smaller cardboard box. Mafulla stopped and said, "I have a feeling we'd better pull this inner box out and set it on the floor."

"Why?" As soon as Walid asked, he corrected himself and said, "I mean, Ok." They both bent over and together lifted out the inner box and set it down gently. Walid closed the flaps on the outer box, and as he did, he noticed a small wooden platform on the bottom of this larger box, on which the small inner one had been sitting.

On the outside of the inner box, instead of abbreviations or Greek letters, there was a simple, written inventory designation like all the ones they had seen in the regular, numbered storage rooms. It was the number, printed by hand, 89.

Mafulla said, "Yes! There it is. You see? This is the missing box I was so sure about. Like I said, all the boxes in all the other storage rooms we just saw were inventoried in numbers that match the Fibonacci series. This is the one box that wasn't where it was supposed to be. And now it's here, and it's been put into another box that's labeled with a nonexistent

Greek Phi." Mafulla looked exuberant and tired and worried at the same time as he said this.

Walid replied, "I guess we have to find out what's inside."

"Yeah, we really do."

"Ok. Here we go."

14

A Big Discovery

Walid opened the flaps of the box, which had been sealed with a light glue. He pulled them back, and what he saw surprised him again: another even smaller box inside. This one was made of solid, light colored wood that was highly polished with a beautiful finish.

"Chinese boxes."

"What?" Mafulla said.

"A box inside a box inside a box. That's called Chinese boxes and I have no idea why." Walid looked around the room quickly and said, "Here, let's pull the outer box over to near that desk across the room and lift out the wooden box onto the desk."

"Ok." They moved the cardboard box over to where Walid had indicated, and picked up the wooden box from inside it.

"Hey, go close the original box, the one with the Greek letters."

"Why?

"I don't know."

"Ok, then. Will do." Mafulla walked back over to the big group of boxes and closed up the larger one that had contained box 89. He then returned and saw that the wooden box was already out on the desk.

"This one has a lock on it," Walid said.

Mafulla moved to get closer to it and bent over to examine what Walid had just seen. "It's a combination lock. I mean, that's what we call it, but it should be called a permutation lock."

"You always surprise me with these odd factoids."

"What can I say? I get around. A combination is any group of numbers in any order. A permutation is a group in one particular order. This lock requires an entry of three two-digit numbers, clicked into place with your thumb. See? It's set on all zeros right now."

"Yeah. I see."

"If you get the right numbers entered in the right order, the lock will open. But otherwise, not."

"What three numbers?"

"Who knows? But, I'd try your birthday."

"Why?"

"What can I say? I just have a feeling."

Walid then took hold of the lock and carefully clicked into place 08-13-21, and then pulled on it.

Click.

Mafulla smiled. "The last time I heard a click, it was a gun not working. Now, this one is a lock, working. I like this one better." The lock had come open.

"Seriously. How did you know that would be the combination?"

"I didn't, I don't think. But somebody used the Fibonacci series in the storage rooms and started with 34. So I just guessed the three numbers before that which, and here we get spooky again, happen to be your birthday and, voila!"

"Voila?"

"Yeah, French for something like: Look! See? Tada!" Mafulla gestured toward the box with both hands, accompanied by his now trademark double eyebrow jump.

"Amazing. So, do you want to open it?" Walid looked up at his friend.

"No, go ahead. You're the prince, the future king, and the one with the strange birthday numbers. I'm just the sidekick, and proud to serve the soon-to-be-famous Golden Viper."

"Ok, Storm, here goes." Walid took off the lock, set it on the desk top, and with both hands slowly began to lift up the wooden lid. Mafulla was leaning over from behind him and to the side in order to see. Just as the top was raised about an inch or less, there was a sudden noise outside the room and then a distinctive sound from the door knob behind them, another click that made Walid drop the lid and both boys jerk their heads around to look at the door that, since they entered the room, had been closed but not locked—until now.

Across town, something else was going on that might at first seem to have nothing to do with these developments in the palace basement. But a sequence of events was unfolding that would end up having major implications for that room, the basement, the palace, and the boys, as well as their king.

Faisul Arambi, the greedy traitor from the desert caravan, the camel train that had originally brought Walid to Cairo, had learned of the recent and sudden political revolution in the palace like everyone else, but with a personal sense of shock, panic, and foreboding, due to his recent actions. He didn't know that the letter he had stolen and delivered to palace officers was a falsified document meant to eliminate obstacles to Ali's plan of retaking the throne. He still didn't realize how his attempted betrayal of the Shabeezar family and their supporters had been prepared for and used by them to forward their own purposes. He had never thought for a moment that Ali could escape arrest by the previous king's army and be able to take power in the darkness of one night. The men Faisul had tried to sell into prison and likely execution for a bag of gold were now ruling the kingdom and he was in hiding, along with a disappointingly modest amount of gold and silver that had been the meager reward for his misinformation. He was terrified, frustrated, angry, and confused. He had been cheated, in his opinion, and to make it even worse, he was in great danger.

Faisul had paid the owner of a small house near the outskirts of the city to evict some tenants and let him stay in the home. He offered additional cash for the man to bring food to him at intervals so that he would not have to go out in public, at least for a time, and expose himself to the likely reprisals he feared he would face for his wicked and despicable actions. He had concocted a story about his need to stay inside for the sake of privacy and had now remained well hidden in his new surroundings since a mere three days after the late night revolution. Those initial days, he'd spent trembling in shadows, in basements, and using the crowds for cover in the marketplace, while wearing a cheap disguise. He'd not given his real name to his new landlord or to anyone else he'd met since the night of the unexpected palace takeover.

He had filled his days cursing his fate and mulling over his limited options, trying to decide what to do. Finally, he realized that the only safe avenue available to him was to leave the city and the kingdom as soon as possible. But he was a wanted man who could be recognized by many of King Ali's followers, as well as by some of the people who had been in the palace when he arrived on his errand of betrayal. So he knew he needed to stay hidden until he could gain help for escaping safely. Since he was now an outlaw, it seemed clear to him that he would need the help of others like him who knew how to evade the legal authorities and military power of the kingdom.

Faisul finally made some indirect inquiries to his landlord concerning how he might meet someone who "lives on the edge of the law, or independently of it," as he put it. He said he needed to make a connection for a friend and didn't know how, since he was only a recent visitor to the city and, he added, a law abiding citizen himself. The landlord nodded his head and told him that, for a price, such an introduction could be arranged. The price was then provided.

So, it was no surprise when there was a knock on his door a day later and a voice could be heard saying, "Mr. Arambi, your landlord asked me to come and see you in case I might be of service to your friend."

Faisul opened the door carefully. A man of relatively inde-terminate age stood in front of him. But the years had not been kind to him. He had badly yellowed teeth and a deep, long scar cut diagonally across his left cheek. His greasy hair was plastered to his head. A scraggly beard almost hid more scars on his jaw and chin. His clothing was dirty and stained. He had a long knife in his possession that was clearly visible and held in place slightly to his side with an old, darkly col-ored but faded belt.

"May I ask who you are?" Faisul was deeply intimidat-ed by the man's appearance and held the door open only a few inches, while bracing it from behind with his foot and shoulder.

"I'm the likely solution to your friend's problem, whatever it might be. I'm here to be of help. My name is of no concern. It might not be safe for you to know it."

"Safe for you, or for me?" Faisul asked.

The man just stared at him. A smile began to appear on his face and he said, in a near whisper, "If you will tell me what your friend needs, I'm sure I can respond and provide the help required."

Faisul thought for a second and then cautiously invited the man in and offered him tea. Cups in hand, they both sat and Faisul mustered the boldness to say, "I should be straight with you. I have the need. It's for me. I'm the only friend I have right now."

The man smiled in a knowing way. "Yes. What do you need?"

"I need a way to get out of the city and the kingdom as soon as possible, without being seen by any of the new king's men, or by anyone who recently served in the palace before the revolution. I sought to be of help to the past regime, to warn them of the revolt. It was for my own financial benefit that I intervened, I can assure you, but my efforts were ineffective. As a result, it would be unfortunate for me to come into contact with any government authorities, whether past or present."

"Assistance can be had for a price. I work for a man who has many connections and can make such things happen. I have a certain reputation in this part of the city, and that's why your landlord came to me. I can help you get started on the path it will take to leave the kingdom in the manner you suggest. But you need a network of assistance that goes far beyond what I alone could provide. I can put you in touch with some associates who together can guarantee your quiet, invisible, and safe departure from the city, as well as from the entire kingdom. No traces of your movements will be available for the authorities to pursue. We can wipe clean the entire trail of your exit and get you to a place where you can live well and without worry. We've done such a thing for others many times before."

"That's exactly what I need. I have only a modest payment that I received from the former regime for services rendered. They cheated me badly and gave me only a fraction of what I deserved, but I'm happy to draw from it to compensate you for your help."

The two men negotiated over a proper price, and Faisul finally agreed to hand over more of his recently acquired wealth than he had wanted to relinquish. But his situation was desperate enough and his life ultimately meant more to him than this treasure for which he had risked so much. He would make half of the payment then and there, which he did in gold and silver, to the great satisfaction of his visitor, and the other half when he had crossed the border of the kingdom. Everything was set. Or, so he thought.

The next day, there was another knock on the door.

"Who is it?"

"The answer to your problems." The response came in a melodious voice, but with the words spoken close to the door, at a low volume.

Faisul carefully cracked open the door. A man he had never seen was standing there, well dressed and almost professional looking. "Greetings." The man smiled. He spoke softly. "One of my local colleagues visited with you yesterday and told me that you have need of my services." There were three much larger men standing behind him and glancing about, all of them much better dressed and more presentable than Faisul's visitor on the previous day. But they still looked like criminals, which is exactly what they were. The man spoke again. "I'm here to finalize the arrangements for you." He looked at Faisul with a reassuring smile once more on his face.

The crime boss, Ari Falma, did not usually involve himself directly in such small dealings. He preferred normally to keep out of the picture, not show his face, and let his lackeys do the work. But he wanted this man out of this house as soon as possible, because he had another and very important use in mind for the property. Plus, in light of recent financial losses that he had incurred, he wanted much more from this transaction than his hasty associate had been able to negotiate.

That man had gone back to see Faisul's landlord after his visit to the house the previous day, and had questioned him about his new mysterious renter. In the conversation that had then taken place, he discovered something he realized would be of great interest to Falma. The landlord told him that when Faisul initially approached him about a sudden house rental of indeterminate length, he was not at all inclined to help. He had one rental house whose contract would be up in a month, but the family in it would likely accept a new agreement at a higher rent and stay in the property. It was an old and established neighborhood. They had been good renters and he liked having them. But Faisul was desperate for a place to stay and he had to have something available in only a day or two, at most.

When the landlord had explained that he could not be of assistance, Faisul opened a bag that he was carrying to show the man what looked like a large, extremely valuable collection of rubies, emeralds, sapphires, and diamonds on one side, with some gold and silver on the other. He also intimated that there was more of this hidden away and that he could pay whatever was needed. The landlord liked what he saw and accepted the equivalent of six months' rent in advance, at the newer high rate, along with a deposit in an equal amount. He then gave his good tenants two days to move, basically enforcing this sudden eviction with a nice bribe and veiled threats.

Rumors about this turn of events caused a stir in the neighborhood, but Faisul's aim was accomplished and he was able to move in at the end of the second day, under the cover of dark. On hearing all this, Ari Falma's dirty associate with the menacing scar knew that his boss would be interested in the story, but especially in the part about the trove of jewels and precious metals the landlord had seen.

Faisul invited the men into his house, and fixed them all some tea, while passing around bread and figs. The room was only dimly lit from some sun coming through an open window. There was a bit of initial small talk about the weather and the neighborhood, and recent political events, during which Ari observed Faisul's face carefully.

"I have good news for you," Ari said as he sat down his cup and smiled again at his host. "There's a sensitive shipment of items that needs to go out of the kingdom soon, and I'll be able to accommodate your need for a departure in connection with this."

"How soon can it happen?"

"Well, very soon, we hope, but we're not sure. The items I need to transport are in storage, unfortunately, and access to them is for the moment difficult. But I'm working on a solution to that problem right now and should have my things relatively soon. When I do, they and you can leave."

"Do you have any idea how quickly it can happen and I can get out of here?" Faisul was nervous and wanted a clearer sense of time.

"I would like to say that it can take place within a few

days, most likely. But the only obstacle is that access to my property, under the present circumstances, will be expensive. And since it's only in association with the shipment of the property that your departure can be effected with all the privacy and protection you desire, you and I will just have to wait until I can gain access to more funds. And that may take a while."

"Is there anyone else who could help me sooner?"

"No. I can assure you of that."

"How expensive will it be to get your property?" This was the question, of course, that Ari was hoping to hear.

He said, "That's the problem I face. The person I'll have to pay in order to gain access to the items I need to send out of town will demand a large price, more than we have in our accounts right now. I will have to borrow the money. As soon as I get my things out of the kingdom and to their destination, I'll be given a huge settlement and can pay back the loan in full and still have a healthy profit for myself. But the only man who can lend us such an amount always demands jewels as security for a loan. He's an avid gemologist and a loan shark. Sadly, I have no jewels available now, for the first time ever. I've taken loans from this man many times in the past, and when I pay him, he always returns the jewels in perfect shape, or offers to buy some of them at good prices. But this time, I simply don't have what he needs. So there's no quick solution to our problem."

"Well, perhaps, I could be of help." Faisul was hesitant and didn't quite know what to say.

"No, I'm sure you can be of no help. You can't even leave this house. I don't know whether you're aware of it, but the king's men are looking for you everywhere and quite aggressively. You're their number one wanted man. So, this will have to be my problem." Ari could lie so smoothly and confidently that he could weave a web of deception around almost anyone. His fabrication here had been just what he needed and it immediately produced the result he intended. Faisul was clearly panicked and motivated to do almost anything to save himself.

He said, "Look, I knew I was in trouble but not that I was being hunted actively and even aggressively. I need to get out of here soon. I have a modest collection of jewels with me that might help. If I can be sure of getting them back, I'll offer them to you as the collateral or security for the loan you need."

"What do you have?"

"Please wait and let me get them." Faisul went into a back room, fished his bag out of hiding, and scooped up about half of the jewels, which he then put into another, smaller bag. It was this smaller sack that he brought into the front room.

"This is what I have. I hope they will be sufficient for your needs." Faisul spoke with a tremor in his voice as he handed the bag over to Ari and then sat back down.

Falma looked inside and was impressed. He plucked out a few of the gems, quickly examined them in the dim light, and put them back into the bag, closing it carefully. "These should do. I'll take this bag to our friend and obtain the necessary loan today. Then I'll be able to get the things I need out of storage and send you on your way. I think we can achieve all this within a few days, at most. Meanwhile, you stay well hidden here. We'll give you half a day's notice when we're almost ready to spirit you away from this dangerous and wretched place."

Faisul was greatly relieved and replied, "Thank you! I'll await your word." They all said their goodbyes, Ari made further reassurances, and the four men left quickly. Falma was extremely pleased with his little ruse and with the resultant treasure in the bag. To have heard what the landlord said about it, though, he expected even more jewels. But this was still impressive. As he turned to walk away, he allowed himself another smile at his own cleverness.

It's for good reason that we have the old saying, "There's no honor among thieves." People who act primarily from greed, and have no intrinsic respect for others or their property, can be trusted only to do and take care of what they think is in their own self-interest. They can deceive as easily as they breathe. But in many cases, they won't breathe as long as they might like, or as easily, as one party to this transaction was soon to discover.

In the palace basement storage room, Mafulla whispered to Walid, "Someone just locked us in here!"

"Should we call out and let them know we're in the room?" Walid asked quickly as he turned around and stood up.

"No, I think they know, and they're trying to keep us here."

"But, why?" Walid had a very concerned expression on his face.

Mafulla said, "Who knows? But we're locked in now. And it's a pretty familiar situation for you and me."

"True."

"Let's just hope it ends as well as the last time."

"Yeah." Walid looked around. "Let's see if there's an interior door, like in the numbered storage rooms." They left the mystery box closed on the desktop and Walid led the way along the far wall and toward the back of the large room. Behind a large pile of stacked boxes, they could just make out the edge of a door frame. Getting to work, they managed to move away all the boxes and gain access to the door which, like the others, was fortunately unlocked.

Walid led the way into another storage room like the first one, but this one looked like it had not been actively used in many years. There were boxes everywhere, but a musty smell announced that the room had been closed for quite some time. They tried the outer door of the room and found it was locked from the outside. Then, right away, they went back to the part of the room where all the other inner doors had been found. And once again, behind two stacks of boxes, they saw a door frame. This time, when they moved the boxes, they were surprised. This door was a bit different from the others, and had four dead-bolt locks on it, spaced a few inches apart, on their side.

"What do you think this is all about?" Mafulla asked.

"I have no idea," Walid said, while he began unlocking the deadbolts, from the top one to the bottom. He then turned the knob and pushed the door open. There were no locks on the other side. He stepped into the room. "Flip the light, Maffie."

Click. A dim glow showed them a room that was not primarily used for storage at all. It seemed to be a hub of plumbing and electrical work. The boys began examining it all around. The ceiling was covered by exposed pipes, with some hissing and clunking going on from inside them. It was warmer in here than in the other rooms, and by quite a bit. There were some small boxes of tools right inside the door. A few feet away was a short stack of pipes. And they could both see across the room that there was a door at the back unlike any of the ones they had seen before. It was a little wider and thicker. It was not wooden but was a heavy metal door with one large bolt lock on it. There was a big latch-style handle on it. "Should we try that door?" Mafulla spoke first.

"Why not? We've gotten this far." Walid was curious as to where this strange doorway might lead. So he walked back over to it. Mafulla stopped for a second to look at something else while the prince got to the door, undid the bolt, which was a little stuck at first, pulled on the handle, and opened it up slowly. He said, "Well, this is a surprise."

Mafulla looked over and said, "Let me see. What's that smell?" He quickly walked the few steps left to get to the opening. By the light of the mechanical room they were in, they could now both see for some distance beyond the door. "Oh, man."

"Yeah, very odd—a tunnel. And the air in it seems warmer."

Mafulla then said, "A tunnel underground should be cool. We must be near the furnace room or something."

Walid added, "And the musty dirt smell is really strong. I wonder what this is for. I wish we could see more. But, there's no light switch here."

Mafulla said, "It looks long."

"Yeah, it does. I want to find out why it's here and where it goes, but first we need to get out of here and figure out what's going on."

"We didn't check the outer door for this room. Let's see if it's locked."

"It may not be, and that could explain why there were so many dead-bolt locks on the other side of the internal door—so people can have access to this mechanical room from the hall without gaining access to the palace guard storage. If this room's outside door isn't locked, we won't have to try the tunnel, yet, to get out of here." Walid was thinking it all through.

Mafulla walked over to the outer door and turned the knob. Click. He pushed. Nothing. He pulled. The door groaned and opened inwardly, unlike all the exterior storage room doors. "It's unlocked!" He whispered enthusiastically. "Let's go."

"Great." Walid quickly came over.

But Mafulla stopped and said, "Wait. We left our bag with the inventory books and flashlights in the first guard storage room with the boxes. Should we go back and get them?"

"No. Whoever locked us in may still be around there. Let's try to get to the stairs without being seen."

"But we still don't know what's in that strange Phi box— the one that was inside Box 89."

"We'll find out later. We need to go tell Uncle Ali what's happened. Either somebody's pulled a big prank on us, or someone's up to no good."

"Those sound like overlapping categories to me. But I actually have a pretty bad feeling about this." Mafulla stepped aside to let Walid go out first and whispered, "Royalty before beauty."

The boys went through the door, closed it, and walked quietly and carefully down a long hallway, then another, and around a corner. They were moving in a direction away from the main stairs at first but they had figured out how to get back to them in a more indirect way. Finally, they caught sight of the stairway across the big open space right ahead of them. There was silence all around. Checking to make sure they weren't being observed, they crept at first across the exposed area and then quietly dashed up the stairs, making their exit through the "Doorway to Disaster" as fast as they could. Slamming it closed behind them, they started to jog down the hallway outside it and toward the royal residence.

"Boys!" A voice shouted out behind them.

Walid and Mafulla twisted around at the same time to

look back, while a jolt of adrenalin shot through their stomachs. They both stopped in their tracks.

"Khalid! What are you doing here?" Mafulla spoke first.

Walking toward them, he replied, "I was going to ask you the same question."

"What do you mean?" Walid said.

Khalid answered, "This is the part of the palace where my wife teaches the girls' classes—well, nearby, at least. I was visiting with her for a short time this afternoon to plan a special event. What brings you two into this area? It's usually more or less off-limits to the boys."

Walid quickly explained, "We were doing some inventory work for the king, at his request, down in the basement."

"Indeed?"

"Yeah. And now we need to get back right away to report to him. He's expecting us and we're almost late. If we aren't back on time, he'll likely send some palace guards to find us."

"Oh, well, you'd better be off, then! I don't want to interfere with the king's business and get the palace guards involved. I prefer to appreciate their work from a distance. I'll see you two later."

"Ok, see you tomorrow!"

"Yeah, see you tomorrow."

Khalid turned around and smiled.

The boys headed off at a brisk walk and, about thirty seconds later, Walid said to Mafulla in a near whisper, "What do you think Khalid was doing down here near the door?"

"I don't know, but it seems odd."

Walid said, "You think it's a coincidence?"

"No. Maybe. I'm not sure. No one else seems to be around."

"Strange."

15

ROYAL INTRIGUE

IT'S A GREAT ADVANTAGE IN LIFE TO HAVE A FAMILY member or good friend who shares with you both a history and a hope. Such people in our lives are precious and rare. With them, we can often feel a sense of solidarity and support. They can help and inspire us to create a life and a legacy worth our work. Without them, our existence on earth can be thin and hollow, however bright its fireworks might seem.

King Ali had now spent nearly the entire day with his brother Rumi and sister-in-law Bhati, catching up on nearly everything that had happened in their lives since the day the big caravan of camels, men, and goods had left their village with Walid along for the first time. They talked of the family and their old neighbors, the past and the present, and dreamed together about the future to come.

Rumi had good news. He had found another expert physician, a man he admired and could trust, to take over his practice in the village. The doctor had even agreed to continue free service for the poor, along with the paid work of his normal practice, as Rumi had provided for years. He and a friend of Hamid would go into practice together, so that Rumi and Bhati could stay in the capital with Ali and Walid. Bhati had closed up the house, but had decided to keep it as a retreat to be used as it might be needed, from time to time. Many of their important personal belongings had been carried with them to the capital. Other things would be brought soon.

Ali welcomed the good news. And in a matter of minutes, they had a plan. Rumi would serve as the royal physician in the palace, for the king and their family, as well as for the top administrators and their own families. He would also take the opportunity to launch some needed new health initiatives for the poor in the capital city and for the general population throughout the kingdom. The king's brother was keenly interested in nutrition, fitness, and the prevention of disease, but most of all, in the whole process of healthy living throughout all its facets.

Ali told Rumi and Bhati about some of his most personal goals for his new reign and for the kingdom in the days and years to come. He talked about the individual men he had appointed to positions of importance already, and mentioned others who would soon be given significant duties in the kingdom. He also spoke of those from the previous regime he had kept on, either because they had been true supporters of the rightful monarchy throughout the years, or at least in the recent time of change. And then there were others who, even though they had been employed by a corrupt administration and had never before known the Shabeezar family, still seemed to be good and highly skilled individuals with a noble sense of purpose that never fit in well with the previous king's policies. In fact, many of the people working in the palace who had not come with Ali on the camel train had been employed in various positions of importance by the previous monarch or else his top administrators, including the chief chef and his entire kitchen staff, who had been entrusted with big plans for two special dinners to be given this very evening.

After great conversation about people and ideas, Ali shared that one of his short-term goals for the evening ahead was to get Rumi and Bhati together with Mafulla's parents at a small dinner for the adults only. The boys would be treated to their own special feast in another dining room elsewhere in the palace, but not far away.

Straight from their adventure in the basement, Walid and Mafulla arrived at the king's office and asked the new young butler on duty if they could see him. He told them that the king was in an important meeting and would not likely be available until either later in the evening, or even the next morning. The butler didn't realize that the meeting in progress was with Walid's parents. He said he had just arrived in the king's personal quarters to give the head butler a break and was simply respecting the closed door and the quick explanation he was given that the king was in a long session and was not to be disturbed.

Walid said, "I remember you from earlier today. You gave me some directions I needed, but I'm afraid we've not yet been introduced. I'm Prince Walid. And there's something I must tell my uncle."

The butler bowed and seemed eager to be helpful. "If you'd like to write a short note, I'll get it to the king when I'm next called in to refresh drinks or bring snacks. I'm sure he'll get back to you as soon as it's possible." The man was smiling and yet standing in front of the closed door that led to the entry area of the king's private quarters as he spoke. He ushered the boys over to a nearby desk and produced some paper and a pen.

Walid was in a hurry to see the king and tell him about what had just happened, but he didn't want to interrupt any important business. So, while Mafulla chatted with the butler, he sat down quickly and wrote.

"Dear Uncle: Maffie and I went into the basement to start our inventory work and when we entered the guard room, we opened the boxes from Mr. Adi's store. Most contained weapons. One box was very strange, and had a surprising label on it. As we started to open it, someone locked us in the room. We escaped through adjoining rooms. And then on the first floor nearby, on our way out of the basement, Khalid called out to us. He said he was in that area of the palace visiting his wife. But we felt strange that we saw him in that part of the building so soon after being locked in the nearby room. There was absolutely no one else around. Can I talk to you about it, right away? I'll be in my room. Walid."

The prince folded the note, put it in an envelope, and wrote on the front, "King Ali, Urgent." He sealed it and gave it to the butler for delivery and explained, once again, "He needs to see this as soon as possible, please."

"Certainly, Your Highness," the butler replied, and bowed slightly, as he took it back to the desk.

The boys then both walked down the hall toward their rooms.

"You should have insisted on seeing the king now," Mafulla said. He was clearly worried. "You're royalty, too. The butler works for you."

"Sort of, I guess. But I don't want to interrupt something that shouldn't be interrupted. We're safe now. It can wait."

"Ok, but the sooner the better. And there's something strange about that butler guy. I got bad vibes from him."

Walid was a bit distracted, but he said, "What was strange?"

"I don't know. He sort of seemed phony in some way. But maybe I've just got the jitters."

They were getting close to Walid's room. The prince said, "Maffie, go get your books from your room and come back to mine and we'll do our homework together before dinner. We'll probably get to talk to the king then."

Mafulla said, "Will do. It's a plan. But after all that time in the basement, I have to go to the bathroom. So, I'll hit the water closet first, then be back here in less than five."

Walid went into his room and saw on the bed a large white engraved envelope. On the front, it said simply, "Prince Walid Shabeezar." He opened it and inside, in a beautiful script in a rich black ink, he read, "You are invited to a banquet to be held this evening in your honor. Please dress for a special occasion and expect company. The dinner will begin at 7:00 PM in The Dining Room off the Main Library." In a contrasting bright blue fountain pen ink, there was also some familiar handwriting beneath that said, "I'm having dinner tonight with your parents and Mafulla's parents, to introduce them. I've had this special dinner prepared for you boys. There will be a nice surprise there for you. I'll see you after it. Uncle Ali."

There was a knock at the door. "Come in."

"Yeah. So." Mafulla entered with a similar invitation in his hand. He showed it to Walid. "What's this?"

"An official invitation to dinner. I didn't know anything about it. I just opened mine."

Mafulla looked back down at his. "It sounds good. I hope the nice surprise is dancing girls."

"You would. But, look, we'd better get to work right now. We don't have long, especially since, I suppose, we'll have to bathe and put on our best clothes for the dinner."

"Have you ever seen The Dining Room off the Main Library?"

"Yeah, briefly one day, and the table is so big it can seat maybe twenty people. Or more. And there's a lot of room around the table."

"For the dancing girls, I hope." Mafulla smiled as he said this and did a little belly dance move that cracked Walid up.

They pulled out their books and got down to business unusually fast, working with a quiet intensity to finish their assignments in time to get ready and change clothes. Within two hours, they had done all the work, gone their separate ways to bathe and change, and were back together, standing in Walid's room. They were both wearing their best clothes, fresh from the cleaner, ornamented with bright blue sashes and they were each sporting handsome new leather sandals. Their hair was carefully combed and Mafulla's favorite cologne flavored the air around them.

"The perfume of the gods," he explained in his inimitable way as he poured just a bit more into his hand to slap on his face. "I suspect it can have a nearly supernatural power of attraction over the ladies that could be almost equal to my own raw magnetism."

Walid coughed twice. "Amazing."

"The combination of cologne and charisma could be, I must say, very dangerous, and perhaps should even be illegal."

"I agree completely. But you mention ladies."

"Yes."

"How do you know we'll see any ladies?"

"I don't, of course, but hope springs eternal."

"I see."

"And, one must always be prepared on the occasion of such ... occasions, which of course happen these days ... only, occasionally."

"Well said."

"Do you need any of this manly scent? I brought it with

me in case you wanted an equal chance with any ladies who indeed might be present, or even nearby. It's good to be ready and at your best."

"No, thank you."

"You're sure?"

"I'll just stay within about ten feet of you, well inside the orb of attraction, and I'll benefit sufficiently in that way, I'm sure."

"You're a wise man. Stay close to the master and learn."

Both boys, laughing, left Walid's room. They walked down the hall, around a corner, and then down another long hall to get to the staircase that took them to a large open area from which they could access the hallway to The Royal Library and its adjacent dining room. The stroll took only a few minutes.

There were festive decorations around the door to the dining room, and inside they could already see Malik and Haji, standing next to a small table in the corner, with a large punch bowl, all spiffed up and looking a bit awkward. The long table in the center of the room was covered with a very large, perfectly white linen tablecloth and was adorned with beautiful china and silver and arrangements of flowers along its entire surface. In addition to the boys, there was one attendant at the punch bowl who had just served the two of them exotic fruit drinks. The second that Walid and Mafulla appeared, the other two boys smiled with happy relief and instantly looked more at ease.

"Hey, Prince! Thanks for having a party for us!" Haji called out.

Mafulla laughed. "Yeah, that's why I keep him around. You never know what's going to happen next. He's the royal ticket to all kinds of excitement." That second, Bafur walked in, looking around the room.

"Bafur!" Haji called out.

He saw the other boys and said, "Do I hear a big dinner calling my name?"

Mafulla answered. "No, that was Haji. I believe the dinner turned around and ran like crazy when it detected your arrival." Everyone laughed and he continued, "In fact, I think the roast goat was just now yelling, 'Save me! Save me!' as it headed out the door for safer pastures." The boys laughed again as Mafulla patted Bafur on the back and said, "Just kidding, my man."

Jabari came in with a happy, expectant look, and the much taller Set followed him toward the cluster of their classmates. "Who else is coming?" Walid asked, to no one in particular. And, at that moment, as if in answer, Khalid entered the room with a big smile on his face.

Mafulla elbowed Walid, leaned over, and whispered, "I hope there's no lock on the door."

"Hello, boys! Welcome! Walid, Mafulla, when I saw you earlier today, this was the event I spoke about that I had been planning with my wife—all the last minute details for this first meeting ... drum roll please ... and a moment of anticipation ... for this first social gathering of the boys' class and the girls' class!"

Mafulla turned to Walid. "I knew it!"

"You didn't know it."

"Well, some part of me knew it!"

"Dancing girls?"

"Well, if a couple of them will dance, then I almost foretold this event."

"Where are the girls?" Walid spoke more loudly in Khalid's direction and looked eagerly toward the open door. And, although his words were plural, his mind was singular.

Khalid glanced back at the door himself and said, "They should be here shortly. Hoda's bringing them in as a group."

Suddenly, from the wide hallway outside the entrance to the room, there was lively music being played by a string quartet that had appeared out of nowhere in a matter of minutes. Mafulla's eyebrows shot up. He turned to Walid and in a lower voice, said, "When the time is right, I may have to bust a move myself."

And just then, the stunningly beautiful Hoda El-Bay walked elegantly through the door, followed by a line of girls who all glowed like royalty. Khalid said, "Boys, let's applaud their entrance," and began clapping his hands, as the boys then in turn followed his lead and did likewise. That brought big smiles to all the girls' faces.

The girls lined up on one side of the room. The boys were clustered on the other side. Khalid faced the girls and said, "Ladies, may I present to you, your fellow palace students, Prince Walid, Mafulla, Haji, Malik, Jabari, Set, and Bafur."

Then Hoda looked over at the boys and spoke: "Gentlemen, I would like to introduce you to your fellow students, Ara, Hasina, Cabar, my daughter Kissa, Bakat, Kit, and Khata."

Walid could not help staring at one of them and barely heard anything except the word 'Kissa' when it was spoken. This was it, he thought—the gift of destiny.

His teacher brought Walid back to reality with his next words: "Now, Prince, ladies and gentlemen, to begin our evening together, each of you must ask each student in the other class two questions: Where were you born, and what is one interesting fact about you or your family? No more than half a minute with each person, then you should move on. We have pens, pencils, and paper in case you'd like to take notes. There will be a quiz later."

Mafulla was the first to grab paper and a pen and go around the table to begin his interviews. To be a good sport, Walid followed him, and then the other boys joined in, with various degrees of reluctance and shyness, except for the other small boy in the class, Jabari, who seemed to share Mafulla's positive energy about this exciting new opportunity.

Within a minute, there was a loud buzz of conversations all around the room, punctuated by occasional laughter that was often heard in the vicinity of either Mafulla or Jabari. The happy chaos continued until Khalid saw that all the interviewing had probably been done and he then asked everyone to locate the seat that had been prearranged for them in an order, boy-girl, boy-girl, around the table.

There were place cards with names written out in beautiful calligraphy, and everyone quickly found their assigned chair with help from their fellow students. Walid had a desperate hope in his heart, and was nearly dizzy in anticipation. Khalid was already at the head of the table and Hoda was at the far end. As chance, or destiny, or a wise mother, would have it, Walid had been put next to Kissa on one side, and her best friend Hasina on the other. But Hasina was also next to Mafulla and she, like Kissa, was very attractive. So, for more than one reason, there wasn't much chance that poor Hasina would have many conversational opportunities to turn to the prince during dinner. The magic of Mafulla would make that suitably difficult. And Walid was magnetically turned toward Kissa. It was clear that there had been plenty of information sharing and planning between Khalid and Hoda in making these seating arrangements.

Walid was floating on a cloud. But he was so nervous that he interviewed every other girl before he could work up the nerve to approach the only one he really wanted to talk to. Kissa knew from her father's reports since the first day of school that Walid was in his class, and that he was the boy she had met in the marketplace. So when he came up and they started interviewing each other with the two questions, she made sure to thank him again for his gallant help on that day so long ago, or so it seemed to both of them now.

"I had no idea you were a prince!" Kissa said, almost embarrassed. "And you were so nice to me!"

"Well, you certainly looked like a princess that day, as you do now, and I didn't want a princess to be without assistance in a difficult situation," Walid explained with a big smile. He hesitated inwardly, but went ahead and said, "The one thing that bothered me that day was that I didn't have a chance to ask your name, and I was really worried that I might never see you again. Then I got kidnapped by large, armed men and I thought I'd never see anyone again!"

Kissa looked stunned. "What? I didn't know anything about that! It must have been terrible!" And that was when her father spoke up loudly over all the conversations and directed them to please be seated, with a further instruction that the informal dinner talk should begin with each of them discovering from their seat partners, on each side of them, what their favorite subject was in school or in life.

Once they were in their chairs, Walid greeted Hasina warmly and found that she loved reading world literature. She in turn learned that he had a special enjoyment of philosophy. He then focused on Kissa to continue their conversation. She loved art and music. And in answer to her questions, he explained his enthusiastic connection with the great thinkers of the past, while relating his love of wisdom to the trip he had made across the desert, and everything that had happened up to the unexpected meeting they had in the market. She asked more about the kidnapping, and he gave her a dramatic summary, explaining how he had met Mafulla because of it.

As anticipated, Mafulla did his best to keep Hasina well entertained throughout the meal, without failing to attend to the very nice girl Cabar, on his other side, as well. In fact, at many times during the dinner, he somehow managed to engage them simultaneously, leaning back and drawing them both into his stories and jokes, and getting them to laugh at the exaggerations and engaging antics for which he was already becoming widely known.

Both boys were asked at some point about their beautiful watches, which were rare for someone their age to own and wear. They each told the whole story, showed how the watch cases flip. And they explained the engravings on the back, with ample references to the Parthenon, the Great Pyramid, and ideal human beauty, hinting that the girls needed to do no more than look in the mirror at any time to see the golden ratio in many of its most enchanting manifestations. The girls were mesmerized by the story, utterly enthralled, and tremendously flattered by the compliment. And the boys were consequently even more grateful for this gift than ever before.

They both temporarily forgot their worries about Khalid and the incident in the basement. They were immensely enjoying themselves in the company of the girls and their classmates. The food was delicious, the talk was great, and the time seemed to fly by as they all eventually relaxed into the warm glow of a very good time.

By contrast, it was a dark, moonless night outside, with a howling wind that occasionally boomed against the glass of the room's large windows. And then, suddenly, all the electricity throughout the palace was cut off and the dining room was plunged into complete darkness so deep that nothing could be seen.

The next moment, many voices could be heard saying, "Whoa!" "Jeez!" "Yikes!" "What just happened?" But in less than five seconds, a voice from outside the door of the room spoke the words, "Ladies and Gentlemen: Your attention, please. There's no cause for alarm. The electrical power throughout the palace is off temporarily and will be restored as soon as possible. Meanwhile, alternative light will be provided." Within a few more seconds, two palace butlers had lit candles for the table and more were being brought into the room.

With the first flicker of renewed illumination, it was clear that everyone around the table was frozen in place, except for Khalid, who was no longer in his chair. There were many whispers, a few nervous laughs, and general stirrings all around the table. As many more lighted candles were brought in, the mood changed back to one of relatively relaxed fun. But now nearly everyone was asking "What do you think happened?" and "Where's Khalid?"

"It's just like my husband, to think it's his job to go solve the problem!" Hoda spoke with a laugh. And then she added, "Well, that just means there's more dessert for the rest of us!"

At that, there were several other laughs and scattered applause around the table and someone said, "Cheers to Khalid! Pass the sweets!"

Across town, a few hours earlier, before dark, an important discovery was made. The criminal mastermind Ari Falma liked to be careful, and he always preferred expert knowledge to amateur opinion. He had taken the jewels that came from Faisul to a gemologist he could trust, for a general estimate of their overall value. The man got out his loop, took the bag over to a table and, under a small light, began looking at one, then another, then a third. "Amazing," He said. "Incredible," he remarked. "Simply beautiful."

Ari smiled and nodded his head.

"I'm actually astonished by what I'm seeing." The jeweler looked up at Ari. "Congratulations, my friend. These are the most extraordinary and beautiful fakes I've ever seen."

"Wait. What did you say?"

"These are the most masterful and incredible fakes. They would fool almost anyone who didn't have my eye and skilled judgment."

"They're fakes? How do you know they're fakes?"

"They're gorgeous, spectacular fakes. I've worked with gems long enough to know how to tell the real from the artificial. But these, my friend, are true works of art."

"Could you be wrong?"

"No. But I'd like to meet the exceptional craftsman who constructed these marvels. They're simply magnificent. Their only real value, of course, is for use in costume jewelry, but they're excellent beyond any other such fabrication I've ever seen. They're works of genius."

Ari could almost feel his blood begin to boil in his veins. A wave of dizziness passed quickly through his brain. His heart started pounding and his eyes narrowed. "The man who gave me these jewels represented them as genuine, as authentic, as the real thing." His voice was rising as he spoke.

"They're incredible, but are not real, I'm afraid. The man who gave them to you could know the truth, or could himself have been fooled by them. Like I say, only a real expert could tell the difference."

Ari took a very deep breath and forced himself to calm

down so that he could think clearly. "Do you believe these fakes would reliably fool the average man?"

"Oh, yes, with certainty. They would even deceive most connoisseurs and amateur aficionados, at least using only the naked eye. Examine them yourself. You've purchased many fine, authentic gems in your life. These are extravagantly beautiful and so much like the real thing." The jeweler held a diamond up to the light for Ari to see.

"Yes, yes, I glanced into the bag and was duped instantly. I came to you not because I suspected anything deceptive, but only to get your official estimate of value."

"Well, they're very valuable as fakes, but not as real jewels."

"What are they worth?"

"Actually, now that I think about it, I'd estimate, perhaps, forty or fifty dollars each, maybe double or even triple that. It's hard to say."

"But if they were real, what would they be worth?"

"The smaller ones would be worth, on the retail market, a few thousand dollars each, and the bigger ones, perhaps even up to twenty thousand or more. But, of course, it varies a lot with the stone—whether it's an emerald, or sapphire or ruby or diamond, and then what the cut is, the color, the clarity, and the size."

"The whole bag, then? I need a rough, general estimate."

The jeweler gazed into the small bag and thought for a few moments. "Well, a wild guess, but an educated guess, would be that if these were real, then you would have here an overall value of between five hundred thousand and a million dollars, and maybe even more."

"Ok, good. So, give me back the bag. I appreciate your expertise. But, first, since you find these stones so impressive, as do I, please keep your two or three favorite pieces, if you'd like, for your trouble. And I'll show you more appreciation later. But for now, I have some other pressing business to attend to."

The gemologist spread a few more of the jewels out on the cloth on his table under the light, picked out an emerald, a sapphire, and a large diamond, and then wrapped up the others, putting them back into Ari's bag and handing it to him with a smile. Falma nodded his head, turned, and left the shop. Just outside the door, three men waited for him.

He walked up close to them and spoke. "Go get the guy in the house. He has a bag with gold and silver and more jewels, I've been told. Make sure he brings it with him. Tell him we've retrieved the items that need to be shipped and that we're going to meet at an old warehouse, from which we can get him to freedom. Take him to the special place." Ari then stared into the eyes of one of the men and said, in a very low voice, "Quietly give him freedom from this world. He gave us fake jewels. No one does that to me and lives. Then, bring me his bag, disposing of all other evidence in the usual way."

In the king's dining room, the intimate dinner for five had been a wonderful occasion. Everyone had gotten along tremendously. Never had parents talked more enthusiastically about their children. And they had all immediately liked each other. Shapur and Shamilar were lavish in their praise for Walid. Rumi and Bhati, for their own part, could not say enough about Mafulla. The king made a toast to all four parents, as well as to their boys. Right after everyone had sipped the delicious beverage with which they were ending the meal, and before their glasses had once more touched the table-cloth, that was the moment the lights went out and they were all plunged into instant darkness. The king's butlers in the room were always prepared for almost anything, though, and they had small flashlights turned on in about five seconds, illuminating the room as the other attendants lit candles and brought them to the table.

Rumi said, "Your Majesty, was this your extremely subtle hint to us that it's time to leave?" Everyone laughed.

"No, no," the king replied. "I just have to remember from now on to pay the electric bill." And that, of course, got everyone laughing again.

Mafulla's dad said, "Well, I'm surprised there's anything left in the royal treasury, the way the previous regime lavished money on themselves."

His wife Shamilar laughed and then made a stern face, saying, "Shapur, you should not criticize in any way even the worst and most foolish past representatives of our exalted monarchy, no matter what ridiculous and criminal things they did!" She then looked quite surprised and said, "Oh, my! I do believe I just did the same thing myself!" She put her hand to her mouth as more laughter danced around the table.

Bhati smiled and said, "I'm sure the king and all his men are working hard to undo the damage that the previous occupants of this building have done both to the treasury and to the kingdom. I just wish I could do more to help."

Ali said, "You'll do plenty! And you've already done much!" He beamed at his sister-in-law and over at his brother. "Good people working well together can accomplish a lot, and often in a very short time. We're busy fixing many problems—at least, those that have nothing at all to do with electricity." At that, everyone smiled again.

Just then a man came into the room and bowed deeply. "Please pardon me, Your Majesty. I just wanted to check on you and let you know that the boys and their friends are perfectly safe."

"Shapur, Shamilar, this is Naqid, head of the palace guard. Rumi and Bhati know him well. Naqid, these fine people are Mafulla's parents."

"It's nice to meet you, Mr. and Mrs. Adi. I've heard many good things about you. And we all love your son, Mafulla." He turned and nodded with a big smile. "Rumi, Bhati, it's so good to see you again. I hope we'll have time soon to catch up. I just wanted the king to know that, prior to the loss of electricity, we had two guards stationed outside the dinner the boys and girls are having." Naqid looked over at the king as he said this. "We've now added four more, just for extra security."

"That's good." The king nodded his approval. And Naqid went on.

"Many candles are lit in the dining room and the party's continuing. The young people were in the dark for only a matter of seconds and there was no obvious dismay. I've been told that there was some appropriate joking, and things are back to normal. Oh, and you have a full contingent of guards in this area of the palace. We're in the process of checking and securing other areas, in a descending order of perceived importance. And we've been assured that maintenance is working on the problem."

"Thank you for the report, Naqid. We shouldn't detain you any longer from your duties. We appreciate your attention."

"Your Majesty." Naqid smiled, bowed, turned, and walked briskly from the room.

It had taken only three jewels each to buy the assistance of the three evening maintenance men. The kitchen staff members and the one jailer were more demanding. Bribing them required six fake jewels each, gems they had been told were to be valued at over five thousand dollars each. In the capital city at that time, the total amount for each of the men would purchase a fairly lavish home, or serve as an ample retirement fund. A downpayment was made in advance, with the remainder of the gems to be provided upon sufficient results.

One maintenance worker cut the power to the entire palace in such a way that it could not easily or quickly be restored. The building would be in darkness for at least an hour's time, and likely more. The other two men instantly descended into the basement and joined him, on the pretext of fixing the problem, but really to make sure that it was not fixed too quickly. And then the second job for all three was to remove about twenty boxes of military equipment from the palace guard storage room, along with an additional special box whose label they had been alerted to recognize.

A few palace guards had initially rushed down to the electrical room in the basement to make sure that no sabotage was going on but, seeing nothing, they redeployed to other parts of the palace, assuming that the power outage was some sort of technical problem not requiring their presence in the basement.

The bribed workers had no keys to the lock of the particular storage room where the boxes were located, but they had been assured that this would be no problem. When Walid and Mafulla had been locked into that room and had escaped through two adjoining areas, they had been forced to leave the door unbolted that led to the electrical and plumbing room. At least, those planning the operation had wagered that would likely happen. And they were right. That allowed these men to reverse the path the boys had taken, and in that way access the room they needed to get to in order to take the boxes, which they resealed and removed from the room, all now covered with tarps labeled "Electrical." In case they were stopped by anyone, they would explain that they were removing faulty transformers, cables, and switch boxes to fix the power problem for the palace, and that they could take no time to talk because of the urgency the king had communicated for the job to be finished. They were depending on the fact that, whenever the king was invoked or mentioned, people typically deferred.

As a cover story, it was a bit of a stretch, and quite thin, but the palace guards were now all busy elsewhere in the vast building, knowing that maintenance was present to deal with the problem. No one was watching either the stairs or the nearest external palace door that led to a loading dock where the masterminds of the theft had arranged a way to hide the boxes and smuggle them out in the next vehicle that was scheduled to deliver food. Their helpers in the kitchen had set this up before undertaking their own main assignment, which was to liberate one small man from the palace jail, an individual having the family name of Falma. His older brother had parted with an apparent fortune in jewels in order to make this happen.

A large catering cart that was regularly used to take food to the prisoners in the special palace jail would be pushed out to the loading dock after its many contents had been removed in the jail and a pig bound in a blanket had been put in their place. But perhaps the term pig here is insulting to the entire porcine family. Idi Falma was more of a weasel, or a skunk, or perhaps an example of some other form of vermin in a turban—the unpleasant, underachieving younger sibling of the crime overlord who would have been better off in many ways just to let him sit in prison. But as someone who had been involved in the attempted murder of a prince, Idi was facing the possibility of far worse consequences, and Ari felt that, for now, he still needed his services.

Some families help and support each other. Others use and despise each other, focusing their animosity inside their closest relationships even more than on anyone outside the family. That was the Falma brood—not at all a happy group of people.

The moment the lights went out, the plan went into action, and everything went exactly as planned. Except for one thing. And it was big.

16

LIGHT IN THE DARK

KHALID NEVER REAPPEARED AT THE TABLE. A MESSAGE was handed to Hoda, who read it quickly with a serious expression and then, smiling broadly, took over the hosting duties completely, without speaking again of her husband and his whereabouts. Within no more than a few minutes, she had thanked all the students for coming to the party and reminded them of classes in the morning. She asked the boys to make their departures first, and explained that she would then walk the girls back toward the formal reception area in another part of the palace where their parents were scheduled to meet them all.

Large candles lighted the hallways and palace guards were stationed at regular intervals. As Hoda began herding the boys toward the door, Walid did a small bow to Kissa and she curtsied back, smiling. Mafulla caught Hasina's eye at a distance and also bowed. She did a quick curtsy, as well. He then pointed to his watch, traced its shape quickly with his right index finger, and wagged the same finger in the air toward her, with a big smile on his face, hoping she would know what he meant. She laughed, so he concluded that he had successfully managed to communicate his recognition of her classic, golden beauty, reflecting the well known attractiveness of the watch.

Then Mafulla turned to Walid and said in a low voice, "Kissa and Hasina just curtsied. And as you may know, curtsies are a part of classic dance; therefore, we had with us tonight … dancing girls. So, in the end and after all, I was right."

Walid just shook his head and smiled.

Everyone said their goodbyes, and as Walid and Mafulla began their walk back to the private quarters, Mafulla said, "Ok, listen, you've got to talk to the king right now. This is too much. We get locked in, then Khalid suddenly appears near the spot. And tonight when the lights go out, he just as suddenly disappears. We need to tell your uncle."

Walid looked concerned, and like he was thinking. And he let out a deep breath. "Yeah, you're right. Uncle Ali might still be with our parents in his private dining room. Let's go straight there."

They were only a short distance farther down the hallway when they suddenly heard quick, heavy footsteps behind them.

"Prince!" The boys stopped and turned around with a little jolt echoing the one they had felt earlier when Khalid called out to them in the far side of the palace. They both looked apprehensive.

"I'm sorry, Your Highness. We've been assigned to escort you both back to your rooms." One of the two palace guards walking toward them explained. "We won't interrupt your conversation further. We'll stay back but keep you in sight for the walk to the private quarters. King's orders. I just wanted to explain."

"Thanks. We appreciate your attention." Walid was always polite with the palace guards. He knew several of the new top officers from their time together on the desert caravan. And the men in the guard all treated him with great respect, as was due the future king. So, he felt genuinely comfortable around them. And yet, tonight, he was a little jumpy.

The boys turned and resumed their walk down the dimly lit hall. Mafulla said, "I really don't understand what's going on with Khalid. He seems like such a good guy, but then all this stuff happens."

Walid replied, "I don't get it, either. I wonder what the message said that Hoda read near the end of the party tonight. She was really serious, and then all smiles."

"I noticed that, too. It was a bit incongruous."

"Incongruous?"

"Yeah. Odd. Out of place, given the surroundings. What's there to smile about with a mysteriously missing husband and all the power out in the palace?"

"Good question. It was something in the note, I guess."

"Yeah. No doubt something … incongruous."

Within a few minutes, they had arrived back at the king's private entry hall upstairs. Walid asked the chief butler if they could see the king. He ducked inside, and came out telling the boys that his majesty would receive them right away and they should come in. When they entered, they could see Ali seated on a sofa, by himself, reading.

He put down the book and smiled at them broadly. "Boys! Come in!"

"Hi, Uncle."

"Hi, Your Majesty."

"Sit, please. Your parents left me just a few minutes ago. We had a wonderful time together. Did you two enjoy your special dinner?"

The boys both sat down and Mafulla said, "It was amazing! Poetry on plates!"

Walid confirmed his report, saying, "It was the best meal ever!"

"I'm glad. I wanted you to meet all the students at your level in the palace and have a good time together. I was hoping it would go well."

"The girls are pretty great." Walid anticipated what Mafulla was thinking. "And it was good to see the other boys in a new setting. But we have something urgent that we need to tell you, right away."

"Oh? What is it?"

Walid launched into the whole story about their trip to the basement earlier that afternoon. He described their inventory of Storage Room One, their examination of the other rooms, Mafulla's discovery about the Fibonacci numbers, and the missing mystery box. When that was mentioned, the king looked very concerned but said nothing. Walid went on and talked about their subsequent visit to the Palace Guard Storage Room where they found lots of weapons in the Adi shop boxes, but were much more surprised to discover the missing box inside another box with a strange label that he now described in detail. And the prince then finished this part of the story by telling how, in turn, they found a beautiful polished wooden box inside the box with the odd label, and were just getting ready to look into it when they were shocked to hear someone locking them in the room.

The king listened intently. He said, "You're sure that someone locked you in there?"

"Yes, absolutely. We first heard a different noise. Someone may have opened the door to the room, and seeing us there, they closed it."

Mafulla added, "Our backs were to the door. And then we heard the click of the lock being set."

Walid went on. "It's a good thing we found the inner doors of that room and the next one, and they were both unlocked—or at least the first one was unlocked and the second was locked only from our side. The room it opened to had lots of plumbing stuff and electrical equipment. And that room's exterior door was unlocked, too. That's how we got out."

"The room you describe is the mechanical and maintenance room for plumbing and electricity," the king explained.

"Yeah, that's what it looked like."

"And you left from that room without, of course, being able to re-lock the bolts on the other side of the door that had led you into it."

"That's right, Uncle. That's the only way we could safely get out. We didn't want to go all the way back into the guard storage room at that point to get our key and then go to a lot of trouble to re-bolt that one inner door before we left, again through the guard door that had been locked."

"Yeah, in case whoever locked us in was still around," Mafulla explained.

"I see," the king said.

Walid added, "We were worried that whoever had locked us in would still be around and might do something worse to us next if they saw us out of the room where they had apparently wanted us to stay. I hope that all makes sense."

The king said, "Yes. It was well reasoned. Did you leave the mystery box sitting with all the other boxes from the Adi store?"

"Box 89?"

"Yes."

"No, we took it to the other side of the room before we got locked in. Box 89 is beside a desk in there, away from the other boxes."

"What of the wooden box?"

"We left it on the desk."

"So that box is on the desk in the room, a good distance from the majority of the boxes?"

"Yes, sir. It's across the room from the other boxes."

"Good. Very good. You did well. But why didn't you bring me this information right away?"

"We tried to. We came back to tell you, but a new butler, the man who was here relieving Kular for his break, said you were in a big meeting and couldn't be disturbed. That's why I wrote you my note outlining some of this, gave it to the butler to pass on to you, and went back to wait in my room, where I saw the fancy invitation. Maffie and I then had to work hard and fast to get our school assignments done in time for the special dinner that just ended. And now here we are, finally telling you everything. But, I gave you the basics in the note."

The king looked thoughtful, and said, "I didn't know that Kular was on break at any time during the afternoon, or that a new man was on duty for him. And I never saw your note. It wasn't delivered to me."

"Oh. I'm really sorry. I marked it as urgent. That's where I told you about being locked in and about the weapons and the mystery box. I knew you'd want that information as soon as possible. The new butler said he'd get the note to you. And I also told you in it about Khalid."

"What about Khalid?"

"When we got out of the locked room and made our way to the stairs to leave through the basement door unseen and unheard—at least, we thought—and we started jogging down the hall to come back here, someone called out to us, and the voice came from behind us. It was Khalid. He asked what we were doing. And he was standing near the basement door."

"He was?"

"Yes. And pretty close to it," Mafulla added.

Then, Walid continued. "We were surprised to see him in that part of the palace where there was nobody else around, and we asked him why he was there. He said he was visiting his wife. And then, tonight at the dinner, when the lights were out, he just as suddenly disappeared from the table. The candles were lit and he was gone, and he never returned. Hoda made some jokes about him having to fix every problem, but then a note was given to her a few minutes later and she smiled and pretty much thanked us for coming and sent us on our way. I couldn't figure out what she was smiling about with no power and no Khalid around."

The king got up, as then did the boys. "Sit. I'll be right back." He walked across the room, opened the door, and conferred in a low voice with the head butler. Within half a minute, four palace guards came into the room. It seemed that at least a couple more were standing outside.

One of them said, "Your Majesty. At your service."

Then Naqid himself entered at a fast walk. "Majesty."

"Naqid. Thanks for coming. Get Masoon. Tell him to bring Hamid to see me as soon as possible. Send at least four of your best men into the basement quickly, to the palace guard storage room. Tell them to be prepared for the possibility of danger and armed resistance. Have them dust the doorknob and the lock and the door for fingerprints. While that's being done, have them check to see if the boxes recently put there from the raid on the Adi Shop are still in place. See if there's anything at all missing. Report back to me on this quickly."

"Yes, Your Majesty."

"And, this is important. If there is a wooden box on the desk in the guard storage room, tell the men to leave it untouched and unexamined for now."

"Yes, sire."

"Also, have the men go through the right inner door from that room into the adjoining storage room and re-bolt the next inner door that opens into the mechanical room. Then they can go around and check the maintenance that should be going on in there."

"Will do, Majesty."

"Find out if anything seems unusual. Something happened in those storage rooms earlier today that resulted in the inner door between them and the mechanical room being left unbolted, and tonight we get a power failure, and the main power equipment is almost all in that room. It may be a coincidence, but it may be more."

At that moment, an additional guard entered the room. "Pardon me King Ali, but there's been an escape from the palace jail."

"Who?"

"The nasty little man who was in Mr. Adi's store, the guy we think works for Ari Falma."

"Anyone else?"

"No, only the one prisoner."

"How did he escape?"

"We don't know. We just now discovered his cell empty. We think he got out after the power went off."

"I see. Find him. Take all the resources you need. Learn how he escaped. Question anyone who was for any reason in the jail today. And do this while Naqid is sending another group of guards into the basement. It's possible that something is going on beyond the power outage and this unfortunate escape. Perhaps something related. We need information now and we need to stop anything nefarious that can be stopped. Go."

"Yes, Majesty." The man with news from the jail turned and left. Naqid reassured the king that he would carry out his orders with haste.

As he bowed, turned, and began to walk out, Ali stood up and took a few steps while motioning for the boys to remain seated. He called out, "Naqid, there's one more thing."

The head guard stopped and turned around. The king said, "There was a substitute butler on duty here today, this afternoon. Find out who he is. Have him brought to me in light custody. He shouldn't realize that he's being apprehended."

"Yes, sire, right away." Naqid bowed again and left while the king returned to the sofa with a very serious expression on his face.

Ali let out a deep breath. Then he smiled. "And up until now, it's been such a fine evening."

"This is all amazing." Walid spoke. The king nodded his head.

"Boys, what you've told me just now is important. I thank you. We're in the middle of something unpleasant, I believe. And I plan to get to the bottom of it quickly."

"Do you think Khalid's involved, and maybe Hoda?" Mafulla asked.

"Actually, no, not at all. I don't think there's even a chance of it, because of his sterling background and credentials, and his well known character, along with his wife's distinctive qualities and wonderful reputation throughout the capital and the whole kingdom as a fine person and good soul. I've known Hoda fairly well, off and on for years, and I trust her completely. But the fragmentary evidence calling this into doubt that you've presented me is, on the face of it, a bit troubling … to both of you, I can tell."

"Should we go to class with Khalid tomorrow morning, I mean, with all this in question and everything?"

"Yes. You should go and observe him. But he shouldn't be made to think he's under any sort of suspicion. Don't reveal that he's caused you any worry. And take a step back, yourselves. Watch him tomorrow with a clear mind. If he has something to hide, the hint of any suspicion on your part will lead him to push it down more deeply and cover it over more carefully. On your part, you have to keep open the possibility that he's done nothing wrong. Surface appearances, as you know, aren't always reliable guides to reality."

"That's something you're often reminding me," Walid said.

"Yes. And by putting aside any dark interpretations of Khalid's recent actions, you give yourself the chance to see more perceptively. What you observe may confirm your suspicions, nonetheless, and in that case, you'll believe with greater evidence that something's wrong. Plus, you'll have more to act on. Right now, you have nothing but a weakly explained presence, perhaps, and a so-far unexplained absence."

"But is it totally safe for us to go to class?" Mafulla had to ask.

"I'll have guards outside the classroom door tomorrow to ease your concern and, if asked, they can tell Khalid that they're there because of some unresolved aspects of the situation tonight, and especially if our escaped prisoner is still on the loose. The need for your protection will be understood. Your classmates are the children of my top administrators. And Walid, of course, you're the future king. And you, Mafulla, are, well ... you're the one and only Mafulla Adi."

"Thank you, Your Majesty." Mafulla almost smiled.

The king nodded and said, "In fact, I'll have more than two guards protecting you. There will be several close by, but two at the door. If you need anything during class time, just call out."

Mafulla suddenly remembered something. "King Ali, Your Majesty, I almost forgot to ask. Did my mother say anything tonight about her recent letter to me and her worries about our neighborhood?"

"Yes. Thank you for reminding me. I did manage to have a few words with her privately while the others were in a lively conversation. I asked about the nature of the strange events she had mentioned."

"What did she say?"

"She reported that a nice family across the street and a few houses up from her had been suddenly and strangely evicted. A single man came to stay in the house that very night. But he never seemed to go outside. It was very mysterious. And then, she said, he was visited by a terrible looking man, and on the next day by four more men. She couldn't see well at the distance, but one of them seemed familiar. He was short and thin and well dressed, like the fellow who was behind the goings on at your father's store."

"Oh, no."

"She had a strange feeling about these men, and thought she might have recognized another one of them, a very tall man, as an individual who had been noticed loitering nearby the family store just prior to the visit at your home made by that criminal Ari Falma, who claimed to be representing me."

"Jeepers. That's not good. Has anything else happened?"

"Well, your mother said another neighbor told her that, last night, some men visited the home in question, in the evening, and the mysterious individual who was living there left with them. He's not been seen coming back since then. We're having your family's house watched even more closely now. Once I heard all this, I sent out word after dinner for the guards there to be on special alert."

Mafulla said, "Thank you so much for that."

"It's my pleasure."

"Please, could you let me know if anything else happens that I might want to hear about?"

"Certainly."

Mafulla thought for a second and said, "It's likely far too big a coincidence that Mom might have recognized a man in the neighborhood who may have been checking out the shop before that guy Ari set up his crime operation in the back. And now, the small creep who worked for Falma there has just escaped, and maybe something is going on with their stuff in the storage room, which they would surely want back."

"I completely agree."

Walid said, "Uncle, do you mind if we hang around for just a little longer to see what news you get about the storage room and the jail break and the butler? Our work for tomorrow is already done."

"I'd enjoy having you here. You boys are both very perceptive. Never hesitate to tell me if either of you has a strange feeling about anything that's going on."

"We won't hesitate." Walid said this right away, although the confidence of his statement went a little beyond the certainty in his heart. He sometimes hesitated about revealing hints or feelings he had about situations or people, especially when the feelings were bad. But Mafulla was helping him with that. He seemed comfortable with being completely open about his instincts, intuitions, thoughts, and feelings. And Walid had realized from his example how this could be good.

Ali leaned back on the sofa cushion. He said, "Something just occurred to me. Have you boys ever heard of the unconscious mind?"

"Not really," Mafulla said, "I mean, I know my mind's unconscious when I sleep, and sometimes in class."

"Maybe I've heard the expression once," Walid said, as he smiled at his friend.

"Well, there are many things stored in our minds, like information learned in the past, of which we're not at this moment consciously aware. It's in our minds for retrieval, but is not now conscious. There are also habits and dispositions that exist in the mind beyond our introspective self-awareness. You can consciously gaze within and not see them. And this is true of many other things that we take in about the world around us but that remain beneath the sweep of full awareness. We have huge resources in the unconscious mind that are not always quickly or easily available to consciousness."

"I hadn't thought about it like that, but this makes sense," Walid said.

"What's most important to realize is the perhaps initially surprising truth that the unconscious mind represents the vast majority of our mental possessions and abilities. Our conscious experience is like the very top few stones of the Great Pyramid. The rest of our mental ability is like the remainder of that huge structure, except that, in reality, the difference in the size and scope of those mental areas is much, much bigger."

"I'd never really thought about that, Your Majesty," Maful-la said. The king nodded and continued.

"Many things go on in our minds that we never consciously realize. There are patterns and indications picked up by deep processes of recognition within us that may or may not enter our explicit thoughts. But we can train ourselves to be more open to this deeper part of our mental activity. We can get to a point where we allow those otherwise hidden thoughts and hints to flow upward. That way, we become aware of much more than most people ever realize. Inventors do this. So do all great explorers and artists and scholars, and athletes. The most innovative scientists are very good at it. The best warriors like Masoon rely on it. Creativity in any walk of life requires it."

Walid spoke up. "That's connected to what we were talking about so much in the desert—the power of our minds."

"Correct. And, Mafulla, in case you and Walid haven't spoken of this, he and I talked much about the mind on our trip across the desert. Most people live in a terribly constricted and reduced circle of being. They're in self-imposed exile from the best that life has for them. They can't make the right decisions or even see the true possibilities that our world offers unless they access this deeper level of the mind. Exiles from their own greatness, they choose unhealthy relationships, pursue the wrong paths, and generally end up living in various levels of either misery, or emotional deadness. They exist on the most basic level as human beings, but they're not fully alive."

The king went on, as he looked over at Walid. "I've talked with you a great deal about the power of the mind. But it's not just that our normal conscious awareness can be powerful. In fact, if it's cut off from the deeper sources of thought and feeling, it will not be powerful at all. Only when we allow the deep parts of our minds and hearts to percolate upward into consciousness, and also directly touch our actions, can we tap into our true power. And only when conscious thought resonates with these deeper resources will it have its proper impact."

He sat for a moment in silence, then said, "We have to get beyond the superficial chatter of our normal consciousness. We need to access all that's available to us beneath the clutter, beyond the chattering voices and distractions of normal thought." The king smiled. "We need to experience what I like to call the thought beyond thought. That's where the deep power is."

"How can we do this?" Walid asked.

"We calm our conscious minds. We relax our bodies and release whatever ordinary thoughts or feelings might be impinging on us. We then become open to allow deeper insights to appear. And they're always near us, available to us, if we'll just notice them and take them in. We'll talk more about this in days to come, but for now, learn to listen carefully to any small thoughts that might seem to play about beneath the surface of your normal consciousness. When one appears, invite it to linger and develop in your mind."

"This is what you do, Your Majesty?" Mafulla asked.

"Yes, it is. All the time. I want you boys to do this as well, to be sensitive to your inklings and feelings about the situations that develop around us. Never just dismiss these hints that sometimes fleetingly appear from the realm of the unconscious mind. Pay attention to them. They're worthy of your notice. And then tell each other and me. That way, we can work together powerfully to resist and restrain those who have given in to the downward pull of evil. And that way, we can also make some very good and creative things happen."

"Ok," Walid said. "This sounds really important."

"It is."

"We'll try to do exactly as you say."

"Sure thing, Your Majesty," Mafulla answered.

"As you seek to tap into your deeper potential, you'll progressively grow in your ability to do so. It's like any skilled behavior."

"I'm sure you're a master at it, Your Majesty," Mafulla said.

"It's very natural for me, and has been for many years. Just remember this. What we can know goes far beyond what most people suppose. And what we can do is just as vast."

Mafulla and Walid both nodded their heads. Walid said, "This is part of why I love being around you so much, Uncle Ali—Your Majesty. You open new ideas and new horizons to me all the time."

The king smiled. "And I'm sure you would admit, I can also be great fun to be around—perhaps even moderately humorous on occasion. Not as clever as you, Mafulla, certainly, but better than most, I would hope."

Walid said, "You have a great sense of humor."

"Yeah, I never knew a king could be a fun person, but you really are," Mafulla added.

"Good. I'm determined not to be dull at my advanced age, or too serious. In fact, my New Year's Resolution this year had been to fit a bit more silly into my life—at least when I'm not too busy with traitors, kidnappers, revolutions, criminals, jail escapees, and the admittedly time consuming business of running a large and complex kingdom."

Mafulla said, "Yeah, that revolution and kingdom ruling stuff can get in the way, I'm sure. But, remember, there's always time for a little Mafoolery." His eyebrows wiggled in their distinctive way, as punctuation for his statement. Both the king and Walid had to laugh.

"Indeed, indeed," the king replied, as his stomach bounced a little more with residual mirth. "Mafoolery! You never cease to amaze me, my young friend."

A knock at the door heralded Naqid's reappearance. "Majesty, there was no resistance around the palace guard storage room, or sight of anyone suspicious there, and its external door was still locked. But all the boxes from the Adi raid were missing, except for one, it seems. On the floor a distance from where the other boxes had been, we found an empty box numbered '89' and there was, as you said, on a nearby desk, a beautiful box of lightly colored wood that no one could remember seeing before. It was a size that could have come from inside the numbered box. It had a lock on it that was closed. And no one has disturbed it, as you instructed."

Mafulla looked at Walid and whispered. "You closed the lock?"

"Yeah, as we were leaving. And I thumbed the numbers so they wouldn't sit there with the combination showing."

"Good man! Brilliant."

The king continued talking with Naqid. "You bolted the doors to the mechanical room?"

"Yes, the guard rooms are now secure. And we're already questioning three mechanics or electrical supply maintenance men about what happened, what they saw, and any possible involvement they might have."

"Good.

"There was one very strange thing."

"What is it?"

"In searching these men, we found on one of them two large jewels that it makes no sense for such a man to have in his possession. I've brought them. They look like gems of great price." Naqid took out from his pocket a cloth napkin and opened it in his palm to display its contents for the king's inspection. There was a big, beautiful emerald, well cut and polished, and an almost equally large ruby, shining brightly against the white cloth. "It's a mystery how they could possess such stones. And when asked, they had no sensible answer."

The king looked at them and said, "Oh, my. This is most unexpected."

"What is it, Uncle?" Walid was paying close attention.

"Unless I'm badly mistaken, and I don't think I am, the mystery is even deeper than it might at first appear. These seem to be two of the flawless fake jewels that we were carrying in that special bag on our camel train, the one that our companion Faisul stole, in his treachery. I have no jeweler's loop here, but I remember stones just like these, among the many others, exactly this size and cut. We had acquired the gems from a master, genius craftsman for the purpose of thwarting any potential treason, in case it were to blight our journey. And it strikes me that these stones have come from Faisul's bag."

He went on. "Someone has likely used these fake jewels to bribe those maintenance men to cut our power and either remove, or allow someone else to remove, the confiscated boxes from the guard storage room, and take them out through the mechanical room."

He put his hand on Naqid's shoulder and said, "Engage the men with more questioning. At this point, let them know that the jewels they were given are all fake, amazing replicas, but fakes. Tell them that these manufactured items were used to dupe them into helping a criminal. Reveal the bad news that these stones are practically worthless, or of small value, compared to appearances. The men have been cheated by someone who knew they wouldn't be able to check the authenticity of gems, but would take appearances for realities. One of them, if not all, will confess out of anger and the desire to implicate their deceiver. Offer a deal to the first one who confesses fully. Propose a reduced sentence of limited jail time rather than decades of prison, and guarantee that justice will be done to their deceiver, if they will just tell us whatever they know."

"Yes, Majesty. Right away." Naqid bowed and began to leave the room.

"Oh, one more thing."

"Yes, Majesty?"

"Masoon and Hamid."

"I've found them and filled them in on everything. They should be here shortly. Masoon wanted to put a special detail on alert and said he would arrive in no more than half an hour, once I assured him that you're well guarded. And we're still looking for that butler."

"Very well. Continue the good work."

The small warehouse was only dimly lit. It was too close to the palace for comfort, but its proximity had allowed all the liberated goods and the prisoner to be transported briefly and hidden away quickly.

Ari Falma greeted his brother with cold disdain. "I should have left you to rot in that prison for your stupidity. It irritates me to no end that I still have need of your services."

"Well, it's good to see you, too, dearest companion. Thanks for springing me out. It's nice to know that you're still doing evil things, even if for the wrong reasons. You may need to be replaced some day by a better man." The weasel, Idi Falma, grinned.

Ari pulled out a long knife and pointed it at the man's face as he hissed, "I should put an end to your disrespect on the spot, as a lesson to the other men. In fact, that's why I really sprang you. I didn't want the palace to execute you. I'd prefer that pleasure myself. If you do one more stupid thing or insult me one more time, you'll join all my other former enemies in another world, where maybe you'll do better for yourself, or else get what's really coming to you."

Idi seemed unperturbed by this outburst. It wasn't the first time he had heard such words. His older brother then turned to the other men. "Did you get all twenty-one boxes?"

"Yeah, including the one with the strange label."

"Excellent. And you've paid off our helpers?"

"Yes, with those great make-believe jewels."

"Good. At least that moron's gold and silver were real. I still can't believe he gave us manufactured gems, and then hid from us half of the ones he had. But now we have them all, and his fakes have ended up coming in handy. It feels nice to pay major bribes in worthless baubles. You know what they say, 'Good things come to those who hate.' And I hate jerks I have to bribe." Two of the men laughed. The others looked like they were trying to understand.

"You know me." Ari continued to speak to his head goon, a man, like the others, with more muscle than mental activity, but sharper than the rest. "I always prefer gaining cooperation through simple deceit or intimidation. But when we have to bribe, we bribe. And this time, we could do so with deceit. So it's all good. Maybe those simpletons can find other lame-brains to take their worthless stones as payment for the equally worthless stuff they want. I really don't care. We have what we need. Now we can take everything to the buyer."

The henchman said, "We'll get on it right away, before any palace guards come snooping around, looking for their stuff. We should have it out of here within three or four days. But there's no big rush. It may be weeks before they even realize the boxes are gone. I was told no one ever seems to go down to that basement on a regular basis, except some kids now and then to play and mess around. And, you know, it was a couple of those kids who gave us our easy access to the room, without even knowing what they were doing. We didn't have to break a lock or even pick one, so there's no sign on the outside of the door that we've been in the room. We even moved some other boxes over to where ours had been sitting. They won't likely know anything's happened for a long time."

"Ok, good. Smart. But still, don't waste any time. And get two men over to the empty house where the loser with the fake jewels was staying. We're going to make good use of the place while it's still rented. I want a rotation there watching the Adi home down the street. Record their comings and goings—all of them. We still might have a use for them. You never know."

"Right, boss. We'll get on it."

In the private royal sitting room, Walid and Mafulla stayed a bit longer, talking to the king. It was nice just to have the time together, even on a night when so many troubling things were happening. As Walid reviewed in his mind the events of the day, it suddenly occurred to him to ask something he'd been thinking about.

"Uncle Ali, maybe this isn't a good time to bring this up, or maybe it is. I've been thinking that Mafulla and I could use some self defense and maybe martial arts lessons from Masoon, if he ever has time. I mean, we get into some pretty sticky predicaments these days and it would be good to know how to defend ourselves."

The king looked impressed, and he smiled. "Masoon has already told me he plans to train you."

Walid was surprised. "Really? When?"

"Whenever you asked. And now I can tell him you've asked."

"Oh, man! That's great. Thanks, so much."

"You couldn't possibly have a better teacher for physical readiness, and the mental side of it, as well."

Mafulla and Walid were both grateful to hear this. But they were also extremely tired. When the younger boy covered a very big yawn with his hand, the king suggested they both go off to their rooms and get some sleep. Nothing more was likely to happen in the next few hours, at least nothing important or urgent. So they should rest. They needed to be fresh for class, especially since they now had to pay close attention to Khalid as well as to their lessons—if Khalid was even going to be there.

And they were getting ready to learn some pretty big lessons.

17

THE ENDANGERED FAMILY

"WHAT?" MAFULLA YELLED THE WORD OUT INTO THE darkness as he fought to come to full consciousness. His entire body jerked violently into a stiff, half-sitting position, with his right hand supporting his weight on the bed. His heart was pounding through his chest.

"Oh. No. What just happened?" He said this aloud, in a lower voice, with his head swimming. He flipped off the side of the bed, clicked on his new flashlight, opened the door, and lurched down toward Walid's room with a sick feeling in his stomach and his mouth sucked dry of any moisture. He knocked, pushed the door, and stuck his head into the dark room.

"Walid! Something bad has happened!"

"What? What is it?" The prince spoke as he fought to shake the sleep from his head. "Come on in." Mafulla stepped into the room.

"Something's wrong. I saw it in a dream. But it was more real than a normal dream. My father was on the floor of our home, bleeding from his head. I saw it!"

"In your dream?" Walid was still not sure what Mafulla was saying.

"Yes, but it was much more than just that. Remember what the king said about deep feelings and thoughts. I think this is real. I think my father is on the floor of our house and his head's bleeding and no one else is there and he needs help."

At that moment, having heard the noise, one of the butlers appeared outside the door. "Is everything all right, Prince and Mafulla?"

"Mafulla has need of a guard, as quickly as possible. He has an urgent concern."

"I'll get one right away. I should be back in a minute or less." The butler strode down the hallway.

"Maffie, go back to your room, dress as quickly as you can, and put your watch on. I'll do the same."

"Ok. But, what can we do?"

"We'll figure that out with the guard."

"I'll be quick." Mafulla dashed back down to his room.

Before he could return, and just as Walid had dressed, strapped on his watch, and slid into his sandals, a palace guard arrived at the room, offering his services. The prince explained that Mafulla had reason to believe his father had just been seriously injured and asked if there's any way the men watching his house from a short distance could be sent to check on him. The guard assured him that they were in radio contact from the palace to every guard outpost or mission in the city and that word could be sent within minutes.

Walid said, "Would you please do that, then, as quickly as possible? And we'll want to hear back, right away."

The guard replied, "Certainly. Or I can escort you down

to the communications room now, if you'd like, to make sure everything's done as you would prefer. Then you could hear immediately."

"Ok. Good idea."

That's when Mafulla walked up. "What are we doing?"

Walid explained, "We're going to follow this man to the palace communications room, radio a message to the guards watching your house, and wait there for word from them."

Mafulla frowned. "I feel like we should be there ourselves, at the house."

Walid said, "That would take too long. We need quicker action. And we need to stay to hear what's discovered and then decide what's to be done. It might take us half an hour to get there in person. The guards can be there in less than four or five minutes."

"Ok. That makes sense. Let's go."

The boys walked quickly down the darkened halls, illumined only by some dimmed electric lights that were now working again, but just at partial power, and descended a flight of stairs, following their guard into an area they had seen but not yet explored. They came to a series of rooms where men in uniform were working or lounging or eating. Many were drinking strong coffee.

Right away, they met the supervisor on duty and explained the situation briefly, but without mentioning anything about a dream. He was a bit puzzled and wanted to ask how they could know or suspect trouble, but this was the prince and his best friend, so he took the boys into the communications room and instructed the soldiers on duty to make contact with the Adi home guards. Within little more than thirty seconds, their concern had been conveyed and two armed men were on their way down the street to the home, which they already had in sight. Walid looked at his Reverso. It was about 5:20 AM. He turned to Mafulla. "Wind your watch."

"What?"

"Wind your watch. We do that when we get up normally, but I forgot to when I put it on, and I bet you did, too."

"Oh. Yeah. You're right. Ok."

A guard brought the boys some juice, which they took gladly, and with thanks. A minute later he came back with bread and figs. They nibbled nervously as they stared at the radio control panel.

Eight very long minutes later, the radio crackled. It was one of the guards with a report. "We have Mr. Adi. He had a nasty blow to the head, but he'll be fine. He's conscious now and the bleeding has been stopped. He's quite frantic, though, and rightly so. His wife and two children seem to have been taken away by unknown assailants."

"Oh, no!" Mafulla said. "Mom and the kids! Oh, no!"

The radio crackled and popped.

The supervisor leaned in and switched on a microphone. "What's happened there?"

The voice responded: "Someone got into the house. Mr. Adi was knocked out. We found him unconscious and there was a note lying on the floor beside him with the message that his family members are going to be held until Mr. Adi retrieves, in whatever way he can, a box that the writer says belongs to his men. It's one that's in the palace, and that they intended on taking from the guard storage room when the power was off, but that they somehow managed to miss. They said it would have the number 89 on the side of it, and they gave a location where Mr. Adi is to leave the box, or have it left. They said the family would be returned when the box is in their possession, and they instructed him to tell no one of this. Does any of that make sense?"

"Yes," Mafulla said, over the microphone. "All of it does." He felt cold inside, and could tell that he was starting to tremble, ever so slightly.

Walid turned to the supervisor and said, "We know what he's talking about. Please send someone to tell the king right away. This must be dealt with immediately. Naqid and Masoon also need to know what's just happened." Walid didn't see him, but his old friend Bancom al-Salabar had poked his head into the room just in time to overhear the transmission, and the second it ended, he was gone.

In the abandoned nearby warehouse he was using, not far from the palace, Ari Falma glared at the man sitting in front of him. "Put your left hand on the table. Spread out your fingers." The man did as he was told, with a look of fear on his face. "You have three days to get the box. At sunrise on the fourth day, one of these fingers will be separated from your body, as the box has been separated from me. Each sunrise after that, another finger will be taken from you as you watch. And we'll fill your mouth with rags when we do this so that your screams can't be heard. If you run out of fingers, there are always the toes. Then we move to other areas. I'll use this knife." He held up a long, curved blade with serrated edges.

"But Ari, please! I've already put into operation the plan you suggested to retrieve the box. The men have taken the Adi woman and her small children. They knocked out the father, and left beside him a note explaining that he'd have to get the box for us to secure their safe return. Since we suspected the house was being watched from the front, our men entered from the back, and I'm sure they got away with no one knowing. They should be here any minute now."

"I'm aware of what you've done. But I've already trusted you once to get what I wanted, and you failed me with the most important item. I'm telling you now in a way you can understand that you have to get the secret box this time, or you'll personally suffer some very permanent consequences."

The man looked desperate. "We'll threaten to do to the family what you've just threatened to do to me! We'll do whatever it takes!" He was stricken with real panic and was starting to sweat profusely.

Falma looked impressed. "That's actually a good idea. I'd give Adi a day to act, just to get his family members back, and then your threat would be a nice extra measure, sure to produce quick and dramatic action on his part. Give him a deadline, one like you have. After this first day passes, if there's no box at the drop spot, put the deadline in a note and pay some street kid to deliver it to his store. We know he has access to the palace and the king. His older son's living there. Surely he can prevail on his son to make this happen. And then we can do what we need to do."

"Ari, I swear I'll make this work."

"I'll expect you to keep your oath. But I'll also sharpen the blade."

Walid and Mafulla left the communications area and walked back to the royal living quarters at a brisk pace, followed by the guard who had escorted them to the radio room. Mafulla felt like every cell of his body was being squeezed by anxiety and fear. His face was ashen. Walid could tell that his friend was under great stress and advised him, as they walked, to breathe deeply and try to make his mind a blank. He pointed out that the emotions of panic and worry would do him and his family no good. They could even block his ability to think well and deeply. He needed to try to let go, release his quite natural concerns of the moment, slow his racing thoughts, and open himself up to deeper guidance.

Walid's many talks with his uncle during their days in the

desert were being brought to bear on the situation and his words were helping. Mafulla listened attentively and tried to do everything he suggested.

When they arrived at the king's rooms, Ali was already up and was being briefed on the situation. It was Bancom. He nodded at the boys as they walked quietly into the room. They went over to the long sofa and sat down. The color had come back to Mafulla's face, but he was shaking his left leg hard and fast, bouncing the heel up and down, toes and fore-foot planted firmly on the floor. His head was calmer but there was a manic nervous energy still coursing through him.

Two guards came in the door, and the king turned to them, giving instructions. Bancom walked over to the boys and put his hand on Mafulla's shoulder. He looked at Walid and then back at Mafulla. "It's good to see you both. I'm sorry about the situation. But we'll act fast and get your family back. Your father's fine and well protected now."

Mafulla said, "Will we have to give the bad guys the box they want?"

"I think we have other options that will be less pleasant for them."

Walid asked, "What can we do?"

Bancom responded, "I was just telling the king that Masoon has already sent five groups of top soldiers, six to a group, to search the city for these people. They're in normal civilian clothing and will pursue every avenue available for finding the men and rescuing Mafulla's family."

"Good."

"Masoon himself is taking his twelve best men with him to pursue the likeliest leads. They're also undercover. It's a strike force that no one can resist. The criminals who did this will soon regret deeply what they've set in motion."

"Can Mafulla and I do anything?"

"I think you'd better talk to the king about that. I need to go right now and get to work coordinating all the incoming information, and get it out to the men who need it."

"Ok, Bancom, thanks for telling us all this. We'll see you later."

The man did a short bow of his head and quickly left the room. The guards had just that second left as well. King Ali turned to the boys.

"Mafulla, I'm deeply sorry that such a thing has happened. We thought our observation post in the neighborhood would prevent anything remotely like this. But apparently, the criminals somehow knew of the post, or at least suspected it, and came in the back way. It seems that Ari Falma will do anything to get what he wants."

"Uncle, are we sure he's behind this?" Walid asked.

"Yes."

"Well, then, who is he, really?"

"He's a man enslaved by greed and corrupt ambition." The king thought for a moment. "Can you boys stay for a couple of minutes?"

"Sure." Walid answered first.

"Yes, sir, if you're certain there's no place we should be, and nothing else we should be doing to help out, right now." Mafulla said.

"I'm certain. We need you here. Please, have a seat."

"Ok." Mafulla let out a deep breath. They both sat down on the sofa but almost at the edge of the seat cushion. The king sat across from them.

"I want to ask you to make your minds blank for a few seconds, and trust that all will be well. Clear your heads and emotions for now." He paused and looked at both boys and then went on. "I like to use moments like this for some reflection. I just characterized Ari Falma as a man enslaved by greed and ambition. I want to explain what I mean."

"Ok," Walid said.

The king explained, "Greed is an overly strong love of money, or anything that money can measure. It's about acquiring and having. Ambition, on its side, is typically all about attaining something that's believed to be of value—whether it might be greater status, power, accomplishment, or recognition." Ali paused again and then said, "There's, first of all, nothing wrong with a good, healthy appreciation for financial resources, or an enjoyment of the positive power they hold. With great resources, we can do great things."

"That makes sense," Mafulla said.

"Good. Ambition, like a proper appreciation of money, can also be perfectly healthy. It's fine to want to do and achieve and be esteemed by others. But when a love of money or an ambition for other externals comes to dominate your life, it can enslave you and cause you to engage in actions that are self-destructive, and even evil. That's apparently what's happened with this man, Falma. I've been told that it was true of his father, and of his grandfather, as well. When you grow up around bad ideas and bad examples, it can be especially difficult to become a good person."

"Why is that?" Walid asked.

"Quite simply, it's because we tend to become like the people we're around," Ali answered. "There's a deep imprinting disposition in us, meant to help us learn when we're very young. But it can cause us to pick up bad habits, thoughts, and attitudes just like good ones."

"That's the principle of the two powers again," Walid commented.

"Yes it is. And it's worked in Ari Falma's life like it does in anyone's life. Unfortunately with his background, he picked up terrible things. I've learned enough about him and his family history to be confident in saying this. And he can be a lesson to you both, a cautionary tale. Always ask yourself: 'What's my main motivation in life?' If it's just money, power, status, or fame, then that will be a little like trying to catch a fast and elusive poisonous snake in your hands. In case you succeed, it may mean your own demise. And yet, in this case, unlike the snake, it's not the nature of the thing caught, but the narrow, focused pursuit of it that's dangerous. It's the effect that such a focal pursuit has. It changes a person."

The king went on. "One of the great surprises of life is that when you focus and fixate on external things like money, power, status, or fame as your main goals, your ultimate ends, the values that drive you, you diminish yourself to the point that, if you actually attain any of these things, you'll be less likely to handle them well than a person who gains them almost by accident, as a by-product of good work that's well done. The individual who pursues things of the spirit, and the well-being of others, is different. If, along the way, any of these other highly regarded external things comes to him, or all of them, for that matter, then he will much more likely be able to act as their master, and not their slave. There will be healthy, and not harmful, results."

"Why do things work this way, Uncle?" Walid was always curious to understand.

"Well, you see, the inner must be the foundation for the outer, or nothing really goes well. Any large building that's without deep and solid foundations is unstable and can collapse in a storm, or when it's otherwise pounded and stressed by external forces. A tent needs no foundation. It's temporary. A tower does. In a similar way, if you want your life to rise high and last long, you must anchor it deeply. Dig down beneath the shifting sands of worldly fortune, glamour, and fame. Establish footings deep in the soul. That way, you can truly flourish. Then, all the riches of the world can come to you, and you'll never be diminished as a result. You will, by contrast, flourish. A man or woman with inner strength can use all outer things for good purpose, and with beneficial consequences. The world works this way to help remind us where the most important things are to be found."

Mafulla appeared to be so entranced by the king's thoughts that he'd temporarily loosened his grip on his immediate worries, or they had at least momentarily eased their hold on him. He said, "Wow. This is really interesting, Your Majesty. And it seems so important. I'm glad to gain new insights like these."

The king replied, "Good. I'm happy to help. So, please ponder these thoughts as you can. Remember them, and they'll steer you well in your lives."

He pursed his lips and lowered his head for a moment, stroking his beard. Then he looked up and said, "Throughout the years, I've been provided with useful perspectives and with answers to many of life's questions. But right now, I do have one question for which I need an answer. Mafulla, exactly how did you know of your father's plight?"

"I had a vivid, scary dream that seemed like more than a dream. I told Walid right away, and he acted fast to do something about it."

"You both did the right thing. And I commend you. I should also say that I'm not at all surprised at your mental access to the traumatic event that's happened. As a result, you were able to be of help to your father and your family tremendously, heroically, and well. But, for now, at this point, I can't imagine anything else that you boys can do here to assist any further—unless, of course, some other vivid dream or vision comes to you. And if that happens, by all means, tell me immediately. For the time being, I should get on to other aspects of this pressing business."

"Yes, sir," Walid said. But then the king went on.

"Mafulla, we'll get your family back, safe and healthy. So, please, try to trust in all of us and do what you can to go about your day to the extent that you're able. I'll send word to you, as soon as we learn anything else."

"Ok, Your Majesty," Mafulla said.

And Walid added, "Thanks, Uncle Ali. We feel more than a little frustrated that we can't do something ourselves at this point. But we're glad so much is being done by everyone else to help."

"Yeah, thanks, Your Majesty." Mafulla looked worn out, and it was just the start of the day. He then said, "Do you really think mom and the kids are going to be all right?"

"Yes, I do," the king replied. "The most obvious interpretation of the situation is that they've been taken to be traded for something the criminals badly want, and so we can be fairly confident that they'll be kept safe as bargaining pieces, at least for a time. And before that time is up, we should have them back, completely unharmed."

"That helps. Thanks again." Mafulla looked at least a little bit relieved. He and Walid stood up and began to say their goodbyes, but just then Walid's father walked through the door.

"Ali, I had to come by as soon as I heard. They told me it was likely the boys were here." He turned and looked at the two of them.

"Walid, are you Ok? Mafulla, are you all right?"

"Yeah, dad, just worried, I guess."

"Yeah, thanks, Dr. Shabeezar, I'm really worried, too, and somehow totally wide awake, and yet exhausted, at the same time."

"That's natural, Mafulla. It's a stressful situation. But rest assured that your family will have the best available help on earth."

Rumi turned to Walid. "Your mother will be in the palace all day. She would love to see you if you have time. Hamid and I will be on duty, in case any medical services are needed for our men in the field."

He put his hand on the shoulder of his son's friend. "Mafulla, I deeply regret that you and your family are going through this. With the men who are out looking for them, they should be returned to safety soon. I'm sure these criminals just don't realize who we are. This is not the former regime. Our men have prepared all their lives to defend the kingdom and everything of value in it. They'll find and free your family soon."

"Thanks, Dr. Shabeezar. I needed to hear that. Our family has never had special protection. Well, we've never needed it, but it does give me some comfort and more confidence to hear what you've just said."

"Good. Boys, I need to be getting to the duty station. We'll make sure you're well informed throughout this operation." Rumi turned and conferred a moment with the king and then left as quickly as he had arrived.

The boys thanked the king again and walked back toward Walid's room.

Mafulla looked at his watch. "6:30. It's still hours until class. Should we even go?"

Walid said, "I think the king wants us to go, you know, to watch Khalid and try to figure out that situation. Who knows? There could be some connections. But as soon as I say that, I somehow really doubt it. I just don't know. This is all pretty confusing."

"Yeah. It is." Mafulla rubbed his face and his closed eyes with both hands. He said, "Have you ever had coffee?"

"No." Why do you ask?

"I maybe want to try some. I feel really worn out from all this stuff, and there still might be a lot happening today. I've got to stay alert."

"I think you have to be older to drink coffee."

"Just a couple of sips might help."

"Ok. We'll ask Kular in a minute, on our way out."

"What do you mean, out? You have a look on your face. Are we going somewhere else, other than our rooms, at this hour?"

"Well, suddenly, I'm having a strong, strange feeling. I think we should go back down to the basement."

"Really? Now?"

"Yeah. There's something there, I think, something we need to find."

"This sounds a lot like The Golden Viper talking."

"Yeah, I know. And I have another really odd feeling."

"What?"

"We need to take our guns. And get that green ribbon, just in case."

"That really sounds like a Viper thing to say. Ok, GV, see you in two minutes."

"Oh, Maffie?"

"What?"

"Just one empty chamber, Ok?"

"Oh, Ok. Will do."

Mafulla jogged down to his room and, walking over to a big dresser, opened the drawer where he kept his small revolver, took it out, checked the chambers, and rummaged around to find the little box the palace guards gave him after the mess at his dad's store. He carefully loaded one extra bullet into the gun, and tucked it into his belt. Then he found the green ribbon which he tied discreetly onto the belt, over to the side where it wouldn't be too prominent. He left the room, closed the door, and went down the hall to rejoin Walid.

Walid noticed the green ribbon right away and whispered. "Not yet with the ribbon. Take it off, for now. We'll put them on when we get down to the basement." Mafulla started to ask why but instead just untied the ribbon and tucked it away in a pocket for the moment.

They walked back down the hall and stopped at the head butler's room. Walid stuck his head in the doorway. "Good morning, Kular."

"Good morning, Prince Walid. Hello, Mafulla. I've heard what's going on. I'm very sorry."

"Thanks, Kular," Mafulla said.

"I'm sure the situation will be resolved quickly and safely."

"I hope so. I've decided to be confident."

"Good. That's the best idea for any situation. Is there anything I can do for you gentlemen this morning?"

Walid said, "Just a quick question, first. Did the king speak to you yet about some break you took in the middle of the afternoon yesterday?"

"Yes, Your Highness, we've discussed it. One of the young butlers, a new man on staff, had heard me talking about some recent knee pain, and he insisted that I go see Doctor Hamid about it. He said he would cover for me. He made the excellent point that every step I took, without consultation, I was perhaps doing more damage to my body. So, I limped right off. I was back in not too long."

"Did the king tell you that I gave the substitute butler an important note for my uncle that he never delivered?"

"Yes, and it was all apparently just a big mistake on the young man's part. Hamaj—that's his name—said that he put the note in a safe place until the king's meeting would end, and when I returned, he had completely forgotten about it. It seems that he had several people interrupting him with things he needed to do and, unfortunately, he just lost track of it. When I came back, he never mentioned the note to me— which, I suppose, confirms his forgetfulness. He's apologized profusely for the oversight, and I've explained to him that it was a serious mistake on his part. He won't be serving again in the king's quarters for a while. When I told him that, he asked to be reassigned to your parents where perhaps, he said, he can redeem himself."

"Oh, Ok. Thanks. I just wondered. But there's one more thing. Mafulla thinks he needs a sip or two of coffee. Do you have any this early?"

"Yes, right here, freshly made." He turned to Mafulla and said, "But aren't you possibly a little young for coffee?" Kular smiled.

Mafulla replied, "I'm much older than I look."

"Oh?"

"I take care of myself, you know, with good nutrition, ample exercise, and I try to avoid too much sun exposure. It's terribly aging."

"I see."

Walid spoke up. "I had told him the same thing. But he says he thinks a sip or two would help him wake up from the exhaustion he's feeling this morning."

"There shouldn't be any harm in it since, now that I've heard his quite mature explanation of the discrepancy between age and appearance, he does strike me as much older than he looks."

Mafulla smiled. Kular said, "Allow me to pour you some coffee, then." He then turned back to the prince and asked, "Would you like a couple of sips as well?"

"Uh, sure, I guess, just to taste it."

Kular walked over to a pantry to get cups with saucers and then pour some hot coffee into them. Walid and Mafulla stepped more into his office and his small kitchen area. He handed them each a cup and watched as they looked down at the steaming dark liquid, so deep brown that it was nearly black.

"It's very hot, even though I poured from holding the pot high above the cups so it would go through more of the morning air on its way down, and as a result cool at least a touch."

"I wondered why you held the pot up so high," Walid said.

"It's an old trick for sensitive or novice coffee drinkers. You'll still need to blow on it to cool it a bit more at first. Or take a spoon and stir it. That exposes more of it to the air, and in addition, the heat will enter the metal of the spoon, and the coffee's temperature will drop."

"Why is that?" Mafulla asked.

"Metal conducts heat well and will draw it out."

"Oh. Interesting."

The boys did as he suggested, taking the spoons he offered, and they stirred, while also blowing. Then, Mafulla carefully sipped.

"Whoa! Hot. Still hot. And, jeez, bitter! But really, actually, not at all completely bad." He took a second sip and made a face, wrinkling up his nose. Now, Walid had to try it, too. He blew into the cup for about five seconds more. Mafulla watched him. Kular smiled.

Then he sipped. "Oh! My! Yuck! That's a little bit awful."

"I'm so sorry, Prince! Others tell me I make the best coffee in town!"

"Gee. I'm glad I didn't try it anywhere else, then!" Kular laughed and Walid asked, "Why do the older men like this stuff so much?"

The older man said, "You get used to it. Over time, you can actually develop a deep enjoyment of it."

"Really?"

"Yes, indeed. Many things in life are like that—strange at first, then they grow on you, and you come to enjoy them. Some foods are that way and some activities. Coffee is often like that for people when they first taste it, and especially if they're your age. Many put in milk or sugar or both to improve the taste. But some drink it black, like you're doing right now. I wasn't sure what to give you, so I gave you black, the straight stuff. Black is the standard for strong men, like the king."

Mafulla raised his eyebrows and said, "Yes, indeed, for strong men like us!" And then he took his third sip, a bigger one. "Ah! I'm liking it better already."

Walid sipped again, and paused, and said, "Well, I'm glad we stopped in to do this. It's been an educational experience, but I think it's back to tea for me. Plus, we'd better get going."

"Just a second." Mafulla took a fourth sip, swallowed, and said, "Yes. Yes. The additional strength now building within me calls out to be used. We must go. A strong man needs action. So, then bring on the world—or, at least, its bad guys who need to be taught a lesson!"

The head butler and Walid both laughed. The boys then handed him their cups and saucers with thanks and walked on.

Mafulla spoke first. "I guess you can tell I'm still really worried."

"Yeah, your coffee-induced wit clued me in."

Mafulla let out a big breath and said, "I'm better, after what the king and your dad said, but, you know."

"Yeah, I know. It's natural. I'd be really surprised you could joke at all, if you were anyone but you."

"If I were anyone but me, while still being the I of whom you speak, and yet someone else at the same time, then that in itself should be as surprising as anything, whether I could joke or not."

"True." Walid just replied with the one word, not wanting to set his friend off into any other craziness.

It took them only about five minutes to make it all the way down to the door of the basement. Of course, Mafulla had to say, "Well, well, The Doorway to Disaster—good to see you again, old friend." Walid opened it and they both proceeded through the short hall and then down the stairway. They seemed to be alone.

Walid whispered, "Now let's tie on the ribbons."

"Oh. Ok."

They both produced the small green ribbons and attached them to their belts. "We need to go straight to the mechanical room." Walid led the way down the dimly lit hall. He remembered well where he was going. The outer door to the mechanical room, as usual, was unlocked. He entered and walked over to the inner door on the left wall and tried it, to make sure it was still bolted. It was. Then he began to look around.

"Maffie, I have a feeling we're supposed to go look at the tunnel."

"I sort of feel that, too, now that you mention it. It's strange."

The boys walked back to the far wall and moved aside some boxes that were now in the way, and then unbolted and opened the old tunnel door. The heat and the smell hit them again, the scent of dirt and stale, warm air. Walid said, "I don't think this has been opened very often. It stinks in here." He then pulled out from a pocket the flashlight he had brought and switched it on.

"Man. I didn't know you had that with you," Mafulla said. "I should have brought mine. But you didn't say anything about the tunnel, earlier. I would have gotten it."

"Yeah. Well, I didn't even know why I grabbed the light when I left the room. But one's enough if we stay together." Walid slowly walked forward in the path of light he was cre-ating. The tunnel was lined in rough stone, and floored in stone as well, and was about seven feet wide, and maybe eight or ten feet high. He moved the flashlight side-to-side to make sure there were no spider webs or anything else in their way. They walked on for about thirty or forty yards, straight ahead, in total silence, other than the sound of their sandals on the stones and their breathing. It got hotter as they went on.

Walid whispered, "We must be near the furnace room now. The tunnel must run next to it. Wait. There's a wall up ahead." They walked on. Within a minute or so, they were facing what seemed to be a dead end, an old stone wall with several ancient wooden barrels stacked up against it. But why would there be this long a tunnel and just a dead end? And why were these barrels here? The questions occurred to Walid right away.

"Maffie, hold the light, I want to check something." Walid gave the flashlight to his friend, and got to work moving some of the barrels. They were empty but still awkward to move and a bit heavier than he had expected. He slid or rolled three sideways, then a fourth, and behind that barrel the edge of another door came into view.

"Turn the light to this. Over here." Mafulla got closer and aimed the light where Walid was standing and pointing.

"What is it?"

Walid answered in a loud whisper, "There's another door here."

He moved three more stacked barrels and the doorway was clear. There was a lock that looked like the one on the special Phi box, a combination lock, or what Mafulla had called a permutation lock. But this was a bit different. There were four small openings, or windows on the lock, and zeros showed behind each one.

Walid whispered, "Maffie, look at this. Bring the light closer. There's a lock with four single places for numbers. My birthday won't work. What should we do?"

Mafulla thought for a second, and said, "Ok. Four single digit numbers." He thought for a second and then said, "The lock is a brass or golden color. Try the golden ratio—the four digit part."

"What?"

"Try 1, 6, 1, 8."

"Ok." Walid slowly thumbed into place those numbers and pulled on the mechanism.

Click.

"Boy, I don't know how you do this, but you always get it right."

Mafulla whispered back, "Well, there are patterns here,

obviously, and once you understand, that's the first thing you try. Somebody's been pretty consistent with all this stuff. It's a lot easier when you're dealing with a guy who's either clearly obsessed, or reliably crazy."

"Well, I wouldn't really call you obsessed or crazy," Walid said.

"No, not me, silly man—whoever's responsible for all these locks and maybe the numbers of boxes in the storage rooms. He's the one who's obsessed."

"Oh, I see." Walid was joking, but with a straight face.

Mafulla continued. "At this point, you at least have an idea down here what to expect. Still, I have to depend a little on something like luck, or my very special, highly developed, extremely spooky extrasensory abilities."

"Extrasensory abilities?" Walid turned to look at him.

Mafulla answered, "How else would I always know the right thing to say to the ladies? Admit it. You see my uncanny skills in action all the time."

"I guess you're right." Walid took the lock off the door, and grabbed the handle. As he pulled it forward, it creaked lightly and groaned, as if it hadn't been opened in many years, or maybe decades. The door was a bit smaller and the tunnel beyond it got a little more narrow at this point. As Walid and then Mafulla stepped forward and twisted the light around, they saw that the space ahead was maybe five feet wide by eight or nine feet tall, still mostly rock, and still dry looking and safe to enter. They walked slowly ahead and saw in front of them a sharp turn to the left. The air was getting much cooler now. They continued to follow the tunnel and suddenly saw up ahead another door. As they approached closer, they could see that it had an identical lock on it. The light had reflected off it, right away. Walid went up to it and entered the magic numbers and, click, he was able to open this one, too. But the door wouldn't budge much. It opened toward the other side, and though he was pushing hard, it wouldn't move.

"There must be something blocking the door on that side." Walid spoke first, and still very softly.

"Or another lock," Mafulla suggested, almost in a whisper.

"Yeah, maybe so. What do you think we should do?"

Mafulla said, "I don't know. But, first, does it seem a little lighter to you on this end of the tunnel? I mean, the darkness isn't as total."

"Yeah, maybe so."

"Let me turn off the flashlight for a minute."

"Ok."

Click.

They seemed to be in almost complete darkness for a second. Then their eyes adjusted. There was a bit of light coming from somewhere.

"Look, right above us," Mafulla whispered. "There's a big square with a line of faint light around the edges. I bet it's a door or something."

"I see it."

"What do you think?"

"I think you're right. It looks like it's made out of wood."

"Ok, I have an idea," Mafulla said. "Give me the Kidnapper's Hotel Hand Boost. Let me get higher and see if I can grab onto these rocks lining the tunnel, and find a foothold. Maybe I can get a hand on something and pull myself up, so I can get closer to the light."

"All right, but first, reverse your watch, just in case you hit it on anything, and I'll do the same."

"Ok. Thanks." At this point, they could both do it in the dark, by feel.

Click.

Click.

"Here's the boost. Can you see my hands?"

"I'll feel my way. Yeah, there they are. Let me put the flashlight on the floor first. Ok, here comes my foot."

Mafulla got his boost and leaned against the rock wall, feeling for a handhold. He whispered, "I got it. One rock sticks out just enough. I'll grab it and search with my foot for a crack or ledge. Just a second. There, there's a little bit of a ledge. I'll put some weight on it, and keep one foot in your hands. If I lift up, raise your hands and keep me balanced. Give me a second. Good thing I'm a wiry guy, and limber."

Mafulla got up closer to the light and whispered back down to Walid. "I was right. It looks like a trap door made from wooden boards, and I can see more light through it, around the edges, and ... wait. Shh."

There was silence for ten or fifteen seconds. Walid's arms started to tremble under the weight of Mafulla's one foot that still rested in his hands. He whispered, "I'm losing it. I can't hold you up much longer."

"Shh." Now, even Walid could hear distant muffled sounds. Then he heard his friend whisper with a new intensity.

"Oh, no! Help me down." Mafulla grabbed Walid's shoulders and jumped down as quietly as he could. He whispered up close to Walid, "I heard two men talking, one angry and threatening, one scared. I couldn't really make out what they were saying, but I heard the words, 'family,' 'box,' and then, 'good.' Where are we? What's above us? I have a scary feeling they were talking about my family."

"I have no idea where we are. But we have to get Masoon down here as fast as we can."

"Ok, let's go back."

The boys picked up the flashlight, clicked it on, and walked as quickly as they could back through the tunnel, around the turn, through the inner tunnel door, and across the longest stretch, toward the mechanical room in the basement of the palace, whose faint light they could see just up ahead of them. At this point, they were almost running, and their sandals were making real noise on the rocky floor, scraping along.

Walid first stepped into the much brighter but still dim light of the room, and then, right after him, Mafulla. There was a noise from across the room, outside the exterior door, that grabbed their attention and their gaze, but at the next instant, there was a scramble from behind the open door at their backs, and suddenly, before they could turn their heads, both of them were seized from behind and some sort of cloth or bag was quickly pulled down over their eyes.

They each struggled and tried to fight. "What? Who are you?" Grips tightened on both of them. They heard a gruff voice.

"Give me their hands to tie." Each of them felt his arms being forced forward.

At that moment, Walid suddenly remembered that no one knew where they were. Mafulla's family had just been taken violently, and now this. A cold sharp fear struck him in the gut. He expected the worst, but had no idea what would happen next.

In fact, it might be no exaggeration to say that he was a single second away from the biggest surprise of his life.

18

A Surprise or Two

BOTH BOYS WERE IN SUCH A PANIC THEY COULD HARDLY think. Their minds were at the moment as blocked as their vision. It was as if the hoods or bags that had been put over their heads had eliminated the possibility of rational thought. Experience was no help. They were both being wrestled and forced into a position where they could be tied up, starting with their hands, which had just been pulled out and away from their bodies and held up to some additional unseen assailant. Then, the next words they heard him say could not possibly have stunned them more.

"Oh no! No, no! The sign of Phi! God help us!" The man sounded frantic and spoke in a loud but hoarse whisper. "Just tie their arms tightly and put them on the floor. We must get out of here to save ourselves! Quickly!"

"They can't be Phi! They're just boys!" An obviously alarmed voice behind them reacted with confusion.

"Yes, you fool! They have the sign on them, on their bracelets! Act fast! We have to get out of here!"

Ropes were looped around their bodies and arms in an

instant, pulled tight, and tied as quickly as possible. Heavy hands shoved them down to the floor, and they could then hear three or four people leaving the room and running down the hall outside.

Walid realized he needed to act fast. He took a breath and said, "Maffie, I'll bend over toward you. Use your hands to get the bag off my head." Mafulla did and then, with their backs together, Walid awkwardly untied his friend and was quickly untied in return. The knots were simple, big, and loose. "Get out your gun and let's go."

Walid led the way out the door and down the hall, running fast in the direction of the footsteps. And they were able to take a short cut. As they approached the stairway, still at a distance, they saw their attackers from behind, dashing up the stairs from the bottom, three men. In two seconds they would be all gone. Walid jumped into a crouch and aimed. Click. BAM! The sound was thunderous.

Mafulla did the same, a fraction of a second later. Click. BAM! The noise of the two shots together filled the basement and slammed into their ears almost painfully as it bounced off the walls.

The last man on the stairs, right before getting to the top, suddenly jerked and lurched forward and collapsed backward, falling, then rolling back down two, three steps, then a few more. He lay sprawled on the staircase, barely clinging to a step, as two dark circles of blood began to grow large and easily visible against his clothing. Walid stood up, panting, his heart throbbing in his ears, and racing. He said one word to himself: 'Control.' He took two deep breaths to try to gain some composure and, turning to Mafulla, said, "Breathe deep, two or three times." He knew his friend would be in just as bad a shape. The adrenaline was coursing through them both, jangling all their cells and neurons into a state of maximal alertness, but with blurred edges of panic and confusion. They seemed to be in a small, tight bubble of time, where the whole world had paused, waiting for their next move.

"Let's go!" Walid yelled as he ran toward the man, his gun held in front of him. Mafulla heard him clearly, although it was as if a pillow or blanket had been stuffed over his ears. He instantly followed Walid, and in the same pose. As they grew closer, they could see the man slowly move to reach for a knife in his belt.

"Stop Or Die!" Walid yelled, shocked at his own voice, as he arrived on the step closest to their assailant.

The man said, "Don't kill me! Please! I didn't know you're Phi! I'm sorry! I didn't know! It wasn't my idea! I was following orders, doing what I was told!"

Walid had no idea what he was talking about and said, "Who told you to do this?"

"Yeah, who?" Mafulla added.

"The but, the new …. hama." As he spoke, his voice trailed off and stopped. He coughed and jerked in a breath. His body convulsed hard, and the overwhelming pain of his wounds caused him that moment to lose consciousness, and go limp.

"Is he dead?" Mafulla looked scared.

"I don't know. Let me see." Walid felt for a pulse. "His heart's still beating. I think he just passed out. Take off your belt. We need to tie him here and go get help."

Mafulla did as Walid had said, and the prince tied the man's arms tightly together behind him, as the blood stain spread even more. That second, the door above them was flung open, with a crashing sound, and two men came to the edge of the stairs, guns drawn, with one yelling, "Stay where you are! Drop your weapon! Hands in the air!"

A jolt shot through Walid's body. It could be the men returning for their downed comrade. But as he twisted his head around to see, while feeling for his gun, which he remembered was close by, but a bit out of reach on a step in front of him, he suddenly recognized their uniforms, even in the dim light, and shouted, "I'm Prince Walid, with Mafulla! We need help!"

"Oh! Prince! We heard shots. Are you all right?" One of the guards called out immediately, and began descending the stairs, followed by his colleague.

"We're fine. We just got attacked by three or four men down here. They grabbed us, bagged our heads, tied us up, and ran away. We got free, gave chase, and saw them escaping. We had to try to stop them, so we shot and wounded this guy. He just passed out."

The second and younger guard exclaimed, "This is a man who works in the palace kitchen! He's a dishwasher." He looked at the older guard. "What's he doing down here attacking the prince?"

"I don't know, but we'll have to find out fast. I'll stay with this guy. You take the boys and get help. Get word quickly to Naqid."

"Yes, sir. Come with me, boys." Walid and Mafulla followed the guard up the stairs. Walid looked back.

"That's Mafulla's belt, tying the guy up. We'll need it back."

"Sure thing, Prince. I'll get it to you."

Even in the dim lighting, and amid all the turmoil, Walid then recognized the guard who was with them, from their time together on the camel train. "You're Omari. I remember you from our trip."

He said, "Yes, I am. We never had much chance to talk

with each other on the journey across the desert. I was up toward the front. And the older men kept me busy. It's an honor now to serve you."

Omari asked Walid and Mafulla to keep their guns out and ready, as they didn't know where the other attackers had gone. The boys went out the door cautiously, and began walking rapidly down the hall, frequently turning their heads and sweeping from side to side with their weapons at the ready, and often looking backward, following the lead of Omari, who seemed to know just how to make a quick, careful exit from a dangerous situation.

In a minute or so, and on a different hallway, they saw two guards up ahead of them. Omari called out to them, and told them his partner needed help on the basement stairs with a wounded suspect who had attacked the prince, and that there were likely other suspects at large, still in that area of the palace. The new men ran off to be of assistance. Omari, Walid, and Mafulla continued on toward the main guard station, where the radio room was located. It was more than a five minute walk, during which time they were extremely alert. But the adrenaline rush was starting to subside in their systems. They could breathe more normally now and their hearts were no longer racing at maximum speed. Still, the boys each felt like they were trapped in a bad dream, and that this could not really be happening.

When they came within sight of the guard rooms, Omari yelled out at the first colleague he saw, "Get word to Naqid, now! The prince has been attacked and is safe, but there are two or three suspects still loose in the palace."

Walid also shouted to him, "Get through to Masoon, too! We have vital and urgent information for him that he needs to hear right away!"

That very second, Bancom stepped out of the communications room, a bit farther down the hall. "Boys? Are you Ok?"

Walid said, "Yeah, fortunately."

"You were attacked?"

"In the basement."

"What were you doing down there?"

Walid said, "It's a long story. We both had a feeling we were supposed to go check out a room there, and we did, and there's a tunnel off the mechanical room that we entered and we went down it."

"Yeah," Mafulla added, "and we think we've found maybe where my family is being held!"

"Really?"

"Yes." Walid continued. "And when we were running back to tell you guys, we were grabbed from behind, right at the entrance to the mechanical room, and we had our heads bagged, and were tied up, just like in the marketplace."

Mafulla again picked up the narrative. He said, "But the guys suddenly panicked or something and left us and we got loose and gave chase and shot one of them in the shoulder and the leg and he's in custody now."

"You did?"

Walid said, "He's unconscious, but before he passed out he said he was under the orders of somebody."

Mafulla added, "All we heard were the sounds, 'the but, a new ... hama,' and then he conked out before he could say more."

Walid suddenly realized something, and said, "Oh, man! It could be the butler, a new man, Hamaj who substituted for Kular the other day in the king's quarters and didn't give him an urgent message I left, and he's now assigned to my parents!

He needs to be arrested and questioned before he can do anything to my mom."

"Wow. That's a lot, all at once. Ok, I'll get on everything
this minute. Is there anything else you can tell me?"

Omari spoke up. "The man they shot works in the kitch-
en. There were at least two others who got away and they may
work there as well. We need to lock down that area and round
them all up. And find anyone who works in the mechanical
room."

Walid said, "And get Masoon on the radio. I have to talk
to him now."

"Are you sure, Prince?"

"Yes, I am. I need to speak to him without delay."

"Ok. You two come into the control room. I'll get Masoon
on the radio." Bancom then spoke to another man about having the guards lock down the kitchen area, and joined the
boys in the radio room. Omari stood at the door, still watchful, as they entered.

They all gathered behind the radio operator who, on Bancom's instructions, tried to find Masoon. They checked the
guard outpost near the Adi home, where he was going to be
canvassing a half mile and then a one mile perimeter around
the house, with his men spread out, asking neighbors for any
sightings of the kidnapping. One of the guards at the outpost
went out to find Masoon.

In about ten very long minutes, the outpost operator
called back in and put the general on the radio. The receiv-
er cracked and popped. There was lots of interference. They
could hardly hear a thing. But when the radio guy turned the
microphone over to Walid, the signal cleared up. The prince
told Masoon the whole story as quickly as he could, focusing
on the part about the tunnel, the door, and the conversation

Mafulla overheard that sounded like it was about his family. Masoon said he'd bring his men back to the palace immediately and meet them at the large entrance hall at the side of the palace closest to the basement stair door. He asked that Rumi and Hamid be sent there to help in twenty minutes. And he instructed that the king should be informed of everything quickly.

Masoon then asked, "Walid, who's with you now?"

Walid answered, "Bancom and Mafulla and a radio operator and another communications officer. And the guard, Omari."

"Good! Excellent. You can trust him. He's strong and true. Have him choose two more guards to go with you back to the big entrance hall near the basement door. I'll meet you there and take just a minute of your time to establish exactly where we're going."

Walid said, "Ok."

Masoon responded. "And, Walid, this is important. Send everyone right now out of the radio room for a minute."

Walid said, "What?"

"Ask everyone else who is there to please leave the room."

"Ok. I will." Walid looked around. There were Mafulla, Bancom, the radio operator, and one other man who worked in communications. Before he could speak, Masoon then said, loudly, over the radio speaker, "Everyone who can hear my voice, except for Walid, please clear the room for at least thirty seconds. Walid, let me know when you're alone."

"Yes, Masoon. Just a second." Everyone looked puzzled but quickly exited the room and Bancom closed the door behind them. Walid then said, "They're gone. I'm alone."

"Is the door closed?"

"Yes."

"Ok. When you tell Omari to pick two men to go with you, tell him quietly that I gave you a signal. Tell him a word, it's actually a Greek letter. Say, 'Phi' and he'll know what you mean."

"Phi?"

"Yes."

"What?"

"I'll explain later."

"I have some more to tell you that involves that letter."

"When I get there and get this done. Now, please, go quickly."

"But also, Masoon, I told Bancom that the new young butler assigned to my parent's quarters may have given the orders for the guys who attacked me and Maffie. You need to get that guy and protect my mom."

"Tell Bancom to have Hamid do that before he comes to the meeting place, but tell him to move fast."

"Ok, I will."

"I'm on my way. Out."

Walid walked to the door, opened it, gave Bancom the message for Hamid, and told everyone the radio call was over. A swirl of events moving in several different directions was instantly set off. The palace was filled with vectors of action that would converge very soon.

Within ten minutes, Hamid was striding into the wing of the palace where the royal family stayed, walking past pairs of guards here and there, and heading straight for Rumi and Bhati's suite of rooms. As he moved through the entrance door, he saw the new young butler sitting at the reception desk and writing. The sound of his footfalls caused the man to look up just as the doctor appeared.

"Please stand up and show me your hands." Hamid said.

"What?"

Hamid glared at him and said, slowly, "Stand up right now and show me your hands. You're under arrest."

As the man stood, he pulled a hidden knife from the bottom of the desk. But then, in a shockingly fast blur of motion, the knife hit the far wall of the room and fell to the floor and the butler was doubled over in pain without any breath remaining in his body. Hamid unleashed one more quick motion and the man crumpled to the ground, unconscious. The older man shook his head and said aloud, but in a low, disgusted voice, "They always choose badly."

He stuck his head out the door and called down the hall, "Guards! Come apprehend this man!" Two nearby palace guards responded right away and took the unconscious butler into custody.

Bhati Shabeezar opened an inner door, looked at the scene in shock, and said, "What in the world is going on?"

"Bhati, this man's a criminal and traitor. We're taking him into custody for questioning. You're safe." He didn't mention anything about Walid, because he was in too much of a hurry and could explain more later.

"Oh, my goodness! Thank you!" Bhati exclaimed. "Does the king know?"

"He will, momentarily. You'll have guards in the room within minutes, just to make sure you're all right while we interrogate this guy."

"Is Walid safe? And Mafulla?"

"Yes, they're at the main guard station talking with Bancom now."

"Good. But shouldn't they be on the way to class?"

"Yes, but they had some information they needed to pass on to us. I suspect they'll be headed to class very soon, with an official guard excuse for tardiness."

"Thank you, Hamid."

"And I'll be meeting Rumi in a few minutes to do some work together."

"You both be careful. The king has let me know about the Adi family. So please, have me informed if anything of importance happens."

"We will."

Hamid turned and left as the two palace guards were lifting the still unconscious butler off the floor and dragging him to a chair, so that he could be suitably shackled and prepared for being moved to an interrogation room in another part of the building.

Right outside the radio room now, Mafulla whispered to Walid, "Why did Masoon send us all out of the room?"

Walid said, "Just a second. Follow me." And then, a few feet down the hall, he turned to the young guard who had been waiting for them, approaching him up close, and speaking to him in a voice that only he and Mafulla, who was just two feet away, could hear.

"Omari, Masoon says you're to choose two men and accompany me and Mafulla back to the entrance hall near the basement stairway door. And he said that when I tell you about choosing the men, I'm supposed to say that he gave me a signal—the Greek letter, Phi."

Omari looked surprised. He said, "Oh! Ok, not a problem, Your Highness. Please wait here." He walked down the hall and disappeared into one of the far rooms.

"Well, that was unexpected." Mafulla spoke in a soft voice to Walid. "What's this all about?"

"I have no idea," Walid said.

"Ok then, let's summarize. Masoon knows something about the name of the golden ratio. And it's somehow a secret signal that has something to do with choosing people for a guard detail. And Omari apparently knows what he means to communicate in this way, by using the Greek letter."

"Yeah, so it seems." Walid rubbed his neck and twisted it side to side.

Mafulla said, "And there's even more going on here than we know about. Those guys in the basement completely freaked when they saw the backs of our watches."

"Yeah, they did."

"They yelled that we're Phi, or that we can't be Phi, or something."

"Yeah, or both those things, whatever they meant."

"All of a sudden, for some reason, they were scared of us, or of something."

"Totally. It was a good thing we had reversed our cases. Who knew that such a small action would save us from a situation that could have been really bad?"

"Well, apparently, you knew."

"Not really. But, yeah, Ok, maybe, somehow, at some level—it's possible, I guess."

"Look, you knew we were supposed to go to the basement and then the tunnel and just when we were supposed to be down there."

Walid replied, "Well, you knew that I was right, and then you knew to get up close to the trap door and listen. And, what about the dream? You knew your dad was hurt and that something was really wrong. You saw him on the floor across town. That was freaky."

"Yeah, we're both freaks. But we're super freaks."

"I guess."

Omari walked up with two men Walid also knew from the camel train.

"Paki! Amon! I haven't seen you guys since we rode up to near the city. You're palace guards now?"

Paki responded, "Yes, Your Highness. It's good to see you. We've heard about your amazing exploits. We've been serving outside the palace and going through special training until a couple of days ago, but we're here now."

"Good," Walid said. "It'll be great to have you around."

Amon smiled and said, "Thanks, Prince. And, hey, congratulations on breaking up the crime operation in the back of the Adi store." Then he turned to Mafulla. "I bet you're Walid's friend, Mafulla."

"That's me."

"Amon at your service. And this much-less-good-looking associate of mine is Paki." Paki laughed and did a small bow.

Mafulla smiled and said, "Nice to meet you both."

"Well," Omari concluded, "Enough pleasantries. Let's get down to the staging area. We need to go now."

"Back to our old friend, The Doorway to Disaster." Mafulla said with a sigh and turned to follow their lead down the hallway.

Walid looked over at the others and explained, "That's Mafulla's little joke about the door to the basement. That's what he's called it since the first time we went down there to explore."

"May I ask why?" Omari looked puzzled.

"It's a phrase our teacher had used in class, about something completely unrelated. But Mafulla has certain intuitions. And the basement seemed like such a harmless place, for a while. We even played bocce ball down there."

Mafulla shot Walid a look and spread his hands out in the universal gesture of, "What? Why are you saying this?" He actually said, "Oh well, good. Now, the next thing you know, everyone will be playing ball down there. We'll have to schedule a hallway days in advance. People are going to set up concession stands. The crowds will be unbearable. The price of bocci balls will go through the roof. There may even be a scarcity of proper equipment. And of course, there will be nowhere at all pretty soon to park your camel. It's all ruined now. The secret's officially out."

Walid grimaced. "Oh, maybe I wasn't supposed to say that."

Two of the guards just looked surprised, but Paki laughed, as the five of them kept walking back at a good pace toward the area of the palace where they'd meet others near the basement entrance.

Omari turned to Mafulla and in a voice mixing kindness, admiration, and perplexity, he said, "It's amazing to me that you can make a joke at all, under the circumstances."

"That's just Mafulla," Walid said.

The younger boy then sighed out loud and said, "I always do it when I'm nervous or worried, and the more intense the situation is, the worse I get. This is so bad that I'm liable to say anything. Just ignore me, like the wise Walid does, at least, most of the time."

"Boys!" A voice called out from behind them. It was Hamid, walking up quickly. They slowed down. He drew close and looked at Walid and said, "I took care of the little problem at your parent's quarters. When the guy wakes up, we'll find out what's going on."

"Thanks, Hamid. But, wait. When he wakes up? What did you do to him?"

"Not a lot. He went for a knife. I had to respond. He should wake up soon. He'll be in some pain, but he'll be able to answer questions."

"Wow. Good deal," Walid replied.

Now the six of them turned and walked briskly toward their next adventure, and the new information that would change the lives of the two boys forever.

19

A HUGE PIECE OF NEWS

WITHIN A FEW MINUTES, THEY WERE IN SIGHT OF THE large entrance hall where Masoon had said that everyone should meet. Walid's dad was already there with a few men, examining maps on a big table in the middle of the space.

"Dad!"

"Walid! Come over here. Mafulla, you, too. I've heard what you've both been through already today. Are you Ok?"

"I am." Walid said.

"Mafulla?"

"Yes, sir."

"Good. I'm glad. You two are always in the middle of the action. And I'm grateful that, so far, you always seem to land on your feet."

Walid said, "I guess you're right. So far, at least."

Rumi continued, "I'm here for more than one reason. Right now, I can use your help. We need to get down to business. Masoon will be with us any minute. Step over to the table and look at this map." The boys followed his lead, as their companions took a few steps forward and then hung back, except for Hamid, who also joined them at the table.

Rumi bent down and gestured. "This is a map of the palace and its immediate neighborhood. Here's roughly where we are." He pointed to a spot near the back and side of the building.

He then motioned to another map on the table, one that was very different. "Now, look at this second map, a rough blueprint of the basement. We have extra blank paper around it for you to use." He pointed a finger. "Here's the mechanical room where you found the door to the tunnel. As you can see, the tunnel and its door are not on the blueprint. I'm not personally familiar with that room, so I need you to show me where the door to the tunnel is, and give me your best guesses as to the distances you walked and the directions you went in, after you entered the tunnel."

Walid and Mafulla easily agreed on the location of the tunnel door, pointing to the same spot on the map. Rumi gave them pencils and they traced where they thought the tunnel went, the straight sections, and the turn. They estimated the distances, and they basically agreed on the place they thought they had ended up. They then went back to the first map, locating the palace in the larger neighborhood, with all the nearby buildings identified, and Rumi helped transpose what they had drawn into the different context and scale.

Their estimated end point was a short distance away from the edge of the walled and fenced palace grounds, and down toward the end of the next city block. It looked like their tunnel came up under what was marked as an old warehouse, one that was once used for supplies that would go to both the palace and some other nearby government buildings. It was not currently in use, as far as they knew. This could be the location of the voices Mafulla heard.

At just that moment, Masoon arrived with his twelve best

men, a fearsome looking bunch. Walid thought to himself that, if he didn't know Masoon, he would be a little frightened by the appearance of these guys, even though he recognized several of them from the camel train, and they were all in civilian clothing. They were big and strong looking, but what was most scary was the focused intensity of expression on their faces that he had never seen, a look that showed they meant business. And, however hard it may be to understand, the air in the room seemed to change when they entered. It was charged with a new and powerful energy that both boys could feel. It was almost like the space around them had lit up with something that was both good and fierce and dangerous, all at once.

Masoon nodded to the boys, but addressed Rumi straight away. "Have you come up with a location?"

"Yes, the boys are in agreement. We think they were under this old warehouse, and we think it was in this section." He pointed to a place on the south side of the building, toward the back.

Masoon said, "Hamid, I'll take six men outside to the front of the warehouse, Team A. You take six through the tunnel, Team B. Check your watches. In fifteen seconds it will be exactly 10:27. Set your watches on my word ... three, two, one: Now."

Walid and Mafulla had reversed their cases again to access the glass side, and they did what the men did, exactly when they did it. Masoon continued, "At precisely three minutes to 11, we'll enter the building from the north and east sides. That will draw the enemy's attention in our direction. As soon as you hear anything, at that time, and no more than five seconds later, proceed up through the trap door and eliminate any threat you see. That probably means anyone who's not a member of the Adi family."

"Will do."

"Mafulla's mother and her two small children may be there as hostages."

"Yes."

"They've been through enough already. Go to extraordinary measures to protect them, first physically, and then emotionally, as well. Precision is necessary. Their safety is our first concern. Dealing with their captors is secondary. Am I understood?"

"Certainly."

"We'll assault them from three sides. From what I see on the map, there's no way out for them. Now, Team B, take the ladders with you, and the lights, and get to the tunnel. Seven from the outside, seven from below ground, first wave at 3 minutes till 11. Shortly after that, or five seconds later, the next wave. That ought to do it. Let's go."

The men broke up into their predetermined units and quickly left the room, half toward the outside, and half around the corner, to proceed to and through the basement door. Walid turned to his father and said, "What should we do?"

"I have to take two men down the street to back up Masoon's assault with emergency medicine. Hamid's going in as the leader of the basement group with one more field medicine guy and two assistants to back him up. You two wait here with the other men. We need you here."

"Why here?"

"One or the other group may have an urgent need of some sort and send a runner here for your help in whatever way is required. We have to have someone on site here, at the operation center, just in case."

"Oh, Ok. What about the guys who attacked us today?"

"They're being pursued. They'll be caught. We're fairly

sure they're no longer in the palace. Naqid has searched well. Omari can talk to you about them, or answer any other questions you have. With him, Paki, and Amon here, you're safe and well assisted. And you can function as our coordinating, backup team, as I've said. But I have to go now."

"Ok, Dad, just be careful."

It was all happening so fast. But it had to. Mafulla's family was in great danger and needed to be rescued.

Omari and the other two guards walked up to the table where at this point Walid and Mafulla were standing alone.

Omari said, "Don't worry, Your Highness, and Mafulla. The fight is already won."

Walid looked puzzled. "What do you mean?"

Omari answered, "It's Masoon, and Hamid, and the rest of them are the right men for the job. It's done already."

Mafulla looked at his watch and said, "But it's just 10:30."

Omari simply looked at him and smiled.

Mafulla responded, "You seem very sure of what you say."

Omari replied, "Your family's already protected. Their future is secure. They'll be returned to you unharmed."

Mafulla raised his eyebrows, not for comic effect, but expressively, and said, "I hope you're right, but how can you say these things with such confidence?"

"The world is an ocean of information. Waves of it surround us. There's knowledge everywhere. You just have to be able to read it. I swim in this ocean. I dive deep. I ride the waves. We can know much more than most people think we can know. You yourself often know things that may seem impossible for you to be aware of. Am I right?"

"Yeah," Mafulla answered hesitantly. "All the time, or—I mean—at crucial times. I seem to get what I need when I need it. One thing I don't know is how any of this works."

"It's because you are who you are that it works. As you

learn more of the universal language of the world, as you become more proficient in reading it, you can access more and more of the information available. Some of us are simply very good readers."

Walid spoke up. "It's so strange. Much of our land is desert and yet I hear the ocean spoken of a lot, just recently."

Omari smiled and said, "So do I. Have you ever seen it?"

"The ocean? Not yet."

"Well most of the earth is ocean, even though not near our little neighborhood, and it contains many lessons for us. I hope you'll see it soon, you and Mafulla. It's vast, and dynamic, and powerful."

Walid could not help himself. He suddenly felt like he had to ask a certain question, even though it seemed like a big change of subject. He said, "Omari, why did Masoon have me pass on to you the Greek alphabet letter, Phi?"

"To tell me what sort of men to take along with me to guard you."

"Paki and Amon?"

"Yes. In this instance."

"How did a mention of the letter Phi lead you to include them?"

Omari was silent for a moment and looked at his colleagues, then back at Walid, and he said, simply, "They're Phi."

"But, what does that even mean, in such a context? I understand Phi, the golden ratio, as it applies to watches and faces and buildings. But how does it apply here, as you just said it? I mean: when Mafulla and I were attacked in the basement, the guys who grabbed us saw the backs of our watches and one of them said, with fear in his voice, 'They're Phi! We must save ourselves!' And then they just took off, running. We had no idea what they were talking about."

Omari looked surprised. "What's on the backs of your watches?"

Walid flipped the case. Click. "We had them like this to protect the glass on the reverse side while we were exploring the tunnel."

Omari looked and laughed out loud. "Oh! Very good. You gave those guys a real scare. Good for you!"

"Why? I mean, how? Why would they get scared and run away when they just saw the Phi symbol on our watches?"

Omari stood quietly for a couple of seconds more. He looked again at Paki and Amon. They both nodded slightly. The boys were perplexed.

Speaking to Walid, and also to Mafulla, but mainly to Walid, Omari said, "Well, it all started long ago. Before the Greeks ever visited Egypt with their culture and language and philosophy, our fellow citizens, a group of highly advanced Egyptians, had gone to Greece. You see, the ancient pharaohs always had at their side certain men with special talents. They were advisors and protectors, wise men and warriors, sages and seers. These men had what were known as golden abilities—special knowledge, and powerful skills far beyond even the dreams of most people. They visited Greece in the early days and saw great potential there for the cultivation of more individuals like themselves, and so imparted some of their knowledge and skill, while they also soaked up much that the Greeks in turn could teach."

"Really?" Walid had heard none of this before.

"Yes. The Greeks were quite advanced in their use of reason. The Egyptians were unusually developed in what's deeper than reason."

He paused, and said to both boys, "You know the whole story of Phi, in Greek mathematics and design? And, since then?"

"Yes. Well, at least some of it."

Omari glanced around them to make sure they were still alone, and he lowered his voice. "There's always been a secret society, a small group of us who have certain knowledge, and talents, and skills, and we're called by the name of Phi. We're chosen by the most advanced members already in the group, who must agree on our selection, when it becomes clear that we have the openness and the ability to carry on the tradition. We're the designated guardians among the royalty of the mind and body who have accepted all the additional responsibilities that such royalty can carry."

The boys were listening intently, but were still puzzled. Omari went on. "In some other parts of the world, Phi isn't organized, and that's too bad. But still, there are Phi. You could find them by looking at any walk of life and asking: Who stands out? Who seems to have extra intuition, instinct, and vision? Who has real power to move others to action? Who can make great things happen? Those people are likely Phi, whether they have ever been recognized as such or not. Some become national or world leaders. Some become professors, others inventors, or discoverers. A few become artists. Some are known as philosophers. There are Phi in business and medicine and in the military. They make a difference on many levels and in many ways. But, in our land, you must be chosen to be included in the organized group of Phi and then trained by those who are farther along the path."

"You're all three members in this society? You're all Phi?"

"Yes."

"Who chose you?"

"Masoon, years ago, chose me. Paki and Amon were chosen by Hamid."

"They're both Phi?"

"Very senior Phi."

"And they chose you?"

"Yes. Many years ago. But that just means that they first spotted the Phi in us, and were the ones to tell the others about us. And then, they were our sponsors, our main contacts, the ones who primarily taught us the things we needed to know. But all active senior Phi had to agree. At least, all in this kingdom who could be contacted at the time."

"How many Phi are there?"

"In our land, there are usually a few dozen, I'd say, give or take. Sometimes, more. Right now, I'm not sure. Only the most advanced members are aware of the exact number. Their identities are not widely known, and are only suspected by some."

"Ok, so why were the attackers so afraid of what they saw on our watches?"

"The letter strikes fear into the hearts of those on the wrong side of the law who have heard of the society."

"But why?"

"Phi are the fiercest warriors of all. It's almost impossible to defeat a senior Phi. This is also, to some extent, true of more junior but intermediate members, like the three of us. And every junior Phi has the close protection of senior Phi. Plus, there are legends among those who follow the path of corruption, and especially the worst criminals and wrongdoers. There are wild stories of the apparently supernatural—myths and beliefs about Phi that would surprise you."

"What, for example?" Now, Mafulla spoke up, completely fascinated by all this. He wanted to know more.

"There is a belief that a top, senior Phi can extinguish the physical life and even the soul of an evil man with a look. And it's a death involving torturous pain."

"Whoa."

"There's a widespread rumor that a Phi can see almost anything happening anywhere. That we have access to inner thoughts and feelings whenever we choose. That a Phi on a mission can't be killed or even escaped—only, at best, evaded and avoided temporarily. And, even then, that any prolonged avoidance is rare. That a deep and powerful force from the beginning of the universe flows through us and can make to be so whatever we will, far beyond the normal structures and strictures of nature."

"Wow," Mafulla said.

Walid added, "That's pretty wild."

Omari paused and replied, "You can see then how the guys this morning were so afraid when they saw your engraving."

"But why did they think, just because of the engraving, that we're Phi?" Walid was still puzzled.

"No one in our kingdom has ever been allowed, by an ancient law, to wear that symbol or display it in any way on, or in connection with, their bodies, even with a bracelet or watch, unless they're Phi."

Walid was confused in a new way. He said, "Wait. Then, did Uncle Ali not know about this law? Why would he engrave it on our watches?"

"Because, and this may come to you as a big surprise: You're Phi."

"What?"

"You're Phi. You're both Phi."

"What do you mean?" Mafulla spoke first.

"Yeah. What do you mean?" Walid could hardly process what he was hearing. He felt nearly as off balance as he had when his uncle, Ali, had first told him of his royal heritage and standing. His mind was nearly blank, as he tried to process what had just been said.

Omari went on. "You've been chosen by the king himself, the most exalted member of Phi in the entire area, and a very senior and advanced practitioner. The honor now falls to me to tell you. That's part of why you and Mafulla both live in the palace. That's a part of why you're being educated together. It's why Masoon will train you. It's one reason the king speaks to you freely about important things."

"But." Mafulla could get out only the one word.

Omari continued, "That's what your watches show. I guarantee you that any serious criminal in this town who saw that engraving would react in the same way that those guys did this morning. It's an amulet of protection for you that you'll need until your training has advanced to a certain point. Then, it becomes almost like a protection for others, a warning to any who would dare seek to harm you, or to physically resist you."

Walid and Mafulla were standing there just totally astonished. Their minds and hearts that had at first been nearly blank were now being slowly filled with a mixture of fear and awe, and pride, and shock, and wonder, and humility, and gratitude, and confusion, and doubt, and seriousness. They were so overwhelmed by this revelation that neither at this point could speak.

Until, at least, Mafulla said, "And I thought all that good stuff was because of my winning personality."

Walid laughed and replied, "I thought it was all because of your choice of cologne."

Everyone smiled. Walid then commented, "Well, this is a lot to absorb all at once. Are you absolutely sure about it?"

"Yes. We're very sure."

"Why didn't the king tell us all this himself?"

Omari said, "He was going to, when it seemed that the time was right, if you hadn't already found out some other way by then. His view has always been that, when the time has fully come, when the time is right, the right information emerges. He doesn't like to force these things, but rather to allow them to happen as they should. And now, it seemed right to inform you, and I'm glad. It's a great thing for me, and for all of us here."

"Welcome to the club," Paki said to both boys.

"Yes. Welcome to the club." Amon nodded and echoed the sentiment.

"And, I suppose … there are dues?" Mafulla said.

Amon laughed and answered, "Yes, big dues, bigger than you can imagine, and you'll pay them all the time. But there are even more benefits. So, on balance, it's a huge win."

Walid looked at his Reverso. "Wow. It's 5 minutes to 11."

Omari looked at his own watch and said, "It is."

"The action starts in 2 minutes."

"Yes."

"What will happen?"

Omari replied, "Masoon will approach and initially enter by stealth. He'll neutralize anyone guarding the entrance. He'll have two others with him, most likely. They're already in position. Their initiative will be followed by action from the second part of their team, whose first job will be to create a commotion, some sudden noise where none of them is located, to surprise and completely mislead the opponents. As soon as that's heard by Hamid, he'll break through the trap door, quietly if possible, but with his own commotion if necessary, and either sneak in or storm in from behind the enemy. The family will be as if in a bubble. They will not be harmed."

Mafulla said, "What do you mean by a bubble?"

"A complete, three-dimensional ring and sphere of protection. There's no other word I can use for it. The good news is that several men on the raid are Phi. A couple are quite senior. All the others have many Phi characteristics and have been specially trained by Masoon. They know how to protect and how to neutralize. It will all happen at lightning speed. The adversaries have no chance. They're common criminals with no training. Your family should be back here by 11:30 or 11:35 at the very latest, and that's only because of the time it may take to find and untie them, reassure them, and bring them safely back here."

"Really?" Mafulla was deeply impressed, but still not sure.

"Yes. I speak the truth."

"So," Walid said, "What do we do now?"

Paki said, "We wait. We relax. We get a snack."

"You can relax?" Mafulla said.

"You can snack?" Walid added.

"We're Phi." Paki shrugged.

Mafulla let out a deep breath. "Well, I guess it's clear that if I'm Phi, then I'm a barely born little bitty baby Phi."

Omari laughed. "Baby Phi is better for such situations than no-Phi, any day."

Amon then wandered off to get snacks for the group. Paki and Omari sat on the floor, and Mafulla and Walid joined them, just to keep from pacing a hole in the floor. They had not yet learned the art of relaxation during what may be violent action, especially when the well-being of people they love and care about is at stake. The minutes elongated like taffy stretched across a table. Amon came back with fruit and juice and some biscuits.

Paki asked to see their watches. He was wearing a simple

round military watch, as were his associates. He had never seen a Reverso, and as soon as he saw the case up close, he laughed and said, "The whole watch is Phi. I can tell the case is the golden ratio. It's nice. Very powerful." Mafulla flipped his and clicked it in place, and Paki admired the engravings. He took off his watch and turned it upside down. There, on the back of the case was also an engraved Phi.

Walid said, "Do you all have the Phi on the backs of your cases?"

Amon said, "Yes. We do. The watches are fairly recent gifts to us from those who chose us and brought us into the club."

Omari said, "When you complete the first two levels of training, it will be marked somewhere on your body, only with a small marking, but clear, and it will be up to you to maintain it, or renew it if it fades."

Mafulla said, "Why?"

"So that if, as a junior Phi who's not yet completed all five levels of training, you're ever apprehended and subdued, however unlikely that might be and, to be absolutely candid, if you ever experience the extreme situation of being stripped down for torture and no one has noticed the back of your watch, or it's not with you, your adversary will still have a chance to see that you're Phi."

"Wait. Torture?"

"Yes. It's not likely, but possible. Most enemies will stop right there, as soon as they see the symbol, and make themselves scarce, as you experienced in the basement. They know that if they continued, they would be hunted quickly and relentlessly by those who cannot be stopped. It's a protection and a warning, like your engraving."

Mafulla thought for a second, turned his head to the side as if he were listening to something, and then he jumped up and ran across the large room. Several men standing across the room looked over at him.

"What? Maffie!" Walid instantly got up and called out after his friend.

Amon, Paki, and Omari had already risen. Omari put his hand on Walid's arm and spoke softly but firmly. "Wait, Your Highness. Prince, Please. Hold steady. Be still."

Walid looked at him and back at Mafulla, as he went through the nearby door, and said, "But, why?"

"There's a vital and powerful reason."

20

QUESTIONS AND ANSWERS

QUESTIONS ARE NORMALLY EASIER TO ARRIVE AT THAN answers. They can just come to us, unexpected and uninvited. Some can almost force themselves on us. But answers we normally have to go looking to find. And some will elude us, no matter how hard we look. And yet, there's a bit of a paradox here. Not all questions are easy. It can take a true genius to come up with the right breakthrough question for any domain of human life or inquiry. That's not easy at all. In fact, the first secret to pioneering accomplishment in most areas of life is to ask the right questions. This is because, once you're inquiring in the right direction, your path will almost inevitably lead you to interesting and important realizations, if you keep at it and don't give up. Great questions often define the creative spark.

And even before any answers materialize, merely living with the right questions can deepen your life, alter your understanding, and make you a different person. Those who can't bear to live with unanswered questions can't function well or dwell at the highest level of existence in this world.

It's been said that a little philosophy is a dangerous thing. That's because a modicum of philosophical reflection gives us most of the ultimate questions but without most of the answers. And many people, learning that the answers aren't nearly as easy to identify as the questions, get discouraged and then despair of finding the truth, or even of there being any truth about these deepest of issues. It's only with extended and persistent philosophy that the answers to our most challenging questions can be pursued effectively and eventually found. They're hard to dig up, and some of them can even seem impossible to attain, as you journey hard in their direction.

There are many lines of basic inquiry about life that have been pursued for centuries, even millennia. Some questions just will not go away. And an initial surprise is that the people who have thought about them the hardest don't often agree. That can be troubling, and even disheartening, because these great thinkers of the past can sometimes even be worlds apart. A conclusion then begins to emerge. The full form of final answers about the ultimate contours and conditions of life may just elude us, even through the entirety of our earthly adventures. But typically, on any deep subjects regarding the core issues of our existence, the harder the answers are to find, the more important they may be. This means that all the work required to seek them out should, in the end, be worth the effort. Yet, this will be true only if we persist.

Using our minds well to chase the truth can be an extraordinarily beneficial activity. If we're open, and genuinely curious, we'll almost always benefit in some way from the pursuit. And with some lines of inquiry, it may be that the most beneficial result of the quest will be not a propositional answer, a statement of truth realized by the mind, so much as a personal transformation, a new lived understanding felt in the heart.

Even practical questions about our individual lives and destinies in the world can be hard to answer. Life is full of surprises and puzzles. And that was something the prince was feeling in his heart at this moment as he stood watching Mafulla run toward the outer door of the palace and he realized in that moment that he didn't know exactly what he should do.

At this point in his life, Walid had many questions, big and small. What would his future hold? Would he actually one day become king? Is it something he would find deeply fulfilling as his true mission in life? If so, could he really be a good king and even a great one? Would he be able to uphold all the hopes and dreams of his family? Or was he supposed to have his own dreams?

Is it possible to be distinctively who you are, while living a dream bigger than just your own creation? Could he, meanwhile, in the midst of all these questions continue to make his uncle and parents proud? There's a vast distance between being thirteen years old and running a kingdom with wisdom and grace. How can it be bridged?

Is Kissa the girl who will become the woman he should marry? And what about her parents, Khalid and Hoda? What's the real story on them? How will the friendship with Mafulla develop? What new adventures await? What role could Maffie eventually play in his life?

Is he really a member of a secret society called Phi? And, what does that even mean? What abilities qualify him for this? What has he yet to discover about himself? Will Phi and the good guys prevail over all the bad they confront? Or is that really possible?

What about the other boys in the palace school? What part will they play in the future of the kingdom? Will the king catch Ari Falma and stop him from continuing to do the terrible things he's been doing? Is Mafulla's family going to be Ok? Why did they have to be dragged into all this? It just doesn't seem fair.

Are there really ways of knowing that operate beyond the normal senses? And if so, can these be mastered, so that you can ever be certain of your feelings and intuitions? Is it possible to develop deep skill in the use of your mind and body so that you can indeed go beyond what most people experience? And if this is possible, then can more of the population be enlightened as to how to do it? Is human nature always the same, or can it be elevated? Can the world in general be improved through a proper use of the mind?

How does Omari know all the things he seems to know?

How many bad guys are still in the palace? And who are they?

What's in the secret box?

How did all the Fibonacci Series and golden ratio stuff get into the palace?

What's the deal about my birthday?

Why did Mafulla jump up and run across the room a moment ago, at 11:27 AM?

And Omari just said, "Hold steady. Be still." But, why? What's going on?

Room 421 of the Grand Hotel had one of the best views in the capital city. Looking out the French doors that opened to a balcony, a guest could see many of the most beautiful buildings in Cairo and, gazing down, could enjoy a view of the sparkling blue water in the hotel's main pool, a large rectangle surrounded by a white stone patio decorated along the edges with live palm trees, shrubs, and flowers. It was possibly the most extravagant structure in the kingdom, aside from the palace, but it was even more showy in its external features.

This was the designated meeting place. Ari Falma had let himself in and was sitting on a chocolate brown overstuffed armchair that faced the glass doors and the great view outside. But he couldn't enjoy the scenery at all on this day. In fact, he hardly noticed it. Inner agitation drained him, and he dreaded the report he would have to give, any minute now. Tea and biscuits sat on the small marble top table in front of him. It was all so refined—blue and white Spode china, a crisp white linen napkin, and ornately designed silver sat there unappreciated, unused, and mute. For ten interminable minutes, he tried to breathe deeply, with thoughts and excuses and promises whirling around in his brain. A newspaper lay on the couch perpendicular to him, obviously read but reassembled and awaiting any guest who had the presence of mind to focus on headlines and actually take in what had been written about the events of the previous day, as well as what was soon to come.

But it was a rare newspaper article that ever said well what was to come. It was hard enough for busy journalists, working under relentless deadlines, to get things right about what had already happened. And then, at least, they had witnesses to rely on, and records, and physical evidence. The future was much harder to get right. And Ari knew the pressure of deadlines. For a man who had wanted through his whole life to feel like a king, he had too often recently felt like a vassal instead, forced to serve another man whose power and fortune far eclipsed his own. In fact, Ari had recently felt even worse, like a disposable pawn in a long and complex game of chess. He was afraid he could be sacrificed at any time, in service to a strategy and an endgame that he didn't even understand.

The door between the two main rooms of the suite creaked open a few inches. He knew not to turn and look. The voice he had heard in person on merely four previous occasions now spoke to him from the other room, but close to the heavy wooden door. "Do you have the boxes—all of them?" It was a low voice, full of gravel, almost guttural, but with no emotion woven into its tones.

"We have twenty of the twenty one, and are getting the remaining box this week, within about three days, I would estimate."

"You would estimate."

"Yes."

"Can you tell me which box is missing from the collection you have in your possession?"

"The special box."

"Oh. The one extremely important box. The box I want the most. The one I truly need. The one worth more than ten thousand of the other boxes. That's the one you don't have."

"Yes. I'm afraid so. Not yet. It was a small glitch in the plan. I'm sorry. But we should have it soon."

"You should have it soon."

"Yes, we thought we had it. The men who took the boxes out of the palace believed on very good evidence that they had them all. They were unfortunately misled by a properly labeled larger box that lacked its expected contents, the smaller box in question. On the night when they took all the boxes, they didn't notice that the bigger box no longer carried its full contents."

"Why?"

"There was a power outage that covered the theft. It was

dark. And the men were rushed. They had no time to double check or investigate. The box felt like it held its contents, and they just assumed it was the right contents. They didn't know. But they couldn't really be faulted. They were very hurried. They did their best. And we're working now to rectify the issue."

This frantic explanation by the man who considered himself, and was widely thought by others, to be a crime lord of international standing, this rushed account of the missing box, was now met with silence.

After a few seconds of oppressive waiting, Ari went on. "I assure you that we're right now implementing a fool proof plan to secure the missing box."

"That's good, since there seem to be many fools involved in your plans. But I'm afraid my patience has run out."

"Your enduring patience will pay off handsomely within three days. I promise. I can guarantee you results within just a few days. You'll very soon have everything you've requested."

"You reveal a basic and dangerous misunderstanding in your words."

"What do you mean?"

"I don't make requests."

"Oh. Yes. I'm sorry. I understand. You've directed me as to what I should do. And you've offered to pay me handsomely."

"I've offered you a greater reward than that. If you had done as I required, I was prepared to allow you to continue to enjoy your position in this city, and throughout the kingdom. But, more than that, I was ready to allow you to enjoy something even greater, continuing to breathe and to see the sun rise, and the mid day blue sky and the sparkling sand of this kingdom, and even new days of intrigue and success and celebration. Your failure has now caused me to reconsider all this."

Ari squirmed in his seat. A visceral fear, a wave of inner shivers, began in his gut and climbed up his ribcage and into his throat as he was hearing these words. He spoke with a faint tremble in his voice. "I assure you that there's no reason for any drastic change of our beneficial arrangement. The difficult task you gave me is almost accomplished. I'll have for you soon everything you desire and rightly demand."

"You know, the chair in which you now sit could be the last throne of your small kingdom. The men you brought with you and left in the lobby as your safety backup, as your personal protection, are no longer in their chairs."

"What do you mean? Where are they?"

"They're no longer anywhere. Those were their last chairs, as this one may be yours."

"No, please. I'll do whatever you say, now and in the future. I'm your servant, the right arm of your power here. My network of associates and safe-houses is, in its entirety, at your disposal for anything you need. I'm the living glue that holds it all together. Without me, things would be immensely more difficult. You know there's no one else who could have done what I've already accomplished for you here in Cairo. That's why you chose me, in all your wisdom. Please don't allow yourself the difficulties you would encounter if you were to remove me from the role I so gladly play for you. We can do great things together, me with my expertise and network developed over the years, and you, with your superior mind and skills. Please, I beg you to allow me to finish this job and prove myself to you."

There were twenty seconds of silence following Ari's plea. Twenty of the longest seconds he had ever experienced. Then, the voice finally could be heard again.

"You have five days. I'll be generous, one last time, because that's what I am, until I'm not. So, you now have more than your requested three days. Get the job done, or get your effects in order. If I don't have my boxes, all of them, by the sunset of the fifth day, then you'll not have your life any longer, either. And, you know me. This is not a threat, or even a prediction. It's merely a statement of certain fact."

"Yes. I understand. Thank you. That's indeed very generous of you. I assure you, I'll not fail you. I'll succeed in the mission."

The only response to these words of gratitude and reassurance was the sound of the door closing. Ari sat for a few more seconds, looked around nervously, and stood up. He glanced at the now closed door, from behind which he had just heard his future foretold, and, with a weight of pressure he had never felt in his entire life, he walked slowly to the outer door of the room, turned the knob, and let himself out. As he made his way down the hall toward the stairs, he could hardly think.

And, even if he could have thought of anything during the time it took him to get back down to the hotel lobby, numb and dazed, there's no way he could have imagined, even in his worst nightmares, what had just happened, not far away. The men he had brought with him were his least loss of the day.

Mafulla had run across the expansive palace rear side entry hall and, jerking open the large exterior door, dashed past two surprised guards and down the marble steps and over across the grounds toward the side gate. "I need to get out to the street," he shouted to three other guards who stood at the closed gate, just outside the gatehouse. With a puzzled look on his face, one of the guards pushed open the wide, white painted, wrought iron barrier and watched the young man flash by it into the street. From there, he could now already see them coming—a group of men, and his mother, and brother, and little sister Sasha, who was being carried by Masoon.

They were half a block away, but it was a very long block. Mafulla continued to jog toward them. When he got close enough, he yelled out, "Is everybody Ok?"

His mother called back, "We're fine, my son!"

As he approached them, he asked, "Are you sure?"

"Yes! We're all fine! We're just shaken up and glad to be free!"

"Oh mom! I can't believe this happened to you! I was so worried!"

There was a big, relieved reunion hug right there on the street, with Mafulla, his mother, Sammi, and small Sasha, who reached out to him while she was still in Masoon's arms. Masoon moved in closer so that the assembled family members could all be touching each other, as Shamilar broke into tears at her happiness to be safe and to have all her children together and with her.

She wiped her eyes and said to Mafulla, "Masoon told me that your father's fine. Have you seen him?"

"Not yet, but I've heard he's in the palace now. Let's go to him!"

"That's a good idea," Masoon said. "We need to get the family inside."

Moments earlier, Omari had just removed his hand from where it was resting on Walid's arm. "I believe your friend saw with his mind, in a flash, his family safe and returning with the men. And he couldn't contain his desire to get to them in person. He's running to meet them now outside on the street. We should let him have this moment on his own, an experience that will accomplish more than one thing."

"What do you mean?"

"He'll have a needed, further confirmation from this that his visions are real and true. That reassurance will help him. He's been seeing things and knowing things on occasion, now and then, throughout his life, things impossible to know with merely the ordinary senses, but he's never fully understood this gift. He needs to know that he can rely on these connections, these openings to information that come to him. By letting him run out, as soon as he had his sudden mental vision of his family, we've allowed him an instant and powerful confirmation that he can trust himself in his unusual awareness. It was good for him to do this alone, and without you or us behind him."

Walid said, "Ok. But … I may be a nuisance, and yet, I have to ask how you know these things."

Omari replied, "That's just part of my gift. I have no other explanation for you. But, be patient for a while more, and you'll see a very happy young man emerge through that outer door, very shortly."

He was right. When the door soon opened, only minutes later, a beaming Mafulla came through with one arm around his mother, and the other holding the hand of Sammi. Masoon was walking beside them still carrying little Sasha, who was also finally smiling, though still with the trace of a tear on her cheek.

All those in the entry hall who had been awaiting their colleagues began to clap for the men and their triumphant errand, as they came back into the large room. Walid's dad, Rumi, was the last through the door. And, within no more than a minute, Hamid and his men were coming back up the steps, through The Doorway of Disaster, as Mafulla would say, and this time, it was exactly that, but for their adversaries. Hamid and the tunnel crew then rejoined their associates around the map table, from where they had embarked on their successful raid.

The big surprise to all was that, just as there were many handshakes and backslappings and words of appreciation around the room while details of the recent events were being shared, someone called out, "The king!" And there he was, in his most beautiful and formal robe, accompanied by four palace guards, in ceremonial attire. They stood, all five of them, side by side, stretching across the stone floor beneath the wide, high archway that connected this entry hall to the rest of the palace.

Everyone then stopped what they were doing, where they were, to turn toward King Ali and bow slightly. The words, "Your Majesty," were uttered at a low volume all over the room and created a whispered rumble of regard and respect for their exalted leader, and what he represents.

King Ali said in a loud, strong voice, "I wanted to see all of you immediately, and congratulate you on a job well done."

Walid looked at Omari and said, "But how did the king know? Oh, never mind."

Omari just smiled.

The king then chose the path of brevity. He said, "Please, everyone accept my grateful thanks, and go back to your celebration!"

A murmur went through the room, with many smiles and looks of satisfaction. And then there was more applause, a clapping of hands for the king, the successful rescue, and for each other. The king smiled broadly, joined in the applause himself, and then walked over to Masoon, who was standing close by, now without the child in his arms. In a lower voice, Ali said, "My friend, a personal thanks to you. Was there any serious resistance?"

Masoon replied, "It was my privilege, Majesty. And, yes,

there was an attempt at fierce resistance. Unfortunately, they all had weapons, but it was nothing we couldn't handle quickly. It was good that we caught them completely off guard, since they had taken their hostages little more than seven hours ago. There were five men holding the family and guarding them. And I use the past tense intentionally. There are no additions to our jail today. The speed of the operation and the vicious nature of our adversaries wouldn't allow for any of the otherwise noble delicacies of restraint and capture."

"I see. I hope the children weren't traumatized by the event."

"No, they were frightened, it was clear, but we kept the worst of it all away from their gaze, and out of their hearing. They were in a room alone and tied up when the worst happened. We were fast, but quiet and very cautious of them, given their age. We didn't want to deepen any damage that might have already been done."

"Very good. I knew you'd do a magnificent job of it, Masoon. Again, I thank you deeply, and I know that Shapur Adi will be forever grateful."

"It was my honor to serve in this way."

Rumi walked up at that point and said, "Your Majesty. Why don't I take the Adi family to where Shapur has been waiting? I could do a little follow up checking on all of them, just to make sure that Shamilar and the children were not injured in any way today, and reconfirm that Shapur is without any ongoing problems from the attack on him. I'd also be very happy to host their reunion."

The king smiled and replied, "That's an excellent idea!" He then turned to the boys and said, "Mafulla, Walid, you should go along. I'm sure Mr. Adi would love to see you. Both of you played a very big role in this happy ending to a traumatic morning, for which I deeply thank you. And I'm sure that he would like the opportunity to do the same. Then, I would ask you to join me in my rooms in about one hour. We can have some lunch together, and it will give me a chance to catch you up on other things that have been happening."

"Good, Uncle, we'll see you then," Walid did a small bow and followed his father down the hall with Mafulla and the rescued members of the Adi family.

It had not taken much to get the palace mechanics who were caught with the jewels to talk. The king was right. Hearing that they had been fooled with fake gems made them very angry, and two of them confessed freely right away, spilling out the whole story of what had happened. They said they had been approached outside of work by a man who offered them a very large payment for what he called a small service.

The story he told them was simple. The man said that there were some boxes in the Palace Guard Storage Room that had been confiscated by mistake from a crime scene and that they contained items that would be of no interest to the king or to the guards, but were very valuable to his employer. He explained that he could use legal means to get them released in the normal course of things, but that this would take far too long, months at least, and his boss needed these items soon. So, instead, he said with a big smile on his face, that for their help he would give each of them some very rare jewels. Each man's payment would be worth more than thirty thousand dollars, and they would be asked only to facilitate the removal of these boxes at a specific time, on a particular evening. They would simply have to turn off all the electrical power to the palace at that time, for just a little more than one hour, and then in the resulting darkness carry off the boxes, which they would need to disguise as power equipment, and take them to a truck that would be waiting at the loading dock, out back.

He presented this proposed theft to the maintenance men like it wasn't really a theft at all, but rather just a way of returning some items to their rightful owner in a fast and expeditious way. He actually even said they'd be doing the palace guards a service by clearing out some cramped space in their storage area. To underline how minor a matter this all was, he told them that even one of the royal butlers would help them out and make sure that all the proper doors were unlocked in advance of the electrical outage. Again, he emphasized that the king would feel bound by legalities to refuse the official release of these boxes until the full process of law had dragged on. But he repeated that this option would take far too long. The men would be doing everyone a favor, in the end, by just going along with this plan and telling no one. They could then, of course, use the money they'd be able to receive from a sale of their jewels in any way they'd like—to buy a great home, or even to retire from their work.

The man was so convincing and the jewels were so magnificent that the maintenance men found his request in the end to be very reasonable, and they complied, fulfilling all the duties they had been assigned. They had cut the power on the day and time specified, and had gone through the inner door from the maintenance room to the two guard storage rooms, through a door that was otherwise always locked, to find, disguise, and remove all the boxes near the Adi sign, as they had been instructed, exactly twenty-one in number.

The kitchen crew had been harder to crack in questioning. Because they had been given more jewels, due entirely to their own greed and stubbornness in negotiating with the mysterious man who had also approached them for help, they were much more reluctant to accept the claim that the stones were fake. Nothing that Naqid could say would even begin to convince any of them, until he snatched up the largest gem that was on the table in front of them, walked over to the window of the room they were in, and flung it out of the building, shouting "Worthless!" And this was all that two of them needed to see and hear in order to be persuaded, at least in that moment. They realized that no one would spontaneously throw a real emerald of that size and beauty from a second floor window. It must indeed be fake.

When Naqid flung the jewel out through the open window, one of the men, a big guy with a thick, bushy mustache, had at first yelled out in a voice of great alarm, "What are you doing? Are you crazy? Are you insane?" The emerald was one of the stones he had been given.

Naqid calmly stood where he was and said, "You see, I would never do that with a real gem. They're fake. They're all very well made fakes. You were played for fools. You were asked to risk your jobs and lives and freedom for artificial stones, so that someone else could get what he really wanted. You were treated like garbage."

The two men who seemed immediately convinced by Naqid's stunt began to curse their luck and the poor excuse for a man who did this to them. But the third individual, the one with the big mustache, vigorously shook his head and said, "No!" He could not believe he had been cheated so badly and had thrown away his career and freedom for a phony gem.

He glared at Naqid and challenged him. "You must have someone outside to retrieve the jewel. You had planned to do that. You think you can fool us. It's not that easy, my friend." He looked at the others and said, "Don't let this man play you like idiots. Don't fall for his fake drama. He's bluffing."

The other two were quiet, and now had a hint of doubt

in their minds. Naqid walked to the door and conferred with a guard outside the room, who could then be heard walking off. The interrogator himself stayed at the edge of the door for a good minute or two, silent. The door then opened, and someone outside handed him an item that the men in custody could not see. He walked over to the table with this thing behind his back, and said, "Diamonds are the hardest of gems, and one of the toughest, most indestructible substances in the world. If this were a real diamond," he picked up one from the table, displayed it to their view, and then laid it back down," it would be impossible for me to do … this!" He raised from behind him a hammer and brought it crashing down on the gem, shaking the whole table and causing some of the other jewels to roll or bounce off onto the floor. When he then lifted the hammer back up, they could all see the dust and shattered fragments of the fake jewel on the table, where a diamond of their dreams had just been sitting, a moment earlier. It was indeed a fake. No more proof was needed.

The man with the mustache looked shocked, and then sick. He was then the first of the kitchen crew to tell their entire story, which in some ways was similar to, but in other ways different from, the account that had been given by the mechanics. These men had been assigned jobs on the night of the heist having to do with boxes, but also involving the prison escape. They were in addition given other things to do in the following days, but these he did not mention. However, it was clear from what he did say that all roads led back to Ari Falma.

When the boys had spent over half an hour together with Mafulla's dad, his mom, and the little ones, along with Rumi and Bhati, who had also come down to visit, Walid remembered that they were expected soon in the king's private quarters, and reminded Mafulla. But knowing it would take them less than five minutes to get there, they lingered as long as they could in the palace infirmary where Shapur had been resting. It had done them both great good to hear and see that he was fine. But now, having enjoyed the time together with all of them, Walid and Mafulla quickly had to say goodbye and jog all the way to the private royal sitting room to see the king.

Kular was at the door, as usual. He invited the boys in and they took up their favorite spots on the sofa and waited for the king to arrive. A couple of minutes later, Ali entered from another room in the suite and they rose to their feet.

"Sit, sit, my friends. It's been a long day for all of us, and there's still much of it left!" The king sat down in his favorite chair and asked Kular to bring in a light lunch for them to enjoy.

Ali started off by thanking both boys again for the crucial role they had played in the day's events. He smiled and said, "Still, it would have been an excellent idea to take a palace guard with you into the basement and down the tunnel, which I think hasn't been used in years. Remember our discussion of courage, my boys. You don't have to leap into the dark to be brave and helpful to the kingdom."

Walid said, "I'm really sorry, Uncle, that I led Maffie down to the basement without taking anyone along with us. I was having feelings about going down there that I just couldn't put into words. And I couldn't imagine at the time trying to explain to anyone else what I was feeling and doing. I knew that Mafulla would come with me without asking questions. It never even occurred to me to get anyone else to go along. I actually didn't know why we were going down there. I sure didn't guess we'd be in any danger. In fact, it wasn't until we got into the basement that I fully realized we should go to the tunnel. I really didn't mean to be taking a big risk."

The king replied, "I understand completely. I know that, like Mafulla, you've had feelings and intuitions about things your whole life, but never with stakes as high as they've been recently. You'll just have to get a little better at recognizing when an intuition may be leading you into a situation that could be challenging or even dangerous, and make sure that you have help available. No one here will question your expression of a need. You're the prince. As you become more accustomed to your special role in kingdom affairs, you'll have more confidence in such things. Of that, I'm sure."

He turned to look at Mafulla. "And, Mafulla, I would address the same cautionary and confidence building remarks to you. Trust your feelings, but also trust the men around you that you know well, or who have been put into positions of great responsibility by those you know and trust. Then you can go into any unknown situation with the support you may need. Even Masoon takes many able men with him when he goes into potential danger."

"Yes, Your Majesty. That's good advice." Mafulla seemed tired but also grateful for the words of the king.

Ali looked back at Walid, and then Mafulla. "Now, I've spoken with Omari while you were with Shapur. And he's told me that he had the great good fortune of sharing some news with you both."

"Yes, Your Majesty, and that was some pretty overwhelming news," Walid replied. "I just wondered why you hadn't told us, and I wanted to ask: Are you sure that you're right about us? I mean, Maffie has some pretty wild insights about things that are going on or that are about to happen. But I feel like I'm just a completely normal person."

"Well, first of all, I'm certain that I'm right. You're both Phi. And if you wonder how I know, it's just because you don't yet fully understand enough about Phi. And that's completely natural. I just know. And I didn't want to tell you and try to explain it to you until you'd had enough real evidence in your own experience that would be supportive of what I was going to say."

"What do you mean?" Walid seemed puzzled.

"Just look at what's happened since we arrived in town. Walid, you and Mafulla survived and escaped a kidnapping. You both helped to break up a criminal operation at the Adi store. You got emergency assistance for Mafulla's dad this morning, and located his mother and the little ones before anyone else could. Consider, by itself, the fact that Mafulla's dream led you to help his dad just minutes after he had been attacked far across town before dawn."

"That was sure strange," Mafulla said.

"Yes, and it was vitally important. And, Walid, your strange feelings about the basement this morning led you to the tunnel and down it. Mafulla then played his role in feeling or knowing the right things to get you both through the entire length of the tunnel and to the trap door where he was able, at just the right moment, to gain evidence of the family's whereabouts. And he recognized what he was hearing for what it was. You then stopped a fleeing assailant as well as any experienced military man could have, and in the immediate aftermath of an attack, you kept your heads enough to get the right information to all the right people."

"Yeah, it's all pretty amazing," Walid muttered.

"I'm sure you must realize that this is not the normal flow of experience for the average twelve or thirteen year old boy, in our kingdom, or anywhere else. Then, after all this, in answer to your questions, and with the concurrence of two of his most trusted associates, Omari told you about Phi, and that you are both Phi. And at about that moment, immediately, as if on cue, Mafulla suddenly knew his family was safe and on their way to the palace, some minutes before they got here."

"How did you know that?" Mafulla asked, stunned.

The king smiled. "I'm very senior Phi. The fact that you're also Phi, both of you, explains all of this. And all of it should confirm to you that you're Phi, now that you understand a part of what that means. I knew this about you, Walid, some time ago. It didn't take me long after first meeting you, Mafulla, to know it about you, too. I can sense how deep a well is as soon as the water comes out. Now the time has come for you both to know this, as well, and to benefit from the growth and training that this new knowledge can allow."

"It's still pretty hard to take in," Mafulla said. "But I'm surprised to say that I guess I really have no doubt about it. I mean, now that Omari's told us, and you've repeated it and reminded us of all the evidence, however strange it is, and however far away I seem to be in knowledge and skill from anyone like you, or Hamid, or Masoon, or Omari."

Walid took a deep breath and said, "I guess I feel the same way, now that you've explained it all so well, Uncle—Your Majesty. But what does it really mean for us, and what happens next?"

"Well, one thing it means is that Masoon can begin to train you both, this very week. And he can be open about what he's teaching you and what its purpose might be. His job will be to bring you up physically and mentally into the best shape a novice Phi can attain. You'll be embarking on what's known as level one training. There are five levels overall. But with Masoon, each of the five will be richly enhanced.

He never does things in an average way, or anywhere near, as you know—not even a Phi average. These levels of training are intended to support the special service you can offer to your fellow man."

"How long does it take to go through all five levels?" Walid was clearly curious about all this.

The king said, "It varies greatly, but it can take years."

Mafulla held up a finger and said, "So, basically it sounds like you're suggesting that I'm not quite ready yet to dispatch an entire room of bad guys by myself?" Despite his words, he looked very serious.

The king chuckled and said, "At this point, you're better off relying on your quick wit, your winning personality, and your access to Masoon."

Walid added, "But as we all know, you can clear any room of bad guys the quickest and most reliably right now with simply an extra dose of your special cologne."

Mafulla frowned. "That's right, make fun of the elixir of the air, the olfactory magnetic field for feminine beauty that's finally entered my domain, the unseen force on which you yourself unknowingly rely for the good graces of the ladies."

Walid laughed. "Olfactory?"

"Having to do with aromas and our sense of smell."

"An intellectual and a joker."

"What can I say? Stay close and benefit in many ways."

"Ok. As far as I know, you may be right. So, I'll continue to stay as close as I can without coughing uncontrollably when you have your special magnetic field going, full power, and I'll just hope for the best."

"The best will come to you, my friend. I'll see to it." Mafulla punctuated his words with his distinctive double eyebrow jump.

"If I may interrupt this extended bit of jocularity," the king said, chuckling himself, "there are a few more things you should know."

"What are they, Uncle?"

"Well, we questioned the mechanics who were caught with the jewels, and the kitchen staff who were likewise apprehended, including the man you two wounded on the stairs this morning. We got them all to talk by helping them to understand that they had been tricked and paid for their services in fake gems. They told a consistent story about how they were involved in the theft of the boxes from the basement, and a few of them, in the jail break."

The king went on to provide all the details that he had gleaned from Naqid, and also talked about the young butler, Hamaj, who seemed to be the local mastermind of the entire operation. It turned out that he was a secret, trusted associate of Ari Falma. And, despite his criminal background, he had managed to get inside the palace on false pretenses, and with a convincingly concocted work history.

The king painted a broad picture of everything that had happened, as it was understood at present. And then he said, "We think, from some things Hamaj told us under questioning, that Falma was going to send the weapons in those boxes to a buyer in a nearby country who may have some connection with the previous regime, or some political ambitions of his own. But what they were planning to do with the weapons, exactly, we're unsure. Certain obvious scenarios suggest themselves, however, and we're on the alert now for any attack on us that may come from abroad."

Walid spoke up. "Uncle, could we ask about some specific things you haven't mentioned yet?"

"Yes, you certainly can," the king replied. He smiled and

added, "I'm fairly sure that, for one thing, you'd like to know about your teacher, Khalid."

"Yes, definitely," Walid replied. "We're eager to find out the whole story about Khalid. But there's one thing that's bothering me even more than that. What's in the secret box?"

"Oh! Yes! I shall tell you both. You'll be surprised, I'm sure. But, look, here's Kular with our food!"

21

THE MYSTERY BOX

"ARI! THEY'RE ALL DEAD! ALL THE MEN ARE DEAD!" THE messenger was breathless and had a desperate, panicked look on his face.

"What do you mean, they're dead?"

"I went there like you told me, to check on everything and take them food and the men are all on the floor, dead. They've all been killed! And the boxes are gone!"

"The boxes are gone?"

"All of them!"

"And, you say every one of the men is dead?"

"All of them!"

"How can this be? Were they shot?"

"I don't know. It's unclear how they died. I saw no wounds or blood. The door was closed and locked from inside like everything was normal. I used the key and got in and saw the first man, Sardi, lying on the floor, face down. A second body was close by. Their weapons were beside them. I went into the first room beyond them. No one was there. I walked into the back room full of fear and then I saw."

"What?"

"There were all three of them, all dead on the floor. And the woman was gone, and the children were gone."

"What happened?"

"I don't know! How could I know? I got out of there as fast as I could!"

"And you say all the boxes are gone?"

"Nothing was there except our men, all dead!"

"No! No, no, no, no. This can't have happened! Not now!"

"Who did this thing and took all the boxes and left the men like that on the floor?"

Ari said, "We've been betrayed!"

"What do you mean?"

"Our client must have seen the secret box left at the drop spot nearby, before we even thought to check, and he's chosen to double cross us!"

"But why would he do that?"

"He's taken what he wanted, everything he wanted, and decided that to kill us is better than to pay us! Which means that you and I are practically dead men, too."

"Why do you say this?"

"He will kill the rest of us now, so that none of us can try to get even with him, or reveal his plans."

"But we don't know his plans."

"He might worry that we do. He's taking no chances! He's covering his tracks. He'll kill us next."

"No! We can't let him! We must leave, now! We have to flee the city and the kingdom!"

"You don't know him. He'll find us. He'll always find us, wherever we go."

"But we have to try to protect ourselves. You're smart.

You can figure out something, but we need to buy time. We should get out of here to buy time, time for us to think."

"You're right. Your words are true. We need time. To stay here is only to stretch my neck across the executioner's block."

"And mine!"

"Yes. We do need time. Only space will buy us time. We've got to put many miles between us and this wretched place where nothing goes right any more."

"What should we do?"

"Gather the remaining men as soon as you can. Tell them to take the most basic provisions possible, enough to last three days."

"Ok. I can do that."

"They should also bring any money or gold or jewels they have. Tell them not to let anyone know they're going anywhere. We'll just leave."

"Yes. That's what we should do."

"We have to disappear. We can return when it's once again safe. But we need to go now. Move fast and tell all the men. Have everyone meet in less than two hours at the north edge of the marketplace, at our friend's stall there."

"I'll do it!"

"Tell the camel man only what we need, and not why we need it. Pay whatever it takes. Get horses for you and me, in case we should need the extra speed. We'll flee as soon as we can."

"But will he find us before we can leave? What's to stop him from killing us in the next hour—in the next few minutes?"

"If we come across him, nothing will stop him."

"That's what I'm afraid of."

"Look. I'll leave here in minutes, as soon as I gather a few things. He knows of this place. I have to get out of here right away."

"I'll go tell my wife."

"You tell her nothing."

"I must tell her something. She'll see me taking my things."

"All right. Tell her you may have to be away for a few days for work, but nothing else, you hear?"

"Ok."

"Nothing else. And then get word to the men and go to the meeting place. Time is the first enemy."

"You're right. Even taking two hours is a great risk. You and I could flee now."

"We'll need all the men, for any chance of protection. You don't know our adversary. We could never face him alone. But, enough talk! Go! We meet in less than two hours! Go!"

Ari's man ran out the door without even closing it. Falma himself stood still, thoughts flooding through his brain, tense all over and dizzy, his lips so dry they stuck together as if glued. He reached into his desk for his gun, then unlocked another drawer and pulled out a large envelope full of money, and put it all into Faisul's old bag, with the remaining fake jewels, gold, and silver.

At that moment, there was a small sound right outside the door. Another man appeared in the doorway. When he heard a footstep cross the threshold, Ari pulled his gun and spun around. He almost shot one of his own men, his personal assistant, a man he would need now and in the near future. "Oh! It's you!"

"Ari, what are you doing? What's happening?"

"All the men at the warehouse are dead and the boxes are gone."

"What?"

"You heard me! I think our client's going to kill us all."

"Oh, no! This is terrible!"

"And we can't let it happen. We're leaving town in two hours, together, all of us who remain."

"What can I do?"

"I need you to go into the kitchen and fill two large bags or more, all you can carry, with provisions for the two of us, enough to last three days in the desert. Then grab any money you have on hand and get my brother, and both of you go to Anwar's stall at the market. From there, we'll leave."

"I can do that, right now."

"Good. We'll talk more of it later, but now we're racing with death. Gather the food quickly and go to the stall."

The man said, "Yes, immediately."

"I'm leaving now." And without another word, Ari Falma walked through the door and down the stairs, out into the afternoon heat. He had the heavy bag hooked over his left shoulder, hanging next to his body. And his right hand was down in it holding the gun's handle that was almost at the top of the bag. He also had his finger on the trigger as he turned his head to all sides to make sure there was no one waiting for him in the street.

In the palace, things were quite different and calm. Kular the butler walked into the room with a large silver tray, bringing in a wonderful, hearty lunch for the king and his two young friends. He set the tray on the big low table that was well positioned between the chair and the sofa, and asked if he could be of any further assistance. The king told him that the lunch looked marvelous, and that they would be in a closed session for the next half an hour. Kular bowed, excused himself, and quietly exited the room, softly closing the large, heavy door behind him.

As the king handed the boys some food and drinks, he said, "Now, let me tell you the tale of Khalid."

Walid said, "We can't start with the box?"

"No, no, we should end with the box. I do like to create a bit of mystery and suspense when I have interesting things to relate."

Mafulla said, "Ok, Your Majesty. So, what can you tell us about our mysterious teacher? Is he now in shackles in the palace jail?"

Ali laughed and said, "No, I believe that instead he may be sitting outside in the garden on such a beautiful day, enjoying a nice lunch with his lovely wife."

Walid looked skeptical and asked, "What did you find out about him?"

"Well, as far as we can determine, when you saw him near the basement door, he had indeed been meeting with Hoda, doing some of the last minute planning for your special dinner. We have an independent corroboration of their separately told and consistent stories about this. They had called one of the porters into their meeting, to instruct him on where to get the nice decorations that met you at the door of the library dining room when you arrived. And one of the musicians had stopped in for instructions, as well. So, two witnesses saw them doing exactly what Khalid said they were doing, and at the time when you would have been hearing the lock turn on the basement storage room door."

Walid seemed relieved, and yet still concerned. "But, what about his disappearance at the dinner?"

"That's a more interesting story, by far. Do you know that his eighteen year old twin sons, Baqid and Shumar, work in the palace kitchen?"

Walid looked surprised. "No, I didn't know that."

"He's never mentioned them in class," Mafulla added.

"He's very proud of them, but Khalid is a humble man, for all his many accomplishments. The older son by ten minutes, I'm told, Baqid, is the Chef Saucier, in charge of cooking meats and meat sauces for all of us. And his younger twin, Shumar, is the Chef Patissier, who bakes all our breads and pastries. These are positions of great responsibility for young men their age, and especially in a kitchen as big as ours here in the palace. We normally have over twenty people employed just in the kitchen and related areas at any given time, and often many more."

"I had no idea." Walid had just never thought about how big a staff it took to keep everyone in the palace fed, including the school students, with their daily lunches.

"Naqid spoke to your teacher about the dinner and the effects of the power outage on the students. He didn't make it seem like he was at all interrogating Khalid, just like he was inquiring into every aspect of the power failure and its effects. He did mention that he had heard about Khalid's disappearance and the note that later arrived at the table, making Hoda smile, and he then gave our friend an opportunity to explain these odd things."

"What did he say?" Walid was at this point almost forgetting to eat.

The king took a sip of juice and continued, "Well, Khalid said his sons had reported to him that, on the previous day, Shumar overheard one of the dishwashers talking to a storeroom employee about 'when the lights go out' and saying how surprised everyone would be. He also heard the man utter the words, 'That's when it's going to happen,' but with no explanation as to what was being discussed. It turns out that those are two of the men we now have in custody."

"Oh."

"Khalid went on to explain to Naqid that he and his sons had speculated on what that strange conversation was about, and they were a bit worried, but really had no idea. Shumar told his dad that one of the men, the one doing the talking, was something of a loner, and given to bursts of anger, an individual that he had harbored doubts about for some time. So, both the boys were concerned that something bad might happen soon, either in the kitchen, or elsewhere in the palace, and maybe even something like a power outage to cover something else going on, but really they had no clue. And yet, they were nervous about it all."

"That makes sense."

"As soon as the power went out during the dinner, Khalid was worried about his sons, since he knew they were at work in the kitchen with that man, and he just got up instantly to go check on them. Mafulla, you certainly know what it's like to get an idea suddenly in your head, and then go running off to do something about it."

"Yes, I do," he admitted.

"Well, Khalid was out the door and down the hall before any of the candles were lit, literally feeling his way toward the kitchen. But the thing is that his boys, of course, knew about the dinner, since they had helped prepare it, and they were as worried about him as he was about them. They knew that you two were at the dinner with the other students and their own parents, and that you might be a target of potential retaliation of some sort, since you had both done so much recently to stop the criminals of the area. So, just like their dad, they instantly left their stations in the kitchen, but with flashlights, to go find Khalid and Hoda and make sure they were unharmed."

"I see," Walid said. "But what about the note?"

The king continued, "Khalid and his sons met up only a short distance from the dining room and, coming back toward it together to check on Hoda, they saw that there were lots of candles and palace guards around. So they decided to go back and look around the kitchen, since that's where the suspicious conversation had been overheard. But first, Khalid quickly scribbled out a short, funny note for Hoda, telling her that the boys were fine and had met him with lights as he was on the way out to check on them. He said that she should dismiss the group as planned, since he was going to get a couple of guards to accompany them to the kitchen to make sure that everything was all right there. So, that was the note."

"Ok. What did they find in the kitchen?"

"Nothing different, except a few of the employees seemed to be nowhere around, including the two men who had been overheard in that odd conversation."

Mafulla said, "So, Khalid left to check on his boys, and at the same time, they went to check on him, and he wasn't involved in any way in the power outage or box theft or anything else?"

The king smiled and said, "That's correct. The explanation he gave made sense to Naqid, who also spoke to the boys independently, and he got the same story from them. There's no reason for any further suspicion of your good teacher, or anyone in his family."

"Oh. Well, that's good," Walid said.

The king went on. "I have to admit to you now that I knew with certainty from the start there was nothing to worry about, but I wanted to gather the evidence that would help you two come to your own conclusions and truly feel better about it all."

"Well, now that we've heard all you've told us, it does totally make sense," Walid admitted. "And that pretty much does away with all my worry."

"I thought it would. You can completely trust your teacher and his wife. I had Naqid speak to him entirely for this reason, to provide you with the full story and the assurance I knew it would bring, but I also figured there might be more to the story that I would also need to hear."

"That's a relief." Mafulla popped a fig into his mouth.

"Yeah, it is." Walid agreed.

Then Mafulla said, "I was worried we'd have to go sit in jail with Khalid just for the continuation of our classes. And classical Greek is punishment enough already, as it is."

Walid said, "Well put. And this is another lesson, of the many we keep getting, that things are not always what they at first seem on the surface. I was truly worried about Khalid, but in the end, my concerns were caused only by appearances—well, the one appearance at the door, and the other disappearance at the table."

Mafulla said, "Mark one up for not jumping the gun and rushing to judgment."

The king nodded. "Yes, it usually pays not to rush to judgment on the basis of surface appearances only, especially when they seem to implicate in some sort of wrongdoing a person you otherwise have good reason to trust. It's always better to hear their side of the story. And then, you may realize there was no reason at all for your worry. I've known Khalid to a good extent, and Hoda much better, for a long time, seeing them on many visits to the city. And I've been long convinced that they're totally trustworthy friends, which is why I have them as the two main teachers in the palace. You can always count on them."

"But you said that we should watch Khalid carefully in class."

"That was for your benefit, and not at all mine. I allowed you to maintain your concerns so that you could come to see for yourselves the truth, as you might learn to watch more carefully, and as a lesson in not allowing appearances to mislead you."

Walid said, "Ok, Your Majesty, I get it, now. Thanks. We did need to learn that lesson."

"Good. I'm glad you agree."

"But, please, can we now turn to the biggest mystery of all?"

"What mystery would that be?"

Walid laughed. "Uncle! Please! What's in the wooden box that was in box 89 that, in turn, was in the oddly and indirectly labeled Phi box?"

"That's what I really want to know," Mafulla said.

Then Walid added, "And what's the whole story about where it was, originally, and the Fibonacci series in the storage rooms, and all the Phi numerical stuff that's all around?"

"Yeah, Your Majesty, all that, too."

The king held up a plate. "Would either of you boys like another roll? They're marvelous today—so soft and buttery! Or perhaps some more fruit?"

"Ha! Uncle Ali, you're driving us crazy!"

"A mystery can be as delicious as a good meal! Am I right?"

"Yes! And there's a time for each to be over!" Walid laughed.

The king smiled broadly and said, "Ok, boys. First, I can tell you the easy part, and then the harder part."

"I'm all ears," Mafulla said.

"Yes, but don't be embarrassed about that," Walid couldn't

help but comment, in the well-established spirit of Mafoolery, adding, "Big ears are often a sign of high intelligence. You hear much more and fill your mind with otherwise unavailable information."

"I'm sure you must be making a joke, since I see the smile on your face, and your mouth is moving, but I'm sorry, for some reason I can't hear a word you're saying," Mafulla deadpanned.

"Ok, Ok, sorry. Your Majesty, please, what were you about to say?"

The king looked amused, and he continued. "I know you have many questions about the mystery box that you two discovered. The easy part of dealing with these questions concerns where the box was, originally, down in the basement, how it got there, who placed it, and all the use of Phi and Fibonacci numbers in the basement area."

"This is easy?" Walid said.

"Yes. And that's because we don't yet know who arranged the boxes that way, or for what reason, or why the various locks that you've come across were so easy to open using numbers from the famous series, or from Phi. We don't yet even know who found the box where it was in the original storage room and moved it to get it into the possession of the men who carried it into the Adi store."

Walid frowned. "We don't know any of this?"

"Not yet. But we're working on it, and the answers we ultimately discover may be very interesting, indeed."

"What do we know?" the prince asked.

"Well, there's a lot, actually. So now, let me get to the hard part—hard only because there are so many details."

Mafulla looked at Walid and said, "I bet this is going to be good."

"Shh." Walid held a finger to his lips and turned back to the king. "Please, excuse my friend here and continue on, Your Majesty."

"Certainly. The beautiful wooden box itself is one that I've seen and used on several occasions in the past. It contains two things that many people with evil intent would give almost anything to own—an old book, and a smaller box that itself contains an even older item, a ring."

"A book and a ring?" Walid was surprised.

"Yes. The book is called The Book of Phi. It contains first the names and biographies of every member of the secret organization for the last eight generations, and some going farther back, in our kingdom and in a few neighboring countries as well, including the last known addresses of all those who are still with us. It needs to be updated, since our recent move here, and for other reasons. The details in the book also include all immediate family members of those who are in the society, all occupations of Phi and family, and many other very sensitive pieces of information, including members' abilities, what battles they've fought, and any exceedingly odd things that might have happened during their lives. For those deceased, there is information about how, when, and where they died."

The king paused for a moment. "What I'm telling you now must not leave this room, except in your minds. It's not known by many."

"No problem, Uncle."

"Yeah, no problem, Your Majesty. You can trust us."

"I know I can. That's why I feel free to tell you that there are also extensive instructions in the book."

Walid said, right away, "What sort of instructions?"

"They're for the most senior Phi. They have to do with

the cultivation and access of our most advanced abilities, and with background knowledge that helps to explain those abilities. No members under level five, and not many at that level, have ever seen these instructions."

"Have you seen them before? I mean, I'm guessing that the book has been here in the palace all these years that we've been far away in our village."

"I have. I've been in the palace on a few occasions throughout the years of exile. It was difficult to enter and leave by stealth, but with the help of friends, I managed. And I've quickly read through most of the book before now, during those visits. For many years, I've also had a copy of that part of the book with the most advanced instructions. But the very highest level of these instructions, given in a very long section toward the end, is written in a sort of code, or a language that it's oddly impossible to decipher, even for someone at my level. No one seems to know where the key to this code is. The rest of the instructions are written in ordinary but quite archaic language. Just the one extensive part at the end is still a mystery."

Mafulla couldn't help but say, "Wow, this is all pretty amazing."

The king nodded and went on. "Any enemy of Phi, anyone who sought to avoid the watchful eyes of Phi, or even who wanted to try to fight or undermine Phi, would crave access to this book. It's been kept here in the palace for generations, although there's no reason to think that the previous illegitimate king knew anything about it. It was hidden away, as you know, in a normal looking box, buried back deep within a rarely used storage room. And it was checked on and updated throughout those unfortunate years of the previous regime by a senior Phi who managed to retain full access to the palace during that entire time, an individual who tirelessly worked undercover to help prepare for our eventual arrival and our late night revolution."

"Who was that?" Walid asked.

"You'll know when the time is right," the king replied. "But let me go on."

"Ok."

The king then summed up what was known so far by saying, "The boxes we've recovered, originally from the Adi store, and now more recently from the nearby warehouse in today's raid, one and all, contain weapons that are presumably for either criminals or enemies of the kingdom. And, of course, the people who took them were still trying to get the box with the book of secret information that they would most need if they were planning something big against us."

"So they know we're Phi," Mafulla concluded.

"Well, they presumably know or suspect that about at least some of us," Ali answered. "So they realize they may need the secrets the book contains."

The prince then asked, "What are we doing with all the other boxes now?"

The king replied, "Masoon determined that we could use most of their contents, which are still in good working order. The weapons from the boxes are already being distributed to our military, from which many had been stolen in the first place. None of them will be kept here in the palace any more. The boxes are all being emptied out, and their contents are being sent securely to many places. It won't be possible for anyone so easily to steal again what was in those boxes."

"What about the special box?"

"It will now be kept in my personal safe, well hidden, and locked up."

"You mentioned a ring in it."

"Yes, the ring."

"What kind of ring is it?"

"It is a simple band of white gold with two narrow, beaded platinum inserts in the middle of it that can be rotated around the base. But the origin of this particular metal and its history may have been special."

"What's special about it? And why's the ring in the box?"

"There are still mysteries surrounding it all. But it's a ring of legend. It's called The Ring of Phi. It's been known and talked about for innumerable generations, stretching back into the hazy mist of those days before history was written. It's rumored to contain immense power, indeed, tremendous power."

"Really?" Walid had never heard of such a thing.

The king continued, "Yes. There are many stories about great men who once wore the ring. When they rotated the platinum bands on it, all manner of things have been said to happen, in accordance with their most urgent needs, or their deepest desires."

"Like what, Your Majesty?" Mafulla was entranced.

"Well, they say that men have vanished because of the ring. The wearer was suddenly whisked out of imminent danger and found himself standing somewhere else altogether, at a great distance from what had threatened him. Or, an adversary has disappeared, right in front of witnesses, while thrusting his sword at the wearer of the ring, and was never to be seen again."

"Wow. Strange. And totally wild." Walid was just as mesmerized by what he was hearing.

"It's even said that a turning of the bands has brought time to stand still so that impossible deeds could be accomplished

before the blink of an eye. There's a rumor that it has prevented in several ways what would otherwise have been clearly
fatal wounds. It's been reported to embody, or else connect its
wearer to, unseen and incredible forces of attraction, creation,
preservation, and destruction."

"Jeepers," Mafulla said.

"How old is this ring?" Walid asked.

"I've heard that it's been worn, off and on, by some of the
greatest men of Phi since even before the time of the earliest
pharaohs. It's been said that the first man we know to have
worn it and used it, the first wearer that we can identify with
any substantive information, was the truly remarkable individual who also conceived and oversaw the building of the
Sphinx in Giza."

"That's amazing," Walid said.

Mafulla had the expression on his face of a much younger
boy sitting around a campfire and listening to ghost stories.
He asked, "Are any of the stories about the ring actually true?"

The king replied, "No one knows what's true and what's
myth, and that's part of the fascination of the ring. To my
knowledge, it hasn't been worn at all for the past three generations, at least."

Walid said, "Why? And why aren't you wearing it, now?"

King Ali took a deep breath. "There has been a legend in
the Phi community, among the most senior members, that
its wearing, and especially its use, may carry a heavy price for
the one who uses it. But I've never met anyone who could tell
me more about what that price is, or why there is such a cost.
In the past, the ring was apparently used in only the most
extreme and dire of circumstances. And you know me well
enough to understand that I'm a careful man. Because the
ring has not been worn for so long, there's no living witness

available to speak of its power, if any, beyond that of producing great myths and legends. So, we just don't know with any certainty what it can do, or the full results of its use on the user and others." The king paused, and sipped some juice.

Walid was concerned. "It's really in the box?"

"It is."

"Then someone could desperately want it and not just the book, someone who has big plans that would require blocking or overcoming the power of any Phi who resisted him."

"Yes," the king answered. "That's the irony of it. Someone could seek to use the chief artifact of Phi, its best known talisman of legend, in order to avoid or overcome those who are currently Phi. Anyone who's trying to steal it must either believe it has great power that they can use, or at least must think that many others hold this view and could easily be manipulated by its possession and the threat of its use."

Walid said, "That's so spooky. I mean the whole story, and the fact that there's someone out there who wants the ring and the book and plans to try to use them, or at least threaten to use them. And it's even scarier that they came so close to getting both things."

"Yes. It's troubling."

Mafulla said, "Do you think it's Ari Falma?"

"We know of course that he's directly involved, but we don't yet know the full nature of that involvement. Understanding what we do about him, though, this likely goes far beyond the scope of his concerns and plans. He may not even be aware of what was in the box that he was so desperately trying to get."

Walid at that moment happened to glance across the room, and said, "Uncle, someone's just put a note under the door."

"Would you retrieve it, my boy?"

"Sure."

The prince jumped up, walked over to the door, and picked up the piece of paper that had just been slid quietly into the room. He walked back, and handed it to the king, who unfolded the paper.

"It's from Naqid. I'll read it to you: 'Majesty: There's word on the street that Ari Falma is leaving town very soon, today, with his entire organization, or what's left of it. Rumor has it that he'll be departing the entire kingdom, as well.' I see." The king paused and looked up. "This is interesting, and not altogether unexpected. We should take it as good news. For one thing, we could do without the likes of him and his enterprise under foot and causing trouble for us. He must know already what happened to his men and the hostages today."

"Shouldn't we go after him?"

"Ordinarily, we'd seek to capture him immediately," the king answered. "But because we suspect that someone else is involved, someone he's working with, or more likely, working for, we've decided to see if he'd flee, and then have someone track his movements."

Walid said, to no one in particular, "I wonder why he's leaving, rather than just trying again to get what he's been after."

Mafulla said, "He must be afraid."

Walid looked at the king and said, "Of us?"

The king replied, "Perhaps, or of something else—and this may complicate our plan. He could be running from a superior, or a feared partner who'll be angry that he didn't succeed. And under that scenario, he may not lead us to anyone else who's involved in this. Or, he could simply be regrouping. He might think that he could have a better opportunity to get what he desires by being somewhere else right now. We can't know. Remember, he's a man motivated by either greed, or ungoverned ambition, or else fear. There are no alternatives for individuals of his mindset. So either he's leaving in pursuit of gain, or else to escape from something he fears. In either case, we're the beneficiaries, at least in the short run. In the long run, we'll see."

After their mid day meal with the king, Walid and Mafulla went on to have a good late afternoon and evening. And then, in the days that followed, they had a string of very good experiences. They soon started training three times a week with Masoon, and augmented those sessions with their own workouts on alternate days. School continued to be fun and interesting, with no underlying intrigue or anxiety to distract them. The boys' and girls' classes met again shortly afterwards for a picnic outside in the palace gardens, and it was once more great fun for everyone.

Walid had a chance to visit Khalid's house and, in the presence of Kissa's parents, he got to know her a little better. Mafulla met Hasina's mother and was able to talk with his new female friend much more. The boys played lots of games outdoors with their school friends, and even incorporated bocci ball into their weekly routine, without always going down into the basement to do so. As the weather cooled a bit, it was more fun to do things outside.

The king made new laws that benefited everyone. He improved education throughout the land, stressed civic engagement in many of his public messages, and began to include more people in basic issues of governance. His general popularity, strong from the start, increased even more because of what he was doing, and especially as the results of his efforts began to have their proper effects.

There were no further mysterious threats against the kingdom, the palace, or anyone's family. Crime in the capital decreased discernibly in the absence of the Falma organization. A sense of peace and safety began to prevail in a new way.

Walid and Mafulla each grew a bit taller and much stronger as they developed their distinctive abilities. They continued now and then to call each other "The Golden Viper," and "Windstorm." They joked a lot about secret identities and saving the world, or at least the immediate neighborhood around the palace. But they also talked of serious things like philosophy and psychology whenever they could. Some of their friends even joined in these discussions, now and then. They got to know Omari better, as well as Paki, and Amon.

The kingdom was seeing a time of abundance. Some said they were entering into a Golden Age for their land. The boys' personal lives were happy and flourishing.

All was well in The Golden Palace.

But, as the ancient philosophers have reminded us in their writings, one of the most constant things in life is change. And there was already a stirring, a rustling, a faint breeze, then an increasing light wind across the desert that would soon bring them a great deal of change—a storm, really, and more challenge than they ever could imagine. Walid and Mafulla both began having symbolic dreams, and inklings, and a sense of something coming that would truly put them to the test. And of course, this was because they are Phi.

APPENDIX

The Diary of Walid Shabeezar

I began this diary, or journal of ideas, at the first oasis we visited during our time of crossing the desert. Uncle Ali had started telling me amazing things about life and the power of the mind. I decided to write a few notes about what he said, to help me understand and not forget. I've continued, whenever possible, to jot down insights and realizations that have come my way since then. Today, I'm starting this new notebook to continue the diary. For a few days after we got here, I was too busy to write much. But I'm determined to keep up this practice of daily reflection during my time in the palace now. I'm going to keep this small notebook where I sleep, and I'm going to use it at the end of the day, whenever I can, to review whatever I've learned. I hope this will deepen and solidify what I gain from each day.

△ △ △

Power is multiplied by purpose. A small group can do big things.

No task is too hard for those who have a noble purpose inspiring and helping them.

It's possible to take emotional ownership of your surroundings, no matter how overwhelming they might seem. When we own where we are, we make great things possible. This is my place right now.

Every day is a test of what we've learned and a classroom for learning more.

The testing that life brings us can make us better and transform us into teachers and leaders.

△ △ △

I learned some things in the marketplace. You can learn anywhere.

Courtesy and kindness are always appropriate. In new situations, they can make a big difference.

A chance encounter can plant seeds in your heart, and you can
often tell something's growing there, even if you don't know what
will result, and whether it will bear the fruit that you want.

△ △ △

Malicious people often snare unsuspecting victims by appealing
to the best in them, then springing a trap.

We can reduce our stress by the use of our minds. We can calm
our hearts by controlling our thoughts.

In bad situations, good people rise up and make a difference.

△ △ △

People come into our lives in strange ways. Good things can
result from bad circumstances.

A hero seeks to serve, and is willing to face a risk to do so.

You don't have to feel like a hero to be one.

△ △ △

When we got to the palace, Bancom told me about his adventures in the desert and what he learned there. In many ways, the most important thing he said to me was this: One person on a mission, committed to a goal, can accomplish much.

He also reminded me that truth is strength. And that can play out in surprising ways. The truth is always among our best resources.

△ △ △

I want to write down some more wisdom from Bancom.

When you're in a tough situation with apparently no way out, there almost always is one. If you can stay calm and focus, you can find it.

The Triple Double is indeed the best way to deal with trouble: Prepare and Perceive; Anticipate and Avoid; Concentrate and Control.

Clear danger focuses the mind. Jeopardy creates clarity. When we most need help, this helps a lot.

In some of the worst situations, time seems to slow down to allow us to think and act well. The expanded moments allow for our best efforts.

Most battles are won or lost in the mind.

Anyone who departs from the truth endangers himself. It's a path to stay on, regardless of what calls you away from it.

Lies never solve our problems—they just create new ones.

△ △ △

Right eventually brings might. When you're on the side of the true and the good and the genuinely beautiful, you're connected with deep power, despite any difficulties you face.

Strong roots produce good fruits. The basic and often unseen foundations of any enterprise are what allow it to flourish.

Breathing and positive visualization can calm the mind and body.

△ △ △

Having a friend doubles the good and cuts the bad in half.

Life often seems random, but there are patterns beneath the surface. People and things come to us when the time is right.

Real friendship requires wisdom. Fools can't be friends.

Life is like a big wagon wheel. Most people live on the outer rim, so as the wheel turns, they go through severe ups and downs. Wisdom centers you at the hub. The wheel will still turn, but at the hub you won't experience such giant swings, up high or down low.

There are two kinds of freedom: a freedom from, and a freedom to—the freedom of release, and the freedom of aspiration. The second freedom is the purpose of the first.

The meaning of life is creative love, or loving creativity. Everything we do should respect that.

We're here to create and to love. Create what you love, so that you can love what you create.

When setting goals for myself and deciding how to use my time, I'll seek always to follow the path of love.

△ △ △

Good families provide great support for all their members. And good friends can be a form of family, as well.

It's important to give, and then you'll get what you truly need.

Maffie's family was very open to the suggestion that he could live here in the palace for his education. I think openness is an important quality to have.

Openness is the most fertile soil for personal growth. To be open is as rare as it is important.

It's strange. I already feel like the Adi family is also my family. It's great how you can feel so accepted by some people. I should always try to help other good people feel accepted by me and my family.

△ △ △

People often reject things they don't understand. But we're always surrounded by such things.

Time is one of the most normal, ordinary, familiar things in life, but in many ways it's hard to understand.

A proper use of time is one of the biggest challenges we face.

It's important to manage time well. But this is hard because we often wrongly guess the time that a job, action, or commitment will take, and we just as badly estimate the passage of time itself.

Time management depends on thought management. We can't control our emotions or our actions without first governing our thoughts.

When we lose control of our emotions, we lose control of our time.

Thieves of time are all around us. Those people we come across who waste the most time always want to include us in their squandering ways.

Time is one of the few things that, if stolen, can't be gotten back.

I should invest time into things worth the investment, and into the people I care most about.

Today, while learning about time, I got my first watch, a great one called a Reverso, from Uncle Ali. It's really beautiful, and was designed in accordance with the famous Golden Ratio, 1 to 1.618.

An accurate watch helps us manage our days and work with others well. It oddly frees us and helps discipline us at the same time.

A beautiful watch is a work of art that can help you work well on the art that is your life.

In this world, some of the hardest things to understand are among the most important, and some of the easiest things to understand are among the least.

Seek the understanding most that's true wisdom.

△ △ △

The wise are willing to improvise. Not everything can be planned in advance.

Mr. Adi told me something interesting. Secrets create problems. Even when their intention is helpful, they often end up being harmful.

Honesty treats people with respect. Dishonesty means disrespect.

Honesty can take courage. Dishonesty often arises from fear.

△ △ △

When something scary happens, we should be calm and confident and act with care.

The best preparation for danger is the support of strong friends.

Aristotle thought of courage as one of the main virtues, or strengths, that we need to bring to everyday life.

Every virtue is a mid-point between two vices, a lack, and an excess. Courage is the mid-point between timidity and temerity, or between cowardice and crazy rashness. It's not good to fall short or overshoot the golden mean in our responses to the world.

Courage and care should go together. A brave person can still be properly cautious.

I need to prepare myself in my mind for various things that can go wrong. What would I do? If I think through this in advance, then I'll be better prepared to deal with a situation that doesn't itself allow time for thought.

Worst-Case Scenario Thinking is helpful. Worse-Case Scenario Believing is not.

△ △ △

There's nothing like a good family to make us feel valued.

Honesty is a great bond between friends, and within a family.

A crazy idea tonight: Crime fighters need secret identities, so the bad guys can't retaliate on their families and friends. When I thought of this, Maffie and I came up with crime fighting names for ourselves. I'm The Golden Viper, and he's Windstorm. It's all just in fun, of course, but—who knows?

△ △ △

We have to assume many things in life, things we can't prove but that we need to believe in order to function. Yet, it's dangerous to make sloppy assumptions when important things are at risk.

Before making an assumption, I should ask myself whether it's safe to do so, and what could be lost if I'm wrong.

A foolish assumption is the doorway to disaster. That's a quote from Khalid.

Wisdom requires prudence. Look before you leap.

My constant motto should be "Proceed Boldly, But Also With Caution."

You can know something strange is going on without knowing what it is. That's what Maffie said today.

Trust your intuition. And check it.

There's something odd about the way the storage rooms are arranged in the palace basement. We need to figure out why, and what's going on there.

△ △ △

When something unexpected and threatening happens, you have to keep your head and come up with a way out.

I'm worried about Khalid. We got locked into a room in the basement today, and when we got out, he was the only person around, near the basement stairs. I know that things aren't always what they seem, but it was pretty suspicious.

Trust is a strange thing. We take it back quickly, but then to return to it once more takes time.

ΔΔΔ

Who can write tonight? I got to talk to Kissa at the dinner … a lot! Tonight may have been a big step in destiny's plan. I sure hope so!

There is this strange positive energy that a girl can have, or can give you. I don't quite understand it, but it feels really good. It's like you're surrounded by light. When I looked around the table at dinner, I could see that some of the other guys were feeling it, too. Maybe Khalid would let me write an essay on it. No, that wouldn't be good. I'd have to say too much about Kissa. And that could get awkward.

One lesson: When destiny—or a kind uncle—puts on a dinner in your honor, make the most of it!

ΔΔΔ

I got interrupted. And this maybe rates a separate entry anyway.

Here's a problem: What do you do when you really like someone but that person is closely related to one or more other people who may be doing suspicious things? Should I say something, or not?

Khalid disappeared from the big dinner when the lights went out. This was very odd. I don't know what to make of it. If we find out that anything bad happened during the power failure, it'll be hard for me not to suspect him of some involvement. But he's Kissa's father! I hope he's not doing anything wrong.

Tonight, I learned some things from Uncle Ali about the mind.

When a situation isn't clear, we need to observe it with a mind that is.

The mind is our greatest tool. To use it well takes skill and effort.

The mind is also like a great pyramid. Our conscious experience is just the very tip of it. Without access to the unconscious, the vast majority of the structure below, we can miss out on most of what's available for us in this world.

The pyramid analogy suggests other insights. It's the unconscious mind that can raise consciousness up high.

When we reduce the chatter of the conscious mind, we can break through to the thought beyond thought, a real source of power.

We can know more than we think. We can do more than we know.

△ △ △

Trust your instincts. Listen to your heart. Take inklings seriously.

Don't worry when you can't explain how you know what you know. You can still know it. And you can act on it with boldness.

Panic never helps. Worry never improves things. A calm and peaceful heart makes everything easier.

△ △ △

I'm Phi. Maffie's Phi. This was a huge surprise. It is a huge surprise.

It's still going to take me a while to understand what it means to be connected to something much bigger than myself, and to have talents and powers that maybe go far beyond what I know.

Uncle Ali spotted something in me and Maffie—an openness of our minds to more of what's going on than most people seem to access.

It looks like Phi can be manifested in different ways. It will be interesting to see how it develops in us.

Is Phi the beginning of Philosophy, or is Philosophy the beginning of Phi?

The myths of Phi are many. Where there are myths, there are usually some deep truths seeking expression.

More of us may have a bigger dose of Phi in us than we ever imagine.

It's important to be able to live with questions. Seeking truth is a lifelong process, and maybe some truths can come to you only when you're deeply prepared.

Deep questions can bring us truth, or can bring us transformation.

Courage can do its best with support. Never hesitate to ask people you trust to help with something you seek.

True friends will walk with you in support even when you aren't sure where you're going.

Uncle Ali said something about people that I want to remember. He said: "I can sense how deep a well is as soon as the water comes out." I need to make sure my well is deep and the water is pure.

The journey of beginnings never ends.

ACKNOWLEDGMENTS

I want to thank my wife Mary for all of her enthusiastic support during the writing of this book. Going far beyond a normal form of spousal involvement, she let me read it to her out loud at night, once chapters were done, and while it was still being written. She asked great questions along the way and sparked in me a lot of new perspectives.

I also want to thank those friends whose encouragement during this writing was so important to me. To the Sports Center gang: You keep me going and help me stay strong. Don, Tony, Tom, and all the others: You're an inspiration. My friend and neighbor, the sculptor and track and field master Ed Hearn also read this carefully to catch many typos and run-on sentences that were produced by my original enthusiasm and haste to write this all down quickly as I saw it play out in the theater of my mind. I love it that I can thank him in the exact sort of sentence that he surely would suggest I shorten. I appreciate his keen eye, dedication, and always helpful notes.

This book came to me as a total surprise, just as its predecessor and prologue, *The Oasis Within*. The present book continues the story started there, but can be read first. If you've begun here, then at some point go find *The Oasis Within* for a backstory. Both books came to me the same way, exactly like a movie in my head. The prologue ambushed me after breakfast one morning, while I was still sitting at the table. As in the most vivid daydream of my life, there were two characters, talking. I ran to the computer and typed. And then in subsequent days, the movie would continue to play. When I made myself quiet and sat calmly, the adventure would start up and take crazy twists that I never saw coming. From the first, I realized that I was not being called on in this process to make any of my own conscious decisions about who would show up or what would happen. My job was just to sit and wait and see what would take place, sentence to sentence, and page after page.

Lots of friends have read *The Oasis Within*, which is indeed the prelude and companion book to the series that fully begins here, an epic journey that my granddaughter Grayson first named *Walid and the Mysteries of Phi*. I thank her for that. The enthusiasm of friends and other early readers has meant so much to me along the way. I'm eager to thank them all here for their encouragement and ongoing assurance that these books can make a difference in other people's lives like they have already in mine. The highly acclaimed thriller novelist and former philosophy student of mine decades ago, Kevin Guilfoile (*Cast of Shadows*, *The Thousand*) was of great support early on and helped give me the confidence to persevere in my most unexpected adventure of writing these books. His words and inspiration were then and are now greatly appreciated.

The artistic eye of my daughter Sara Morris has benefited me greatly in the cover concepts of both *The Oasis Within* and the current book. In addition, Abigail Chiaramonte has worked tirelessly on all the other elements of design, as well as on preparing the final product for print. I want to thank both of them for their ongoing help.

There will be more books on these characters and their adventures. Without giving anything away, I can tell you that when one person in this part of the story threw something out a window, I suddenly realized that he was throwing it all the way into a next book. As soon as this awareness came over me, I couldn't wait to see what would happen! And as the movie continued to play, I was amazed as I discovered what's to come. I hope you feel the same.

And last, but not least, I thank you, the reader, for caring!

AFTERWORD

Beyond *The Golden Palace*

First, there was *The Oasis Within,* a short tale about a series of deep conversations and surprising events that took place as a group of men and camels crossed the desert in Egypt in 1934. The present novel is the official Book One to an exciting new series of subsequent stories about these remarkable individuals collectively entitled:

WALID AND THE MYSTERIES OF PHI

If you've read the prologue to the series, *The Oasis Within,* or you've enjoyed this longer book, you'll likely love the entire series, which presents a sprawling epic account of action, adventure, and ideas, set in and around Cairo, Egypt in 1934 and 1935, with a few sojourns farther abroad. Its books contain captivating tales about life, death, meaning, love, friendship, the deepest secrets behind everyday events, and the extraordinary power of a well-focused mind. The events they relate will interact with such classics as Plato's *Republic, The Epic of Gilgamesh, Beowulf, Frankenstein,* and *Moby Dick,* among many other seminal texts. With unexpected humor and continual intrigue, you'll gradually discover in these books the outlines of a powerful worldview and a profound philosophy of life.

To find out more, visit **www.TomVMorris.com/novels** or go to **www.TheOasisWithin.com.**

The companion book, *The Oasis Within*, as well as this book, is available for large group purchases at special discounts. To find out more, contact the author, Tom Morris, through his oldest and most reliable email address, **TomVMorris@aol. com** or through his website. Tom is also available to speak with book groups via email, Skype, or any other means that would help in the discussion of these stories. Make a request, and speak directly to the author himself.

About the Author

Tom Morris is one of the most active public philosophers and business speakers in the world. A native of North Carolina, he's a graduate of The University of North Carolina (Chapel Hill), where he was a Morehead-Cain Scholar, and he holds a Ph.D. in both Philosophy and Religious Studies from Yale University. For fifteen years, he served as a Professor of Philosophy at the University of Notre Dame, where he was one of their most popular teachers. You can find him online at **www.TomVMorris.com**.

Tom is also the author of over twenty pioneering books. His twelfth book, *True Success: A New Philosophy of Excellence*, launched him into his ongoing adventure as a philosopher working and speaking throughout the world. His audiences have included a great many of the Fortune 500 companies and several of the largest national and international trade associations. His work has been mentioned, commented on, or covered by NBC, ABC, CNN, CNBC, NPR, and in most major newspapers and news magazines. He's also the author of the highly acclaimed books *If Aristotle Ran General Motors*,

Philosophy for Dummies, The Art of Achievement, The Stoic Art of Living, The 7 Cs of Success, Twisdom, Superheroes and Philosophy, and *If Harry Potter Ran General Electric: Leadership Wisdom from the World of the Wizards*, as well as the philosophical prologue to the current series, the book, *The Oasis Within*. He just may be the world's happiest philosopher.

Φ

Made in the USA
Lexington, KY
08 April 2016